THE FLAMETHROWERS

A NOVEL

RACHEL KUSHNER

SCRIBNER

New York   London   Toronto   Sydney   New Delhi

SCRIBNER

A Division of Simon & Schuster, Inc.
1230 Avenue of the Americas
New York, NY 10020

First Scribner hardcover edition April 2013

SCRIBNER and design are registered trademarks of The Gale Group, Inc., used under license by Simon & Schuster, Inc., the publisher of this work.

For information about special discounts for bulk purchases, please contact Simon & Schuster Special Sales at 1-866-506-1949 or business@simonandschuster.com.

The Simon & Schuster Speakers Bureau can bring authors to your live event. For more information or to book an event contact the Simon & Schuster Speakers Bureau at 1-866-248-3049 or visit our website at www.simonspeakers.com.

Book design by Ellen R. Sasahara

Manufactured in the United States of America

1 3 5 7 9 10 8 6 4 2

Library of Congress Cataloging-in-Publication Data

Kushner, Rachel.
The flamethrowers : a novel / Rachel Kushner. —1st Scribner hardcover ed.
p.   cm.
1. Women artists—Fiction. 2. Motorcycles—Fiction. 3. Futurism—Fiction.
4. Brigate rosse—Fiction. 5. New York (N.Y.)—Fiction. 6. Italy—Fiction.
I. Title.
PS3611.U7386F57 2013
813'.6—dc2   2012027350

ISBN 978-1-4391-4200-4
ISBN 978-1-4391-5417-5 (ebook)

Chapter 4 appeared in *The Paris Review* Winter 2012 issue. Chapters 1 and 3 appeared, in slightly different form, in *Animal Shelter*.

Page 387 constitutes a continuation of the copyright page.

This book is for Cynthia Mitchell.

And for Anna, wherever she is (and probably isn't).

FAC UT ARDEAT

THE FLAMETHROWERS

1. He killed him with a motorbike headlamp (what he had in his hand).

Valera had fallen back from his squadron and was cutting the wires of another rider's lamp. The rider, Copertini, was dead. Valera felt no sadness, strangely, even though Copertini had been a comrade in arms, someone Valera had sped along with under the Via del Corso's white neon, long before they both volunteered for the cycle battalion in 1917.

It was Copertini who had laughed at Valera when he'd crashed on the Via del Corso's streetcar tracks, which could be so slippery on a foggy night.

Copertini considered himself a better rider, but it was Copertini who had been going too fast in the dense woods and slammed head-first into a tree. His bike frame was mangled, but his headlight bulb had an unfractured filament, which now weakly illuminated a patch of dirt and stiff grasses. Copertini's motorcycle was a different model than Valera's, but they used the same lamp bulb. Valera wanted a spare. A spare would be handy.

He heard the faint whoosh of a flamethrower and the scattered echo of shelling. Combat was on the other side of a deep valley, near the Isonzo River. It was peaceful and deserted here, just the silvery patter of tree leaves moving in the breeze.

He'd parked his motorcycle, left his Carcano rifle fastened to the rear rack, and was working to free the headlight, twisting to loosen the lamp nestle from its socket. It resisted. He was tugging on its anchoring wires when a man darted from behind a row of poplars, unmistakably German, in the green-and-yellow uniform, and helmetless like a rugby player sent into battle.

Valera pulled the heavy brass casing free and went for a dump tackle. The German was down. Valera tumbled after him. The German scrambled to his knees and tried to grab the headlamp, which was just about the size and shape of a rugby ball but heavier, with a braid of cut wires trailing it like a severed optic nerve. Valera struggled to regain control of the headlamp. Twice he grubber-kicked it but somehow the German ended up in possession. Valera grounded him, kneed the German in the face, and pried his fingers from the headlamp. There was, after all, no penalty here for foul play, no one to flash him a red card in the quiet woods. His own platoon was miles ahead, and somehow this lone German was loosed from his pack, lost among the poplars.

The German reared up, trying to shoulder-charge him.

Valera brained him with the headlamp.

2. SPIRITUAL AMERICA

I walked out of the sun, unfastening my chin strap. Sweat was pool-
ing along my collarbone, trickling down my back and into my nylon
underwear, running down my legs under the leather racing suit. I took
off my helmet and the heavy leather jacket, set them on the ground,
and unzipped the vents in my riding pants.

I stood for a long time tracking the slow drift of clouds, great fluffy
masses sheared flat along their bottom edges like they were melting on
a hot griddle.

There were things I had no choice but to overlook, like wind effect
on clouds, while flying down the highway at a hundred miles an hour. I
wasn't in a hurry, under no time constraint. Speed doesn't have to be an
issue of time. On that day, riding a Moto Valera east from Reno, it was
an issue of wanting to move across the map of Nevada that was taped
to my gas tank as I moved across the actual state. Through the familiar orbit east of Reno, the brothels and wrecking yards, the big puffing power plant and its cat's cradle of coils and springs and fencing,
an occasional freight train and the meandering and summer-shallow
Truckee River, railroad tracks and river escorting me to Fernley, where
they both cut north.

From there the land was drained of color and specificity, sage-tufted dirt and incessant sameness of highway. I picked up speed. The faster I went, the more connected I felt to the map. It told me that fifty-six miles after Fernley I'd hit Lovelock, and fifty-six miles after leaving Fernley I hit Lovelock. I moved from map point to map point. Winnemucca. Valmy. Carlin. Elko. Wells. I felt a great sense of mission, even as I sat under a truck stop awning, sweat rolling down the sides of my face, an anonymous breeze, hot and dry, wicking the damp from my thin undershirt. Five minutes, I told myself. Five minutes. If I stayed longer, the place the map depicted might encroach.

A billboard across the highway said SCHAEFER. WHEN YOU'RE HAV-ING MORE THAN ONE. A bluebird landed on the branch of a sumac bush under the high-clearance legs of the billboard. The bird surfed its slack branch, its feathers a perfect even blue like it had been powder-coated at the factory. I thought of Pat Nixon, her dark gleaming eyes and cer-emonial outfits stiff with laundry starch and beading. Hair dyed the color of whiskey and whipped into an unmoving wave. The bird tested out a short whistle, a lonely midday sound lost in the infinite stretch of irrigation wheels across the highway. Pat Nixon was from Nevada, like me, and like the prim little state bird, so blue against the day. She was a ratted beauty-parlor tough who became first lady. Now we would likely have Rosalynn Carter with her glassy voice and her big blunt friendly face, glowing with charity. It was Pat who moved me. People who are harder to love pose a challenge, and the challenge makes them easier to love. You're driven to love them. People who want their love easy don't really want love.

I paid for my gas to the sound of men in the arcade room playing a video game called Night Driver. They were seated in low-slung cockpits made of sparkling, molded fiberglass, steering jerkily, pale-knuckled, trying to avoid the guardrail reflectors on either side of the road, the fiberglass cockpits jiggling and rocking as the men attempted to steer themselves out of catastrophe, swearing and angrily bopping the steer-ing wheel with the heel of a hand when they burned and crashed. It had been this way at several truck stops now. This was how the men rested from driving. Later I told Ronnie Fontaine. I figured it was something Ronnie would find especially funny but he didn't laugh. He said, "Yeah, see. That's the thing about freedom." I said, "What?" And he said, "Nobody wants it."

My uncle Bobby, who hauled dirt for a living, spent his final moments of life jerking his leg to depress the clutch while lying in a hospital, his body determined to operate his dump truck, clutching and shifting gears as he sped toward death on a hospital gurney. "He died on the job," his two sons said, unmoved. Bobby was too mean for them to love. Scott and Andy had been forced to oil Bobby's truck every Sunday and now he was dead and they had Sundays to themselves, to oil their own trucks. Bobby was my mother's brother. Growing up, we'd all lived together. My mother worked nights, and Bobby was what we had as a parent. Done driving his dump truck, he sat inexplicably nude watching TV and made us operate the dial for him, so he wouldn't have to get up. He'd fix himself a big steak and give us instant noodles. Sometimes he'd take us to a casino, leave us in the parking lot with bottle rockets. Or play chicken with the other cars on I-80, with me and Scott and Andy in the backseat covering our eyes. I come from reckless, unsentimental people. Sandro used this against me on occasion. He pretended I was placed in his life to torture him, when it was really the other way around. He acted smitten but I was the smitten one. Sandro held all the power. He was older by fourteen years and a successful art-ist, tall and good-looking in his work clothes and steel-toed boots—the same kinds of clothes that Bobby and Scott and Andy wore, but on Sandro they added up to something else: a guy with a family inheri-tance who could use a nail gun, a drill press, a person not made effete by money, who dressed like a worker or sometimes a bum but was ele-gant in those clothes, and never hampered by the question of whether he belonged in a given situation (the question itself was evidence of not belonging).

Sandro kept a photo above the desk in his loft, him posing on a couch next to Morton Feldman in his Coke-bottle glasses, Sandro looking cool and aloof, holding a raised, loaded shotgun, its barrel one long half of the letter *X* crossing the photograph diagonally. Slashing it. It was a black-and-white image but you could see that Sandro's eyes were the whitish-blue of a wolf's, giving him a cold, sly intensity. The photo was taken in Rhinebeck, where his friends Gloria and Stanley Kastle had a place. Sandro was allowed to shoot guns on their property, various handguns and rifles he had collected, some of them made by his family's company before they got out of the firearms business. Sandro liked shotguns most of all and said if you ever needed to actually kill someone, that was what you'd want, a shotgun. That was his way, to tersely let it be known in his light accent, barely Italian, that he could kill someone if he had to.

Women responded to this. They came on to him right in front of me, like the gallerist Helen Hellenberger, a severe but beautiful Greek woman who dressed as if it were permanently 1962, in a black shift and with upswept hair. We ran into her on Spring Street just before I departed for Reno to pick up the Moto Valera for this trip. Helen Hellenberger, in her tight dress and leather flats, holding her large black pocketbook as if it were a toolbox, had said she wanted so badly to come to Sandro's studio. Would she have to beg? She'd put her hand on his arm and it seemed as if she wasn't going to let go until he said yes. Sandro was with the Erwin Frame Gallery. Helen Hellenberger wanted to steal him for her own gallery. He tried to redirect her by introducing me, not as his girlfriend but as "a young artist, just out of school," as if to say, you can't have me, but here's something you might consider picking up. An offer she had to maneuver around in order to press on and get him to commit to the studio visit.

"With an art degree from . . . where?" she asked me.

"UNR," I said. I knew she wouldn't be familiar with the school's initials.

"She's influenced by Land Art," Sandro said. "And her ideas are great. She made a beautiful film about Reno."

Helen Hellenberger represented the best-known Land Artists, all midcareer, blue-chip, and so I felt especially self-conscious about Sandro's insistence that she learn about me, my work. I wasn't ready to show with Helen Hellenberger and in his pretending that I was, I felt

Sandro was insulting me without necessarily intending to. It was possible he knew this. That he found some perverse humor in offering me in lieu of himself.

"Oh. Where did you say—" She was feigning a low-level politeness, just enough to satisfy him.

"Nevada," I said.

"Well, now you can really learn about art." She smiled at him as if depositing a secret between them. "If you're with Sandro Valera. What a mentor for someone who's just arrived from . . . Idaho?"

"Reno," Sandro said. "She's going out there to do a piece. Drawing a line across the salt flats. It's going to be great. And subtle. She's got really subtle ideas about line and drawing."

He had tried to put his arm around me but I'd moved away. I knew how I looked to this beautiful woman who slept with half her roster, according to Ronnie Fontaine, who was on her roster himself: I was nothing but a minor inconvenience in her campaign to represent Sandro.

"So you'll be going out West?" she'd asked before we parted ways, and then she'd questioned me about the particulars of my ride with an interest that didn't quite seem genuine. Only much later did I think back to that moment, look at it. *You'll be going out of town?* Reno, Idaho. Someplace far away.

When I was getting ready to depart, Sandro acted as if I might not be coming back, as if I were leaving him to solitude and tedium, a penance he'd resigned himself to enduring. He rolled his eyes about the appointment Helen Hellenberger had wrangled.

"I'll be here getting eaten by vultures," he said, "while you're tearing across the salt flats, my unknown competitors drooling over you like stunned idiots. Because that's what you do," he'd said, "you inhibit thought. With your young electricity."

When you're having more than one. I sat at the truck stop, facing that billboard, naively thinking my young electricity was enough.

Helen Hellenberger's stable of Land Artists included the most famous, Robert Smithson, who died three years earlier while I was a student at UNR. I had learned about him and the *Spiral Jetty* from an obituary in the newspaper and not from my art department, which was provincial and conservative (the truth in Helen's snub was that I *did* learn more from Sandro than I had in art school). The foreman who built the *Spiral Jetty* was quoted explaining how tricky it had been to construct it on such soft mud, and that he had almost lost some very expensive equipment. He was risking men and front loaders and regretted taking the job, and then the artist shows up in the Utah summertime desert, it's 118 degrees, and the guy is wearing black leather pants. Smithson was quoted declaring that pollution and industry could be beautiful, and that it was because of the railroad cutoff and the oil dredging that he chose this part of the Great Salt Lake for his project, where the lake's supply of fresh water had been artificially cut, raising the salt content so high that nothing but red algae could grow. I had immediately wanted to see this thing made by a New York artist in leather pants, who described more or less the slag-heap world of the West I knew, as it looked to me, and found it worth his attentions. I went there, crossed the top of Nevada, and came down just over the Utah border. I watched the water, which pushed peculiar drifts, frothy, white, and ragged. The white drifts looked almost like snow but they moved like soap, quivering and weightless. Spiky desert plants along the shore were coated in an icy fur of white salt. The jetty was submerged but I could see it through the surface of the water. It was the same basalt from the lake's shore, rearranged to another form. The best ideas were often so simple, even obvious, except that no one had thought of them before. I looked at the water and the distant shore of the lake, a vast bowl of emptiness, jagged rocks, high sun, stillness. I would move to New York City.

Which was an irony, because the artist himself had gone from New York to the West to make his specifically Western dreams come true. I was from the place, the hard-hat-wearing, dump-truck-driving world the Land Artists romanticized. So why did Helen Hellenberger pretend to confuse Idaho and Nevada? It was an irony but a fact that a person had to move to New York City first, to become an artist of the West. If that's what I was going to be. Sandro declared it, "she's influenced by

Land Art," but this also served to explain away the fact that he was with a woman so young, with no detectable pedigree or accomplishments. Just his word.

When I was little, skiing in the Sierras, I felt that I was drawing on the mountain's face, making big sweeping graceful lines. That was how I had started to draw, I'd told Sandro, as a little girl, five, six years old, on skis. Later, when drawing became a habit, a way of being, of marking time, I always thought of skiing. When I began ski racing, slalom and giant slalom, it was as if I were tracing lines that were already drawn, and the technical challenge that shadowed the primary one, to finish with a competitive time, was to stay perfectly in the lines, to stay early through the gates, to leave no trace, because the harder you set your skis' metal edges, the bigger wedge of evidence you left, the more you slowed down. You wanted no snow spraying out behind you. You wanted to be traceless. To ride a flat ski as much as possible. The ruts that cut around and under the bamboo gates, deep trenches if the snow was soft, were to be avoided by going high, by picking a high and graceful line, with no sudden swerves or shuddering edges, as I rode the rails to the finish.

Ski racing was drawing *in time*, I said to Sandro. I finally had someone listening who wanted to understand: the two things I loved were drawing and speed, and in skiing I had combined them. It was drawing in order to win.

The first winter I was dating Sandro we went to the Kastles' place up in Rhinebeck for Christmas. It snowed heavily one night, and in the morning I borrowed cross-country skis and skied across a frozen pond, made tracks that went across it in an X, and photographed them. "That will be good," Sandro said, "your X." But I wasn't satisfied by those tracks. Too much effort, the plodding blobs of ski poles every ten feet. Cross-country skiing was like running. It was like walking. Contemplative and aerobic. The trace was better if it was clean, if it was made at some unnatural speed. I asked the Kastles if we could borrow their truck. We did doughnuts on the snow-covered meadow beyond the frozen pond, me spinning the steering wheel like Scott and Andy had taught me, Sandro laughing as the truck's tires slid. I made broad, circular tracks in the meadow and photographed those. But it was only about having a good time upstate. I thought art came from a brooding solitude. I felt it had to involve risk, some genuine risk.

My five minutes at the truck stop were almost up. I rebraided my hair, which was knotted from the wind and crimped in odd places from the padding in my helmet.

Drivers were arguing about truck color. A purple rig shone like a grape Popsicle among the rows of semis. A cup of cola sailed toward its grille, casting a vote with a slam and clatter of cubes. The men laughed and started to disperse. Nevada was a tone, a light, a deadness that was part of me. But it was different to come back here now. I'd left. I was here not because I was stuck here, but to do something. To do it and then return to New York.

One of the truckers spoke to me as he passed. "That yours?"

For a moment, I thought he meant the truck. But he tipped his chin toward the Moto Valera.

I said yes and kept braiding my hair.

He smiled in a friendly way. "You know what?"

I smiled back.

"You won't look nearly so good when they're loading you off the highway in a body bag."

ALL VEHICLES WITH LIVESTOCK MUST BE WEIGHED. I passed the weigh station, breezed through third gear and into the midrange of fourth, hitting seventy miles an hour. I could see the jagged peaks of tall mountains, stale summer snow filtered by the desert haze to the brownish tone of pantyhose. I was going eighty. Won't look nearly as good. People love a fatality. I redlined it, still in fourth gear, waiting.

Light winked from the back of something silver, up ahead in the right lane. I rolled off the throttle but didn't downshift. As I got closer,

I recognized the familiar rounded rear corners of a Greyhound. Builds character, my mother liked to say. She had ridden buses alone in the early 1950s, an episode just before I was born that was never explained and didn't seem quite wholesome, a young woman drifting around on buses, patting cold water on her face in gas station bathrooms. The footage ran through my mind in high-contrast black and white, light cut to ribbons, desperate women accidentally strangled by telephone cords, or alone with the money, drinking on an overcast beach in big sunglasses. My mother's life was not so glamorous. She was a switch-board operator, and if her past included something akin to noir, it was only the gritty part, the part about being female, poor, and alone, which in a film was enough of a circumstance to bring in the intrigue, but in her life it attracted only my father. He left when I was three. Everyone in the family said it was good riddance, and that uncle Bobby was a better father to me than my own could have been. As I approached the Greyhound, ready to pass, I saw that the windows were meshed and blacked. Exhaust was blowing out carelessly from its loose, lower pan-els, NEVADA CORRECTIONS on its side. A mobile prison, with passengers who could not see out. But perhaps to see out was worse. Once, as a kid, riding my bicycle around the county jail, I had seen a man staring down at me from his barred window. A fine-grade rain was falling. I stopped pedaling and looked up at his small face, framed by a gravity-flop of greasy blond hair. The rain was almost invisible. He put an arm through the bars. To feel the rain, I assumed. He gave me the middle finger.

"Save your freedom for a rainy day," someone had written on the bathroom wall at Rudy's Bar in SoHo, where Sandro and Ronnie liked to drink. It remained there at eye level above the washbasin all summer. No retorts or cross-outs. Just this blank command as you angled and turned your hands under the faucet.

I passed the bus, shifted into fifth, and hit ninety, the orange needle steady on the face of my black speedometer. I tucked down into my little fairing. I loved that fairing the moment I saw the bike at the deal-ership in Reno, where I picked it up. Metal-flake teal, the color of deep freeze. It was a brand-new 650 supersport. It was actually a '77—*next* year's model. It was so new no one in the United States had one but me. I had never seen a Moto Valera this color. The one I'd owned in college, a '65, had been white.

I'd ridden motorcycles since I was fourteen. I started out riding in the woods behind our house, with Scott and Andy, who had Yamaha DTs, the first real dirt bikes. Before I learned to ride, I'd ridden on the back of my cousins' scramblers, which were street bikes they customized, no passenger pegs, my legs held out to the sides in hopes of avoiding an exhaust pipe burn. They were not street legal, no headlight or license plate, but Scott and Andy rode with me on the back all over Reno. Except past the front of our house, because my mother had forbidden me to ride on my cousins' motorcycles. I held on for wheelies and jumps and learned quickly to trust. It wasn't Scott and Andy I trusted, one of whom angled a wheelie too high and flipped the bike with me on the back (he had not yet learned to tap the foot brake, to tilt the bike forward), and the other took a jump over a pile of dirt at a construction site and told me to hold tight. That was Andy. He landed with the front end too pitched and we went over the handlebars. I didn't trust their skills. I had no reason to, since they crashed regularly. I trusted the need for risk, the importance of honoring it. In college, I bought a Moto Valera and then sold it to move to New York. With my new life in the big city, I thought I'd lose interest but I didn't. Maybe I would have, had I not met Sandro Valera.

I was going one hundred miles an hour now, trying to steer properly from my hunched position, as insects ticked and thumped and splatted against the windscreen.

It was suicide to let the mind drift. I'd promised myself not to do it. A Winnebago towing a Volkswagen Beetle was in the left lane. The Winnebago must have been going forty miles an hour: it seemed to stand still on the road. We were in separate realities, fast and slow. There is no fixed reality, only objects in contrast. Even the Earth is moving. I was suddenly right up on the towed VW's rear and had to swerve into the right lane. The road was in bad shape, and I went into a divot. It threw the front wheel off balance. I bounced and swerved. The front end of the bike was wobbling like crazy. I didn't dare touch the brake. I tried to ride out the wobble. I was all over my lane and thinking I was going to wreck, and I hadn't even gotten to the salt flats yet. But then the front wheel began to calm and straighten out. I moved left again onto the better road surface. The wobble I'd been thrown into was my wake-up call. I was lucky I hadn't crashed. "Speed is every man's right" was Honda's new ad slogan, but speed was not a right. Speed was a causeway between life and death and you hoped you came out on the side of life.

I stopped for gas at dusk. The broad sky had turned a cold medium-blue with one star burning, a lone pinprick of soft, bright white. A car pulled up on the other side of the pumps. The windows were down and I could hear a man and woman speaking to each other.

The man removed the car's gas cap and knocked the nozzle into the opening of his tank as though it required force to get it to fit correctly. Then he waggled it in and out of the tank in a lewd manner. His back was to me. I watched him as I waited for my tank to fill. When I was finished, the woman was getting out of the car. She looked in my direction but seemed not to register me.

"You made your choice," she said. "And I'll make mine. Creep."

Something about the light, its dimness and the deepening blue above us, the commencement of twilight insects, made their voices close, intimate.

"You call me a creep after what you asked me to do? And now it's nothing? *I'm* a creep?"

The man pulled the nozzle from the gas tank and jerked it at the woman. Gasoline sloshed on her bare legs. He resumed filling his tank. When he was done, instead of putting the nozzle back on its resting place on the side of the pump, he dropped it on the ground like it was a garden hose he was finished using. He retrieved a book of matches from his pocket and began lighting them and flicking them at the woman. Each lit match arced through the dim light and went out before reaching her. Gas was dribbling down her legs. He lit matches one after another and flicked them at her, little sparks—threats, or promises— that died out limply.

"Would you quit it?" she said, blotting her legs with the blue paper towels from a dispenser by the pumps.

The angled sodium lights above us clicked on, buzzing to life. A truck passed on the highway, throwing on its air brakes.

"Hey," he said. He grabbed a lock of her hair.

She smiled at him like they were about to rob a bank together.

Night fell in an instant here. I rode on, as darkness changed the desert. It was more porous and vast now, even as my vision was limited to one tractor beam fanning thinly on the road in front of me. The enormity of dark was cut rarely and by a weak fluorescence, one or two gas stations. I thought about the man trying to light the woman on fire. He wasn't trying to light her on fire. Certain acts, even as they are real, are also merely gestures. He was saying, "What if I did?" And she was saying, "Go ahead."

The air turned cold as I climbed in elevation to a higher layer of the desert's warm-to-cool parfait. The wind leaked into my leathers wherever it could. I hadn't anticipated such cold. My fingers were almost too frozen to work the brake by the time I reached my destination, a small town with big casinos on the Utah border, Diamond Jim lettering glowing gold against the night. Only a killjoy would claim neon wasn't beautiful. It jumped and danced, chasing its own afterimage. But from one end of the main drag to the other was NO VACANCY in brazier orange. I stopped at one of the full motels, its parking lot crowded with trucks towing race cars, hoping they might take pity on me. I struggled to get my gloves off, and once they were off, could barely unbuckle the strap on my helmet. My hands had reduced themselves to two functions, throttle and brake. I tried to lift money and my license from my billfold, but my still-numb fingers refused to perform this basic action. I worked and worked to regain mobility. Finally I got my helmet off and went into the office. A woman said they were booked. A man came out from the back, about my age. "I'll handle it, Laura." He said he was the owner's son, and I felt a small surge of hope. I explained that I'd ridden all the way from Reno and really needed someplace to sleep, that I was planning to run at the salt flats.

"Maybe we can work something out," he said.

"Really?" I asked.

"I can't promise anything, but why don't we go have a drink up the street at the casino and talk about it?"

"Talk about it?"

"There might be something we can do. I'll at least buy you a drink."

It was always the son of power, the daughter of power, who was most eager to abuse it.

"I don't think so," I said. "Where's your father?"

"In a rest home." He turned to walk away. "Okay, final offer, just one drink."

I said no and left. Outside the motel office another man addressed me.

"Hey," he said. "He's a twerp. That was bullshit."

His name was Stretch. He was the maintenance man and lived in one of the rooms. He was tan as a summer construction worker but didn't quite emanate a sense of work. He wore jeans and a denim shirt of the same faded blue, and he had a greaser's hairstyle like it was 1956, not 1976. He reminded me of the young drifter in the Jacques Demy film *Model Shop,* who kills time before turning up for the draft, wandering, tailing a beauty in a white convertible through the flats and into the hills of Hollywood.

"Listen, I have to stay out all night guarding the twerp's race car," Stretch said. "I won't be using my room. And you need a place to sleep. Why don't you sleep there? I promise not to bother you. There's a TV. There's beer in the fridge. It's basic, but it's better than having to share a bed with him. I'll knock on the door in the morning to come in and shower but that's it, I swear. I hate it when he tries to get over on someone. It makes me sick."

He was extending actual charity, the kind you don't question. I trusted it. Partly because he reminded me of that character. I'd seen *Model Shop* with Sandro just after we met, a year earlier. The tagline became a joke between us, "Maybe tomorrow. Maybe never. *Maybe*." It begins with oil derricks jerking up and down beyond the window of a young couple's Venice love shack, the drifter and a girlfriend he doesn't care about. The beginning was Sandro's favorite scene and the reason he loved the film, oil derricks right outside the window, up and down, up and down, as the girl and boy lazed in bed, had an argument, puttered around their bungalow, decrepit and overshadowed by industry. After that we both used the word *bungalow* a lot. "Are you coming up to my *bungalow* this evening?" Sandro would ask. Though in fact it was a glass and cast-iron building, four thousand square feet on each floor.

Stretch showed me his room. It was tidy and a little heartbreaking. The owner's son had his collection of vintage cruiser bicycles crowding out half the space, as well as stacks of wooden milk crates filled with wrenches and bicycle parts. Stretch said he was used to it. On one side of the washbasin was a hot plate and on the other, a shaving kit and Brylcreem. It was like a movie set for a film about a drifter named Stretch who lives in a small gambling town on the Nevada border.

At a Mexican restaurant across the road from the motel, I ordered fish, which came whole. I picked around, not sure of the appropriate method, and finally decided to cut off the head. It sat on my plate like a shorn airplane fuselage. In its cavern, instead of menthol-smelling pilots, the dark muck of its former fish mind. I had to turn away, and watched two men who sat in a booth across the room, probably also here to run vehicles on the salt flats. Big mustaches, faces barbecued by sun and wind, suspenders framing regal paunches. The waitress brought them two enchilada plates, vast lakes of hot cheese and beans. As she set the plates down, the men stopped talking and each took a private moment to look at his food, really look at it. Everyone did this in restaurants, paused to inspect the food, but I never noticed it unless I was alone.

Stretch's sheets were soft cotton flannel, surely not the motel's. It always came as a surprise to me that men should want domestic comforts. Sandro slept on the floor when he was a boy, said he felt like he didn't deserve a bed. It was an asceticism that was some way of rejecting his privilege, refusing it. I didn't care whether I deserved a bed or not but I had trouble settling. Trucks from the highway rumbled through my airy sleep. I couldn't warm up and lay with my jacket splayed over the blanket, leather side up like a heel of bread. I worried that Stretch was going to sneak into bed with me. When I had convinced myself he wouldn't, I worried about tomorrow, and my speed trial on the salt. What would happen to me? In a way, it didn't matter. I was here. I was going through with it.

In the depths of cold motel sleep, I dreamed of a gigantic machine, an airplane so large it filled the sky with metal and the raking sound of slowing engines. I was not in Nevada but home, in New York City, which was shaded and dark under the awful machine, a passenger jet enlarged hundreds of times. It moved slowly, the speed of a plane just about to land, but with no lights under its wings. I saw huge landing flaps, ugly with rivets, open on greasy hinges, as the plane came lower and lower, until there was nothing left of the sky but a gunmetal undercarriage, an enveloping screech.

In the morning, Stretch came in and took his shower. While the water ran, I hurriedly pulled on my leathers. I was making the bed when he emerged, a towel around his waist. Tall and blond and lanky, like a giraffe, water beading on skin that was ruddy from the hot shower. He asked if I minded covering my eyes for a moment. I felt his nudity as he changed, but I suppose he could just as easily claim to have felt mine, right there under my clothes.

Dressed, he sat down on the bed and combed his wet hair into its seventies version of a duck's ass, severe and tidy, but down the nape of his neck. The important matter of small-town hair. I laced my boots.

We talked about the speed trials, which were starting today. I said I was running in them, but not that it was about art. It wasn't a lie. I was a Nevada girl and a motorcycle rider. I had always been interested in land speed records. I was bringing to that a New York deliberateness, abstract ideas about traces and speed, which wasn't something Stretch needed to know about. It would make me seem like a tourist.

Stretch said the motel owner's son had a Corvette running but that he could not so much as check the oil or tire pressure, that mechanics worked on it and a driver raced it for him.

"I have to fill out his racing form because he doesn't know what 'displacement' means." He laughed and then went quiet.

"I never met a girl who rides Italian motorcycles," he said. "It's like you aren't real."

He looked at my helmet, gloves, my motorcycle key, on his bureau. The room seemed to hold its breath, the motel curtain sucked against the glass by the draft of a partly opened window, a strip of sun wavering underneath the curtain's hem, the light-blocking fabric holding back the outside world.

He said he wished he could see me do my run, but he was stuck at the motel, retiling a rotten shower.

"It's okay," I said. I was relieved. I felt sure that this interlude, my night in Stretch's bed, shouldn't overlap with my next destination.

"Do you think you might come through here?" he asked. "I mean, ever again?"

I looked at the crates of tools and the jumbled stack of the owner's son's bicycle collection, some of them in good condition and others rusted skeletons with fused chains, perhaps saved simply because he had ample storage space in poor Stretch's room. I thought about Stretch having to sit in a parking lot all night instead of lie in his own bed, and I swear, I almost decided to sleep with him. I saw our life, Stretch done with a day's work, covered with plaster dust, or clean, pulling tube socks up over his long, tapered calves. The little episodes of rudeness and grace he'd been dealt and then would replay in miniature with me.

I stood up and collected my helmet and gloves and said I probably wouldn't be back anytime soon. And then I hugged him, said thanks.

He said he might need to go take another shower, a cold one, and somehow the comment was sweet instead of distasteful.

Later, what I remembered most was the way he'd said my name. He said it like he believed he knew me.

On occasion I let my thoughts fall into that airy space between me and whatever Stretch's idea of me was. He would understand what I came from, even if we couldn't talk about movies or art. "Were you in Vietnam?" I'd ask, assuming some terrible story would come tumbling out, me there to offer comfort, the two of us in the cab of an old white pickup, the desert sun orange and giant over the flat edge of a Nevada horizon. *"Me?"* he'd say. "Nah."

On the short drive from town out to the salt flats, the high desert gleamed under the morning sun. White, sand, rose, and mauve—those were the colors here, sand edging to green in places, with sporadic bursts of powdery yellow, weedy sunflowers blooming three-on-the-tree.

The little gambling town's last business was a compound of trailers orphaned on a bluff. LIQUOR AND DANCING AND NUDE WOMEN. I thought again of Pat Nixon, of underthings in a Pat Nixon palette. Faded peach, or lemon-bright chiffon. As a teenager in Reno, when I heard the words *Mustang Ranch* I pictured a spacious lodge with gold-veined mirrors and round beds, velvet-upholstered throw pillows shaped like logs. The actual Mustang Ranch was just a scattering of cruddy outbuildings, gloomy women with drug habits inside. Even after I understood what it was, it seemed natural enough to hear Mustang Ranch and imagine country luxury, sunken living rooms with wet bars, maybe someone putting on Wanda Jackson, "Tears at the Grand Ole Opry." But they were listening to Top Forty in those places, or to the sound of the generator.

Beyond the access road off the interstate, a lake of white baked and shimmered, flaring back up at the sun like a knife blade turned flat. Pure white stretching so far into the distance that its horizon revealed a faint curve of the Earth. I heard the sonic rip of a military jet, like a giant trowel being dragged through wet concrete, but saw only blue above, a raw and saturated blue that seemed cut from an inner wedge of sky. The jet had left no contrail, just an enveloping sound that came from no single direction. Another jet scraped the basin, high and invisible. I must have heard them in the night. There was a base nearby, Area G on my map, a gray parenthesis. I thought about satellites, Soviet ones, whose features I borrowed from the vintage globe-shaped helmet of a deep-sea diver, a blinking round orb scratching its groove in the sky like a turntable stylus. Everything in Area G put away, retractable roofs closed, missiles rolled out of sight for the scheduled appearance of the probe, the military changing theater sets for the next act.

I wondered why the military didn't claim the salt flats for themselves, for their own tests. I don't know what kind of tests, but something involving heat, speed, thrust, the shriek of engines. American legend Flip Farmer had shot across these flats and hit five hundred miles an hour, driving a three-wheeled, forty-four-foot aluminum canister equipped with a jet engine from a navy Phantom. Why Flip, an ordinary citizen, and not the military? You'd think they would have wanted this place, a site of unchecked and almost repercussionless speed. But the military didn't want an enormous salt desert. They gave it, more or less, to Flip Farmer, world land speed record holder.

Growing up, I loved Flip Farmer like some girls loved ponies or ice skating or Paul McCartney. I had a poster above my bed of Flip and his winning car, the *Victory of Samothrace*. Flip with his breakfast cereal smile, in his zip-up land speed suit, made of a silvery-blue ripstop cloth that refracted to lavender at angles and folds, and lace-up racing boots that were the color of vanilla ice cream. He had a helmet under his arm, silver, with "Farmer" in fancy purple script. I'd found that image again recently, in preparation for my own run on the salt flats, in a book about his life I'd picked up at the Strand. The *Victory of Samothrace* was just behind him on the salt. It was painted the same lavender as the refracting undertone of Flip's flameproof suit, hand-rubbed color lacquered to a fine gleam, silver accents on the intake ducts and tail wing. Pure weight and energy, but weightless, too, with its enormous tailfin, a hook for scraping the sky.

When I was twelve, Flip came through Reno and gave out autographs at a casino. I didn't have a glossy photo for him to sign, so I had him sign my hand. For weeks I took a shower with a plastic bag over that hand, rubber-banded at the wrist. It wasn't quite a romantic infatuation. There are levels of readiness. Young girls don't entertain the idea of sex, their body and another's together. That comes later, but there isn't nothing before it. There's an innocent displacement, a dreaming, and idols are perfect for a little girl's dreaming. They aren't real. They aren't the gas station attendant trying to lure you into the back of the service station, a paperboy trying to lure you into a toolshed, a friend's father trying to lure you into his car. They don't lure. They beckon, but like desert mirages. Flip Farmer was safely unreachable. He was something special. I chose him from among all the men in the world, and he signed the back of my hand and smiled with very white, straight teeth. He gave us each that same smile, the children and adults who lined up at Harrah's. We weren't individuals but a surface he moved over, smiling and remote. The thing was, if he had returned my gaze, I probably would have washed his autograph from my hand.

The year he came through Reno, Flip had barely escaped death as he'd made his land speed record on the salt. Just after he hit 522 miles per hour, his rear chute prematurely released. It blew out the back of the *Victory* and snapped off, sending the car veering to and fro between mile markers. He recovered, but with no chute, he had no way to slow down. He was still going five hundred miles an hour. He knew that if he even so much as tapped the brakes they would melt and burn out, and then he'd have no brakes. They were designed for speeds of less than 150 miles an hour. He would have to let the car slow itself, but it wasn't slowing. He realized, as he flew across the salt, almost frictionlessly, that it was all going to be over anyhow. Whether he used the brakes or not, it was all about to end. So he used them. He tapped ever so slightly on the pedal with his left driving shoe. It sank to the floor. The car sailed onward, its speed unchecked. He pumped the brake, and nothing. Just the thunk of the pedal hitting the floor, the flat world running liquid beyond the clear plastic bubble-canopy.

He flew past mile zero, the end of the official racecourse. His crew and several teams of newsmen looked on. He was going four hundred miles an hour. The surface, here, was ungraded. The engine was off, and all he heard was the knocking and slamming of the *Victory*'s suspension as it thudded over the rough salt. He had time to think, as he sat in the cockpit, soon to be tomb, time to notice how small and familiar a space it was. How intimate and calm. The car was filled with a white smoke. As he waited for death, having given up pumping his nonbrakes, it occurred to him that the smoke was salt, aspirated to an airborne powder, having been ground by the wheels and forced up through the axles into the cramped cockpit of the car.

Through a mist of white, softening his view out the canopy, a row of electricity poles reared up. He tried to steer between them but ended up mowing down several. Then he was riding straight into the shallow salt lake, water spraying high on both sides of the *Victory*. The car finally began to slow—to three hundred, to two hundred. But then he was shot up a ten-foot-high salt dike, which had been built when a drainage ditch was dug across the southern edge of the flats. The world went vertical. A quadrangle of plain, cloudless sky. A forced contemplation of the heavens, crisp and angelic blue, a classic prelude to death. If there had been just one puffy trawler, a little tugboat of a cloud, even so much as a cotton ball of vapor against the blue, he would have hoped. There was only blue. He was headed for the drainage ditch on the other side of the dike. It was filled with rainwater. The *Victory* slammed into it. As it sank, nose first, Flip desperately popped the canopy. There was no way he'd get the canopy open once the car was underwater. He tore off his oxygen mask and tried to unfold himself from the driver's seat. He was caught. He could not get himself out from behind the steering wheel. The car was sinking. His fireproof suit was snagged on the afterburner levers. The *Victory* was deep underwater, and he was still trying to unhook the fabric of his suit-sleeve from the levers. Just as his brain was losing its last bit of oxygen he untangled himself and swam toward the wavering brightness above him, where sun penetrated the water. He emerged in a slick of hydrazine fuel that was collecting on the surface. Emergency workers came running. They dragged him to safety just before the hydrazine ignited, sending a boom, and then a far bigger boom, followed by a violent bubbling, as the *Victory of Samothrace* exploded underwater like fuel rods in a reactor pool.

The next year, Flip built another car, *Samothrace II*, with a bigger jet engine and beefy rear disc brakes, at his shop in the Watts area of Los Angeles. It was 1965. The riots came and his warehouse caught fire, or maybe it was torched. The *Victory of Samothrace II* was badly damaged. He couldn't rebuild in time for the season at the salt flats, which only lasts from August to September or October, before the rains come and turn the ancient lake bed into a huge shallow bowl. That year the rains came early, and the *Samothrace* was not yet ready. I read about all this in his autobiography, *Winning*. Riots and rain were presented in the book as misfortunes of the same order: one and then another. Riots in Watts, rain at the flats. Smiling, suburban Flip talking about how he and the crew had entertained themselves with an improvised version of miniature golf, barricaded inside their workshop as marauders flung homemade bombs. "Golly," Flip or his ghost author wrote, "what a year of random bad luck."

Flip recaptured the world record the season after the Watts riots and kept it until last year, 1975, when an Italian stole it away in a rocket-fueled vehicle and Flip officially retired. Now he does television commercials for after-market shocks. The Italian, Didi Bombonato, is sponsored by Valera Tires, which is where the lines begin to cross. Didi Bombonato would be at the Bonneville Salt Flats to set a record. Sandro is Sandro Valera, of Valera Tires and Moto Valera motorcycles.

*   *   *

At the flats, the sun conspired with the salt to make a gas of brightness and heat pouring in from all directions, its reflected rays bouncing up from the hammered-white ground and burning the backs of my thighs right through my leathers.

I parked and walked along the open pits. People were wheeling race cars and motorcycles from flatbed trailers and up onto workbenches, unlooping cable to plug into power generators, transferring gasoline from larger canisters to plastic jugs with funnel dispensers. Pink gasoline and synthetic red engine oil soaked into the salt like butcher shop residue. The salt itself, up close, was the color of unbleached sugar, but the sunlight used it as if it were the brightest white. It was only when a cloud momentarily shifted over the sun and recast the earth in a different mood, cool and appealingly somber, that the salt revealed its true self as a light shade of beige. When the cloud moved away, everything blanched to the white sheen of molybdenum grease.

I heard the silky glide of toolbox drawers, the tink of wrenches dropped on the hard salt. Tanned little boys darted past me on bicycles, wearing mesh baseball caps propped high on their heads, in mimicry of the fathers and uncles who crowded around workbenches, bent over vehicles, their belts buckled off center to avoid scratching the paint. Beyond the workbenches, large women fanned themselves and guarded the Igloo coolers. Each pit site had one of these women, seated in a frail aluminum lawn chair, her weight distending the woven plaid seat, legs splayed, monstrous calves like big, blank faces. Opening and shutting the Igloo cooler to retrieve or simply monitor the soft drinks and sandwiches, as their husbands opened and shut the red metal drawers of stacked and rolling toolboxes. The women seemed deeply bored but proudly so, as veterans of this event.

Cars were being rolled from the test area, salt piled in a ring around the tread of each tire like unmelting snow. I filled out my registration form and waited to have the bike inspected. The Valera motorcade arrived, a convoy of trucks, trailers, and air-conditioned buses with tinted windows and industrial-grade generators. They parked in their own separate area of the salt. It was roped and off-limits. I turned in my form. I had a couple of hours before they would run my class. I walked over to the start line. The men who clocked the start were like the men I'd seen in the Mexican restaurant the night before, big mustaches, wearing sunglasses and ear protection headphones, walkie-talkies strapped to their chests, over their officials' jackets.

For land speed records, each driver has the course to himself. You race by yourself, but your time is relative to whatever class you race in—in my case, unmodified 650 cc twins. No one else shares the course, so vehicles run endlessly throughout the day, a coming and going in the bright white heat, each calamity or success on the scale of individuals. There were two long lines, short course and long course. In the lines were every kind of car and bike, dragster cycles with eight-cylinder motors, streamliners like warheads put on wheels, the drivers coffined flat on their backs in tiny horizontal compartments, inches above the salt, and the elegant lakesters in polished aluminum, rounded and smooth like worn bars of soap, their fender skirts almost grazing the road. There were old-fashioned roadsters with gleaming new paint, roll bars, and big stenciled numbers on the doors. Vintage American muscle cars. A pink-and-yellow 1953 Chrysler Town & Country, a Technicolor mirage bouncing along on shot springs.

After my one year in New York I had practically forgotten there was a world of elsewheres, people who lived outside the city and recreated in their own style. There were a lot of family-based teams, and in a few cases, the mother was the driver. Not many, but I was not the only female, though I may have been the only woman on a motorcycle. There was the joke of the bump-start vehicle, which gave the racers a boost from the start line. Anything on wheels and that ran could work: A school bus. A just-married jalopy, trailing cans. An ice cream truck. The more elaborate and professional the race car, the more ridiculous and lavishly impractical its bump-start vehicle seemed to be. Although I was wrong about the ice cream truck. It pulled up and opened for business, pencil-necked boys lining up at the window. An ambulance came, and I wondered what happened, and how serious the injury was.

But the ambulance was a bump vehicle, pushing a lakester off the start line, the ambulance driver wearing a white medic's shirt and costume bandages soaked in fake blood.

Every few minutes an engine screamed as a vehicle flew off the line, spewing a rooster tail of salt from under each rear tire. A few seconds into its run the vehicle began to float, its lower half warbled. Then the whole thing went liquid and blurry and was lost to the horizon.

One after another I watched the scream, the careen, the rooster tail, the float, and then the shimmer and wink off the edge of horizon, gone.

Careen, rooster tail, float, gone.

Careen, float, gone.

There were lots of us watching. Drivers, kids, wives, technicians. All we had, to track the action, after the vehicle twinkled and melted into nothing, was a crackle on the timing officials' two-way radios. I felt myself bracing for bad news after the crackle. Anticipation was structured into the logic of the place. We weren't waiting to hear the run was routine, that it was solid, that there were no problems. Standing behind the start line, there was nothing to see as a car entered the measured mile. We weren't there to see. We were waiting on news of some kind of event, one that could pierce this blank and impassive and giant place. What else could do that but a stupendous wipeout? We were waiting on death.

My final project in art school was a film about Flip Farmer. I'd contacted him at his shop in Las Vegas to request an interview, but he wouldn't agree to it unless I paid him five thousand dollars. He seemed to make no distinction between an impoverished art student and *Look* magazine. I took a risk and knocked on his door. He lived on the bluffs above the strip. A curtain was pulled aside and quickly shut. No one was going to answer. I had a super-8 camera that I panned around the premises, past a tire swing, unmoving in the breezeless day, broken toys, lawn chairs that someone was stripping of upholstery and bending into scrap aluminum. Several project cars up on blocks—shade tree work, as Scott and Andy called it. "Hey, you can't film here! Hey!" It was a woman's voice, from beyond a window screen. I figured I'd better go.

A friend of mine from school named Chris Kelly had tried to make a documentary about the singer Nina Simone, a similar scenario of knocking on her door. He had tracked her down to the South of France. Nina Simone opened her front door in a bathrobe, saw that the visitor was holding a camera, lifted a gun from the pocket of her robe and shot at him. She wasn't a good shot. Chris Kelly, who had turned and run, was only hit once, a graze to the shoulder, as he tore through the high, wet grass beyond her farmhouse. He got no footage of Nina Simone but I somehow saw this robe from which she had produced her gun. Flowy and feminine, pink and yellow flowers with greenish flourishes, semi-abstract leaves. Nina Simone's brown legs. Her flat, calloused feet in a pair of those unisex leather slippers that Europeans like Sandro wore around the house. She shot Chris Kelly, after which he became a legend at UNR. Or at least he was a legend to me. Being fired at with a gun made an impression; it elevated what he did from a student project to actual art. It was somehow better than if he'd filmed her in a typical documentary style. Chris Kelly moved to New York City a year later and became doubly a legend to me, the guy shot by the singer and also the one who moved to New York.

After I'd left Flip Farmer's place on the bluffs I drove along the Las Vegas Strip at dusk, the camera filming my own departure, casino neon flashing beyond the windshield of the car I'd borrowed for the trip. Stoplight. Man in a white cowboy hat, crossing. Signs stacked up against high mountains. Chapel, Gulf, Texaco, motel, family units, weekly, pawn, refrigerator, fun. A slow proceeding through town and out. No Flip. A Flipless film about Flip. It wasn't bad, and when I first got to New York, I mostly made short movies that were like the tracked retreat from Flip's. They were wanderings, through Chinatown at night, or into abandoned buildings on the Lower East Side. I didn't know what I was looking for. I filmed and then looked at the footage to see what was there.

Sandro had told me about one of Helen Hellenberger's artists who had done a drawing by walking in a straight line across a mile of the Mojave Desert and marking it in chalk. It was almost feminine, Sandro joked, to *walk*. Contemplation, nature, submitting passively to the time it took.

The time it took: that was when I had gotten the idea to do this. What about going as fast as you possibly could? I'd thought. And not marking it in chalk. Drawing in a fast and almost traceless way.

I'd spent half a day among those waiting on death and now I was in line for the long course and hoping I was not the sacrifice.

Perhaps because I was one of the few women running a vehicle that day, the timing officials let me store my knapsack and camera with them while I did my run. Everyone loved the bike. It was brand-new, there was a waiting list to order them from every dealership in the United States. Even the Valera people came over to admire it. I didn't explain that I was Sandro's girlfriend. I simply let them admire the bike, or admire the idea of an American girl riding it. Didi Bombonato was not among the Valera people who came over to say hello, see the bike. Didi Bombonato was in the air-conditioned bus. He would make his run later, when the salt was closed to everyone else.

No bump vehicle? The timing official asked me.

Street bike, I said, with electric start.

They would mark my time at two miles, but I was planning to sustain it for longer. For the entire ten miles, and so I had lots of time and space to get up to top speed. I wanted to feel the size of the salt flats. When I'd requested the long course instead of the short course, the timing association secretary had asked if my vehicle went over 175 miles an hour. I lied and said yes, and she shrugged and put an *L* next to my name.

It had rained recently, which was why everyone's tires were ringed in salt. The salt was still rain-damp and sticky, which meant I'd leave tracks to photograph after my run.

Take it easy, the timing official told me. We're expecting wind gusts. At mile three the course gets funky for several hundred feet, didn't get completely smoothed out when they graded. He was kind. He didn't belittle me for being a woman. He gave the pertinent information and then nodded that it was okay to go.

I was reminded, as I prepared to accelerate out of the start, of ski racing, and the many hundreds of moments I'd spent counting down seconds in the timing shack, my heart pounding, hunched at the start on the top of a course, squeezing the grips of my ski poles, planting and replanting them for the kick out of the start, surrounded by timing officials—always men, all men, but who took me seriously, spoke gravely about the imperfections of the course, what sorts of dangers to watch out for, a courtesy they gave every racer. At Bonneville, the sensations at the start were almost identical, the officials' neutrality, the same people who surely had made this course, painted its three oil lines, dragged graders up and down it behind trucks, just as the officials at ski races prepped the course surface and set the gates. The beep of timing equipment, waiting to trip a red wire suspended over white. And the quality of light, pure reflecting white, like a snow-glinting morning above tree line.

Beep, beep, beep. I was off.

I moved through the gears and into fifth. The wind pushed against me, threatening to rip my helmet off, as though I were tilting my face into a waterfall. I hit 110 on my speedometer and went low. The salt did not feel like a road. I seemed to be moving around a lot, as if I were riding on ice, and yet I had traction, a slightly loose traction that had to be taken on faith. I was going 120. Then 125. I felt alert to every granule of time. Each granule *was* time, the single pertinent image, the other moment-images, before and after, lost, unconsidered. All I knew was my hand on the throttle grip, its tingling vibration in my gloved fingers: 130, 138. Floating Mountain hovered in the distance, a mirage at its skirt. Hazy and massive. Whatever happened, it would watch but not help. Pay attention, it said. You could die.

The trucker had said it more or less, telling me I'd look worse in a body bag. Probably I'd passed him, my loud exhaust pipes catching him off guard.

My left hand was cramping from tension. I slowed to 120 and lifted it off the grip, steering with my right hand. I felt the wind through my deerskin glove, heavy and smooth like water. Wind gets thickest just before an airplane breaks the sound barrier. The sound barrier is nothing but air, an immense wall of wind. Was wind one thing or a thing of many parts, millions or billions of parts? It was one thing, one wind. My two hair braids had worked themselves free from under my jacket and were flapping behind me, stinging my back like two long horse's tails.

The photographs would be nothing but a trace. A trace of a trace. They might fail entirely to capture what I hoped for, the experience of speed.

"You don't have to immediately become an artist," Sandro said. "You have the luxury of time. You're young. Young people are doing something even when they're doing nothing. A young woman is a conduit. All she has to do is *exist*."

You have time. Meaning don't use it, but pass through time in patience, waiting for something to come. Prepare for its arrival. Don't rush to meet it. Be a conduit. I believed him. I felt this to be true. Some people might consider that passivity but I did not. I considered it living.

I tucked in and pegged the throttle. The salt stretched out in front of me. I saw the real ambulance, there in case of accidents, parked along the side of the course. I was going 142 miles an hour now. Two oil lines painted on either side of me marked the track, with a third down the middle. I flew along the centerline. I was going 145 miles an hour. Then 148. I was in an acute case of the present tense. Nothing mattered but the milliseconds of life at that speed.

Far ahead of me, the salt flats and mountains conspired into one puddled vortex. I began to feel the size of this place. Or perhaps I did not feel it, but the cycle, whose tires marked its size with each turn, did. I felt a tenderness for them, speeding along under me.

A massive gust of wind came in. I was shoved sideways and forced down.

The bike skipped end over end. I slammed headfirst into the salt, a smack into white concrete. My body was sent abrading and skidding and slamming before flipping up and slamming down again. I almost crashed into my own salt-sliding motorcycle. We barely missed each other. I skidded and tumbled.

There's a false idea that accidents happen in slow motion.

The crash test dummy careens into the steering column, the front end folds inward, car hood accordioned, glass showering up and then collapsing gracefully like those waterfalls at the casinos exploding into confetti. ("*Confetti*," Sandro says, "confetti is hard almond candy. No one throws it. We say *coriandoli*, a more beautiful word anyway.")

What happens slowly carries in each part the possibility of returning to what came before. In an accident everything is simultaneous, sudden, irreversible. It means this: no going back.

I know the wind gusted and that I crashed.

What came after was slower, but I wasn't there for it. The lights were out.

3. He had come a long way to that moment of quick violence,

to braining a German soldier with a motorbike headlamp, and then taking the soldier's dagger, his pistol, his gas mask, no longer of use to him. Such a long way.

From a placid childhood that faced the African sea, in which every young boy's game was a set of silhouettes against a clean division of water and sky, vast and limitless, a sea smooth and convex as a glassmaker's bubble, stretching and welling as if the aquamarine water were a single molten plasma.

Valera spent hours on his family's balcony in Alexandria, looking for ships and pissing on the Berber merchants who trundled below with carts of sticky dates and ostrich plumes. Flaubert had done this before him, on his trip down the Nile in a felucca with Maxime Du Camp. Coptic monks had swum up to the boat, naked, begging alms. "Baksheesh, baksheesh!" the monks cried out, the felucca's sailing crew hollering back this or that about Muhammad and attempting to cudgel the monks with frying pans and mop handles. Flaubert couldn't resist taking his prick from his trousers, waving it and pretending to piss on their heads, and then delivering on the threat as the wretched monks clung to the rigging and prow. "Baksheesh, baksheesh!"

Valera was more furtive, sending a patter over the balcony railing and ducking behind a potted plant as the merchants yelled up,
indignant, and then briskly wheeled their carts away, leaving Valera
to read in peace, without the irritating clang of handbells and the
distracting grind of wooden cartwheels on the paving stones. He was
busy supplementing his strict lycée education with Rimbaud and
Baudelaire, with Flaubert's letters, volumes he purchased on trips to
Paris with his father. His father proudly paid the extra customs fees
for Valera's crates of literature, unaware that some of it was not only
improper but downright lewd, like Flaubert's letters from the year
he went down the Nile, 1849. Pages were passed among schoolboys,
creased and underlined, depicting a life that confirmed the essential
goodness of everything the boys had been told was bad, a life that
involved fucking before breakfast, after lunch, before dinner, all
night, and then again the morning after, ill with hangover—the best
yet, by Flaubert's own account. Valera memorized Flaubert's reports
and dreamed of his own sentimental education of see-through pants
and sandalwood, of the endless succession of breasts and velvety
cunts that Flaubert encountered.

Valera longed for a French girl named Marie, closing his eyes to
close the physical gap between their two bodies, as he pretended his
own hand was Marie's lips, mouth, and tongue. Dark-eyed, pale-
skinned Marie, who lived at the convent next door. She was older than
Valera, but she let him hold her hand and even kiss her, though nothing more. The promise of her warm body was buried under layers of
no and not yet. Every morning the girls were taken into the convent
courtyard by the nuns, and Valera would strain at the kitchen window
to see them doing their knee bends and stretches. On occasion the sun
angled in such a way that it penetrated the girls' thin white cotton
blouses, and he was able to glimpse the shape of Marie's breasts, which
were round and large. They were not suspended in any kind of undergarment, like the complicated muslin-and-elastic holsters his mother
wore, and he wondered if brassieres were only for married women.
When he looked in the mirror he felt unfree, a hopeless entwinement

of longings and guilt. His private pleasures were wrecked by the specter of guilt, even with the door locked, the covers pulled up: a fortress of privacy breached by his mother's voice, calling his name. He figured he'd stored up a lifetime of lust and that upon its first real release he would unburden himself in one violent salvo and then settle into a more manageable state. He imagined that physical proximity would instruct him in so many things—first of all, the real distance between people. He was willing to pay to begin this education. He strolled the Rue de la Gare de Ramleh, where the whores worked in the open, but the truth was that he could not distinguish male from female, even as he'd been told that men were on one side of the street and women on the other. But which side was which? He was embarrassed to ask. They looked the same, wore their scarves knotted and wrapped the same way, trailed the same perfume. He longed for his own sexual delinquency, but he had no taste for surprises if he should accidently choose the wrong side of Ramleh. On the night of his fourteenth birthday he mustered his courage and visited a brothel on Rue Lepsius, where native women—maybe they were Jews—yawned and adjusted their hairpins. A large doll lay on a chair, its legs splayed wide. Valera quickly selected a woman in gold-slashed bloomers whose curly hair reminded him of Marie's. Together they entered a little chamber with threadbare rugs and a rickety settee. The woman flopped on the settee and began puffing on a hookah in a mannish and private-seeming fashion, eyes closed, mouth like a trumpet bell exhaling smoke toward the ceiling in O's that floated virginal and then frayed and collapsed. When she was done with the hookah she took off her bloomers. The settee creaked loudly as she pulled Valera down and wrapped her legs around him. Soft pressures enveloped him. He ignored the symphony of creaks from the settee and moved into a drifting sea, felt a sensation of a boat and waves, but whether he was the boat and she the waves did not matter, only the pleasure of movement mattered. Suddenly the woman bore down, activating ridiculous muscles. He didn't know that females possessed such muscles, which were like a hand that grabbed him and squeezed until there was nothing left to squeeze.

The salvo he'd been dreaming of was not violent, though it produced a strange aftershock of trembling. Most unexpected was the sadness that followed on the heels of pleasure, like smoke from an extinguished candle. But like smoke, the sadness quickly dissipated, and a week later, behind the open bazaar, he paid a native woman to let him touch her bosom. He'd been so consumed with the mechanics of the act with the woman in the brothel that he'd all but forgotten to investigate her breasts, which had stared up at him, jiggling softly in rhythm with the creaking settee. Behind the bazaar, he prodded and handled the breasts of the native woman as if they were fruits for purchasing. They felt, to his horror, like farmer's cheese with gravelly bits buried deep inside. He was sure that Marie's breasts would not be lumpy and unpleasantly complicated. Marie's would be springy and consistent, like two water balloons. He would wait for hers and hers alone.

One late afternoon on his way home from rugby practice, Valera saw a strange machine parked on the seawall, a cycle with odd compartments, painted black. He supposed it was technically a bicycle—two wheels, a seat, handlebars. But it had a motor like an industrial machine. Its surfaces gleamed, showing none of Alexandria's pervasive dust, road dust, brick dust, lime dust. As if it had just been transported from a trade show or museum, and yet it ticked with life, metal expanding as the cycle cooled: someone had just ridden it. Over its solid black rear wheel was sprung an odd upside-down sluiceway or gutter with interior machinery. German names were lettered in gold on its rear, "Hildebrand & Wolfmüller, München," in fussy and old-fashioned cursive stencil like on the Prussian War–era sewing machine his mother kept for the seamstress. The place name, München, made him think of workmen whose lives were organized around haptic knowledge and early wake times, tinkering away as the Bavarian sun rose over narrow cobblestone streets. The cycle's frame was thick and looked made of iron, to which a giant canister was bolted, a sort of metal keg that must have been the engine. There were no pedals, just two rigid pegs. The front wheel was spoked, the rear an opaque black disc like a factory flywheel. A young man came around the corner, and by the tap and click of hard-soled, well-made city shoes, Valera understood that he was the owner of this weird cycle. The sun was already low over the sea. The man's hair was slicked and wet with the possibilities of evening. Valera had never seen him—a Frenchman, he guessed. The man got on the contraption. There was nothing athletic in the attitude of his body, as if he would get the cycle going without physical effort, as a horseman swings his leg over, settles in the saddle and digs his spurs. He compressed a crank with one of his fancy shoes, to start the motor. After a few tries, it caught with a rumbling bub-bub-bub, coughing smoke, banging and backfiring, almost sputtering out, but then it seemed to find itself, and idled evenly again. Oh, but what happened next. Above the din of the engine Valera had not heard the broad, heavy door of the convent sing shut on its hinges. Had not heard the soft slap of a young woman's espadrilles. Marie, walking along the seawall. She was glancing nervously at the convent's open casement windows, moving quickly as if to avoid detection. She did not notice Valera. She approached the man on the bubbing cycle, threw her arms around his neck, and kissed him. Is this real? Valera asked himself. Or am I dreaming this absurd betrayal? Marie hopped onto the seat of the cycle behind the man, her legs wrapped around his, her arms clutching his waist, the side of her face pressed against his back, her skirt bunched up around her knees. Off they went on the black machine, a thin looping trail of white smoke unfurling behind them.

Marie, were you not a virgin after all? Did you refuse me because you were taken, and not because you were pure? Or was I not good enough?

They rode along the seawall, Marie's skirt and the man's jacket flapping erratically in the warm wind. The cycle picked up speed until they seemed to be darting into the horizon, an orthogonal razor across Valera's eye. Valera shouted. He used everything he had. He knew they could not hear him. He needed to enter the space of air, too, as that machine had, as that man had, taking Marie with him, man and bike and Marie making an obscene double-humped centaur's profile that moved along the seawall.

Watching its smug glide, Valera was in pain, but he felt a strange exhilaration around the edges of his pain. "The world is unknown to me," he said out loud. "It is unknown."

The cycle quieted to a distant throgging whine and then he could no longer hear it or see it. He was abandoned to his own sudden urge. He felt like a baby snake with too much venom. Afraid he would do something rash if he went inside his family's apartment just then—defiling melons smuggled from the pantry was only half-pleasurable and led to an empty and disgusted sentiment, not worth the momentary joy—he instead descended the crumbling stairs along the seawall. Above the railing were smudged blue handprints, placed there by superstitious Egyptians to ward off the evil eye. No one was around, and he could have attended to the matter discreetly but decided against it. This erection, he felt, meant something. He wanted to use it, somehow. He disrobed, and with the calm thrill of entering a woman, he entered the ocean.

The sun was already half-melted, its redness spilling like cassis over the horizon. Valera pumped his legs in the water and composed. Composed! He made a poem, his first, to commemorate the black machine and to condemn the man who rode it.

When the sun had sunken completely under the horizon, the whole of the ocean's visible surface turned an opaque silver. His body disappeared at the waterline and he felt bifurcated. Two halves, above the water and below it. He could hear everything acutely, as if the silvery light were fine-tuning all his senses. He was aware of tiny nuance in the lap and slurp of water against his body as he was raised and lowered in the swell.

He wrote a very fine poem in that swell. But with no pencil, no paper, he had only his memory to commit it to. He practiced it viva voce in the waves. But dazed by the awful truth that young Marie had a secret life, that someone else was holding and squeezing her perfect water balloon breasts, and stunned by the silver surface of his sea—his, where he'd swum every day of his childhood and yet had never seen it turn this . . . not quite a color, but the colorless shine of mercury—the reverie was a crucible of forgetting. An hour later he could not recall his poem. Only a few fragments, like broken seashells caught in a dragnet. OIL OF POSSIBILITY and REMORSELESS, SPEEDING SHADOW BELOW BLUE UNBROKEN SKY, and LOVE AND HATE THE SAME, FORGED IN YOUR FLYWHEEL / BLACK AS MELTED PRUSSIAN CANNONS / NO TAINT OF DEFEAT. Strung together, they were not a poem. The unity and cadence were lost. Later this happened to him repeatedly, not in the ocean but in sleep. He would wake up with an understanding that he had just generated, in the final crepe-thin layers of active dreaming, the greatest poem of his life—objectively great—and that it was lost forever, sacrificed to the process of waking.

As Valera swam toward shore this occurred to him: If Marie was getting on strange cycles and spreading her legs for strange men, it meant Valera, too, had a chance with her.

Don't despair, he told himself. Be patient. And get a cycle with a combustive engine.

When his family left Alexandria for Milan, six years after he'd composed his poem and then lost it to the ocean, motorcycles were becoming common. It was 1906. His father, who had quickly built a vast construction empire in the newly industrial Milan, would have gladly purchased him one if he'd asked, but Valera expressed little interest. French-made, German-made, even American-made, the cycles in Milan were newer, sleeker designs than the one from München with its giant metal-keg engine, but none gave him the same thrill. At first he knew why. Later he forgot. The reason was in his own fragment: unbroken sky.

Valera had grown up in a world of long and empty afternoons in the African heat, and he succumbed to Milan's noise, chaos, and frenetic schedules poorly. The city was overrun with screeching electric trams, shuddering violently to their scheduled stops as though their rigid wheels were being forced over piles of lumber and debris. The trams were chained to one another like bulky oxen, with a gripman whose only choice was to pull the lever or to jam it shut and stop the tram. The dour gripman. Pull the lever, jam it shut. Pull the lever, jam it shut. Lunch break. Dry ham panino and scalded espresso thimble. Pull the lever, jam it shut. The trams were powered from overhead by electricity, via a wand that attached magnetically to a wire strung above each route. Wires crisscrossed the sky like a great ventilator through which the city exhaled its polluted breath. The explosions and smoke from automobiles and motorcycles were a war fought on his nerves. The electric lights, burn holes in his vision. Most depressing were the rush hour masses, darting like rats down numbered trackways, clutching sacks that contained mass-produced snacks they would eat without pleasure as they were conveyed to their outer-rung apartment blocks.

The cycles that putted along coughing their blue smoke took people to work in street-level shops and upper-level offices, not into the bosom of pink sunset, into Marie's arms. It was discord that had struck him so many years earlier. Cycle against honking and crowds and wires was nothing. Girl against pale laundry and waves, well, something, but a lust doomed to boredom. It had been the frisson of the two, cracked limestone wall and gleaming motor parts, Marie's skirts fluttering, her knees wrapped around the back of some asshole Frenchman, the loud machine farting a trail of exhaust into the calm, vast blue, that had made its impression.

Valera with his elegant leather satchel, a student in Rome, was not part of any Bohemian rabble. It was 1912 and he was just about to finish his university degree and move back to Milan, to work for his father. But he nursed a secret interest in this rabble, young men who gathered at the Caffè Aragno on the Via del Corso, arguing and penning manifestos instead of going to their classes at the university. He spied on them daily, lurking at one of the Aragno's outdoor tables, pretending to read, scribbling silly poems, or openly staring at these little clusters of subversives who spoke to one another in low tones. To spy and to participate are separate worlds, and when the little group had something important to discuss, they retreated to a back room of the café, which the proprietor let them use. They'd glance at one another and say, "Third room," and as they filtered inside the secret back room, Valera, the sole voyeur, was left with no group on which to eavesdrop. He longed to be among them.

One night, motorcycles converged on the corner beyond the café, motors revving, goggled grins exchanged among the cyclists. No one had clued him in.

What was happening?

"A race, pal."

The young people smoking at the outdoor café tables cheered. Someone threw a full bottle of Peroni, which smashed in the paved intersection, leaving a great wet stain that glittered with broken glass.

The drivers all backed out simultaneously and squealed off down the Corso.

Two men crossing the avenue with evening newspapers under their arms and a woman in a black toque carrying packages were all sent diving for the curb. A tram came, and the brakeman had to pull the lever and let the gang of motorbikes pass. Pedestrians and vehicles halted for these renegades, their cycles growling like a convoy of hornets. The atmosphere had changed. The quick looks, the retreats to the secret meeting room, there was none of that. This was an open celebration, and Valera, too, was lifted by the festive spirit. He felt that he was part of it, even as he wasn't sure what they were celebrating.

Twenty minutes later he heard the far-off noise of cycles accelerating in sync. The racers, returning.

The motorbikes came streaming down the Corso, their light beams diffused by fog into iridescent halos, each a perfect miniature of the colored ring that appeared around the moon on rare occasions, an effect of ice crystals in the clouds. Scores of moon rings laced and interlaced. Valera knew they were cycles with riders, but all he saw was glowing rings. They sent a seditious crackle through the air, those headlights, promising that something would happen.

The drivers collected along the curb near the café, some popping up onto the sidewalk, spoked wheels and hot exhaust pipes in one tangled mass under the orange neon letters CINZANO. The shiny metal of gas tanks, fenders, carburetor covers, headlamp rings, and wheel rims sent the orange neon skidding over chrome and steel and suffusing everything—the atmosphere and the charge in the atmosphere, this feeling of sedition—in ember orange. For the first time in his life he found the neon, and the way it bathed those shiny machines parked below it, dazzling. Something was coalescing, an energy transfer from the cyclists to his own spirit. Life is here, he thought. It is happening now.

People were trading cycles, letting others take turns.

Valera stood.

"You want to give it a go?" A chrome pudding-bowl helmet was placed in his hands by a rider who had just dismounted.

Valera put on the helmet, looping the chin strap. He climbed onto the cycle with what he hoped was the élan of Marie's companion on the seawall in Alexandria, with his wet hair and those hard-click shoes, who had seemed completed by his machine, as if together they made one thing.

You start it like this, see? It's in neutral. Pull the compression lever. A downward thrust of the body's weight on the kick-starter, and release compression. Bub-bub-bub-bub. Careful not to pop the clutch. Ease off it gently. First is down. Second, third, and fourth are up. Here's your hand brake and there's your foot brake. Don't pull the hand brake alone without your foot brake, or you'll be over the handlebars like a pole vaulter.

Valera stalled the motor trying to shift from neutral into first. His face went red.

It's okay, just put it back in neutral and give it another kick start. . . . Yes, good. . . . Now into first. Pull in the clutch so you'll be ready—

The cycles began to move and thin. They were off!

Go! That's it—go!

The cycles were dispersing. Valera pushed on the shifter with the sole of his shoe, gave the throttle gas, and eased off the clutch, understanding, this time, that it was a two-part invention: the gas flows and the clutch releases as one movement, but each part is controlled independently, the two meeting at a fluid halfway point.

The cycle burped forward, not at all gracefully, but he felt the essence of what was required, control with the wrists. After a few erratic lunges, learning the stiff springs of clutch and throttle, he was able to go along more smoothly and to follow the movements of his fellow riders, each reacting to the next as fish do, swimming in a school, auto-choreographed in one undulation, fish to fish, rider to rider, as they threaded the narrow streets beyond the Corso.

He grew bold and began moving forward between riders, under neon signs that looked like bright, hard candy, reflecting from the tram wires and the tracks in smears and gleams. He was making his way to the front of the pack.

As they cornered the roundabout of the Piazza Venezia, Valera reached the front. He and three others formed a motorcade. Light and noise, and the damp air on his face, the helmet making him feel like a brave soldier. Four cycles across, vanguarding.

As if they were both in an official capacity and yet undermining all.

Hunched over the handlebars above a blur of paving stones, flinging off their burdens behind them.

A night junta.

Amid the growls of so many engines echoing through the streets, the rider next to Valera yelled, "Let's take the city!"

They swerved down Via di San Gregorio, past glimpses of the exterior wall of the Colosseum, whose massive belly was lit with electric light leaking through its dark and crumbling walls, turning the Colosseum into a broken and blazing lantern.

They were on Via Nazionale, streaming through the dark in a cavalcade of motorbike headlights, under the glow of argon and neon.

RINASCENTE FARRINI FALCK

BAR TABACCHI CAFFÉ

CINZANO CINZANO CINZANO

He could see the dim lights in the fountain up ahead, in the vast Piazza Esedra. The night felt like it would burn. It was burning. Why had he waited so long?

He surged into it.

4. BLANKS

I had moved to New York from Reno just over a year before my Bonneville trip. I'd found an apartment on Mulberry Street and planned to make films with the camera I never returned to the art department at UNR, a Bolex Pro. I arrived with the camera and Chris Kelly's telephone number and little else. I was twenty-one. I figured I'd wait to call mythical Chris Kelly, shot in the arm by Nina Simone. I'll get situated first, I thought. I'll have some sense of what I'm doing, a way to make an impression on him. Then I'll call. I knew no one else, but downtown New York was so alive with people my age, and so thoroughly abandoned by most others, that the energy of the young seeped out of the ground. I figured it was only a matter of time before I met people, was part of something.

My apartment was about as blank and empty as my new life, with its layers upon layers of white paint, like a plaster death mask of the two rooms, giving them an ancient urban feeling, and I didn't want to mute that effect with furniture and clutter. The floor was an interlocking map of various unmatched linoleum pieces in faded floral reds, resembling a cracked and soiled Matisse. It was almost bare, except for a trunk that held my clothes, a few books, the stolen or borrowed Bolex, a Nikon F (my own) and a men's brown felt hat, owner unknown. I had no cups, no table, nothing of that sort. The mattress I slept on had been there when I rented. I had one faded pink towel, on its edge machine embroidered PICKWICK. It was from a hotel in San Francisco. I knew a girl who had cleaned rooms there and I somehow ended up with the towel, which seemed fancier than a regular towel because it had a provenance, like shoes from Spain or perfume from France. A towel from the Pickwick. The hat was a Borsalino I'd found in the bathroom of a bar. I wrapped my jacket around it, rather than giving it to the bartender. It decorated the empty apartment. Each morning I went to a coffee shop near my apartment, the Trust E on Lafayette, and sat at the counter. The same waitress was always there. The men who came into that coffee shop tried to pick her up. She was pretty and, perhaps more importantly, had large breasts framed in a low-cut waitressing smock.

"Hey, what's your name?" a man in a yellow hard hat said to her one morning as he stared at her breasts and dug in the pocket of his work overalls to pay his check.

She glanced at the radio behind the counter. "My name is . . . Zenith," she said, smiling at him with her slightly crooked teeth.

That was the precise moment I wanted to be friends with Giddle— her actual name, or at least the one I knew her by.

There are no palm trees on Fourteenth Street, but I remember them there, black palm fronds against indigo dusk, the night I met the people with the gun.

That was how I thought of them, before I knew who any of them were. *The people with the gun.*

I had been in New York two weeks, and the city to me seemed strange and wondrous and lonely. The summer air was damp and hot. It was late afternoon. The overcrowded sidewalk, with young girls standing along Union Square in shorts and halters the size of popped balloons, electronics stores with salsa blaring, the Papaya King and its mangoes and bananas piled up in the window, all made Fourteenth Street feel like the main thoroughfare of a tropical city, someplace in the Caribbean or

South America, though I had never been to the Caribbean or South America, and I'm not sure where I saw palm fronds. Once it became familiar, Fourteenth Street never looked that way to me again.

I remember a rainbow spectrum of men's wing tips parked in rows, triple-A narrow, the leather dyed snake green, lemon yellow, and unstable shades of vermilion and Ditto-ink blue. All of humanity dresses in uniforms of one sort or another, and these shoes were for pimps. I was on the west end of Fourteenth. My feet, swollen from the heat, were starting to hurt. I heard music from the doorway of a bar, soft piano notes, and then a singer who flung her voice over a horn section. *What difference does it make, what I choose? Either way I lose.* A voice so low it sounded like a female voice artificially slowed. It was Nina Simone's. A piano note and a man's baritone voice percussed together, and then higher piano notes came tumbling down to meet the low ones. I went in.

The music was loud and distorted by the echoing room, where a man and woman sat close together at the far end of a bar, the sole customers. The woman had the kind of beauty I associated with the pedigreed rich. A pale complexion, cuticle thin, stretched over high cheekbones, and thick, wavy hair that was the warm, reddish blond of cherrywood. The man conducted the song with the tiny straw from his drink, jerking his arm in the air to the saxophone and the cartwheeling piano notes, which fell down over us as if from the perforations in the bar's paneled ceiling. The horns and strings and piano and the woman's voice all rode along together and then came to an abrupt halt. The room fell into drafty silence.

The woman sniffled, her head down, hair flopped over her face, curtains drawn for a moment of private sorrow, although I sensed she was faking.

"Why don't you sit down," the man called to me in a nasal and Southern voice, "you're making us nervous." He wore a suit and tie but there was something derelict about him, not detectable in his fine clothes.

The woman looked up at me, a glisten of wet on her cheeks.

"She's not making anybody *nervous*," she said, and wiped under her eyes with the pads of her fingers, careful not to scratch herself with long nails painted glossy red. I realized I'd been wrong. She was not the pedigreed rich. He was and she was not. Sometimes all the information is there in the first five minutes, laid out for inspection. Then it goes away, gets suppressed as a matter of pragmatism. It's too much to know a lot about strangers. But some don't end up strangers. They end up closer, and you had your five minutes to see what they were really like and you missed it.

"Come on, honey," she said to me in a voice like a soft bell, "sit down and shithead will buy you a drink."

I'd thought this was how artists moved to New York, alone, that the city was a mecca of individual points, longings, all merging into one great light-pulsing mesh, and you simply found your pulse, your place. The art in the galleries had nothing to do with what I'd studied as fine art. My concentration had been film, but the only films the galleries seemed to be showing were films scratched beyond recognition, and in one case, a ten-minute-long film of a clock as it moved from ten o'clock to ten minutes after ten, and then the film ended. Dance was very popular, as was most performance, especially the kind that was of a nature so subtle—a person walking through a gallery, and then turning and walking out of the gallery—that one was left unsure if the thing observed was performance or plain life. There was a man in my neighborhood who carried a long pole over his shoulder, painted with barber stripes. I would see him at dusk as I sat in the little park on the corner of Mulberry and Spring. He, too, liked to sit in the little park in the evening, in his bell-bottoms and a striped sailor's shirt. We both watched the neighborhood boys in their gold chains and football jerseys as they taunted the Puerto Rican kids who passed by. They were practicing for the future war. The Italians were going to exterminate the Puerto Ricans with the sheer force of their hatred. Or maybe they would just remove all the Italian ice pushcarts and the pizza parlors and the Puerto Ricans would starve. The man sat there with his striped pole jutting over his shoulder like an outrigger, one leg crossed over the other, his sun-browned toes exposed in battered leather sandals. He smiled foolishly when the Italian kids asked what his pole was for. When he didn't answer, they flicked cigarette butts at him. He kept smiling at them. Once, he walked past the Trust E Coffee Shop, holding the pole over his shoulder as if carrying construction materials to a work site. "There goes Henri-Jean," Giddle said.

"You know him?"

"Yeah. He lives in the neighborhood. It's his thing, that pole. No sellable works, just disruption. Goes to gallery openings, bonks people on the head by accident."

The children who taunted him in the playground all had fathers in the Mafia. Every Sunday, the fathers exited their social club on Mulberry, next door to my building, and got into black limousines. There were so many limousines they took up the entire block, lined up like bars of obsidian-black soap, double-parked along Mulberry so that no traffic could pass. The chauffeurs stood next to the open passenger-side doors all afternoon. It was summer, and sweat rolled down their faces as they waited for the men to emerge from the social club.

Every morning I sat at the counter of the Trust E on Lafayette, hoping Giddle and I might talk, and if business was slow, we did. I paid my rent to a Mr. Pong, who said I should contact him only if I was moving out or if the city showed up to inspect. I spent each day looking at the want ads and walking around. As I came and went from my apartment, I would say hello to the two teenage girls who cut and styled each other's hair in the hallway. Sometimes they were in the courtyard between the two buildings—one building was behind the other, and I lived in the front—working out dance routines under the wet flags of hung laundry. Each night I went to a pizza place on Prince. The kind of young people I hoped to know, women and men in ripped, self-styled clothes, smoking and passionately discussing art and music and ideas, were all there. I didn't interact with them except for once, when one of the men called me cutie, he said, Hey, cutie, and a woman near him became upset, telling him that the street was not his pickup joint, and the other women laughed, and none of them asked if I needed friends. Which was something people never would ask. I ate my pizza and went to lie in bed with all the windows wide open. The trucks rumbling down Kenmare, the honking, an occasional breaking of glass, made me feel that I was not separate and alone in my solitude, because the city was flowing through my apartment and its sounds were a kind of companionship.

I had met Giddle, but she was of little real help. The stream of New York, at least the one I imagined, moved around her as it did around me. She seemed as isolated as I was, which was troubling, because she'd been in New York, as far as I could tell, for many, many years. She would tell me about herself but it often contradicted something she'd said on a different day. Once she said she was raised in a Midwestern Catholic orphanage. We wore green skirts, she told me, white blouses, white bobby socks, saddle shoes, green jackets. We watched the nuns shower. But on another quiet morning at the diner, she told me her father sold appliances. They'd lived in Montreal. Her mother stayed home, was always there when Giddle returned from school. She had three brothers. Got an F in French. And I looked at her and nodded and realized she had forgotten she'd told me about the nuns a few days earlier.

Something would happen, I was sure. A job, which I needed, but that could isolate a person even further. No. Some kind of event. "Tonight is the night," I later believed I'd told myself on that particular night when I heard the music and Nina Simone's voice, walked into the bar on Fourteenth Street, and met the people with the gun. But in truth I had not told myself anything. I had simply left my apartment to stroll, as I did every night. What occurred did so because I was open to it, and not because fate and I met at a certain angle. I had plenty of time to think about this later. I thought about it so much that the events of that evening sometimes ran along under my mood like a secret river, in the way that all buried truths rushed along quietly in some hidden place.

*   *   *

"This is my wife," the nasal man in elegant clothes said as I sat down next to them at the bar. "Nadine."

He said it again. "Nay-*deeen*," and looked searchingly at her.

She ignored him, as if she were used to this audible pondering of her Nadine-ness in bars, for the benefit of strangers.

"We were at a wedding," Nadine said, turning to me. "They asked us to leave. They asked Thurman to leave, I mean. But I don't like weddings anyway? They make my face hurt?"

That was how she spoke.

"Why did they want you to leave?" I asked, but I could sense why. Something about their presence in an empty bar many levels below what the man's clothes might suggest.

"Because Thurman lay down in the grass?" Nadine said. "He started taking pictures of the sky. Just blue sky, instead of the bride and groom. He'd had a few too—"

"I did not have *a few too*. I was looking for something decent to photograph. Something worth keeping. For posterity."

"Oh, posterity," Nadine said. "Sure. Great. If you can afford it. You could have just told Lester you didn't want to be the picture taker."

There was a camera sitting in front of him on the bar, an expensive-looking Leica.

"You're a photographer?" I asked him.

"Nope." He smiled, revealing a tar stain between his two front teeth.

"But the camera—" I couldn't think of how to say it. You have a camera but you aren't a photographer. I sensed he would only keep meandering away, like something you are trying to catch that continually evades your grasp.

"Better to say yes," Thurman said, "and then disappoint people. I mean really let them down."

"Lord knows you're good at that," Nadine said in a quiet voice.

"I'm talking about building a reputation."

"So am I," she said.

"All I want," Thurman said, "is for people to stop asking me to come to their weddings. And funerals."

"I don't mind funerals?" Nadine said. "Except when they buried my daddy in a purple casket. That was awful." She turned to me. "Thurman knew my daddy? Daddy was a mentor to him? A teacher?"

"A mentor," I repeated, hoping this might lead somewhere, to some explanation of who she and Thurman were. Because they were someone or something, I was sure of it.

"Well, my daddy was a, I guess you could say pimp. *Pimp* is acceptable—I mean now that he's dead. And you know what? People don't say *procurer* anymore."

I thought of the narrow wing tips in tropical bird colors. Who knew what was true.

"And my mother was a whore, so they got along perfect."

Probably nothing was true, but I liked the challenge of trying to talk to them. I had spoken to so few people since arriving that it felt logical to interact in this manner. It was direct and also evasive, each in a way that made sense to me.

"May he rest in peace," Thurman said. "A gentleman. I wanted to ask him for your hand in marriage. You were fourteen and goddamn. I wanted to just marry the pants off you." He grinned and showed the ugly stain on his teeth. "But then there was no point. It wasn't marrying to get in your pants, since you were allowing it. Not with me. That motherfucker you did marry, later on."

Nadine frowned. "Do you want a purple casket, Thurman? Because Blossom might have one all picked out for you. With a copper millennial vault, to preserve your—"

He got up, walked to the end of the bar, and aimed his camera at a sign above the register. SORRY, NO CREDIT.

Three or four drinks in, still they hadn't asked me anything. But what interesting thing did I have to tell? I was content to listen to their stream of half reports on people I'd never heard of, stories I could not follow, one about a baby named Kotch. "This lady was nursing him," Nadine said, "and then another lady and you begin to think, wait a minute, whose baby *is* Kotch? I don't know who was his mother and who was a wet nurse—"

"I'll make you a *wet nurse*," Thurman said as he grabbed Nadine and put his hand between her legs. She twisted away and then she was prattling about a McDonald's she once went to in Mexico. I had been in a McDonald's commercial when I was in high school, and I thought, as Nadine spoke, that it might be a story I could share with them.

"McDonald's is supposed to be the same everywhere, right? Well, not in Mexico. They Mexicanize it. *Hamburguesa con chile*. No fries—*fri-jol-es*. I was with my ex. We were starving and I was ready to eat beans. We're at the counter and find out we have no money. He had lost his wallet."

She went on about this ex, the revolution he had been fomenting that never took place and had led to their harsh and vagrant life in the mountains of northern Mexico, the hole in his pocket that his wallet wriggled through, leading to his inability to provide for her the most fundamental thing—a McDonald's hamburger. That was how she put it, that he couldn't provide *even a hamburger*. After which she left him and went to Hollywood, where the nightmare really began, a series of episodes and hard luck that involved rape, prostitution, and an addiction to Freon, the gas from the cooling element in refrigerators.

"What you get," Thurman said when she was finally finished, "for marrying a motherfucker."

"I don't want to talk about him. And stop calling him that, would you?"

"You brought him up."

"Only to tell her about the Mexican McDonald's."

"I was in a McDonald's commercial," I said.

"Oh, you're an actress!"

"No, I just did the one thing, I was sixteen and it was just something, an ad our coach answered and—"

"Thurman, she's an actress."

"Well, I . . . we did act, I guess. But that's not . . . they needed a girl who could ski, and so I—"

"You're an actress and a skier! I never meet anyone who skis."

"Do you ski?" I asked, only vaguely hopeful.

"Do I ski. No, honey."

The commercial's director and crew had come to Mount Rose, where we trained. They talked to our coach and ended up choosing me and a racer named Lisa, a quiet girl no one really knew. There was a long day of takes and retakes. They wanted two girls with hair flying, snow bunnies on a brisk, sunny afternoon. A week later they flew us both to Los Angeles, to a strange McDonald's in the City of Industry where they only filmed commercials. It looked like a regular McDonald's, with cashiers in paper hats, a menu board, the plastic bench tables where Lisa and I sat across from each other and smiled as if we were friends although we weren't, each of us holding a hamburger in our fingers with hot lights on us, in this fake restaurant that looked real except they didn't serve customers. I tried to explain this to Nadine, but she kept interrupting me.

When we finished shooting the ad, I flew home to Reno. Lisa was supposed to be on the flight but she wasn't. She was eighteen, an adult, and I didn't wonder. She had apparently gone to a bar near the fake McDonald's in the City of Industry. No one ever heard from her again.

"Freaky," Nadine said. "There's no telling. Once I met the serial killer Ted Bundy. Can you believe it? He was real handsome. Real smooth. I was on a beach and here comes this hunky college guy. I was *this* close to ending up like the gal in that commercial with you."

It hadn't occurred to me that Lisa had been murdered. I assumed she'd been impatient to meet her future and had just fled into it and never bothered to let anyone know where she was and what she was doing. The representative who paid me could not track her down. He called to ask if I knew anything and I'd said no.

"I miss Los Angeles," Nadine said. "Don't you?"

"I was only there the one night," I said. "In the City of Industry, which isn't really Los Angeles, and so—"

"The way the palm trees shake around," she went on, "and it sounds like rain but everything is sun reflecting on metal. I once went to a house in the Hollywood Hills that was a glass dome on a pole, its elevator shaft. Belonged to a pervert bachelor and he had peepholes everywhere. He was watching me in the toilet. Same guy drugged me without asking first. Angel dust. I was on roller skates, which presented a whole extra challenge."

Thurman was laughing. I understood she was his airy nonsense-maker, a bubble machine, and occasionally he would be in the mood for that.

"How the hell did you manage, drugged, on skates?" he asked her.

"Like I said, there was an elevator. Anyhow, there's some use in being doped against your will. Before it happened I didn't have my natural defenses. Some people don't get the whole boundaries thing until they've had their mind raped by another person. It helped me to establish some kind of minimum standard."

She turned to me. "Did you see *Klute*?"

"Yes," I said, "I did, I—"

"I liked it," she said. "He didn't." She gestured at Thurman. She wasn't curious what I thought of *Klute*. But that very film had been on my mind, this portrait of a woman who is alone and isolated in the dense and crowded city. In my empty apartment I'd been thinking of the scenes where her phone rings. She answers and no one is there.

Perhaps because I was so isolated, as darkness fell outside that Fourteenth Street bar, and more drinks were ordered, and a sense of possession over time faded away, a sense of the evening as mine loosened, one in which I would eat my habitual pizza slice and lie down alone, I began to cling in some subtle way to these people, Nadine and Thurman, even as they were drunk and bizarre and didn't listen to a word I said.

I heard the sound of a motorcycle pulling up on the sidewalk in front of the bar.

A man walked in wearing jeans tucked into engineer's boots and a faded T-shirt that said MARSDEN HARTLEY on it. He was good-looking and I guessed he knew it, this friend of Thurman and Nadine's whose name I did not catch. He walked in knowing he was beautiful, with his hard gaze and slightly feminine mouth, and I was struck. He had the

Marsden Hartley T-shirt and I loved Marsden Hartley. He rode a motorcycle. These commonalities felt like a miracle to me. I realized when he
sat down that he had made his T-shirt logo with a pen. It was not silk-
screened. He'd simply written MARSDEN HARTLEY. He could've written
anything and that was what he wrote.

Compared to Thurman and Nadine it was like reason had stepped
through the door. He didn't speak in rambling non sequiturs or take
pictures of the ceiling. Thurman started acting a bit more normally
himself, and he and this friend of his had a coherent exchange about
classical music, Thurman demonstrating a passage of Bach by running
his hands over the bar as though it were a piano, his fingers sounding
pretend notes with a delicate care and exactitude that the rest of him
seemed to lack. There were several rounds of drinks. Their friend asked
if I was an art student. "Let me guess," he said. "Either Cooper or SVA.
Except if you were at Cooper your enlightened good sense would keep
you away from dirty old men like Thurman Johnson."

I said I'd just moved to New York.

"You had a college sweetheart who is joining the military. He was
also in fine arts. He'll use his training to paint portraits of army colo-
nels. You'll write letters back and forth until you fall in love with someone else, which is what you moved here to do."

These people seemed to want to have already located the general
idea of the stranger in their company, and to feel they were good guess-
ers. It was somehow preferable to actually trying to get to know me.

"I didn't move here to fall in love."

But as I said it, I felt he'd set a trap of some kind. Because I didn't
move here not to fall in love. The desire for love is universal but that
has never meant it's worthy of respect. It's not admirable to want love,
it just is.

The truth was that I'd loved Chris Kelly, who'd gone to the South of
France to find Nina Simone, only to be shot at with a gun she'd lifted
from the pocket of her robe. We were in an Italian film class together.
He looked at Monica Vitti like he wanted to eat her, and I looked at
her like I wanted to be her. I started cutting and arranging my hair like

hers, a tousled mess with a few loose bangs, and I even found a green wool coat like she clutched to her chin in *Red Desert*, but Chris Kelly did not seem to notice. He was graduated and gone by my second semester at UNR and mostly an impression by this point, a lingering image of a tall guy who wore black turtlenecks, a cowlick over one eye, a person who had risked himself for art, had been shot in the arm and then moved to New York City.

A few days earlier, I'd finally tried the number I had for him, from a pay phone on Mulberry Street. I'd gone downstairs, passing the teenage girls styling each other's hair in the hallway, trying not to breathe because the Chinese family one floor below me slaughtered chickens in their apartment and the smell of warm blood filled the hallway. I'd dialed the number from the phone booth, nervous but happy. Someone was yelling, "*Babbo,* throw down the key!" It was the morning of the Fourth of July and kids were lighting smoke bombs, sulfurous coils of red and green, the colors dense and bright like concentrated dye blooming through water. I was wearing Chinese shoes I'd bought for two dollars on Canal Street. The buckles had immediately fallen off, and the straps were now attached with safety pins. Sweaty feet in cheap cotton shoes, black like Chris Kelly's clothes. It was sweltering hot, children cutting into the powerful spray from an uncapped fire hydrant. As the phone began to ring, I watched an enormous flying cockroach land on the sidewalk. A woman came after it and crushed it under the bottom of her slipper.

The phone was ringing. Now there was a huge mangled stain on the sidewalk, with still-moving parts, long, wispy antennae swiping around for signs of its own life. A second ring of the telephone. Mythical Chris Kelly. Third ring. I was rehearsing what I would say. An explosion echoed from down the block. An M-80 in a garbage can. The key sailed from a window, inside a tube sock, and landed near the garbage piling up because of the strike.

A voice came through the phone: "I'm sorry. The number you have dialed is no longer in service."

It was true: I didn't move here not to fall in love. That night, I watched from my roof as the neighborhood blew itself to smithereens, scattering bits of red paper everywhere, the humid air tinged with magnesium. It seemed a miracle that nothing caught fire that wasn't meant to. Men and boys overturned crates of explosives of various sorts in the middle of Mulberry Street. They hid behind a metal dumpster as one lit a cigarette, gave it a short puffing inhale, and then tossed it onto the pile, which began to send showers and sprays and flashes in all directions. A show for the residents of Little Italy, who watched from high above. No one went down to the street, only the stewards of this event. My neighbors and I lined our rooftop, black tar gummy from the day's heat. Pink and red fireworks burst upward, exploded overhead and then fell and melted into the dark, and how could it be that the telephone number for the only person I knew in New York City did not work?

I had asked Giddle if she knew an artist by that name and she'd said, "I think so. Chris. Yeah."

We were on Lafayette, outside the Trust E Coffee Shop.

"I can't believe it," I said excitedly. "Where is he? Do you know what he's up to?"

She tugged the foil apron from a new pack of North Pole cigarettes and tossed it on the sidewalk. I watched it skitter.

"I don't know," she said. "He's around. He's on the scene."

The wind blew the discarded foil sideways.

"What scene?" I asked, and then Giddle became cryptic, like, if you don't already know, I can't spell it out. That was when I first sensed, but then almost as quickly suppressed, something about Giddle, which was that there might be reason to doubt everything she said.

I told this friend of Nadine and Thurman's that I was from Nevada and he started calling me Reno. It was a nice word, he said, like the name of a Roman god or goddess. Juno. Or Nero. Reno. I told him it was on the neon archway into town, four big red letters, R-E-N-O. I made a film about it, I said. I set up a tripod and filmed cars as they came to a stop at the traffic light under the archway.

"Spiritual America," he said. "That's Thurman's thing, too. Diner coffee. Unflushed toilets. Salesmen. Shopping carts. He's about to become famous. He's having a show at the Museum of Modern Art."

Thurman was not listening to us. He was nibbling on Nadine's ear.

The friend said, "He's a great artist."

"And what are you?" I asked.

"I turn the hands on the big clock in the lobby of the Time-Life Building. Twice a year it has to be reset, to daylight savings and then back to standard time. They call me. It's a very specialized job. If you push too hard, you can bend the hands of the clock."

There were tacit rules with these people, and all the people like them I later met: You weren't supposed to ask basic questions. "What do you do?" "Where are you from?" "What kind of art do you make?" Because I understood he was an artist, but you weren't allowed to ask that. Not even "What is your name?" You pretended you knew, or didn't need to know. Asking an obvious question, even if there were no obvious answer, was a way of indicating to them that they should jettison you as soon as they could.

"I was in Nevada once," he said. "To see something a guy I knew made, the *Spiral Jetty*. The artist, Smithson, had just died. He was a friend, or something like one. Actually, he was an asshole. A sci-fi turkey, but brilliant—"

I said excitedly that I'd been there, too, that I had read his obituary, I knew who he was, but he didn't seem to think it was a remarkable coincidence.

"He had a hilarious riff about the 'real authentic West,' pretending he's Billy Al Bengston, you know, gearhead who makes paintings, and he'd say, 'You New York artists need to stop thinking and *feel*. You're always trying to make concepts, systems. It's bullshit. I was out there chrome-plating my motorcycle and you're, like, in skyscrapers, reading books.' Smithson was a genius. There are two great artists of my generation," he said. "Smithson is one and my friend Sammy is the other."

"What does he make?"

"Nothing. He makes nothing. He's living outside this year. He doesn't enter any structures. Right now he's camped in a park in Little Italy. He had been out in the Bronx sleeping on a construction scaffold and they were shooting at him."

There was another man, besides Henri-Jean with his pole, who was often in my little park at Mulberry and Spring. He slept there sometimes and I figured he was homeless but he didn't quite look it, this young Asian man with shoulder-length hair. There was something too careful and precise about him. I asked if his friend Sammy was Asian and he nodded and said Taiwanese, and I told him I thought I'd seen his friend. He said Sammy had come to New York as a stowaway on a merchant vessel, and that whenever this came up people assumed it was an art project, a performance he had done, and Sammy would have to explain the obvious, that he did it like millions of others, to come to New York. To be an American. And people would laugh as if there were a deep irony under the words.

"We have a bond, Sammy and I," the friend said. "In having spent a lot of time on boats. In having been delivered from that into a realm where everyone thinks we're kidding. But it's the other way around. Life is kidding us."

I pictured a shore at night. Dark water like the edge of a curtain. A nighttime sea where he and his friend Sammy had both spent time.

At some point Thurman and Nadine decided we were going to another bar. "You're coming?" I asked the friend. I sensed his hesitation before he nodded sure. Under it, *Why not? There's nothing better to do.* He left his motorcycle in front of the bar because it turned out Thurman had a car. Not just a car but a car and driver—a mid-1950s black and brushed-metal Cadillac Eldorado with a chauffeur who looked about fourteen years old, in a formal driver's jacket that was several sizes too large, and white gloves, also too large. I thought of the drivers on Mulberry. I said it was like Little Italy on a Sunday but no one heard me or they didn't care.

We piled into the car with drinks in our hands. Nadine had picked hers up and carried it toward the bar's exit, and following behind, I thought, Yes, of course. This is how it's done. Thurman paid our tab, and I was with them, in a Cadillac Eldorado, heavy rocks glasses in our hands, damp cocktail napkins underneath, the ice in our glasses ta-tinking as the car turned slow corners, honking so people would get out of our way, because we were important in that car, me on their handsome friend's lap, our drinks going ta-*tink*, ta-*tink*.

"This is my favorite," the friend said, pulling a leather datebook from a pocket in the door. "It actually comes with the car: the 1957 Brougham's own datebook. And this," he said, pulling out a perfume bottle from a little cubby in the armrest. "The Lanvin cologne atomizer with Arpège perfume. You could order this stuff at the GM dealership when these models were new. Thurman, what else is this thing loaded with?"

"Beats me," Thurman said. "Blossom was willed the car. It belonged to Lady von Doyle."

This Blossom had been mentioned several times now. I didn't ask who she was, who any of the people they mentioned were. I wanted to study the way they spoke. Not interrupt the flow, be the person they had to stop and explain things to.

Their friend reached back into the armrest and retrieved a leather-bound flask with a big GM symbol on it, opened it, and sniffed.

"Scotch," he said. "This is true post-Calvinist delirium. Like the Jews at Sammy's Roumanian, eating steaks that hang off the plates, a big pitcher of chicken schmaltz on the table. It's all about never going hungry again."

He poured from the flask into our glasses. I felt the presence of his body as he leaned.

"I think Lady von Doyle was Jewish," Nadine said. "Thurman, wasn't she Jewish?"

The friend said that seemed about right, for a Jew to drive a Cadillac. "In a sense," he said, "there is simply this axis of General Motors and Volkswagen. I myself have a VW Bug, a car we associate with Eugene

McCarthy and flower power and not with Hitler, who created it. The VW doesn't make you think of Hitler and genocide. It's a breast on wheels, a puffy little dream. The Cadillac, now, that's a different dream. Of the two, you'd expect the Cadillac would represent some unspeakable horror, crimes against humanity. Look, here's the Brougham powder puff. The lipstick case. The pill dispenser. The Evans pocket mirror. All that's missing is the Tiffany cocaine vial and a chrome-plated .44 Magnum."

"Keep looking," Thurman said.

"Ha-ha. Right. But you would never be tempted to chrome a .44 Magnum, Thurm. That's strictly for rednecks and off-duty cops. My point is that compared to the humble little folks-wagon, the GM seems guiltier, more dissolute, and yet there's no genocide or forced labor camps under this leather upholstery. Just cotton-wool batting. Itself, unlike the beautiful car, not built to last. But these days, only people in the ghetto think it's uptown to drive a Cadillac. In fact, only people in the ghetto think in terms of uptown and downtown. Are you aware there's an oil crisis? I don't even drive my Bug anymore, with the price of gas," the friend said. "I got my little Harley."

"I ride motorcycles," I said. "I mean I used to, but I sold mine."

He looked at me. I was seated sideways on his lap.

"You do have a kind of tomboy allure, I might call it. Yeah."

Okay, I told myself. Something is starting to happen.

"What kind?"

"What?" I asked.

"What kind of bike did you ride?"

"Oh, a Moto Valera."

"See? This fits in with my general thesis. It just so happens I know one of them, though he's not involved with the company. I like to rib him about those calendars they print. They pretend this name, Valera, is about firm Italian tits and desmodromic valves, but actually, they used Polish slave labor to make killing machines for the Nazis. Perhaps not specifically. Not exactly. But they used some kind of X to make a Y; fill in your human cost and slick modern contraption of choice."

"Mine was a '65," I said. "Way after the war."

"Which makes it innocent," he said. "Just like you." He touched his hand to my cheek, quick and glancing. "You don't have it anymore? The Moto Valera?"

"I sold it to move here."

"X for Y."

He had placed his hand on my waist, and I felt heat issue from it, and with that heat, something else, something sincere flowing from him to me, a message or meaning that was different in tone from the way he spoke.

I turned toward him.

"Do you want to know something funny?" I said quietly, not wanting Nadine and Thurman to hear.

"Yes," he whispered back, and moved his hand from my waist to my leg. There wasn't really any other place for him to put it in that crowded backseat. And yet I read the gesture of his hand on my leg as exactly that. A man's hand on a woman's leg, and not a hand that had no other place to rest itself.

"I don't remember your name," I whispered.

"That is funny," he whispered back.

It seemed we'd been driving for quite a while, the teenage chauffeur working the wheel smoothly, readjusting the comb that was wedged in his Afro like a knife in a cake, as if he'd trained his whole life to drive an enormous Cadillac and retouch his hair simultaneously, and in white gloves whose fingers sagged at the tips, too large for his young hands. We must have been traveling in circles. Only later did I realize we were on Twenty-Third Street in Chelsea, just a few blocks north of where we'd started.

We carried our drinks into a crowded bar, a Spanish place on the ground floor of a hotel, full of color and noise and people they knew. A man called Duke, with root beer–colored chandelier lusters hooked onto his shirt, came rushing toward us. He said the lusters were from the Hotel Earle.

"You're the Duke of Earle," Nadine said.

"I'm the Duke of Earle," he said, and shimmied his crystals.

People crowded around them to say hello. I had the sudden feeling they would shed me. I was a stranger they had picked up in an empty bar, and I was irrelevant now that they'd found their place in a familiar scene. I scanned the faces, wondering if this were the sort of place I might find Chris Kelly. I wasn't completely sure I'd recognize him. Pale skin, dark hair over one eye. This might be a place he'd go to. I asked Thurman and Nadine's friend if he knew an artist named Chris Kelly. "Who?" he said, cupping his ear. I repeated the name. "Oh, right," he said. "Sure, Chris."

"You know him? He's from Reno. I've been trying to find him."

"Chris the artist, right?"

It took me a moment to realize he was joking. As I did, I felt that he and his friends were unraveling any sense of order I was trying to build in my new life, and yet, strangely, I also felt that he and his friends were possibly my only chance to ravel my new life into something.

He steered us to an empty booth. I slid in next to him. The Duke of Earle joined us. We ordered drinks and the friend punched in selections on the remote jukebox console. Roy Orbison's voice entered the room like a floating silk ribbon.

"My mother had his records," I said to the friend.

"Your mother had good taste, Reno. That voice. And the hair. Black as melted-down record vinyl."

Someone passed the duke a big bottle of soap solution, and he and Nadine took turns dragging on their cigarettes and then blowing huge, organ-shaped bubbles. The bubbles were filled with milk-white smoke from their cigarettes, quivering and luminous, floating downward as Thurman photographed them. The next table over wanted the soap. The duke blew one final bubble of plain lung air. It was clear and shiny, and everyone watched it as it drifted and sank, popping to nothing on the edge of our table.

"You chose this, didn't you," Thurman said to their friend as a new song came on.

It was "Green Onions" by Booker T. and the M.G.'s.

"It's still a good song," the friend said. "Even if it was stuck in my head for almost a decade." He turned to me and said he'd been in jail. Not a decade, just thirty days.

I asked what for. He said for transporting a woman across state lines, and Nadine erupted in laughter. I smiled but had no sense of the coordinates, of what was funny and why.

"The Mann Act," he said. "*Impure intent*: what is impure intent? I did some time. And then I was free but my head was jailed in this song, so it was like I did a lot more time."

He hummed along with "Green Onions," nodding his head.

"At first, it wasn't so bad. 'Green Onions' was this special secret. Something I was hiding, like a pizza cutter up my sleeve. I was pulling one over on them, jamming out to 'Green Onions' while my fellow inmates were getting their cold shower, eating their pimento loaf, reading letters from women who wanted husbands on a short leash. A really short leash. The men wrote back to these lonely women and did push-ups and waited for the women to come a-courting on visitors day, with their fried chickens and their plucked eyebrows."

He had helped the other inmates write their letters to the women. "*Reach out to your loved ones, 39 cents,* a sign in the common room said. You got an envelope, paper, and a stamp. These guys would be working away with a little pencil like they give you for writing down call numbers at the public library. 'How do you spell *pussy*?' they'd ask. 'How do you spell *breasts*?' 'Does *penis* have an *i* in it?'"

"What was the pizza cutter for?" Nadine asked.

"For cutting pizza, sweet Nadine." He gave her a puppy-dog smile.

"When I got out, I thought, okay, unlike a lot of my friends, I know what the inside of a prison is like. Most people don't even know what the outside of a prison is like. They're kept so out of sight. You only know signs on the highway warning you in certain areas not to pick up hitchers. While I know about confinement and boredom and midnight fire drills. Amplified orders banging around the prison yard like the evening prayer call from the mosques along Atlantic Avenue. I know pimento loaf. Powdered eggs. Riots. The experience of being hosed down with bleach and disinfectant like a garbage can. I know about an erotics of necessity."

"Oh, baby," the Duke of Earle said.

"There's something in that. You think you're one way—you know, strictly into women. But it turns out you're into making do."

"I am going to melt," the duke said, "just puddle right in this booth. I had no *idea*—"

"I don't want to disappoint you, Duke," the friend said, "but I'd have to be in prison, and I don't plan on going back."

His arm was around me. I was in the stream that had moved around me since I'd arrived. It had moved around me and not let me in and suddenly here I was, at this table, plunged into a world, everything moving swiftly but not passing me by. I was with the current, part of it, regardless of whether I understood the codes, the shorthand, of the people around me. Not asking or needing to know kept me with them, moving at their pace.

"When you get released, they dump you in Queens Plaza at four a.m. Guys are darting in and out of the doughnut shop, wedded in some deep way to prison cafeteria code, drinking coffee, holding a doughnut in a greasy bag like they've got a bomb, strutting, but unsure who they're strutting *for*, now that there's no guard, no warden, no cell-mate. They are just random dudes in Queens Plaza, wonderfully, hor-ribly free. That same hour of the night women and children line up in midtown to get bused out to Rikers for visitors day. Buses letting out felons here, collecting visiting-day passengers there, while most people are sleeping. The prisons must stay hidden geographically, and hidden in time, too.

"After I got out," he said, "I was incredibly happy. Freedom after confinement is different from plain freedom, which can sometimes be its own sort of prison. The problem was 'Green Onions.' Weeks turned to months and it hung around. That surging rhythm was always in my head and I mean always."

He hummed it. "It woke me up in the middle of the night, like someone had turned up the volume and there I was, lying in the dark listening to the tweedling 'Green Onions' organ riff, waiting for the guitar parts to cut in, stuck inside its driving rhythm, this groovy song boring out the canals of my brain. It was so unfair, because I had paid my debt to society."

"Green Onions" came on again, for I think the third time, and it felt to me that the whole room was conspiring in some kind of hoax. The friend hummed enthusiastically.

"If you had to hear it for ten whole years," I said, laughing, figuring if I laughed openly, he would stop putting me on, "how can you stand to listen to it now?"

"Because you have to know your enemies," he said. "How can you fight if you don't know what you're up against? Who are *your* enemies?"

I said I didn't know.

"See? Exactly."

Later we danced. My arms were around his neck, his Marsden Hartley T-shirt clinging to his broad shoulders in the heat and sweat of the bar. I had not kissed him but knew I would, and he knew that I knew, and there was a kind of mutual joy in this slide into inevitability, never mind that I didn't know his name or if anything he said was true.

"You're pretty," he said, brushing my hair away from my face.

How did you find people in New York City? I hadn't known this would be how.

"They could put your face on cake boxes," he said.

I smiled.

"Until you show that gap between your teeth. Jesus. It sort of ruins your cake-box appeal. But actually, it enhances a different sort of appeal."

Some women wouldn't want a man to speak to them that way. They'd say, "What kind of appeal do you mean?" Or, "Go fuck yourself." But I'm not those women, and when he said it, my heart surged a little.

The hotel, it turned out, was the Chelsea. I don't know whose room it was, maybe it was Nadine's, a room that Thurman got for her. There was the sense that Thurman helped her out when he felt like it and that perhaps she was out on the street when he didn't. We were drinking from a bottle of Cutty Sark and Nadine was not, it turned out, Thurman's wife. From a phone pulled into the hallway he spoke with his actual wife, Blossom, or maybe he just called her that, not at all tenderly, a nasal, "Blossom, I will call you in the morning." He enunciated each word like the sentence was a lesson the wife was meant to memorize and repeat. "In the morning. I will call you tomorrow, after I've had my Sanka." Which sent Nadine into hysterics. "*Sanka!* After he's had his *Sanka!*"

After he got off the phone, Thurman seemed energized by a new wildness, as if the compromise of the phone call had to be undone with behavior that Blossom, wherever she was, might not approve of. He put on a Bo Diddley record with the volume turned all the way up, and when it began to skip he pulled it from the turntable and threw it out the window. He put on another record, a song that went "There is something on your mind," over and over, with this clumsy but sexy saxophone hook. At the friend's suggestion, I danced with Thurman. He smelled like aftershave and cigarettes and hair tonic. There was something synthetic and unnatural about him, the way his hair formed a perfect wave and the crispness of his fitted suit, clothing that kept him who he was, a person of some kind of privilege, through whatever degraded environment or level of drunkenness.

> *There is something on your mind*
> *By the way you look at me*

The friend was dancing with Nadine. Her arms were slung around his neck, her strawberry hair over his shoulder. She pressed her hips against him, and he pressed back.

> *There is something on your mind, honey*
> *By the way you look at me*

Watching their bodies make contact, I wished we could trade partners.

"Well, look at that," Thurman said. "Take your eye off her for just a minute—"

I felt him fumble for something in his suit jacket. Nadine and their friend turned as a unit, slowly one way and then the other.

Before I understood what it was Thurman had retrieved from his coat pocket, something body-warm, heavy, he was aiming it at them, at the friend and Nadine, who danced to the slow rhythm of the song, pressed together and unaware.

I heard a click. He was pointing it at them. A deafening bang ripped through me.

The friend laughed and asked for the gun and Thurman tossed it in his direction. The friend opened it and took out the bullets and inspected them.

"Blanks," he said, and gave it back to Thurman, who grabbed Nadine by the neck in mock violence and stroked the front of her dress up and down with the gun barrel. It seemed a stupid and ridiculous gesture but she took it seriously and even moaned a little like it turned her on.

I remembered my cousins Scott and Andy saying blanks could kill a person. Thurman put the gun in a cabinet and brought out a new bottle of Cutty Sark. He poured us fresh drinks and then played "Will the Circle Be Unbroken" on the little electric piano that was in the room. The friend took me up to the roof of the building and narrated the New York skyline. "It's up here on roofs where all the good stuff is taking place," he said. "Women walking up the sides of buildings, scaling vertical facades with block and tackle," he said. "They dress like cat burglars, feminist cat burglars. Who knows? You might become one, even though you're sweet and young. *Because* you're sweet and young."

"What are you, some kind of reactionary?" I said.

"No," he said. "I'm giving you tips. But actually, the roofs are somewhat last year. Gordon Matta-Clark just cut an entire house in half. It's going to be tough to beat that. What now, Reno? What now?"

Back downstairs, Thurman barged into the bathroom while Nadine was peeing, for some reason not in the toilet but in the bathtub. He looked at her, sitting on the edge of the tub with her minidress hoisted up.

"You know what I love more than anything?" he said.

"What?" she asked with quiet reverence, as if the whole evening were a ritual enacted in order to arrive at this moment, when he would finally tell her what he really loved.

"I love crazy little girls." He grabbed her and hoisted her over his shoulder, her underpants still around her ankles. Carried her into the bedroom and shut the door.

"You know what they do?" the friend said. "They shoot each other with that gun. In the crotch. Bang. Pow. It makes your eardrums feel ripped in half the next day."

"Isn't that dangerous?" I asked.

"Of course. That's why they do it."

The gun went off. Nadine shrieked with laughter. The telephone in the room began ringing.

The friend and I sat quietly, either waiting for the next gunshot or for the phone to stop ringing, or for something else.

"Hey," he said. "Hey, Reno. Come here."

But I was already right next to him.

We kissed, his pretty mouth soft and warm against mine, as the phone kept ringing.

When we'd finally lain down on my bed, the early sun over the East River filling my apartment with gold light, I told him I didn't want to know his name. I didn't think much about it. I just said it. "I don't even want to know your name."

He was wearing the brown Borsalino I'd found at the bar near my house. He took it off and put it on the floor next to my mattress, peeled off his homemade Marsden Hartley T-shirt, and pinned me down gently. My heart was pounding away.

"I don't want to know yours, either," he said, scanning my face intently.

What was he looking for? What did he see?

What transpired between us felt real. It *was* real: it took place. The things I'd heard and witnessed that evening, their absurdity, were somehow acknowledged in his dimples, his smirk, his gaze. The way he comically balled up the Marsden Hartley T-shirt and lobbed it across the room like a man fed up with shirts once and for all. Surveyed the minimal room, nodding, as if it were no surprise, but information nonetheless that he was taking in, cataloguing. And then surveying me, my body, nodding again, all things confirmed, understood, approved of.

I had followed the signs with care and diligence: from Nina Simone's voice, to the motorcycle, to the Marsden Hartley shirt. All the way through the night, to the gun and now this: a man in my room who seemed to hold keys to things I'd imagined Chris Kelly would unlock had I found him. I never did.

When I woke up in the late morning, he was gone. The day was already midstride, full heat, full sun. My head pounded weakly. I was tired, hungover, disoriented. The brown felt Borsalino was gone, and I remembered that I had wanted him to have it, had told him to have it.

I sat on the fire escape. It was Sunday. Down below, the limousine drivers were in front of the little Mafia clubhouse, waiting next to a long line of black cars. They looked sweaty and miserable and I envied them. To wait by a car and know with certainty that your passenger would appear. To have such purpose on that day.

I had said something embarrassing about the Borsalino being *already* his, that it had been waiting for him in my apartment. I was doing that thing the infatuated do, stitching destiny onto the person we want stitched to us. But all of that—me as Reno, he as nameless, his derelict friends against whom we bonded, and yet without whom I never would have met him—all of it was gone.

I had said I didn't want to know his name and it wasn't a lie. I had wanted to pass over names and go right to the deeper thing.

Rain fell. Every day, heavy rain, and I sat in my apartment and waited for sirens. Just after the rain began, there were always sirens. Rain and then sirens. In a rush to get to where life was happening, life and its emergencies.

Do you understand that I'm alone? I thought at the unnamed friend as I stood in the phone booth on Mulberry Street, the sky gray and heavy, the street dirty and quiet and bleak, as a woman's voice declared once more that I'd reached a number that had been disconnected.

It was just one night of drinking and chance. I'd known it the moment I met him, which was surely why I was enchanted in the first place. Enchantment means to want something and also to know, somewhere inside yourself, not an obvious place, that you aren't going to get it.

5. Valera is Dead

was what he'd written in his notebook late that night, his hand trembling, the pen trembling. He had lain down in his clothes and trembled.

Valera is dead.

Here lies a different one.

As he savored the too quickly degrading images, his memories of the Great Ride the night before, its moments slipping away as if it had been a rare and precious dream, receding in the way the best dreams, the erotic ones, must, he looked at his note to himself, which he'd written exhilarated and shaking, the wobbly hand declaring his death.

From now on, he thought, leaves tremble. Not men. Only leaves.

The death was over. The birth had begun.

The little gang he'd met at the Caffè Aragno had a leader, Lonzi. If not officially the leader, Lonzi was the most belligerent and original among them. Like Valera, Lonzi was from a rich Milanese family, his own father in timber and real estate, with a big, beautiful house in the Brera, near Valera's family villa. Like Valera, Lonzi had fled that and enrolled in the university in Rome. Both were young men who had been told to work hard and claim what would be theirs, to remind the world of their names and behind the names their power and prestige. Lonzi was a dropout, using the name to disgrace it and what it stood for. Though Valera understood this, the call of it, using one's training in self-importance to turn power on its head, he had no interest in giving up on becoming an engineer. Instead, he added Lonzi to his studies, the world of things that could instruct. Lonzi said inherited wealth and stature meant sloth, comfort, and nostalgia. Lonzi detested sloth and nostalgia and said he had no interest in aristocratic splendor, in rotting under the sun as he was meant to, wallowing like a hog in the thick, warm mud in which the Italian upper classes were trapped, in which all of Italy was trapped, lives structured around tradition, custom, sameness.

Valera pictured Egypt when Lonzi talked like this. His hours upon hours on the balcony, gazing out at the steady blue lid of the Mediterranean, pushing his face against the leaves of a potted date palm, trying to feel some scratch, some sharpness.

Lonzi and the little gang hated tourists, Sundays, torpor. They wanted speed and change. For his own quickness, Valera was becoming known among the motorcycle riders. He had a talent and feel for the two-wheeled machine, for how to corner it, braking as he angled into a turn, jutting his foot out to the side to steady and counterbalance the cycle, and then blasting open his throttle to straighten the bike, accelerating out of a curve as the others were still on their brakes, worried about crashing. He pulled ahead of the other riders without fail. He didn't yet have his own cycle—he'd asked for the money but the wire had not yet come through from Milan—so he was always having to wait on the curb outside the Caffè Aragno, hoping to grub a ride on someone else's. Some of the gang were proud to have their cycle ridden by Valera, who would always pull to the front, and others were annoyed by it and tried to avoid him when they saw him on the curb.

When the money arrived, he purchased his first motorcycle, a Pope V-twin, American made, and by far the fastest in the group. Its engine was 999 cubic centimeters, its tube frame painted a stunning, lurid gold. It was powerful and scary, vibrating his hands and arms numb, its suspension and handling not suited to its speed. It was an unruly thing and he loved it. He was officially part of the little gang, and when they whispered, "Third room," and headed to the secret back area of the Aragno, they said it also to Valera, and this tiny gesture, a whisper, strengthened his resolve to be like Lonzi, to fill himself with the spirit, the pneuma, as he thought of it, of the group.

"Don't say words like *pneuma* around here," Lonzi said to him, embarrassing Valera when he expressed this idea in front of the others. "That's crap. Ancient Greece. We're not gazing into the sewer grates of history, Valera."

They were smashing and crushing every outmoded and traditional idea, Lonzi said, every past thing. Everything old and of good taste, every kind of decadentism and aestheticism. They aimed to destroy czars, popes, kings, professors, "gouty homebodies," as Lonzi put it, all official culture and its pimps, hawkers, and whores.

Lonzi said the only thing worth loving was what was to come, and since what was to come was unforeseeable—only a cretin or a liar would try to predict the future—the future had to be lived now, in the now, as intensity.

You can't intuit the future, Lonzi said, even the next moment. He talked about a sect in the Middle Ages who believed that God reinvented the world every moment. Every single moment God reinvented the whole thing, every aspect and cranny, all over again, this sect had believed. All you can do is involve yourself totally in your own life, your own moment, Lonzi said. And when we feel pessimism crouching on our shoulders like a stinking vulture, he said, we banish it, we smother it with optimism. We want, and our want kills doom. This is how we'll take the future and occupy it like an empty warehouse, Lonzi said. It's an act of love, pure love. It isn't prophecy. It's hope.

The little gang hosted evenings at the Aragno, where Lonzi and others, Copertini, Cabrini, Caccia, Bompiello, Papi, read poems about speed and metal, recipes for soufflés of wire and buckshot, a diet that was part of the general call to metalize themselves, their bodies turned metal, into machines, their spirits no longer lethargic and fleshily weak, but fast and strong. Lonzi never seemed to be kidding. Valera took him as a kidder anyway. Lonzi was a fabulist. He made clothes out of screws and mesh, books out of sheets of stamped tin. Many among the little gang drew—dream machines and swift-moving men, or they arranged typed words to look like explosions on paper. Valera drew, too, but with his engineer's training it was hard for him to turn away from the laws of the universe. He drew what he felt was actually possible. Real machines.

The little gang played amplified noises on these evenings at the café, sounds that had been recorded at Lonzi's apartment by hitting sledgehammers on anvils, or snipping giant hedge shears attached to pickup microphones, SNIP SNIP, open and closed, which they announced to the audience were the sounds of the pope's feet being severed at the ankle. The king's fingers sawed off at the knuckle. The optic nerve of God's one big eye cut. Lonzi's shears cutting off the pope's feet brought Valera to an image of young Marie's foot, tan, in her little cloth espadrille, dangling over the rear wheel of the motorcycle that Alexandrian afternoon. A delicate feminine foot that had been carried away on a smoke-puffing beast. As Valera became a part of Lonzi's gang, the image of Marie's young foot, summoned by Lonzi's performance of mock amputations, stayed with him. The foot belonged to Valera, an appropriation that had something to do with being virile, metalized, and part of a group of men also virile and metalized. He had not thought of Marie in years, but in the heat and craziness of those nights at the Aragno, she appeared, a vivid image, its colors unfaded, Marie on the rear of a motorcycle, a figure in loose, white flapping cotton, her dangling foot tanned by the African sun, she and the unknown man flying along the seawall like those wooden figures that slide past a painted panorama in a carnival shooting gallery, the sky above them a broad silk banner of blue.

Standing on a chair at the front of the café, Lonzi said that in the future women would be reduced to their most essential part, a thing a man could carry in his pocket. Valera thought of Marie, how he'd reduced her to her own foot, to a thing he could carry in his mind, like a rabbit's foot. Not so much a gift as a sacrifice. She'd gone from love lost to something he'd loved but had to cut down. The foot was his. Yes, Lonzi, you understand, thought Valera. Woman reduced to parts. But after various of Lonzi's digressions, mostly about the Great War—Lonzi felt that joining the war would be the perfect test and triumph of their metalized gang, who would be their ultimate selves in war, vanquish the putrid Austro-Hungarian Empire and wake all of Europe from its slumber—after all that, Lonzi returned to talk of this essential female part, and it turned out he was speaking specifically of a woman's vulva. A good example of how it was Lonzi had come to be leader. He was willing to think to extremes and name them.

Women will be pocket cunts, Lonzi said. Ideal for battle, for a light infantryman. Transportable, backpackable, and silent. You take a break from machine-gunning, slip them over your member, love them totally, and they don't say a word.

What had actually been in Valera's haversack: not a woman's vulva but grenades, a gas mask, a gun that constantly jammed.

The little gang all volunteered for assault regiments, the Arditi, and ended up in motorcycle battalions that engaged in advance-guard trickery along the Isonzo River. Lonzi was shot in the groin and had to return almost immediately from the front. Valera and Copertini ended up in the same squadron, before Copertini struck a tree and died. Valera rode his Pope, which he'd modified for war, welding on a machine gun rack and adding mudguards, a larger gas tank, rear panniers. Due to a shortage of the standard-issue Bianchi 500s, his Pope had been allowed and it was a good thing, because it was a hell of a lot faster than a Bianchi, since Valera had bored the cylinders. Quickness, as he discovered, was vital for remaining alive. War should be mobile, he felt, and it was not. Most soldiers were stuck in the trenches, waiting on death. While the cycle battalions of the Arditi raced along, flashing their white skull-and-crossbones chest patches as they pulled safety pins from grenades and dropped them. All Arditi, all on cycles, none in trenches. Still, in just two years, 1917 and 1918, half their little gang died.

The war over, one night he and Lonzi, recovered from his battlefront injury, were cruising between the Aqueduct of Nero and the Botanical Gardens when Lonzi hit a stone that must have rolled down from the Neronian ruins. Lonzi wrecked his cycle, shattering his wrist. Afterward, Lonzi felt that dumping his motorcycle because of a chunk of antiquity was a clear enough message that they should vacate Rome. (Despite his insistence on godlessness, Lonzi was always on the lookout for signs and symbols, and once Valera had seen him in the Piazza Navona, sitting at a flimsy card table with a palm reader. Lonzi's eager posture, his open face, waiting and hoping to receive auspicious news from the woman and her cheap crystal ball, had embarrassed Valera so deeply that he repressed, for years, having witnessed this maudlin scene.)

Shortly after Lonzi's wipeout, the gang had a meeting at the Aragno and decided to head north. Rome was tumbling into creep and rot, with its mobs of tourists, its piles of garbage, its shabbily constructed slums encroaching from all sides as the economy bottomed out. Food shortages and unemployment and workers' strikes were rampant. Italy had been all but ruined by its involvement in the war. Rome's slum inhabitants were overrunning the city, zombie lumpen who seemed, to Valera and Lonzi, as if they were living in the Middle Ages, miserable people in faded black clothes, toothless by age twenty, stirring fires of scrap wood in oil drums to stay warm. For all they knew it was the year 800. The gang would make Milan (where most of them were from anyhow) their headquarters. Milan was not the capital, but it would be the capital of the new.

To the north! Lonzi shouted, raising his mangled, plastered hand. To progress! he added, which is always right. It may be a traitor, thief, murderer, or arsonist, but it is always right.

What had he meant? No one cared. They cheered.

*   *   *

They returned en masse, Valera, too, who vowed privately to out-Pope Pope, whoever he was, the American who had designed Valera's bike, whose name meant "pope" in English, and Valera found this wonder-fully funny, that some guy in America had the name Pope. He, Valera, would design the fastest, most unique and elegant motorcycle yet, and his father had pledged the money to put it into production if his pro-totype was a success.

Milan was the same city Valera had experienced as a boy arriving from Egypt, but now the trams and their intricate overhead wires seemed beautiful. Neon was electric jewelry on the lithe body of the city, and he and the little gang were the marauders of this body. They zoomed over it, their engines roaring, their horns ricocheting against the high buildings along narrow lanes. The city was theirs, with all its metal and glass and auto traffic, its cranes and diggers and smoke-stacks. Lonzi talked of a future in which the city would be built to the size and scale of machines and not of men. Houses would be razed to make way for car racing and airplanes. Speed, Lonzi said, gives us, at last, divinity in the form of the straight line. We reject sluggish rivers and zigzagging humans and their flophouse designs! Lonzi said hare-brained things about straightening the rivers of Europe, the Rhine, the Danube, the Po. The gang joined a racing club at a track on the wooded outskirts of Milan. They argued over the exact terms for the sensation of cornering, their motorcycles feeling as if they would split in two, accelerating out of turns as speed come to life, a violent but controlled surplus of itself. This was the difference between Valera and his gang. Valera was the only one with the training to conceptualize speed. The only one who truly appreciated the fine lubricated violence of an internal combustion engine, as he understood precisely how one worked. Valera spent his time designing his cycle and made plans to open a factory with his father's backing. The others went to the track to race their cycles but less and less often, as they were too busy writing poems about motorcycle racing, busy making paintings of the velocity they'd felt. None was interested in generating actual speed: of putting a motor together, clamping it to a frame, filling its tank with gas, and riding the thing. Lonzi and the others scribbled poems that made the sounds of guns, while Valera was busy designing cycle mounts for actual guns. He himself never wanted to enlist in war again. But he saw money in designing the machines for it.

Valera still pictured Marie on the back of that beastly crude bike built by Hildebrand & Wolfmüller of München. He had recovered from his youthful lust, her rabbit's foot foot, his haversack keepsake. He was thirty-two years old and had experienced many other women by now, mostly for hire but some for free, and he couldn't have cared less about Marie, understanding that she was, in any case, surely no longer the person he'd desired. Not burgeoning youth. Probably she's squeezing out children, he thought, her big breasts heavy with milk. While I am changed only for the better. And still a lover of girls. Ready for Marie's daughter, soon enough. Women were trapped in time. This was why men had to keep going younger. Marie's daughter, or someone else's. Because men, Valera understood, moved at a different velocity. And once they felt this, their velocity, all they had to do was release themselves from the artifice of time. Break free of it to see that it had never held them to begin with.

6. Imitation of Life

A month after the night I met the people with the gun and gave one of them my stolen Borsalino, I answered Marvin and Eric's ad in the *Village Voice*. I wasn't planning to. It had sounded so odd I'd read it out loud to Giddle, who was behind the counter at the Trust E.

> YOUR FACE AS UNIVERSAL STANDARD
> Young, good posture, good grooming, with rudimentary film knowledge, able to follow directions please apply.

"You do have nice skin," Giddle said, looking at me in an assessing way that made me blush.

"But what is it?"

"Modeling of some kind is my guess," Giddle said.

"You don't think it's nude, do you?"

"Would you have a problem with that?"

"I don't know."

"Well, you shouldn't," she said. "All kinds of things can happen in people's lives. You can't predict and you might as well keep your options open."

She went to take someone's order.

"Oh, cheer up," she said when she returned. "I was kidding. I don't think they want you to pose nude. That's a legitimate film lab. I've heard of it."

Giddle offered to help with the good grooming part, and although it was a little condescending of her to presume I needed that sort of help, I was eager for friendship, and it was a next step. She came to my apartment bearing hot rollers, a hair dryer, and a small red vinyl suitcase filled with makeup. We had mostly been on either side of a counter from each other, and suddenly she was leaning over me, so close I could smell her perfume, cucumber oil that rubbed off on me and infused the whole experience of applying for the job with her smell. She separated portions of my hair with a fine-toothed comb and then rolled each section onto a hot roller and secured it with a metal clip. It felt ticklish and a little erotic to have her touching my scalp with the plastic teeth of her comb. But I think she forgot about me as she was doing this, lost deep in the act of transforming hair. Never mind whose hair, for what purpose. I ended up with a kind of beehive, all the stray hairs plastered like icing around the shape of the hive with aerosol spray. It wasn't clear why I needed a beehive to apply for a job at a film lab, but that's how it was with Giddle. She got lost in what she was doing, and practical questions were beside the point and in the wrong spirit.

"You look so gay!" Giddle said when she'd finished my makeup and the final adjustments of my hair. In the word *gay* I suddenly saw Catherine Deneuve's bright-colored raincoats and matching little dresses, her sad songs and delicate joy in *The Umbrellas of Cherbourg*.

"I'm gay!" I said back. "Oh, so gay!" And I flew through my tiny apartment like a young girl in a French movie running to meet her lover and accidentally broke a cup. I paused to look in the mirror at the new, gay me. Giddle rushed in and drew a beauty mark near my mouth, painted more gloss on my lips with a brush, and blotted my face with a powder puff the size of a rat terrier.

"Rice powder," she said, "just a dusting."

It gave my skin a kind of moon glow, and my lips seemed redder.

We looked at me in the mirror. Something had changed in my face, or in what I saw there. It wasn't that I was prettier, exactly. It was that the whole charade of getting me ready to be looked at by whoever had placed that ad had exposed me to something. In myself. I looked at me as if I were someone else looking at me, and this gave me a weightless feeling, a buoy of nervous energy. I wanted to be looked at. I hadn't realized until now. I wanted to be looked at. By men. By strangers. Giddle must have known.

"Oh my God," she said. "Your chin cleft is showing—look, it's so prominent!"

I had never noticed I had a chin cleft, prominent or not.

"It's a sign," she said.

"Of what?"

"Luck," she said. "There can't be better luck."

I looked closer. There was a little depression in the center of my normally rounded chin. I had a chin cleft. It was showing. Maybe it was the powder but I think it was Giddle. She said the right kind of chin cleft was one that came and went, that you didn't want a permanent cleft. It brought too much luck, and forced a terrible burden of joy on its bearer. Like Robert Mitchum, she said, who navigated a pussy wagon all over northern Mexico and drank paint thinner when he ran out of *mezcal,* and would be destroyed by his cleft. Too deep, she said. Too strong. Giddle had a cleft like mine, emerging only on certain days and in the right light, as I discovered, once I'd formed the habit of recognizing clefts. Hers was like a shallow thumbprint in dough. Those first few months as we became friends, I'd tell her that her cleft was showing and she'd lean over the chrome sandwich press on the rear counter of the diner to confirm the news, and then run off to buy lottery tickets or play a round of Fascination. If it was the end of her shift she'd throw on a black velvet jumper she kept in her work locker, daub oily swaths of cucumber scent on wrists and neck, fog her armpits with aerosol deodorant, and head uptown to the Carlyle. I figured Giddle was into businessmen. "Not how I'd put it, exactly," she said, reaching into her bra to adjust each breast. She did have beautiful breasts. She was pretty, too, with large green eyes and a soft, pillowy mouth, even if her face was often creased with sleeplessness and her teeth were stained from tobacco, as were her fingers. Between her pointer and middle finger on her right hand was a yellow smudge of nicotine residue from her endless smoking.

"It's like what they don't say in the movie version. I sleep with them, and they give me money, gifts, assistance with rent. It was supposed to have starred Marilyn, did you know? Marilyn Monroe and not Audrey Hepburn, who apparently would not touch the pastry to her lips in take after take outside of Tiffany's. Marilyn loves a pastry and so do I, and she would have been a much better fit but it's too late. It's Audrey Hepburn who is the iconic thing you don't name."

"You need the money?" I asked.

"Yes, I need the money. I mean no, I don't. It can't be reduced to money. I can't explain why I do it. It's a kind of impulse."

At about that same time, I went to see a movie about a Belgian widow turned prostitute. I looked for signs in it of this occasional impulse of Giddle's, but the film was all claustrophobic domesticity, a woman moving around an oppressively ordered space, shining her son's shoes and making coffee in a percolator. Taking things out and putting them away. Opening cupboards. Closing cupboards. Dusting, polishing, whisk whisk whisk with a stiff brush over her son's black shoes, as she prepared him for each samelike day wherever he vacated himself to, a technical university for vocational training on the other side of a series of metropolis gray zones, half-lit in dawns and dusks. The shoes, shined correctly, would pull them out of this. A situation that, perhaps like Giddle's situation, didn't pertain directly or exclusively to money. The bind the woman was in, or wanted to escape from (and never would), was a kind of trouble linked to women and Europe and Jews, not in an obvious way, but it was all there in the film, somehow: history, hatred, cleanliness, and the costs of survival, surviving while drowning, whisk whisk whisk as she shined the shoes. The ring of intimacy tightened after the son exiled himself for the day, and the apartment became the woman's work space. She went into her bedroom and put a small threadbare towel over her bed's coverlet in preparation for the arrival of a customer. A thin terry cloth layer between her two realities. As thin as the difference between a gesture that was dignified and one that was pathetic. Better, I thought, just to have one reality, to put everything on the same surface. To explain to the boy, almost a man, that money came from someplace, that she earned it the hard way, that there was no magical account at the Bank of Belgium. She was sorry there wasn't, but more important, there wasn't.

So there I was with my beehive and my rice powder. Giddle grabbed me and steered me toward the front door of my apartment.

"Go go go!" she cried. "You've got to go now, while your cleft is out!"

Marvin and Eric both wore welder's glasses with thick, greenish prescription lenses, and they both snorted when they laughed. They ran a processing lab, Bowery Film, and after giving me the basic rundown of the job, mostly helping customers, answering the phone, restocking, they steered me to a pile of clothes that made me think of the term *sportswear*. You saw it on the second and third floors of department stores. It wasn't clear what it referred to. Not athletics. The dresses Marvin and Eric gave me were knit, with big gold buttons. There was a sort of bathing suit made of a fabric that looked as if it were not meant to get wet. More like a baton twirler's bodice, black velvet and rickrack. There were coffee-colored pantyhose in a plastic egg. They left me alone. I put on the hose and the black velvet bodice, which was the only garment that fit, because the others were all petite-sized, the shoulders too narrow, the sleeves too short. I stretched out on a white vinyl divan. Eric came in and moved a potted plant behind the divan.

"Look down. Okay, look up. Left. Then right. Sit sideways but face front. Turn your head just slightly toward my hand, here, but follow the camera with your eyes. Yes. Exactly."

I would be looked at, but by people who didn't know who I was. I would be looked at and remain anonymous.

Every movie had what was known as a China girl on the film leader. The first one wasn't Chinese. None of them were. No one was quite sure why they were called China girls, since they were a printing reference for Caucasian skin, there for the lab technicians, who needed a human face to make color corrections among various shots, stocks, and lighting conditions. If the curtains in a film looked tennis-ball chartreuse and not some paler shade of yellow, it made no difference to the viewer. There was no original set of curtains they needed to resemble. Flesh is different. Flesh needs to resemble flesh. It has a norm, a referent: the China girl. Curtains can be acid-bright but not faces. And if faces look wrong, we question everything. Some of the China girls smiled. Most stared into the camera with a faint, taut bemusement just under the surface of their expressions. *Who knew I'd be a model? But here I am, modeling flesh tones.*

My own face, smiling shyly (who knew I'd be a model?), ended up on many films distributed in the United States and Canada. If the projectionist knew what he was doing, loaded the film properly and wound it past the leader, viewers did not see me. If they did see me, my face strobed past too quickly, leaving only an afterimage, like those pulsing colors that mosey across the retina after you stare at a lightbulb. Me then gone, me then gone. There might have been some unconscious effect, if you believed in that. Giddle often claimed the power of the subliminal. She said a voice whispered, "Do not shoplift. Do not shoplift . . . ," over the PA system in her grocery store on Second Avenue, but so low it was not audible. It wasn't clear to me how Giddle heard it if it wasn't audible, except that Giddle was a shoplifter, and like dog whistles were meant for dogs, she was the intended audience.

Most people didn't know China girls existed. The lab technicians knew. The projectionists knew. They had favorites, faces of obsession, and even if I liked the idea of my own fleeting by, I knew the technicians looked at the frames more closely, and I liked that, too. I was and was not posing for them. Pieces of film leader were collected and traded like baseball cards. Marvin and Eric preferred a polished look. "The problem with the girl-next-door thing," Marvin said, "is that with recent

Kodachrome it's *actually* the girl next door. Her name is Lauren and we grew up together in Rochester." The girls, mostly secretaries in film labs, weren't exactly pinups, but the plainer-looking China girls were traded just as heavily. The allure was partly about speed: run through a projector they flashed by so fast they had to be instantly reconstructed in the mind. "The thing suppressed as an intrusion," Eric said, "is almost always worth looking at." Their ordinariness was part of their appeal: real but unreachable women who left no sense of who they were. No clue but a Kodak color bar, which was no clue at all.

Twice in the first few weeks of working at Bowery Film, a waste container of nitrate film spontaneously burst into flames. Marvin said that when nitrate film decayed, it turned into a flammable, viscous jelly, which then solidified into crystals, and finally crumbled to dust. Jelly to crystals to dust. Marvin had been employed for a while by the Technicolor plant on Santa Monica Boulevard in Hollywood. His job sometimes involved getting rid of huge quantities of old and flammable file copies of films the studio had processed and released over the years. They were reference copies, Marvin said, for the studio to have a record of the correct densities and color for prints they had manufactured. All day long, Marvin and two other men took rolls of film out of canisters and mutilated the film rolls with meat cleavers, and then tossed them into a gigantic trash bin behind the studio. Marvin spared a few things from the meat cleavers for his own private collection. A thousand-foot roll of trailers for *The Naked Dawn,* by Edgar G. Ulmer, one identical copy after another. Pieces of imbibition stock, or IB, which was a different texture than regular film, according to Marvin, thicker, but still pliable. He also got a roll of "scene missing," which was cut into a print to mark a gap.

I learned a lot about film working with Marvin and Eric, and they let me process my own films basically for free, so I was coming in with sixteen-millimeter footage I shot with my Bolex from the film department at UNR, mostly scenes I filmed from the fire escape on Mulberry. The films weren't all that good, but they did capture something. I made panoramic sweeps of the Sunday morning chauffeurs, one to the next to the next, black limousines and white drivers, their faces on zoom revealing little, just dulled patience, as if nothing could surprise them and nothing did. Did they wait like that out of loyalty? Fear? Good wages? Or was it pride, docility, boredom? Who knew why they waited, I thought, understanding that I, too, had it in me to wait. To expect change to come from outside, to concentrate on the task of meeting it, waiting to meet it, rather than going out and finding it. My camera grazed their faces as they stood at attention, a secret parade on public view, pretending as they waited that time had no value and what a lie. A lie they didn't mind. They were on the clock, being paid to forsake time's value by standing under the sun like they had all day.

The filmed footage of their patient faces reminded me of how I felt that morning after the unnamed friend of Thurman and Nadine's had departed while I slept, leaving me alone, hungover, bereft.

Marvin and Eric loaned me a projector, and I showed my film to Giddle on the wall of my apartment. She liked it, but said it might be better to get a job as a chauffeur. To have to wait like they did, she said. As a kind of performance. But who would be the audience? I wondered.

"No one," she said. "You'd merge into an environment. Film it and you will never join it. You'll never understand your subject that way."

This was her own method, I was beginning to understand. Giddle, who was a waitress but also playing the part of one: girl working in a diner, glancing out the windows as she cleaned the counter in small circles with a damp rag. Life, Giddle said, was the thing to treat as art. Once upon a time she had hung around Warhol's Factory and would have been too cool to speak to me, much less serve me a meal in a hole in the wall with a grease-coated ceiling, handwritten signs ("cheeseburger and fries $1.25"), and humpbacked men and women lurching toward each other in the vinyl booths. *"Personne,"* that Factory crowd had said to one another, assessing people as they filed into Rudy's. "No one. Don't bother." Giddle had been offered a role in one of Warhol's films, of a girl sleeping on a bed. "How do I prepare?" she'd asked him, and he'd shrugged and said maybe sleep a lot, or don't sleep much so you'll be tired. The day her life changed she was in Hoboken, New Jersey, going to thrift stores, looking to find the right outfit for the role, a lace peignoir. Giddle went into an old chrome diner for coffee. It was winter and freezing. She started talking to the waitress. There was something suspicious about this waitress, Giddle told me. She wore glasses and had a dour and educated New Englandy face. She didn't seem like someone who would work at a diner in Hoboken.

"So I pressed her," Giddle told me. "And she admitted she was actually *not* a waitress, but a sociologist, and that she was living for one year on minimum-wage jobs to gather data on how difficult it was to get by in that life, to understand and expose a kind of American ugliness." So it's like a performance, Giddle had said to the woman. You're performing the role of a waitress. Giddle was a performer herself, and it was what most interested her. The woman insisted, No, it's sociology—I don't care about performing. I infiltrate to study this world.

"But that *is* performance," Giddle said to me. "She didn't see that, but I did. She was performing, as a real but not *actual* waitress. She was rushing from table to table and clipping orders on a little metal wheel that the cooks spun around, and calling out sides of biscuits and gravy and carrying stacked dirty plates one-two-three up the inside of her arm, which I still have not learned to properly do. I can't quite explain what happened next. I was in a strange mood that day. I was all alone. It was February. The sky was very white. The trees were bare. The diner was warm and humming with a kind of life that seemed new to me. I watched the sociologist smooth her apron and slide a pencil in her hair and share a knowing smile with the cook, who called her by her server number, forty-three. When she came to refill my coffee cup, I said, 'I'd like to work here. Are there any openings?' And she said that there would be, because her research was almost finished, and to come back in a week. I had a strange feeling, like I'd decided to go over a waterfall in a barrel. I rented an apartment nearby, a studio with a Murphy bed. It was over an old shoe-repair shop. Neon blinked into my window all night long, startling me from sleep. At first I thought I would hate the neon, but I began to like it, the way it lent this air of tragedy to my so-called life, my performance as a waitress, neon flashing into the room, making me feel as if I were living inside a film about a lonely woman who threw her life away to work in a diner. And I *was* that woman! But the whole thing was in quotes. I styled my hair in a bouffant, like the white women in the South who responded to civil rights by teasing their hair higher and higher and lacquering it into place. I wore a uniform, not actually required. The other ladies just wore black pants and an apron, but I purchased a pink uniform with a white Peter Pan collar. I thought I was very camp and ironic. The sociologist had finished, although she still came in now and then, sat at a table and did follow-up interviews. She didn't want to talk to me because I was a downtown hipster and I might screw up her data. She pretended I was invisible since I wasn't authentic.

"But the thing is, I *became* authentic," Giddle told me. "Little by little. My performed life grew roots. I was lonely, and the work was demeaning and hard. I wanted to go get drunk as soon as I was off shift, and so I was always hungover and barely keeping it together. I discovered that being a waitress was not about the uniform, or the cook calling you twenty-six, which at first I thought was cute. I even thought, what if I fuck the cook and he calls me twenty-six? Hilarious, right? What a riot. I did sleep with him and he called me Patricia, which was what I'd put on my name tag, and it was unpleasant. The next morning I had to face him every five minutes to pick up my orders.

"I moved back to New York a year later. Everyone asked where I'd been. Andy thought it was amusing, or so he claimed, but perhaps he was only making fun of me. Andy preferred the Automat, where there were no waitresses, just clear display windows for meat loaf and pies that slid open when you inserted coins. Never again did he ask me to be in a film, and something in me had changed. I no longer had the drive to make it with that Factory crowd. I told myself I was more extreme than they were, these haughty upper-class bitches who didn't have to work. There was no risk for them. They could always go home to Mommy and Daddy's on Park Avenue. One or two pitched themselves off Mommy and Daddy's Park Avenue balcony, but seriously, *anyone* can do that."

*   *   *

New York was getting colder. I went to a bar in the Meatpacking District with Giddle one October night, my birthday, actually. There were bagels scattered all over the sidewalk, a heavy and rancid animal smell in the air. We stepped over puddles of lamb's blood as we crossed the street to the other side, where there were more bagels. Giddle began kicking them like hockey pucks, and so did I. We were on Gansevoort Street, where carcasses were loaded into the meatpacking plants on pulleys. Giddle led us into a bar around the corner on Ninth Avenue, a dive filled with men who probably worked in the meatpacking places and I thought, Why are we here? Giddle opened her purse and tried to buy our drinks with fake money she'd gotten in Chinatown, oversized bills with a denomination of ten thousand. The bouncer came over to speak with her. She insisted her money was good and that it was my birthday, and as she made more of a scene, he escorted us out.

Why is she my only friend? I wondered, this woman who is so alone. I meet no one through her and she thinks I should forget making films and become a Mafia chauffeur.

Giddle herself was considering her next act, another life, a new performance. She was planning to go to mortuary school, she told me. She went to see an autopsy as research and came to my apartment after. She glowed with excitement and stank of formaldehyde. I kept back a certain distance, and asked how it was.

"Difficult to even talk about," she said. "I feel changed. Like, say my mind is a sweater. And a loose thread gets tugged at, pulled and pulled until the sweater unravels and there's only a big fluffy pile of yarn. You can *make* something with it, that pile of yarn, but it will *never* be a sweater again. That's the state of things."

Winter came early. It was November and the water jeweled itself to a clear, frozen dribble from the fire hydrant in front of my building. Sammy, who had been sleeping outside, was gone. Henri-Jean, with his striped pole and sandals, no longer sat in the park, only hurried along in a ratty peacoat. Once I saw him dart into a building on Mott Street with groceries from the cheap bodega where I also shopped. The Italian kids wore big puffy jackets and blew into their hands to keep warm. I had been in New York four months. I had my job, and I was making films and learning a lot from Marvin and Eric, but I was lonely, eating candy bars for dinner with my coat buttoned up because my radiator was broken and Mr. Pong did not return calls.

One day Marvin mentioned that there was a guy asking about me. I wondered if it was the unnamed friend. When Marvin saw the pleasure in my face, he rolled his eyes. Marvin and Eric were verging on neuter. They didn't want girlfriends. They got excited over discontinued Koda-chrome stock. Imbibition stock. Scene missing.

"He wants to meet you," Marvin said distractedly as he examined prints for imperfections.

"How does he know who I am?"

"The girl cut into the leader, wouldn't you say she's as much a part of the film as its narrative? Her presence there in the margin, her serving to establish and maintain a correct standard of appearance, female appearance. These are aspects of a single question that deserve thought."

"What is that question, Marvin?"

No answer. I went out for my lunch break.

"He saw you coming in," he said when I returned. "It's this guy Sandro Valera. Artist. Italian. Lives around here."

It wasn't the unnamed man. But I knew the name Valera, of course, because of the motorcycles. The unnamed man had mentioned know-ing one of them. I didn't know who Sandro Valera was, but when I asked Giddle, she said, "Oh, for fuck's sake. He's famous. Go to Erwin Frame Gallery—he has a show up right now."

I went to the gallery. The woman behind the counter nodded toward me severely as I came in, glancing up through eyeglass frames that were black and round like little handcuffs. Sandro Valera's artworks were large aluminum boxes, open on top, empty inside, so bright and gleaming their angles melted together. I knew enough to understand that it was Minimalism, meant to be about the objects themselves, in a room, and not some abstract or illusory thing they represented. The boxes had been made in a factory in Connecticut. As I got to know Sandro, I understood that even if the works were stamped by the factory that produced them, they had little to do with the assembly line imagery they implied: the factory, Lippincott, only fabricated artists' works, by hand, and very, very carefully. One of the aluminum boxes was being moved by two gallery assistants in white cotton gloves. I thought of the gloves the boy driver of the Cadillac had worn, too large for his young hands as he worked the giant wheel of that car. The difference was the difference of this warm, quiet, bright place, this snobbish woman behind the counter. Calm reserve. The creak of old wood floorboards. Art that was four metal objects that shone like liquid silver. The gloves the assistants wore were not a curious nod to old-fashioned ideas about service and formality. They were to protect the milled aluminum from fingerprints, which, because of the oils on human hands, would be impossible to remove from the delicate finish. The gloves fit the assistants' hands. They picked up one of the boxes. Moved it a few inches and set it down, stepped back. Looked at it.

Giddle chided me again when I told her I'd seen the show and realized he was a major artist, with work that was subtle, mathematical, grand, and expensive, everything in the gallery sold, the air of the place making me feel like an interloper just being there. I didn't understand why an older and famous artist was seeking out someone young and invisible. "Hmm. Let's see. Why is an older man seeking out a younger woman? Who isn't established in the way he is? Gosh. What a mystery. Oh, for fuck's sake once again," Giddle said. "He's a *man*. Practically middle-aged, and you're young."

"You're saying he's the type who is into younger women?"

"Sweetheart, that's all men," she said. "All men are that type."

I might have been proud to be the object of universal attraction, at least according to Giddle, but I only felt irritated for being treated as if I were too naive to understand. Giddle sensed this and added, as if to soften her condescension, that Sandro Valera was hot for a middle-aged man. By the time I met and began dating him, I chose to forget Giddle's theory. Like all people who fall in love, I took the attraction between me and Sandro as singular and specific, not explainable to types and preferences. Once I asked if he preferred younger women and he said he preferred me. He said he saw me come and go from Bowery Film and I looked so open and lovely that he could not resist. "Could not resist what?" I had asked. "Becoming your boyfriend before someone else did," he said. Which bothered me but I let it go. He had a way of talking about our courtship that presumed there was choice to it. Perhaps this was simply a difference between us. I did not experience love as a choice, "I think I will love this or that person." If there was no imperative, it was not love. But Sandro spoke as if he'd seen me on the street and simply made his selection.

The woman in the handcuff eyeglasses at the gallery that day was Gloria Kastle. Gloria who haughtily said, when I later met her properly through Sandro and mentioned I'd seen her working at Erwin Frame, that she most certainly was not *working* at Erwin Frame that day. She was merely helping him out, just as she sometimes helped Sandro out, "when it's useful to him," she'd said. Sandro had given her a quick, cold look. Their exchange was oblique to me, and I did not try to interpret it beyond assuming she had some proprietary attachment to him, sisterly, perhaps, since she was married to Stanley, who was one of Sandro's oldest friends. But then again, maybe not sisterly, and yet I knew she was not a threat to me, and that it would be a mistake to consider her one. Not even after I began dating Sandro in a serious way did I worry about Gloria. Not even when I moved in, six months after we began dating, and Sandro left a box by the door for Gloria to pick up, items that were personal—a scarf, some books. I did not care to speculate on their friendship. If there was some complicated dimension to it, that aspect was being ended by Sandro when I moved in. She came to get the box and glared at me like we were two tomcats facing off in an alley. I was replacing her in some way. I didn't understand quite how but I didn't need to. I was with Sandro, and our relationship was neither secret nor illicit nor complicated. Whenever I saw Gloria, I smiled and hoped not to get scratched or bitten.

With my permission, Marvin gave Sandro my telephone number. He called. We met. He was beautiful, which I hadn't expected, with a strange stillness, curiously both present and remote, with those eyes that were blanched of compassion but magnetic all the same.

On our first date, we walked through Chinatown, stopping for lotus paste buns. "Diaphanous," he said, and had me take a bite of his. It was the closest our two bodies had been, in an afternoon of walking side by side, each careful not to touch the other. The lotus paste had more fragrance than flavor. Later, I was never able to re-create that taste, after visits to bakeries all over Chinatown.

None of it could be re-created. We'd eaten the lotus paste buns on a cold, damp November day, on which the sun shone and rain fell simultaneously, the strange, rosy-gold light of this contradiction intensifying the colors around us as we walked, the fruits and vegetables in vendors' bins, green bok choys, smooth, sunset-colored mangoes packed into cases, the huge, spiny durian fruits in their nets, crushed ice tinged with fish blood.

As we walked, he kept staring at me. I looked over at him and he continued to stare.

When the rain won out and darkened the sky, he led me into a Chinese movie theater.

The movie careened and clanged along, an old-fashioned opera full of cymbal crashes and agonies, the occasional gong, stringed instruments wearily entangling and detangling. Sandro watched attentively, as if he were riveted by the drama being narrated in thunderous bursts of a language we couldn't understand. It was subtitled, but the subtitles were Asian characters of some kind. The theater was almost empty. We still had not touched. I kept my arm in my lap instead of putting it on the armrest, to avoid his. But then Sandro reached over and rested his hand on my knee, his gaze fixed on the screen. Just like that, he placed his hand on my knee. The feel of it sent electricity through me. I had been with almost no one—just the nameless friend to whom I gave my Borsalino. This was different. This was a man who wasn't playing some kind of parlor game, a cat-and-mouse pretend seduction, which, I now understood, was what Thurman and Nadine's friend had played, and I had been too naively hopeful to understand. It may go without saying that I was the type of person who would call a disconnected number more than once.

While the movie played, Sandro leaned over and whispered to me.

"Do you want to be friends?"

I whispered back that I had a requirement for friendship.

"I'm glad," he said. "It's good to have standards. What is it?"

"Sincerity," I said.

He sighed and squeezed my hand, then put his own back on my knee.

As we continued to watch the movie he began to unbutton my skirt. One button at a time, slowly, methodically, with no hesitation. He knew how to unbutton buttons. There was no fumbling, which was part of why I couldn't find the courage to say, "Hey, what are you doing?" The other reason I didn't find the courage to stop him was that I didn't want him to. No one was in our row, or behind us. My skirt unbuttoned, he took off his coat and placed it over my lap, chivalrous and careful. His hand slipped under the coat that covered me, and found its way through the unbuttoned skirt. He pressed his warm palm firmly against my underwear. I looked at him. He looked straight ahead, his face suggesting only that he was engaged in watching this Chinese movie, in Cantonese or Mandarin, who could say? I tried to watch, too, but was distracted by the warmth of his hand, and the protective sensation of being covered by his coat, denim lined with wool, its unfamiliar scent and feel, which promised a whole world, one I wanted a place in. He concentrated on the film, or seemed to, never looking at me once, as his fingers crept into my underwear. In this manner, both of us watching the film, the act of what he did with his hand was not just erotic but also slightly melancholy, even a little grave. I leaned my neck against the back of the seat and tried to relax, to not be nervous or self-conscious. I focused on the round gold of the gongs, the rice-white faces and wax-red mouths, bleached complexions with artificially rosy cheeks that looked pinched or slapped or scalded. I watched these images in gold and red and white as Sandro's fingers fluttered and moved.

When my body began to tense, his hand understood and slowed itself down, its rhythm matching mine.

After, he rebuttoned my skirt and moved the coat up over my chest and shoulders, as if to redignify its purpose. We both pretended to be absorbed in the inscrutable opera that flickered on the screen.

The gold and red crashes, a gratitude to this person, his wolf eyes and confidence and skill, the feel and smell of his chivalrous coat. On that day, nothing could have seemed more romantic to me, no other scenario more like real courtship, than a Chinese movie and a hand job under a coat.

It would have to be late autumn and the coat would have to be Sandro's. The hand his. The voice his. The movie followed by a walk west, the rain having ceased, the walk led by him. I wanted to be led. To see the city as he wanted me to see it. He had a way of leading, I later understood, by not stating we were going anywhere in particular. By seeming to wander when he wasn't, we weren't.

We were on Gansevoort Street, where Giddle and I had kicked bagels. At the end was an old pier building of corrugated metal. Sandro pulled on the doors, which were locked. We walked around to the side of the pier, and Sandro explained that the artist Gordon Matta-Clark had cut holes into the building. Into the floor, the walls, the ceiling, one large half moon on the end facing the river, converting the place into a kind of cathedral of water and light. Sandro said Matta-Clark was clever, that he'd done everything so perfectly, and then someone tried to get a film permit, which tipped off the cops.

"What does it mean to do this kind of thing perfectly?" I asked.

"There was no bravado," Sandro said. "He didn't storm in, have a big party, get immediately raided." Matta-Clark had cased the building quietly and with discipline for weeks before sneaking in and changing the locks, then slowly, stealthily, he'd moved in equipment, power saws, acetylene torches, pulleys, and ropes to make his cuts. He had noted when, if ever, there was security around the pier. When, if ever, the building was in use. He had learned that its only use was for discreet sex acts between men.

"If we could get in," Sandro said, "we could see about illicit use."

It was cold, the light waning. I wanted to be someplace warm, and I resented this presumption that I would be willing. I saw how easy everything was for Sandro. I felt it, all at once. That he simply found a girl he liked and incorporated her. And because I was attracted to him, his charisma, his looks, and his knowledge, if I didn't form an attachment it would be my loss.

We walked down West Street and viewed the building from the side, water slapping up against the pilings.

Sandro said the police tried to arrest Matta-Clark for the cuts he'd made, so Matta-Clark had fled the country, gone to Milan. There he found a recently closed Valera factory and sawed holes in the building, had an illegal show inside. Invited young kids to turn it into a squat. Sandro laughed as he told me about this.

"You don't care?" I asked. "He's squatting something that belongs to you?"

"Does it belong to me?" he asked. "More like *I* belong to *it*. I think it's great," he said, "that's all it means to me. I think it's great."

We walked along the water, buffeted by wind, an occasional glass beer bottle rolling past like an escapee. Sandro bent to pick up a piece of paper, wet from the rain, a torn page from a magazine, an image of a picnicking couple, an advertisement for something but it wasn't clear what. He'd give it to his friend Ronnie, he said, and carried the page between two fingers as we walked, absentmindedly waving it dry. Sandro liked to collect images and messages from the sidewalk. Some he gave away, but the best things he kept for himself, like the piece of paper he'd found on Canal Street, an awkwardly worded letter written by someone whose first language was not English, about selling something for a fair price and wiring payment to a sister in Switzerland. The letter was signed Alberto Giacometti.

We watched a huge container ship being towed by a tug. I noticed something in the waves, rising up and down with the sloshing wake of the container ship's passage. The bobbing thing was a person in the water. A man.

"People swim here?" I asked.

"I'm not sure he's swimming," Sandro said.

Sandro waved his arms over his head stiffly, to get the man's attention. "He can't swim," he said.

The man was barely keeping his head above the waterline. Only his face emerged, water rolling over it from the ship's wake.

"He looks like he's going to drown."

Sandro took off his coat. The chivalrous coat, removed for the second time that day. There was no choice but to try to save this person. "Go call 911," he said.

I ran until I found a pay phone that was not broken and dialed. The operator told me she couldn't send anyone until I gave her the street address. The address is the Hudson River, I said, Gansevoort and West Streets. A man is drowning. She needed a street address. I repeated myself. She must have alerted someone because I heard sirens, louder and louder. When I got back to the pier, firemen were there. The sound of radios, of heavy coats and boots. The truck's clattery, loose-valved idle.

"There's a guy in the water?" one of them asked me in a Staten Island twang, nasal and flat, looking at me from crotch to neck.

Sandro had managed to secure the man to the edge. He'd found a length of wire and had used it to lasso the drowning man, but he couldn't pull him out. The man was wearing so many layers of wet clothing that he weighed about four hundred pounds. Sandro was pulling on the wire around the man's middle to try to keep him afloat when the firemen and I arrived. They swarmed around to take over. The man looked up at us. In his face I saw confusion and misery, and I understood that we had interrupted him. He'd been trying to kill himself. He looked up, helplessly alive, swaddled in his drenched clothes. He must have been wearing twelve overcoats. It could be that it was necessary to taste the experience of dying to know you wanted to live. Or that you didn't want to live. The man's face said he didn't want to, but he'd had to come this far to learn it.

The firemen had secured a proper rope and were lifting him out, little by little. He dripped like one of those cars they winch from the end of a pier in television police dramas. Drip drip drip.

I picked up Sandro's jacket.

"Let's go," I said.

The events of that first date with Sandro, the curious, distant intimacy in a Chinese movie, the almost-drowning, were two bars that crossed to form an X, and the X pinned us to each other. Sandro walked me home, kissed me on the side of the head, and said he was going to stand on Mulberry outside my building until it was time to see me again.

"You can give signals from the window," he said. "Just a hand, a bare arm."

I went upstairs, took a bath to warm myself, watched the light through the windows turn the bleached gray of winter dusk as the radiator, finally repaired by Mr. Pong, clanged and banged and hissed, its steam carrying a curious feeling of safety, of comfort, as well as the complete unknown thrill that love was, these things filling the room through the rattling valve on the radiator. (Later, Giddle's response when I told her I was in love: "Oh God, I'm so sorry. Love is awful. It ruins every normal thing, everything but itself. It makes you crazy and for nothing, because it's so disappointing. But good luck with that.") I let the bath drain while I was still in the tub, a habit I was attached to, the way the receding water pulled at the body, dragged it down while returning its substance, gravity, density, making the body heavier and heavier as the waterline sank. Finally, there was no water, just bones like lead.

Flushed from the hot bath and sleepy, I looked out the window.

Two kids leaned against a car, an Italian boy and a Puerto Rican girl who lived in my building, one of the girls who practiced dance routines in the breezeway. She was on roller skates, and as she and the boy talked, she rocked silkily from side to side on her skates. Sandro was gone. I didn't really expect him to stand there all night, and yet, at twenty-two years old, part of me was buoyant with silly fantasies, capable of disappointment that he had actually gone home.

To be young was to be more closely rooted to the thing that forms you, Sandro said to me on our second date. We were at an Italian restaurant in my neighborhood where he pretended to speak no Italian, pronouncing menu items with an accent that sounded like John Wayne, a voice Sandro always used to imitate an American way of speaking. We all sounded like John Wayne to him.

He wanted to know about me. Not just the usual things, small-town Reno stuff, giving out ribbons at rodeos, growing up with Scott and Andy, Uncle Bobby, who left the three of us, eight, nine, and ten years old, in the back of his car, gave us Cokes and cherry cigarettes to occupy us while he banged an old lady's box, as he put it. Sandro liked those stories, but he also drew from me, that night in the Italian restaurant, things I hadn't spoken about to anyone before. What I thought about as a child, the nature of my solitude, the person I was before I went through puberty and became more readably "girl." The person I was before I became more readably "person." We seemed to share certain ideas about what happens in childhood, when you have to place yourself under the sign of your own name, your face, your voice, your outward reality. When you become a fixed position, a thing to others and to yourself. There were times, I told him, at the age of five, six, seven, when it was a shock to me that I was trapped in my own body. Suddenly I would feel locked into an identity, trapped inside myself, as if the container of my person were some kind of terrible mistake. My own voice and arms, my name, seemed wrong. As if I were a dispersed set of nodes that had been falsely organized into a form, and I was living in a nightmare, forced to see from out of this limited and unreal "me." I wasn't so sure I occupied one place, one person, and Sandro said this made sense, this instinct of a child, to question the artificial confines of personhood.

I tried to relay to him an almost inexplicable trauma, standing in my mother's yard, in our tiny house in Reno, being unconvinced I was myself. He understood. He *wanted* to understand. At about that same age, I put short little pieces of string in a bottle. Each New Year's Day I took one string out of the bottle and let the wind carry it away. If I looked which way it floated off, I would bring myself bad luck. I told Sandro how I used to sit for hours and stare at the kitchen stove, concentrating on the burner knobs, sensing, at a certain point, that I was ready to turn them on with my mind. That I could do it. I was on the verge of doing it, of finally turning on the stove with my mind, waiting for the coils to glow orange, and then I would ask myself, Are you ready for this? Are you ready to have your entire world turned upside down? (Because what happens once you know you can turn on the stove with your mind?) I wasn't ready. I always pulled back from the brink. I told Sandro about the shortcut from school to home, the man I'd seen. He was standing in the bushes, which had an empty space about waist height, so that his face was hidden behind leaves, but I could see him from the waist down. He was masturbating. We both laughed at the ridiculous geometry of the bush, but then he said, "I really want to hurt the bastard for doing that to you."

I told him how I ran all the way home, as if I were being pursued, in physical danger. Which of course I wasn't.

"No," Sandro said. "You *were* in danger. You absolutely were. It's okay to let go of innocence. But when you're ready," he said. "On your own terms."

Telling Sandro these things collapsed the layers between me as woman and me as child. Sandro saw both, loved both. He understood they were not the same. It was not the case that one thing morphed into another, child into woman. You remained the person you were before things happened to you. The person you were when you thought a small cut string could determine the course of a year. You also became the person to whom certain things happened. Who passed into the realm where you no longer questioned the notion of being trapped in one form. You took on that form, that identity, hoped for its recognition from others, hoped someone would love it and you.

We were the last customers to leave the restaurant. Sandro walked me home under the holiday lights of Little Italy, little frosted bulbs glowing white in the cold air. I invited him up.

I didn't have to be recognizably one thing. Even his touch relayed this. It almost restored some lost innocence.

Sandro's strong, heavy arm stayed wrapped around me all night. Whenever I stirred, he pulled me closer. Later I saw this gesture, the pawing habit of Sandro's sleeping limbs, as a blindness, an unconscious registration: body. Body that's near. But in those first months I thought he was reaching for *me*.

For our third date, Sandro said he wanted to have me over, show me his place.

"What will I find there?" I asked, assuming he'd say dinner.

"Justice," he said, in that half-joking, half-grave way of his. "I've got justice."

It was a cold winter day. When I arrived, he had company. A friend just about to leave, who was sitting on a couch in Sandro's loft, flipping through an art catalogue. He wore a peacoat and scarf, and his hair was darker, from winter light, or because it needed to be washed, but he looked otherwise just the same. Just the same.

Rain began to fall, wet darts hitting the windows of the loft. The rain fell harder and harder until the sound rose to an incredible crescendo, like glass beads pouring down over the front of Sandro's building. The sky beyond the windows was dense and gray but with the curious buttery quality of daytime darkness, as if there were a yellowish light lurking behind the rain clouds. Time had slowed to an operatic present, a pure present.

"My very best friend," Sandro said as he introduced us.

This friend of his stood.

In that strange light, the showering-glass-beads rain, I felt that I was seeing this person before me in two ways at once. Again—finally. And also for the very first time. His smile was simple and open. If there was the faintest edge of knowingness in it, it was purely of this type: *my friend digs you*. That was all.

I don't want to know your name, I'd said to him that night, when he was one of the people with the gun, Nadine and Thurman's friend.

But now I did know his name: Ronnie Fontaine.

7. The Little Slave Girl

The year I turned four, Ronnie and Sandro were shining their flashlights along the planes of a young girl's face.

She was a Greek slave girl carved in marble. She held a dove in her hands that she drew toward her lips, as if she were about to kiss the light little bird. Sandro and Ronnie had studied the girl night after night, tracing her time-softened contours with the directed glow of their flashlight beams. They were night guards at the Metropolitan Museum, eighteen years old, and they spent their evenings roaming the echoing and dark galleries, looking and narrating. The slave girl was a shared object of contemplation and fascination, the thing that marked the birth of their friendship and lifelong conversation.

We went together to see her, running through a downpour, water clattering from every shop awning, splashing us as taxis plowed through lakes of rain and barreled down Fifth Avenue, no one on the steps of the Met, the lobby filled with the echoes of people holding dripping umbrellas. It was our first outing as a threesome. Strangely, there was no awkwardness. I was sure Ronnie had said nothing to Sandro about his one night with me. Nor did I say anything. Ronnie had made it clear, in the purity of his smile that evening in Sandro's loft, that it was not going to come up. We acted like we'd never met before we met through Sandro. Or as if whether we had or hadn't was of no relation to the present.

Which gave it, the past, a kind of mystery I couldn't unknot, a certain meaning. Because if it meant nothing, why could it not be acknowledged? Why did it have to be erased?

We huddled in front her, this slave girl I'd already heard so much about from Sandro. She was a carved marble relief in full body profile. Thick, ancient feet in typical Greek sandals and a draping garment that attached to one shoulder. Ronnie and Sandro took turns speaking about her in serious tones, their voices somehow precisely calibrated to the low lights of the deserted hall where she was displayed. What fascinated them was a pocket of real air that flowed into and around the girl's mouth and the dove in her hand, the bird's small beak raised toward the girl's lips.

Sandro pointed to the little recess between the bird and her mouth.

"This is the only part of the relief that's three-dimensional. So what about the rest of her? Its flatness holds her away from us. She doesn't share our space. She's from another world, lost forever. Only that promise of the kiss shares our space."

It was the kiss of life, he said, of energy, somehow activated and eternal, and I looked and wanted to feel that, the life breath of a dead slave that somehow bonded these two men to whom I was also bonded and in ways that didn't feel exactly simple.

Ronnie said he loved her because she was so . . . *modern*. She interfered, he said, with the fantasy she was there to create. Slipping between the two, like everything in life worth lingering over. Real and false at once.

I stared at the private space between her lips and the bird she held. I looked at the cord around her neck, adornment of the most modest sort. Every aspect of her a modesty. All I could think was "This is a young slave."

Later, when I said this to Sandro, he told me not to feel bad about her. Think of all the anonymous slaves in history, he said. *This* one has been immortalized. She made her way through an unthinkable chasm of time. We are talking about her *now,* he said, and that in itself was a rare and special kind of emancipation.

I spent a lot of time with them looking at art. My tutors, Giddle said condescendingly. Your tutors are here, she'd say, as Ronnie and Sandro hopped on stools at the counter of the Trust E. They started going there and that was perhaps my influence, making the Trust E into a kind of destination.

Giddle treated them with patient indifference. They ordered hamburgers and coffee, always the same thing, and she attended to them last, gave them lousy service. That was yet another thing I misread, Giddle's indifference to them. I attributed it to her general feelings in regard to the art world—that part of it where people made art, sold the art, got in return money, fame, recognition. Success was highly overrated, according to Giddle. "*Anyone* can be a success," she said. "It's so much more interesting to *not* want that."

As I started to get to know Sandro and Ronnie and their friends, exactly the group of successful artists Giddle considered most compromised, I had her standards in my head. Not as my own standards, just a voice. The voice of a woman who said the three most cowardly acts were to exhibit ambition, to become famous, or to kill yourself.

By the time Sandro introduced me to Helen Hellenberger on Spring Street, just before I was set to depart for Reno to pick up the Moto Valera, that voice of Giddle's, my first friend and New York influence, was as quiet as the trees above me. I wanted to make artworks and show them in a gallery. It was what I'd moved to New York to do.

It was through our conversations that I ended up wanting to go to the salt flats, but Sandro had his own ideas about roads and speed and land. He'd written a proposal when he was young, to make paintings by the yard to be laid out over the entire length of the Autostrada del Sole, which connected the north and the south of Italy. Practical and industrial methods in service to something of no use. The autostrada was built by the government with funding and encouragement from the Valera Company. Sandro had a photo of his father and the Italian prime minister standing together to celebrate its inauguration in 1956. Its name, Autostrada del Sole, made it sound hopeful in a fascist kind of way. Anything "of the sun," Sandro said, was code for fascism. "My family helped ruin Italy," he said, "by building this superhighway, Milan to Bologna to Florence to Rome to Naples, but it made us rich." Sandro said highways primed us for a separation from place, from actual life. The autostrada replaced life with road signs and place names. A white background and black lettering. MILANO. A reduction, Sandro said, to nothing but names.

"No different than here," I said. "You might as well deplore all highways."

He conceded it was true, but said America was *supposed* to be a place ruined and homogenized by highways, that that *was* its unique character, crass and vulgar sameness.

"It's your destiny," he said, smiling, his eyes filling with cold light.

"What's your destiny?" I replied.

"To become an American citizen, of course."

Sandro had encouraged the general drift of what I was after, doing something in the landscape relating to speed and movement. But when Ronnie suggested that Sandro should come through for me—use his connections to get me a Moto Valera to ride—Sandro's enthusiasm all but ceased.

The only legitimate way to go to the Bonneville Salt Flats was to ride something truly fast, Ronnie said. "It has to be like she's testing out a factory bike."

Sandro was annoyed at Ronnie. I quietly hoped Ronnie would keep pressing him. I wanted to do a project at Bonneville, but I needed a bike. I didn't have the money to buy one, nor did I want to ask Sandro myself. I wasn't sure if Ronnie was advocating for me out of some old affection or if it was about Sandro, ribbing him. A form of competition. Ronnie had Moto Valera calendars tacked up as a kind of joke, the girls with big breasts straddling gleaming machines, an upholstering of flesh over the entire back wall of his studio. He claimed it was in homage to Sandro, but it was also a kind of mockery, to flaunt imagery that Sandro wanted to forget. Or maybe it was a love of something that Sandro himself could not appreciate in such a dumb and direct way. Which wasn't heckling, exactly, but something else, to fetishize elements of a friend's life that the friend could not see—Sandro, who pretended to mispronounce Italian dishes on a restaurant menu. Twice I had heard Sandro tell someone he was Romanian when they asked where his accent was from. He felt that Italy was a backwater. He claimed he had almost no connection to it.

When I told him I'd loved Florence, where I had spent my junior year of college, he said, sure, as an American woman it's fine. But try being an Italian woman. It's a piggish and abhorrent culture. If a man rapes you but is willing to marry you, the charges are dropped. Rape was not even a criminal offense but merely a "moral" one. He read about the country's financial woes, some directly relating to Valera, the way my cousins and uncle read the statistics of a baseball team they weren't rooting for, a team they hoped would lose, reveling in scandals and injuries and poor performances. With Sandro, it was Italy applying for an IMF loan. Inflation, unemployment. Valera getting hit especially hard by the oil crisis. Suffering work stoppages. Sabotage. Wildcat strikes. Sandro claimed that his older brother, Roberto, who ran the tire company, was as unknown to him as any other asshole businessman.

Italy was too provincial, Sandro said, too closed and familiar, almost preordained, for someone like him, from a family like his. He'd been in New York almost twenty years, so long that his Italianness seemed merely a way to be a unique New Yorker, as if he were more that, a New York artist with a faint accent, than he was Italian. His English was perfect, his friends, mostly American. Sandro had left Italy as soon as he could, refused the money that flowed from the faucets of his name, and worked at the Met alongside Ronnie, from whose name no money flowed, since Ronnie came from a working-class family and was estranged from them anyhow, having been separated in his childhood in some mysterious way you weren't supposed to bring up. Apparently he had worked on boats, but he never spoke about it. When I asked Sandro, he was protective of Ronnie, shook his head mildly, changed the subject.

He and Ronnie shared something in their longing to reinvent themselves as having no provenance, no Pickwick. I, on the other hand, was known to them as being distinctly and precisely a girl from Reno. I was the girl they expected things of. I was meant to find some way to use my origin in an interesting manner. Not like Smithson's spoof of the "real authentic West Coast artist," chrome-plating motorcycle parts and refusing to think. I was meant to form a concept that had rigor. I would listen to them, discussing me as if I weren't present but as a joke, for my amusement. "The girl," Sandro said. "You mean Reno," Ronnie replied, as if in direct taunt of the past—see, I can summon it, that's how little it means. *What now, Reno?*

Speed Week, when they ran various cars and motorcycles over the salt, was happening in September.

One June morning I woke up to hear Sandro speaking quickly in Italian to someone on the telephone. He'd arranged for me to have a Moto Valera.

"You can thank your friend Ronnie," he said.

8. LIGHTS

When I crashed, darkness folded around me like thick felt. I've been waiting all my life for it, was my thought. For this darkness, an absolute silence.

But then underneath it, the strangest, most curious scene came into view.

I saw glowing yellow spheres. They were moving in an elaborate formation, garlanding their way down a mountain face. It was almost dusk, and alpenglow was tinting the snow-filled glades to blush pink. Stands of evergreens marched up the deep folds between each glade in steep triangular formations. The lights swung over a high peak and down the mountain in zigzag, from one side of an open ski run to the other. As the run split into two runs divided by a rock face, the pills of light became two streams and then three, some going around a clump of trees in one direction, and others in the other direction, streams splitting and spilling in a slow waterfall, the slowness giving the sense that these lights were performers in some kind of show.

Night was verging. A last, thin vein of daylight hovered over the jags of the mountain's crest. Those lights pouring down over the front of the mountain were brighter now, as the alpenglow disappeared and the snow faded to the blue-pale of moonlight.

They were skiers, I realized. The lights were affixed to ski poles, a search party descending over the high peak.

The hollows on the mountain's face where trees huddled in their dark vigil had gone black.

When snow slides from an upper branch down the lowers in a great laddered weight-collecting sweep, it's enough to kill a person.

Now it was dark. A cloud was settling in, blotting the moon and cottoning the mountain in damp. I heard the distant beep of snowcats. They appeared through the mist with their huge rolling paws, golden eyes in binocular movement, crawling up the mountain in rows. Night workers, grooming. Above, strung in steep lines, were chairlifts, empty midair silhouettes with their exact and repeating angled geometry, still lifes on steel cable.

I remember a leather ski glove being rubbed over my frozen face. The sound of rubbing, loud, but no sensation of it. Then I was on the stretcher with the emergency blanket over my ski clothes. They had to get me down a mogul field. The patroller snowplowed right over the mogul's tops but shunted the stretcher into the groove between them. I closed my eyes as he picked his line. Slide, plant, pivot. Slide, plant, pivot.

I had fallen into the marrow of some other, long-ago emergency. The sensation of movement continued, me in the toboggan, bumping and sliding over hard-packed snow as the patroller took me down the hill. But as we slid, I heard people around me undoing the straps, as though we had come to a stop. I heard a loud zip, and the cutting of thick fabric with scissors. The sliding had ceased but I didn't know when. Maybe I had stopped sliding a long time ago.

"It might not be broken," someone said.

My body hurt. My eyes were closed, but I'd fallen back into myself with a hard thud.

I heard the rip and tear of engines.

"Hey."

A hand nudging my shoulder.

"Hey, can you hear me? You've had an accident."

There were faces above me, backlit in brightness.

My left ankle throbbed, but I could move my fingers and toes. Two men helped me to the side, across the oil line that marked the edge of the course. Race officials picked up pieces of fiberglass bodywork. The beautiful teal fairing. I was mortified to see it cracked and pulverized on the salt, turned to sudden garbage.

The gust, they said, shaking their heads. You can't fight wind like that. Eighty miles an hour.

But I blamed myself, watching them stack the motorcycle's fiberglass parts, which looked like cracked insect hulls now, and place them in the bed of a pickup truck.

Staticky communications surged from the race techs' radios. An ambulance siren wailed toward us from the direction of the start.

"I'm okay," I said. "Just a little bruised up." I'd be charged a fortune just to get looked at. Once they get you in the ambulance, it's too late.

"We're supposed to have you examined by the medics," one of them said. "It's standard procedure."

"I'm here with the Valera team."

It seemed only partly a lie, and the part that was a lie was quickly replaced by truth, because an hour later I was propped on pillows in the Valera mess trailer, and one of the team technicians had gone off to gather my knapsack from the timing officials' shack.

"You can feel this?" Tonino, their team doctor, was tapping the pads of my toes with his fingers in soft Morse code. He held an ice pack to my ankle, gently moving my foot this way and that. The Valera mechanics had already claimed the motorcycle and the pile of destroyed bodywork that went with it, as if picking up the pieces of my accident were part of their job, or some kind of instinctual chivalry I'd triggered. *La ragazza,* they kept saying. Me, *la ragazza.*

"I need to go back to the crash," I told Tonino as I pulled my camera from the retrieved knapsack.

"Don't be stupid. You're injured. You have a bad sprain," he said. "You need to keep it elevated."

I explained I was here to take photographs. I stressed this with Tonino, and afterward with all the other Valera people. Not only because without their help, I wouldn't be able to make it over there to take photographs, but because it made me feel like less of an impostor. The truth was I didn't know all that much about land speed trials, and crashing proved this. I had owned one motorcycle, and I always needed Scott and Andy's help to maintain it, unless the task was to change a simple spark plug. There was a whole range of knowledge and experience I lacked, and to these people whose life was motorcycles, I said I wasn't really a motorcyclist, but an artist. I'd come to photograph my tracks as an art project. Which was the opposite of how I'd presented myself to Stretch, as a girl into motorcycles and nothing more.

Tonino felt sorry for me and convinced one of the team technicians to ride me over to the inspection area on a little put-put bike they had for running errands in the pits. With my camera over my shoulder, I rode sidesaddle to the racecourse. Because of my crash the long course was still closed. I took photos at the start, hobbling on my sprain. I was ashamed to see the timing association people, remembering how calm and kind they'd been, imparting crucial information about gusts to someone who could not, it turned out, use their warning to prevent a mishap. But I faced them to get my photographs. I could not go home empty-handed. The Valera tech rode me along the side of the course's oil line. A truck was just ahead of us, dragging a metal grader, probably to repair the surface where I went down. When we arrived at the crash site, I saw that I'd broken through. What seemed like endless perfect white on white was only a very thin crust of salt. Where the crust had been broken by the force of impact, mud seeped up. I photographed all this, a Rorschach of my crash.

For five nights I slept in the Valera trailer, on a daybed in the lounge area next to the kitchen. I was visited by Tonino, ate the spaghetti their team cook brought to me on a paper plate, and practiced the Italian I'd learned on my year abroad, studying in Florence, and had been too embarrassed to use with Sandro (in any case, Sandro was so disinterested in Italy that my competence would not have impressed him). Tonino was amused by the way I spoke, the idioms I'd picked up. He wanted to know how I'd learned to speak such Florentine Italian. Telling him about Florence brought everything back. The biker crowd I had hung around with, who rode Triumphs and emulated a kind of London rocker look, unwashed denim and pompadours, the girls with liquid eyeliner and nests of teased hair. I had managed to meet Italians who weren't all that different from the people I'd grown up with in Reno. I didn't blend well with the other Americans who were there to study art history. They were mostly from the East Coast, from a culture I didn't understand, wealthy girls who seemed to be in Florence to shop for leather goods. We were all housed with local families, and somehow the others were put in rambling homes with maids and had the spacious rooms of children who were away at college. I was put in a walk-in closet with a family who owned a fruit stand near the train station. Every morning when I went to use the bathroom it was opaque with the husband's rank cigarette smoke. At dinner, the wife served tiny portions of fried rabbit and eyed me suspiciously to be sure I didn't serve myself seconds. When the wife had gone to bed, the husband got drunk and tried to engage me in conversation about the beauty of women's asses. I began avoiding dinner with them and instead ate french fries and drank tap beer at a pool hall near the train station called the Blue Angel, which often had British motorcycles parked in front. I started hanging around with the bikers and their girlfriends instead of going to my classes at the exchange program in which I was enrolled. We'd stroll the flea market at Le Cascine, drink at bars that seemed identical to the Blue Angel, or I'd go to their apartments, where we smoked hash and listened to records, Faces and Mott the Hoople. I wasn't learning much about Masaccio and Fra Angelico, but my Italian was good by the time I left.

Tonino corralled everyone around to witness this fact that seemed incredible to him, that I spoke Italian. I was something of an instant mascot, although mostly to Tonino, the mechanics, and the team manager, and not Didi Bombonato himself, who had opposed taking me in. Didi Bombonato came across as vain and irritable, but who knows how Flip Farmer would have come across had he answered the door that day in his prefab on the bluffs above Las Vegas.

"Girlfriend of *who*?" I had heard Didi ask when they first brought me back to their encampment. "One of the brothers," the team manager said. "He lives in New York City."

"Never heard of him," Didi said. "We're not an orphanage." But the team manager made his own decision that I could stay.

Didi and I avoided each other, which was fine. Maybe I didn't like him all that much, either. The main problem being that he was not Flip Farmer. No open American smile, no bright white teeth, no fancy purple script, nothing of whatever it was about Flip Farmer that had moved me when I was young.

Almost as bad as not being Flip, Didi was short, and short men so seldom liked me. I'm relatively tall, which seemed to count against me, and I was once even told by a short man that I was retriggering his youthful nightmares of being ridiculed by tall girls in school, and I sensed he wanted me to apologize for this, for his adolescent trauma, and I didn't, and moreover, I gave up on short men partially if not totally, sometimes even preemptively disliking them, though seldom admitting this to myself.

Each morning, I watched Didi out the window of the trailer as he put on his driving gloves and stretched his fingers, open and fisted, open and fisted, as if he were communicating some kind of cryptic message in units of ten. After his hand stretches, a crew member brought him a little thimble of espresso, which he took between deerskin-gloved finger and thumb, tilted his head back, and drank. He had pocked, sunken cheeks, thin bluish lips, and eyes like raisins, which made him seem angry and also a little dimwitted. Not everyone can be a great beauty, and I'm not exactly a conventional beauty myself. But there was a special tragedy to Didi's looks: his hair, which was lustrous and full, feathered into elaborate croissant layers. Somehow the glamorous hair brought his homeliness into relief, like those dogs with hair like a woman's. There was that advertisement on television where you saw a man and a woman from behind, racing along in an open car. The driver and his companion, her blond hair flying on the wind, the American freedom of a big convertible on the open highway, and so forth. The camera moves up alongside. The passenger, it turns out, is not a woman. It's one of those dogs with long feathery hair, whatever breed that is. Didi's breed. After drinking his espresso, Didi would flip his hair forward and then resettle it with his fingers, never mind that he was about to mash it under a helmet. It would have been better to skip the vanity and primping and instead use his face as a kind of dare, or weapon: *I'm ugly and famous and I drive a rocket-fueled cycle. I'm Didi Bombonato.*

For two long days Didi and the crew did test runs in their rocket-engine vehicle, the *Spirit of Italy*. There was a steering issue, which they solved by relenting to a curious handling feature: under two hundred miles an hour, the steering wheel of the *Spirit* was turned right in order to go right. Over two hundred miles an hour, it had to be turned *left* to go right. And over three hundred miles an hour, once again, the wheel was turned right to make it go right.

The moment had finally arrived for Didi to make his run. I was under the Valera awning, my foot propped up. Beyond, spectators packed against a rope. Many of those who had been around for the weekend of various classes of machine had stayed at the salt flats to see this. It was both a private affair, the flats officially closed, and the main event, because Didi Bombonato was favored to beat his own time and set a new world record for land speed. It was late morning, a pleasant day, clouds wind-pushed toward Floating Mountain, their shadows like big weightless vehicles. Soon, heavy rains were expected to arrive— by the middle of next week. The season would end, the salt soaked and mushy and unusable for land speed trials.

Didi put on his deerskin gloves. He performed his hand signals and then waved at the people who pressed in behind the rope to watch him make his run. He drank his single espresso. Flipped his hair. Put on his helmet and bent low to get into the *Spirit of Italy,* a chrome, white, and teal canister—the same silvery teal as the motorcycle I'd crashed.

His techs were about to attach the bubble canopy when the team manager came running out of his trailer, its door slapping closed behind him, waving his arms over his head in an X. "Stop!" he yelled. "Stop! Hold it!"

Didi turned around in the tight little compartment of the *Spirit* and scrunched his raisin eyes in the direction of the manager, who came toward him with a walkie-talkie to his ear, listening.

"We have a problem," the manager said.

"What is the problem?" Didi called back.

"A strike," the manager said. "In Milan."

The manager called everyone under the awning, around the work-benches. Didi hunched over the steering wheel in the *Spirit of Italy,* scowling, as if impatience alone could get his vehicle powered up and motoring along the flats, while his team decided that as loyal members of the union, which was in contract negotiations and had voted to strike, they were obligated to strike as well.

The mechanics in Milan were conducting something called a work-to-rule strike, so the mechanics on the salt flats conducted their own work-to-rule strike. It was a way of striking without striking, as Tonino explained it to me. They were still getting paid, and not at risk of being fired and replaced. They simply went absolutely by union and company code on every single procedural element of their jobs, and their unions and procedures being Italian and deeply bureaucratic, each task, if accomplished according to code, took much longer than it normally would.

Didi, not in the union, not a company employee, but a celebrity racer with an independent contract, was furious.

"You'll do your run," the manager assured him. "But there are a few procedures we have overlooked in the interest of time and efficiency. But really, we should not have skipped them."

For starters, there was meant to be a fully stocked first aid box or no work could commence. Someone was sent into town to buy iodine and tweezers, which were absent from the first aid box. While this errand was run, the crew waited under an awning on the white salt, in absolutely no hurry, certainly not any hurry that would tempt them to disregard official company procedures or compromise safety. They sat and smoked cigarettes. Someone put the Moka on a butane burner.

With the first aid box finally restocked, they were ready to do a safety check on the *Spirit*. But then it was discovered that another procedural rule had been ignored: each screw from the *Spirit of Italy* was to be labeled upon removal, but not by hand; labels were to be printed on tags in lowercase Garamond with an Olivetti typewriter, which they did not possess, nor did they have any tags, so no screws could be removed from the *Spirit of Italy*. Long discussions commenced on what was to be done in light of this problem. The team manager said he felt they could hand-print the labels, but tidily, "As if our *hands* are machines," he said. Just make the letters very uniform, he said. But they didn't have tags, and so someone had to figure out how to make tags.

Didi sat under the awning of his trailer, his deerskin gloves drooping from his pocket, his hair losing its feathery loft, his race suit unzipped to the waist, the sleeves tied around his middle. His eyes seemed to be getting smaller, dimmer, more raisinlike, his lips more bloodless and thin, like the edges of a cooked crepe, as if he were becoming uglier as the day stretched toward dusk and he was not allowed to make his run, set his record, be the famous and glorious (if short and ugly) Didi Bombonato.

The next day was similar, time stretching full with long discussions of how to interpret the employee codes and rules, talk that was punctuated by many cigarette and Moka breaks. Hours waiting under their Valera awning while the team manager filled out a series of forms they usually ignored, and then one man was sent into town to notarize the forms, and having forgotten to collect passports, had to return, and then go again, and suddenly it was time for their company-allotted break, and they would all quit working as one of them prepared the afternoon espresso. Didi was indignant. He fumed. Performed stretches and hand exercises and glared at the others with his opaque raisin eyes.

Morning and evening, Tonino helped me to ice my ankle and dress my road rash, broad lakes of which were drying into big itchy scabs. He asked about Sandro, and said he hadn't been aware there was another brother.

"Do you know Roberto?" I asked.

"We don't *know* him," Tonino said, laughing. "Roberto is the face of the company. The president."

Outside the trailer window, the techs were discussing some new problem.

I'd tried to relay a message to Sandro through one of the mechanics who'd gone into town, to tell him what had happened. The mechanic had called the loft and said a woman answered and told him Sandro was out. A woman? I figured there was a language barrier, or that he'd dialed the wrong number. Or maybe someone from Sandro's gallery had come over, not unusual, to photograph artworks or prepare them for shipment.

"Does Sandro Valera tell you about the company situation?" Tonino asked.

"Not really," I said. "He's an artist, he's not involved."

"Lucky for him, perhaps," Tonino said. "The company is at war with its factory workers."

I knew only a little about this war that Tonino referred to. Sandro did not call it that. It wasn't something he talked about often. The previous spring, an Italian artist he knew from Milan had a gallery show on West Broadway that was about factory actions and the Red Brigades. The show was called *S.p.A.*—a play on words, Sandro explained. In Italy, the acronym meant joint stock company, but literally, "society for actions." The artist had made huge pencil tracings from newspaper photographs of three Red Brigades victims and one Red Brigades member, Margherita Cagol, killed in a shoot-out with police, slumped on the ground in tight jeans, a purse strewn at her side, blood leaking from her mouth. Sandro seemed unhappy to confront the material. The press release mentioned that the Red Brigades were Italian militants who got their start in the Valera factories on the industrial outskirts of Milan. Sandro put the sheet down. "Sensationalist crap," he said.

When I asked Tonino about the Red Brigades he said, "That's just one group. The most visible one. There are so many groups at this point. Many of them come together only after an action, to give those who committed the action a name, and then they disband, disappear. You can't know who is part of what. They don't know, either. They might not know they are *in* a group until the action is done and the group claims it."

Late on the evening of the second day of the work-to-rule strike, word arrived that the mechanics in Italy had declared theirs over.

The next morning, Didi emerged bright and early from his trailer, fully suited and ready to go. He lifted a leg and did a few sets of athletic lunges, then switched legs and lunged again in taut sets. He flicked his hands into open tens, shut fists, open tens. He jumped up and down in a controlled dribble like a prizefighter.

He was ready to claim his empire, be Didi Bombonato, world land speed champion, break his own record, and—

Wait. What was happening?

The six technicians and their team manager emerged from the tool and equipment trailer with extreme slowness, as if the baking white salt were a kind of thick gel that offered great resistance, as they moved toward the workbench onto which the *Spirit* had been wheeled for a maintenance check. The team manager picked up a drill in curious slow motion.

Didi yelled at them. "What are you doing? What is this? Come on!"

The team manager turned toward Didi and lifted his hand to his face. He removed his sunglasses, brought them downward with sustained slowness, and cleaned each lens thoroughly with a handkerchief. Then he put his sunglasses back on.

"I'm preparing for your run," the team manager said. He spoke these words very, very slowly.

He and the others moved around underneath the awning, picking up tools and gauges in slow motion. They spoke with big swaths of silence between words.

Didi let out what I can only describe as a roar. He kicked the side of his trailer and seemed to have injured his toe (his driving shoes, like Flip Farmer's, were of soft leather, not for protection but sensitivity).

The team was now engaged in something called a slowdown, in solidarity with the Valera workers back in Milan. The mechanics no longer followed the rule book so perversely and exactly but instead distended time, taking longer to perform each task, and punctuating their activities and communications with great pauses. As I watched all of this, I felt both closer to Sandro for all I was seeing of this company crew, and also far away. I still hadn't talked to him.

That night, lying on the daybed in the trailer, I listened to the wind and felt like a stowaway.

As we had left the gallery on West Broadway, after seeing the drawings of the Red Brigades victims, Sandro had begun to tell me a story about M, an Argentine friend of his, a man I'd only met briefly on a couple of occasions. I immediately sensed from the quiet, serious way he spoke about M that Sandro was trying to tell me something about himself, his family, and those drawings, people slain in the streets of Rome and Milan, the woman killed in a shoot-out with police. Sandro was protective of M, and the particular burdens that M carried because of his father, who was part of the notorious new military dictatorship in Argentina.

"People are always interested in M when they find out his father was part of the junta," Sandro said, so respectful of his friend's privacy that he didn't want to say his name in the context of M's family. "You hear them practically bragging about it. *You know his father is in the dictatorship, right?* Everyone excited by their two-degree removal from death squads. They don't care what M's relationship to any of it is. They want to know him because he's connected to corruption and murder, even if M moved to New York City to get away from all that. Away from his family and its tarred name, away from the place where it matters."

M, Sandro told me, actively avoided friendship with anyone who asked about his father, and at a certain point, anyone who seemed interested in Argentina or Latin American politics generally. Even a vaguely left-wing orientation, Sandro said, could scare off M. And yet M himself was a Marxist, and also gay, and hated his own father and the culture from which he'd come. But he didn't want to atone for it to anyone else.

"All these people just want to be near him because they're fascinated by the novelty that a military henchman in a government known for torture and murder has a son in the New York art world," Sandro said.

Having suffered the complicated weight of guilt for his father's sordid power, M felt it was his right not to discuss it with anyone, not to explain it or apologize for it. M had to be his father's son, and wasn't that enough, Sandro said, as we'd turned up Spring Street, heading to Rudy's for a drink. "He doesn't have to explain his background to onlookers, or worse, the self-declared morally outraged."

M and Sandro had a very particular bond over these things. M's father's enemies, the leftist guerrillas, had even torched a Valera plant outside of Buenos Aires, which Sandro and M had laughed about together, on one of the two occasions when I met M. It was one of the few times I saw Sandro find anything humorous about being a Valera.

The next morning, the slowdown was over. Everyone was ready. It was finally time.

But Didi did not emerge from his trailer suited up, limbering himself to set records in the *Spirit of Italy,* as he had done each previous morning. At about noon he finally appeared, wearing street clothes, his hair oily and uncombed, a bored and deadened expression on his face. It seemed the spirit of Didi had been maimed or stalled by all the waiting. But a couple of hours later, the vehicle ready to go, he recaptured his Didi fire, suited up, and did two runs, setting a new record at 721 miles an hour.

Because the strikes had dragged on for four days, by this time there were no longer any spectators. Just the six techs, Tonino, me, and a few reporters. There was a formal toast, a press conference with the reporters, and then Didi was taken to the airport in Salt Lake City, to depart for a European tour to promote Valera tires. He didn't stick around for the impromptu party that night, when the mechanics whooped and drank and hugged one another.

I was propped on a couch as the techs celebrated. I could not dance on my sprained ankle, but since I was the only woman, I danced with each of them by being scooped up and swung around, then delicately placed back on the daybed. We had only an AM radio, tuned to Top Forty—"Hooked on a Feeling" and that song about a woman's brown eyes turning blue, which I'd assumed meant she was declaring she would make her eyes the blue of the woman who'd replaced her. "I'm gonna make my brown eyes blue." Replace my replacement. That night, I realized it was not *I'm gonna*, but *don't it make them* blue, which changed the meaning. It was a stupider song than I'd imagined.

The Valera mechanics and Tonino toasted one another and Didi in absentia and said the Americans could go do a *bel culo.* Someone said Didi, too, could go do a *bel culo,* and then their voices hushed and they were, I imagined, talking politics. They were still outside after I went to bed. I heard the dry pop of one or two more champagne bottles uncorking, low voices, and then quiet. Wind whistling across the flats, the snap of canvas awnings, and a periodic light clink of something metal faintly hitting something else metal.

The next morning the team manager came in to speak with me. I was hoping to catch a ride with them to Salt Lake City, and from there fly home to New York. He said of course, and that they had a favor to ask of me as well. It was actually a bigger favor. A magnificent one, in its way, but it would also be a kind of honor, and he wanted me to think carefully before responding.

"We want you to drive the *Spirit of Italy,*" he said.

"But why? In any case, I can barely walk."

"All you need is your right foot, for gas and brake. Didi needs to keep the salt occupied so the Americans don't come back and beat his time; there's a team from Ohio on its way here. It will take a few days to prepare, to train you, and by the time you've done your run, the rains will arrive. We can shut them out for the whole year. A woman's record is easy; the current one is two hundred and ninety miles an hour. That's nothing in the *Spirit.* If you go three hundred and five you'll feel like you're coasting, then you tap the brakes and that's it."

I had always admired people who had a palpable sense of their own future, who constructed plans and then followed them. That was how Sandro was. He had ambitions and a series of steps he would take to achieve them. The future, for Sandro, was a place, and one that he was capable of guiding himself to. Ronnie Fontaine was like that, too. Ronnie's goals were more perverse and secretive than Sandro's, but there was a sense that nothing was left to chance, that everything Ronnie did was calculated. I was not like either Sandro or Ronnie. Chance, to me, had a kind of absolute logic to it. I revered it more than I did actual logic, the kind that was built from solid materials, from reason and from fact. Anything could be reasoned into being, or reasoned away, with words, desires, rationales. Chance shaped things in a way that words, desires, rationales could not. Chance came blowing in, like a gust of wind.

From zero to two hundred, turn right to go right.

From two hundred to three hundred, turn *left* to go right.

Faster than three hundred, turn right to go right.

9. It was milk

and Valera was learning all about it. Not the kind you drank. There weren't even any cows in this jungly part of Brazil, except for the repulsive sea cows he'd seen in photographs, flopped up on muddy riverbanks. They tapped this milk from trees, a liquid that dried to rubber.

The rules in the Amazon, he learned, were different. You had to wait longer. A tree was damaged if you tapped it before it was fifteen years old. In Asia, where most rubber had come from before World War Two had begun, a year earlier, the trees could be tapped at the tender age of eight or nine, brought directly into service like very young girls, and they withstood it. But the biggest difference was that in Asia you planted trees and harvested them. It was farming, industrial farming. In the Amazon, you cultivated the stuff from the wild. The jungle was like a standing army, a reserve that would summon forth a product, become something other than green, useless, hostile nature, and Valera liked this idea, of conscripting nature into service.

The way it was going to be arranged was a kind of perfection. Like a wooden box put together without any nails, joists, screws, or even glue. Just jigsawed pieces designed to perfectly interlock and hold one another in place. The rubber tappers would work on credit. They would be held in place by the need to be paid. All variety of middlemen, nec-

essary to move the stuff downriver to port, also would work on credit.
It was all indebtedness and credit, zero outlay of actual money. Credit
came from *credo,* which was to believe. Cre-do. I believe. He could cite
Latin all he wanted, unencumbered now of Lonzi, no Lonzi correct-
ing him for calling on the root of things. The root of things mattered.
Cre-do. The Indians in the jungle were going to work for free.

Harvest and smoke the rubber, send it back to Europe, and make a
lot of money. A *lot* of money. That was the plan when Valera expanded
into tires in 1942.

"You smoke it? To make money?" six-year-old Roberto had asked
him.

"No, *piccolino,* you don't *smoke* it. You smoke it like you'd smoke
cheese, or meats. To preserve."

This smoking of rubber: they did it over huge outdoor fires, on
enormous paddles, with rags tied over their faces, not only over the
nose and mouth but the whole face, to protect their eyes as well. They
can see enough, the overseer he'd hired assured Valera. They see just
barely, through the weave of coarse cloth. He pictured them moving
around the fire, faceless mummies bumping into one another. Men in
gray, blank, woven masks, adding rubber to form great balls. The balls
were called biscuits. Biscotti. Each weighed one hundred pounds.
That was the weight unit Valera's overseer set. A good comfortable
crushing weight, carried on the head, the maximum. You set it at
150 pounds, the overseer said, and they cannot carry it. A hundred
pounds on the top of an Indian's head, they suffer but they manage.
Not impossible—that was the idea. He understood that this was the
overseer's main skill, to recognize what was within human limits, but
just barely. "Within, but just barely" was the optimum calibration,
the unit of profit. One-hundred-pound biscuits of smoked rubber,
overland, on heads. Big biscuits of rubber, head-crushing but not
impossible. Men loading the smoked rubber biscuits on boats that
would travel a thousand miles to the river's mouth, the coastal port
of Belém. At Belém they would be cleaved in half with hatchets. To
judge their quality. Split like brains, and the lighter the shade of the

biscuit's insides, the higher its value and price. The darker, the poorer its quality. Dark rubber was less pure. "Like everything dark," said the overseer, laughing in a vigorous way, as if instructing Valera to laugh with him, but Valera didn't.

They're going to make me rich, Valera thought. And in any case after spending his boyhood in Egypt he was not unaccustomed to dark-skinned people. It was backward to hate them. He and Lonzi divided ways on this subject. Lonzi had gone off to participate in the invasion of Abyssinia, in '35, to "wrestle negroes to the ground." Lonzi sounded like a missionary, as if he'd forgotten what had been so critical to the spirit of the group: you don't recruit. You never recruit. You act, and those who want to act as you do simply fall in. Nothing was gained through force. Wrestle away, Valera thought. Your entire battalion will be riding my motorcycles. That year, while Lonzi was off fighting in Abyssinia, the thousand-cc bike Valera had designed won the world land speed record, on the autostrada between Brescia and Bergamo. A simplified, street version was in production at his factory outside Milan.

He and Lonzi were no longer close, but they had shared something Valera would never forget, a youthful recognition that vital life was change and swiftness, which only revealed itself through violent convulsions. Sameness was a kind of stupor, a state of being in which people thought the world had always been as they knew it and would always stay that way. Cotton laundry and waves. Blue handprints on a wall. Time had worn a mask. It had hidden itself, and he and Lonzi and the others in the little gang would tear off its mask. It was their destiny to do so. To know that life meant cataclysmic change, exceptional and monstrous to most people but not to them. They embraced the monstrosity of it. Like volume to the ancient Egyptians, who depicted everything flat, in two dimensions, because volume was terrifying unknowability. Yes, it *was* terrifying, Valera agreed with the Egyptians, and that was why he wanted it.

While Lonzi was busy prostrating himself over the map of Ethiopia, fighting the British and buffing the Duce with war poems, Valera was deep into business. Cycles, scooters, a three-wheeled car, and now rubber. Rubber had been coming mostly from Malaysia, until the Japanese overran the place on bicycles. An incredible attack, Japanese on bikes. Italian operations ground to a halt. Valera was not in the rubber business then. It was what got him into it, the rubber shortage that began when the Japanese overran Malaysia, in December 1941. A month later Valera was in Brazil.

In São Paulo, he spent a lot of time waiting in a hotel lobby for men who arrived hours late in creamy linen. They sat in wicker chairs, he and the men in linen, the woven caning of their chairbacks blooming up behind them like gigantic doodled wings. Nearby, something called an umbrella bird crouched inside an enormous cage, a shiny black thing that kept fanning itself out, menacing and ugly. Valera knew that a good business deal is made from patience. From waiting as if you have all the time in the world, your wicker doodle wings creaking, knowing you hate the umbrella bird and that you don't need a reason to hate it, as you sit in a swamp-climate lobby and fan yourself with a map of northern Brazil. Place was gigantic. Obscenely so. This, Valera had not understood. But no matter, a good business deal had little to do with maps. It was about looking other men in the eye in a way that made them feel they were part of a complicit and elite minority.

The minister of industry said there would be no problem rounding up enough labor to harvest the rubber. Brazil had joined the Allies and was sending men off to the war. Or pretending to, the minister of industry said, to convince these men that harvesting rubber was better than going to fight in the war. Except you don't have to convince them, he said. Because it's easier to get a snake to smoke than to get an Indian to enlist. Valera rather liked the image of a snake in the act of smoking, one oblong tube sucking on another, smaller oblong tube. It distracted him momentarily until he realized what the minister of industry meant. A snake would not smoke. An Indian would stay home and harvest rubber. He'd taken it literally, as Roberto had the smoking of rubber—like father, like son.

*　*　*

Down in South America, they had apparently been the last to know about this thing called the wheel, and yet they were the people who had first discovered rubber, and Valera found poetic excellence in these two tandem facts, the place where they had first known of rubber and last known of the wheel. The stupidity of it gave his new endeavor a bright aura, bringing progress to Brazil, last earthlings to discover the wheel.

What had the Indians there done with this rubber they discovered? They made a game, *pok-ta-pok,* which sounded like what it was: you bounced the ball back and forth between two players.

They used rubber in torches to make an ominous, greasy smoke. They dipped cloth in rubber to make it waterproof. And for shoes. They used their feet as molds in a straight-over dipping process to form perfect, custom-fit galoshes. The *original* fit, Valera observed with a certain delight, was *custom* fit. One size fits all was something that came later, with mechanization. He wasn't going to have them making the tires. They would harvest raw rubber and mold it into the great big biscotti, which would then be shipped to Switzerland, to a company he'd set up to operate without the interference of Mussolini, whom Valera increasingly considered a bungler and hooligan.

If he could sell enough tires, he could devote all of his own time to motorcycles, which didn't have the same kind of profit margin. Especially now that Mussolini had requisitioned Valera's entire stock for the military, and all his factories did was make replacement parts for German troops, who were forever ripping out clutches.

He set things up and returned to Milan, anxious to see his youngest child, Sandro, almost three now. Roberto had been sent to boarding school in Switzerland, and this had made Alba lonely enough that she'd trapped him into creating a second. He was practically an old man and had told himself the younger one wasn't his, but while he was in Brazil, playing, as he thought of it, pok-ta-pok, he missed the little thing, its sweet, open face. It was his child, he knew this intuitively, but he felt he had surpassed, in seniority, a direct relation to it. He could be more removed, something like a great-uncle, a godfather. His wife had wanted it and he'd consented by not unconsenting. Who was it who said decision was indecision crystallized? He couldn't recall but in this case it certainly had been.

In those short, intense years of pok-ta-pok, Valera's rubber business flourished, while his motorcycle factory was flattened by Allied bombs. The family moved up to their villa, on a little hill above Bellagio. Safer, even if the area was overrun by crude and abrupt Germans, with their loud voices and their meat breath. It was only a matter of time until everything changed. Mussolini was just north of them, in the Feltrinelli villa on Lake Garda, where he apparently puttered around, depressed, played *scopone,* and looked through a viewfinder at the lake. Made incoherent radio broadcasts about the selfish Italian industrialists who were ruining Italy. We'll see who has ruined Italy, Valera thought at his radio set.

Lonzi turned up in Bellagio, wounded. He was convalescing at a lakeside hotel. He was the same age as Valera—fifty-seven—and still the fool had been with the Alpini, on the Eastern Front.

Valera and Alba went to visit him at the Hotel Splendide. Lonzi, his leg blown off, was packing ice around the remaining stumped mass, but the thing was septic, sending up slow and wretched bubbles, which shone as if blown of mucus. As each bubble of gas-filled ooze on Lonzi's stump stretched full and popped, it sent a smell of rot and death into the closed hotel room, and Valera wished he hadn't brought Alba. He nudged her back, and she stood by the door.

"This doesn't matter," Lonzi said, gesturing to his leg stump as if it were a maimed dog that needed to be shot. He was wearing his Alpini hat, its feather angled like a crooked fence post. "The real issue is that my heart is still human, that's the fix I'm in. I want to dig it out. If I can live without a leg, why not this thumper? It's as bad as hers," he said, pointing at Alba. "That hideous good-looking woman you brought here. Did you learn nothing, Valera? I don't want to see women tarted up for sex. I want to fight for my pleasure. Don't parade that here."

The sepsis must have gone to Lonzi's brain. A grisly adventure, and for what? Valera wondered. There was no future in ground combat, fighting people with daggers and guns, cutting through barbed wire, bleeding and suffering and rolling around in the mud. Mussolini spoke over the radio about a secret weapon of some kind: the Germans would unveil it, whatever it was, and they'd all be saved. And if they lost, Mussolini declared, justice would eventually be served. There would be a grand trial, he said. Mussolini was convinced the Allies would try him in Madison Square Garden—where the world would come to know the truth, and see things as he did. The truth would be revealed, Mussolini said, in Madison Square Garden.

Where is it? Valera wondered. "Alba, where is Madison Square Garden?"

She said England, probably. It sounded English.

Mussolini could do nothing about Valera's secret little pok-ta-pok, Eugen Dollmann assured him. Dollmann, a liaison for the Germans, had helped Valera set up the Swiss operation, part of an elaborate program of Dollmann's to undermine Mussolini's half-witted plan to socialize Italian industry. In truth, Valera's pok-ta-pok was a major operation. He made the drive regularly through the mountains and into Switzerland to oversee things, wearing, for those drives, an officer's dress uniform in case he was stopped. The hat, a black fur Colbacco-style fez with gold fasces, and a heavy wool MVSN coat with its patchwork of badges and emblems. Together they kept him warm and gave his missions an official appearance.

One moonless night, descending in elevation on the switchback curves that took him down toward Bellagio from the Swiss border, he saw artificial light of some kind over Lake Como, a marvelous bursting pink, bright as day. It was tracer fire.

A few days later, Mussolini was executed and hung from the girders of an Esso station in the Piazzale Loreto in Milan. He was next to his lover and a small coterie, all hung upside down from the gas station's girders like Parma hams.

Crowds began to maul the bodies. The images in the newspaper showed people with dirt-smeared faces, the particular face of hunger, hollowed and angular with bright, stuperous eyes, this rabble grabbing at the bodies, tearing their clothes, tugging on the corpses, pulling them down from the girders. The bodies dense and inert, the clothes coming off to reveal a curiously inhuman nudity, not like animals and not like people, lacking in any kind of dignity, pale flesh poked and prodded and spilling fluids from inside. Some of the corpses had been tied behind motorcycles—Valera motorcycles!—the Esso signs on the petrol pumps behind them round and bright as lollipops, the bodies dragged down the Corso Buenos Aires like bags of sand.

logic of the steering, the speedometer, the gas pedal. I knew the world, now, from inside the *Spirit of Italy*.

I knew that feeling. To be the driver. To watch the mechanics in their white jumpsuits leap over the blinding salt toward the vehicle, faces jubilant. Toward me, behind the wheel.

Fall had arrived, and a feeling of hope and freshness suffused the city. The sky was a vivid, seersucker blue. I was finished with my first day back working with Marvin and Eric at Bowery Film, strolling under a canopy of green leaves that were big and floppy, a few gold or ruby-red around the edges, one twirling downward as I crossed Washington Square Park. The light cut a sharp shadow instead of summer's fuzzy outlines. Autumn had brought in definition, a sense of gravity return-ing to a place where it had been chased out by the sun, by the diffuse rule of humidity. There was a late-September crispness in the air. I thought of smashed horse chestnuts on the sidewalks of Reno. The feel of new corduroy. Of course I had a great story to report, and the hopefulness I sensed from the gold-edged leaves above me could have been my own.

I had run an errand for Marvin, dropping off processed film to an address on lower Fifth, and was on my way to meet Sandro. The NYU students loafing around the empty fountain in the park were trying out the fall fashions, the boys in sweaters of wholesome colors, orange, brown, and green. The girls in pleated, brushed-cotton coats and suede clogs or those oxfords with the wavy soles. Lace knee socks and hand-tooled leather purses with a long strap worn crosswise between the breasts. A few berets. In light, dry gusts, the air riffled the leaves, yellow as wax beans, and a few floated softly downward. In such hopefulness, even a beret seemed like a good idea.

"Did you ever notice that three-quarters of China girls have a wid-ow's peak?" Marvin had asked me that afternoon, as he was setting up the lights to take my picture holding the color chart. Mostly I helped customers and ran errands, but twice a year or so they needed new pic-tures for different emulsions and densities of film.

10. Faces

I.

I did it. I set the record.

I was, improbably, the fastest woman in the world, at 308.506 miles an hour. An official record for 1976, not beaten until the next year.

There was an article in the *Salt Lake Tribune*. I'd been interviewed by a reporter from *Road and Track* who was there to write about Didi. And by a reporter for the Italian television station Rai.

And yet it was the beginning of the end for me, some kind of end, although I didn't see things that way at the time.

I returned to New York triumphant. I had crashed going 140 miles an hour and more or less walked away unharmed, mostly because of the helmet and the leather racing suit I'd had on. Just a sprain, bruises, and road rash of which I was secretly proud. I'd been allowed to drive the *Spirit of Italy*. I had been in the cockpit, which held the faint residue of Didi Bombonato's aftershave. I had breathed his aftershave and pretended it was Flip Farmer's, or that I was Flip Farmer. The speed had felt right, even if I had been afraid: to go fast was to conform to the

"I mean a pronounced one," he said. "But you—you have no widow's peak."

It was true. For some reason many of them had a widow's peak.

I have no widow's peak.

I liked the little brushed-cotton coats, very retro-1940s, but soon I would have the Moto Valera, which was being repaired at the dealer in Reno and would be shipped back to New York, all at Sandro's expense. (Did I care? No, I didn't. The money was practically nothing to him.) It might take months for it to be repaired, because they had to order parts and bodywork from Italy since it was a 1977 model, not yet released, but eventually I'd have it, at which point the dainty cotton jacket would be useless. I would need leather. And not just leather but tight leather. Since my crash, I understood its use, which had nothing to do with the kids in leather who packed into Rudy's Bar after midnight. The leathers I had worn on the salt flats were too big, and where they sagged they rubbed my skin off as I rolled and skidded. The scabs were just now beginning to fall off, revealing pink skin, not ready for the world. As the bruises on my legs and hip healed, dead matter just under the skin drained downward in blackish streaks, sedimenting around my ankles like coffee grounds. I hadn't known the body's methods were so crude. The streaks itched terribly. Sandro liked them. He said they looked like paint pours on a Morris Louis canvas. I heard him telling people about my trip to Bonneville, the crash, the ride in Didi's jet car. Neither of us acknowledged that had it not been for Ronnie's taunts, Sandro never would have made the trip possible for me.

The night I'd returned, Sandro said, "Did I tell you I'm doing a show with Helen Hellenberger?" He smiled happily.

"You are?"

"I've been with Erwin too long. I think it's time for a change. He doesn't really get the work anymore. He can't take me to the next level at this point in my career."

I sensed he was repeating Helen's argument to him. I'd seen how persuasive she could be. We were in the kitchen, which always felt like Sandro's kitchen, because I'd lived there all of five months, in a place that had been his for several years, where he had his own finicky way of arranging things and where all the things were his and I felt more like a guest, one who navigated her domestic surroundings with only partial knowledge. Over the course of the first six months we were dating, the boiler in my building broke and was not fixed. "Why stay there when there is heat and hot water at my place?" Sandro said, and soon I was practically living with him, and then the question was why pay rent on my apartment when legally I probably had a right not to, since the place was overrun by roaches and there wasn't hot water? Why not just move in with him? It was hard to argue with. Sandro's place was never homey to me, but it was a lot nicer than mine.

As he and I spoke about his move to Helen's gallery, my eyes drifted to the sideboard, where two dirty wineglasses and several empty wine bottles stood. I had been gone two weeks, and I assumed he'd had a friend over, Ronnie or Stanley, maybe Morton Feldman. When I'd first walked in, he'd looked directly at the glasses, the empty bottles, and said he'd missed me terribly. Now I understood that Helen had been here.

"I'm really happy about this move," he said. "I think it's a bold change. An important one."

If I had expressed jealousy over him having invited Helen to the loft for drinks, our loft, I sensed he would have become the wise father, attributing jealousy to youth, which was how he spoke of jealousy in others, as a kind of fretting that Sandro, the elder, wouldn't indulge.

A couple of days after returning, I'd taken my film to be developed. Sandro had given me part of a huge room to use as my studio, where I spread out photos on a long table. They weren't at all spectacular. They were the detritus of an experience, ambiguous marks in the white expanse of the salt flats.

Ronnie came over and looked at the photographs. He said I should keep the bike as it was when I crashed it. Wheel it into a gallery and place it in the middle of the room, with the photographs of my tracks on the walls.

I'd rather have the bike, I said, to ride it. And he said that was a choice I'd have to make. I agreed with him that the photographs by themselves were too ephemeral. But I was on, now, to the next thing, what the crash had given way to, which was my new and curious association with the Valera team. They had contacted me through Sandro, and had invited me to come to Italy the next spring for a photo shoot at Monza, Didi and I on the famous racetrack outside of Milan. And after Monza, a publicity tour for the tire company. It was, I felt, way beyond what I'd hoped for with the attempted film on Flip Farmer. I would have total access, and they said I could film and take my own pictures.

Sandro had acted as if it were a ridiculous proposal that I go to Italy under the auspices of his family's company. And not only that, but to end up reduced to the ignominy, he said, of a calendar girl. He scoffed at the idea that the company actually thought his own girlfriend would agree to such a thing.

"But calendar girls don't drive race vehicles," I said. This was something else. I'd actually gone fast enough. And he had to consent that yes, it was true, but promoting his family's company was too far. I tried to keep my attitude casual. I wasn't going to pass up the chance to go to Italy and tour with the Valera team, but I didn't push things with Sandro. I simply knew privately that I was going, and hoped he would eventually see things my way.

I was on the trail of land speed racers, as if everything—my childhood with Scott and Andy, my early attempt to interview Flip Farmer— had all been logical training.

Except I was no kind of racer myself. Flip and Didi were actual racers, with actual talent. And the truth was that in participating in some kind of promotional tour, I would be more like what Sandro said, a calendar girl. But if I were an actual racer it wouldn't be art. It would be sport. This, the infiltration, as I thought of it, was a way of drawing upon myself, my life, just as Sandro had encouraged. You lived your art if you were serious, according to Giddle.

"Another thing about the majority of China girls," Marvin had said that afternoon, my first one back at work, as he adjusted a round silver

reflector, "is they don't ride motorcycles. And their portraits don't suggest trauma. They don't show up covered with bruises."

He and Eric were annoyed with me.

"The problem with the bruises is they make you not anonymous,"
Eric chimed in.

"You're not supposed to evoke real life. Just the hermetic world of a
smiling woman holding the color chart."

"Yeah. Anonymous. Friendly. Comely. Various -ly's."

Marvin and Eric had me do my hair and makeup and try on outfits
as if each of our minor, in-office photo shoots were my one chance to
make it in Hollywood, when in reality it didn't matter what I looked
like. Technically they could have used any face. All they needed was a
natural skin tone—any living female would do—in contrast to the color
chart. But the film industry tradition was that reasonably attractive
young women did this work, posing for film leader so the lab technicians could make color corrections. I didn't just hold up the color
chart. I placed it lovingly in my hands like it was the answer to a television game show question. I smiled in a tentative but friendly way, as if
some vaguely intimate possibility might exist between me and whoever
caught a glimpse of me on film, just the slightest possibility.

SAVE YOUR FREEDOM FOR A RAINY DAY

It was still there on the wall of the women's room at Rudy's.

Also: "Long live the king."

"Who?"

"*Le roi.*"

"Roy who?"

"Roy G. Biv."

"Fucker owes me $$$."

On another wall: "Looking for an enemy. Tall. Slim. Ruthless. With
a sense of humor."

SO HOW DO WE FIND EACH OTHER? Someone had written
underneath in big hasty block letters.

I went to rejoin Giddle and Sandro, who were probably stiffly await-ing my return, having exactly nothing in common but me. I felt a hand on my shoulder and turned around. It was Ronnie. He was wearing mirrored aviator glasses. He smiled and I saw that his front tooth was chipped.

"What happened to your tooth?"

He ignored the question, which was very Ronnie.

"Ronnie, you look like a Nuremberg defendant in those glasses," Sandro said, motioning to the waitress. "Could we have four slivovitz? And what happened to your tooth?"

"I was riding a mechanical bull. Oh, shit. Saul is here."

"You went to Texas," Giddle said. "Is that what they really do there? Ride mechanical bulls?"

Ronnie ignored her. He and Sandro both had little patience for Giddle, less than she seemed to have for them.

"Skip the bull," Sandro said. "Ha-ha. Tell us about the trip."

Ronnie had gone to visit the artist Saul Oppler in Port Arthur.

"It was a disaster. I shouldn't have gone. But he called me up one night sounding desperate. Three a.m. and he's complaining bitterly about how much he hates Port Arthur. He's stuck down there for some kind of family stuff, and whines that he misses his pet rabbits, which he'd left under the care of a New York assistant and blah-blah-blah. 'Saul,' I said, 'do you want me to get those rabbits and bring them down to you? Would you like me to do that?' 'Gosh, Ronnie,' he says, 'I don't want to put you out. But the truth is, it would mean so much to me if you were able to do that. You could take my Jaguar.' I thought, why the hell not?"

"Uh-oh," said Sandro.

"I left that same night. I'd never driven an E-type Jaguar before, and I had to stop and get different *shoes* because my goddamn sneakers were too bulky or puffy or something to handle the tight little Jaguar pedals. Twice I almost drove off the road because I couldn't get to the brake adequately. The pedals on that car were so close together they were designed for like Italian driving moccasins. You know, really supple kidskin leather. Buttery little shoes that barely have a sole, just a faint slip of leather, so you can feel every nuance of the accelerator and clutch. Professional dance slippers would have been best. I couldn't find any of those. Nothing even close. I was at a truck stop in Maryland. They had key chains with crabs in sunglasses. Stun guns. Packages of tube socks, which everyone knows are for the truckers, for no-mess masturbation while driving. They didn't have any Italian shoes. I bought women's bedroom slippers, Dearfoams, size thirteen. After I slit the heel they fit me perfect. I was ripping down I-85 in Oppler's E-type with his rabbits in the back, wearing my Dearfoams, and somehow managed not to get pulled over. I felt like Mario Andretti. I understand that Reno here set a record and dazzled the Italians, but let's not forget Ronnie's death race through Texas. Wasting people. Like the two fruitcakes in a souped-up Monte Carlo who tried to overtake me. Later I almost hit an armadillo. I drove all night. Got to Port Arthur in the late afternoon. Horrible place, by the way. Big, squat refineries, air that smells of burning tires. Snakes dangling from the trees, trying to stay cool, I guess. And dead ones, flat paddles of jerky fused to the road. In the middle of the gravel drive into the property was a giant lizard eating a baguette, one of those really cheap and fluffy grocery store baguettes. Sickening, this lizard tearing off hunks of bread and devouring them. I park, and Oppler comes out of his studio and starts limping toward the car, I guess his leg was asleep or something. He's calling to those rabbits like they know their names and are going to be happy to see him. I'm thinking, isn't he amazed by how quickly I got here? Isn't he going to at least mention it? I was redlining his Jaguar. I pissed in a Dr Pepper bottle. When it was full I pissed in a potato chips bag. I broke the law. Gave up a night's sleep. Forwent the tube socks at the truck stop."

"Incredible self-control," Sandro said.

"All in the name of doing Saul a favor. I mean, you try to help a person. He opens the car door and leans in the back and makes this sound. A wailing. High-pitched."

"Oh, no," Sandro said, and put his hands over his face, feigning a brace for disaster.

"Yeah, that's right. Those goddamn rabbits were dead."

"You forgot to check on them."

"My job was transport. And I didn't hear any complaints from back there. But I had the windows down and there was a lot of truck traffic—especially on the 10. I don't know what happened. They just . . . died."

"That's why you're wearing those sunglasses," Sandro said. "The guilt is doing you in. Did you give them any water, Ronnie?"

"No, I did not give them any *water*. Listen, if he'd wanted a night nurse he should have called one. He called me. And there I was, in this hellacious armpit of the gulf and Saul is not speaking to me. He refuses to come out of his living quarters. He's got these black drag queens working around the property, feeding chickens, running his tea tray. They look like football players. Local Texas high school football players, in nightgowns. Biddy and Pumpkin Ray. They don't serve me any tea. Just dirty looks for killing Saul's rabbits. I figured I'd get a quick night's catch-up and leave at the crack of dawn. Put his car back and pretend the whole thing never happened. I was in the guest cottage and had to listen to birds screeching and chirping all night. Apparently it was mating season for something called the ovenbird. All night long I heard this teacher teacher teacher. Teacher teacher teacher. I was fantasizing about calling the sheriff and getting these ovenbirds hauled away in a paddy wagon. I got up in the morning, shook the scorpions out of my boots, opened the cottage door, and there was a rooster, staring me down. It was tall. I could tell what it was thinking: *You're my size.* An unusually tall rooster and it would not let me pass. It lunged and all I could do to save myself was grab something from a nearby lumber pile and swing. I ended up having to go for broke. Double down. Thing just would not let up. Saul came out in his pajamas. Didn't say a word. Just picked up the dead rooster and started plucking. Then he lit barbecue coals. All very methodical, as if it had been in the plans from the beginning that I kill this rooster and we eat it, and that's what we did. I killed it, he cooked it, we ate it. Seemed like he wasn't mad at me anymore. Thing tasted like rubber bands."

Sandro beamed. Ronnie made him happy. He loved these stories. They were part of Ronnie's artistic genius, even if Sandro didn't always like Ronnie's actual art, which was sometimes thin, he felt. Too flatly ironic, the magazine images he collected, slogans and slickness and advertising reformulated for camp effect. Sandro's favorite piece of Ronnie's was a blithe declaration Ronnie once made that he hoped to photograph every living person. Sandro said it was Ronnie's best work and something on the level of a poem: a gesture with no possible rebuttal. It didn't matter that it was never made. That it was unmakeable was its brilliance.

"Let me ask you something," Sandro said. "How many scorpions were in your boots?"

"Just one. Drunk. Waddled under a bush and went back to sleep."

It was my turn to report on my trip. I left out the part where the man tells me I won't look as good in a body bag. He'd meant to shame me and I wouldn't give him the satisfaction of shaming me again, in front of my friends. I also left out the part about the invitation to go to Italy in the spring. I told them about Stretch, and the wind knocking me sideways, and how I ended up driving the *Spirit of Italy*.

"To Stretch," Ronnie said, holding up his slivovitz. "Poor guy is probably waiting for you now. He'll wait for years. He'll tell everyone, this girl came through town—"

"All right, all right," Sandro said.

Ronnie smiled at him. *"Jeal-ouseee, is there no cure,"* he sang. "How exciting that Sandro and Stretch are going to have a log pull. A hay-bale-tossing contest. A proper duel."

"We've moved on from Stretch," Sandro said.

It hadn't occurred to me that a guy living in a motel would make Sandro jealous. I was touched.

Giddle hadn't gone anywhere. Only to Coney Island. "But it *felt* far away," she said. "The far-awayness tugs at you as you rumble out there on the F train. You finally reach Coney Island and think, I'll never see home again. I went several days in a row. It was like taking tiny vacations to Europe."

"Place is a nightmare," Ronnie said. "It's nothing like Europe. It's awful to go there even once."

"Once is good," Sandro said. "Maybe once a year, even."

Sandro had taken me there in winter, just after we met. All the rides were chained down. Guard dogs barked at us, mean and lonely, behind fences. We'd walked out on the beach, which was covered with snow. The moon was out and full, and the waves pushed glowing white piles of snow up onto the shore. We'd gone to a Russian restaurant farther down Brighton Beach Avenue. The waiter set down a bottle of vodka frozen in a block of ice. Sandro ordered caviars and creamed salads and steaks like it was our wedding night. The restaurant was darkly lit, with a spinning mirrored ball and a tuxedoed Bulgarian entertainer playing a mellotron. There was a party of Russians on the dance floor. They gave off a feeling of hysterical doom as they danced, the men circling a woman in a short sweater dress who looked eight months pregnant. Later, they all returned to their table and took turns pouring vodka down one another's throats. Sandro and I stumbled out late, our minds cold and hazed with winter vodka, snowflakes in our hair. Sandro said he loved me. The way he kissed the snow from my eyelashes, wrapped me in his warmth, I believed him.

"It's not a nightmare, Ronnie," Giddle said. "The thing about Coney Island is you have to go with goals in mind. I wanted to win something. A hot-dog-eating contest. A big stuffed purple panda. Once I'd actually won it, I dragged it up and down the boardwalk until it was so dirty it looked like something I'd found in the Holland Tunnel. You have to ride the Skydiver and win a big ugly prize and live on Nathan's hot dogs or you will never understand Coney Island."

"Well, I guess it's my loss," Ronnie said, but in a distracted way. I could tell he wished she'd shut up. Not that the details Ronnie shared were all that different. There was not enough separation between Giddle's basic reality and Coney Island. That was the difference. She gave it a patina of irony, but Coney Island was probably the only Europe Giddle could afford, while Ronnie and Sandro did not have those limitations. Sandro because he was a Valera. Ronnie was self-invented, some kind of orphan, but he knew precisely how to make rich people feel at ease. Which was to say, he made them feel slightly insecure and self-doubting. As a result, they wanted something higher than Ronnie's disdain, for which they were willing to pay a great deal to collect his artwork, and win his approval and even friendship, or what felt to them like friendship.

"Saul," Ronnie said, as Saul Oppler passed our booth. The great Saul Oppler. I'd never seen him in person. He was not the kind of artist you ran into at Rudy's. You read about him in magazines, alongside photo-essays on the homes he kept in Nantucket and Greece and Ischia. He was huge and powerful-looking but very old, with strangely smooth, rubbery skin, a deep tan like you saw on people who wintered in Florida, and crisp, sherbet-colored clothing, also like you saw on people who lived in Florida.

Ronnie stood and offered his hand to Saul, but Saul wouldn't take it. He looked at Ronnie, his gaze bright and sharp and wounded. He was breathing in a labored way.

"Stay away from me," he said. He turned and moved toward the back of the room.

"Ronnie," Giddle said, "I thought you ate a chicken together. Patched things. He looks really pissed."

"Yeah, well, you know what, Giddle? I made that part up."

"Why?" she asked.

"Because people like a happy ending."

We left Giddle at the bar and headed for Ronnie's studio, where he wanted us to stop en route to dinner at Stanley and Gloria Kastle's. Ronnie lived above a fortune cookie factory on Broome and Wooster. When we turned down his street, I spotted the White Lady up ahead. The White Lady was not always in white, only sometimes, and always at night. A white wig. White makeup. White cotton gloves. There were few lights on Broome, but she stood out.

"She's a beacon," Ronnie said after we'd passed her.

Once, Giddle and I had followed her into a grocery store. She bought milk, white bread, a can of hominy, and two jars of mayonnaise. All white products. Giddle had leaned over as we waited behind her. "Oh my God. Guess what perfume she's wearing?" Giddle had whispered to me. It was White Shoulders.

"The show is going to be called *Space*," Ronnie said as he unlocked his studio to show us his new work. He'd photographed the black-and-white-speckled interior of his oven and then blown up the photographs and titled each "Milky Way (detail)." They really did look like photos of outer space, but knowing they were his oven, the inky background and blurs of light made me think of Sylvia Plath more than of the universe. Sandro loved her poems, which was endearing to me because it was so girlish to love Sylvia Plath.

"What's this?"

Sandro was looking at a snapshot of a woman staring intently at the camera, young and blond, and clearly smitten with her picture taker.

"That's not part of my show."

"Just something for you to look at," Sandro said.

"Something for me to look at. Pretty in the face, as they say."

I turned away from the image. He would slip from this young girl's grasp, of course. The way he treated his lovers bothered me, though whether it was sympathy for the girls or a reminder that I had been one of the discarded, I couldn't say.

"I'm keeping her on layaway," Ronnie said, "a layaway plan. She's on reserve, held for me, and I pay in small increments. Actually, I'm supposed to see her tonight."

"You're not coming to dinner?" Sandro asked.

"I'm coming. I'll see her later."

"After dinner," Sandro said.

"Does it matter? I'll see her later. When I'm through with the other parts of my night."

He stood next to Sandro and gazed at the photo, angling his head to match Sandro's, as if Sandro's perspective might afford Ronnie some alternate or deepened view.

"I don't know," Ronnie said. "Could be actual love. I'm starting to think so. Because I'm using all the levers to suppress what puts me off about her."

Sandro laughed. "If it was love, Ronnie, you wouldn't be aware you were doing that," he said, and pulled me toward him.

"I'm always aware," Ronnie said. "That's why it never works out."

I tried not to look at the photo of the girl, who stared at us, meaning to stare at Ronnie, hoping for his pity. Sandro's warm hand was on my shoulder. How lucky I was, and yet I didn't want to see the young and hopeful face of the girl on layaway.

Ronnie and his women were a bit like Ronnie and his clothes. That was Sandro's theory. When Ronnie sold out his first show at Helen Hellenberger's gallery, Sandro figured Ronnie would quit his job at the Met. Sandro had quit long before. Of course he didn't need the tiny salary like Ronnie needed it. Sandro had stayed on as long as he had for Ronnie. To engage in a study together. Night guards figuring out the flows of art history and what they themselves were going to do. Ronnie kept his job and spent the money Helen gave him in large all-cash bursts. He hired a Checker cab on retainer. Paid up front for a year's worth of steak dinners at Rudy's. A year's worth of rent on his studio, because he said you never knew when you'd go from big-time asshole to homeless. He went down to Canal Street in his private Checker cab and purchased a hundred pairs of shrink-to-fit Levi's 501s. Five hundred white T-shirts. Five hundred pairs of underwear and socks and said he was never doing laundry again.

When I had first heard the story, I saw Ronnie balling up his homemade Marsden Hartley T-shirt and lobbing it into the corner of my studio apartment on Mulberry. But I was grafted to Sandro now. We were a project, a becoming, a set of plans. He was invested in what I'd be. But that did not erase an attraction I'd had for Ronnie, on a long night when I never learned his name. I could see now what theater it was, the gesture of balling up the shirt like he would never retrieve it. But of course he had, and with such stealth that he'd sneaked out as I slept, without even saying good-bye.

It was a form of seriality, Sandro said, the clothes, and also the girls. Moving forward in a pattern of almost sameness. But it seemed to me more like a running away. Sandro himself owned precisely two pairs of jeans. Everything was scaled down to simplicity and order. One pair of work boots. One nice jacket. One set of materials (aluminum and Plexi). One girlfriend.

The next image Ronnie showed us was rephotographed from the cover of *Time* magazine, a woman sitting at her kitchen table, pulling down the waist of her stretch pants to expose her hip, revealing the outlines of a huge bruise, like a cloud was crossing the kitchen ceiling, darkening an area of her body in its shadow.

"Meteorite," Ronnie said. "Only human ever to be hit by one."

The woman's expression was of calm, satisfied wonder. As if there were some secret logic to what had taken place, to her having been selected for this unusual fate. *Time* had posed the woman where the meteorite had hit her, seated at her kitchen table. Above her was a torn hole about the width of an oven rack, a shaft of sunlight boring straight through like an inward punch of God's hand.

Sandro said something about matter mattering. And Ronnie countered with a comment about single-story homes, the incident being really *about that*. And then they were talking about what it means to call a magazine *Time*. The latent heaviness there. Infinity parceled into the integers of humans, the integers of death. These random events, according to Ronnie, were the straw that stuffed the mattress of time. I tuned them out. I was thinking about the woman and how it had happened. It was morning, and her husband, maybe a contractor, a man in a hard hat and big, suede, mustard-colored work gloves, had gone. She was in her quilted robe, getting the kids ready for school, standing in the front doorway watching them mount the steps of the county school bus, waving as the bus pulls away trailing a plume of black diesel. Then relief. The hours are hers. For what? Smoking cigarettes at the kitchen table, perhaps with a neighbor who comes over to visit. Instead of making the beds, or doing a load of laundry, instead of marinating some kind of meat or at the very least brushing food crumbs and other debris from between couch cushions, she and the neighbor sit and drink coffee. Sometimes one tells a story, about what her husband said the night before, or didn't say, and the other listens.

Sometimes they just sit. Sometimes one turns on a radio and they listen to music, or to the news, but they don't care about the actual news, just that the radio is issuing a steadyish sound whose particulars they do not have to follow to understand what the radio is actually telling them: life is being lived. No need to be a part of it as long as you know it's streaming. These are their days, the woman and her neighbor/confidante. The job of a housewife is a little vague and it's easy to just not cross anything off the long list of semi-urgent chores. The woman senses that time is more purely hers if she squanders it and keeps it empty, holds it, feels it pass by, and resists filling it with anything that might put some too-useful dent in its open, airy emptiness. Better to smoke in your robe, talk or not talk to the neighbor woman, turn on the television, which, with the sound muted, is like a tropical fish tank or lit hearth: a rectangle of moving color bringing life inside the house. And with life brought successfully in, she is free to sit and gaze at a ringing phone, remaining perfectly still. Free to nap on the couch, because doing nothing is tiring. At five, still somewhat exhausted, she puts onions in a hot pan, to fool her husband. "Smells good," he says, taking off his hard hat.

On one of these ordinary days she and the neighbor woman are at the breakfast table and blam! A heavy message arrives from above. Heavy and dense. It crashes through the ceiling and hits her thigh before clattering to the floor, a dimpled and puckered metal hulk.

"No," she says, when the neighbor woman goes to touch it. She has a feeling it might be *hot*. She knows somehow that it must be from space. We better call and get somebody out here. Some kind of . . . meteorologist.

And what were the chances?

There were practically no chances. The chance was almost zero, and yet it happened. To her. The thing about news was that it never touched you. You could turn off the radio mid–urgent warning and know the escapee was not going to be in your bushes, not going to be peeping in on you in your shower. The news never reached anybody in a real way. The meteorite did, and a radio announcer never could have predicted it. All the world's uncanniness in that thing that came crashing in from deep, unknowable space, and the proof that it left on her, a tremendous bruise (if only it had lasted!). The person to whom something so unlikely has happened is allowed to think it wasn't an accident, that a meteor fell through space and into Earth's atmosphere and didn't stop falling until it had passed through her ceiling and hit her and you can say accident, but she doesn't have to.

The neighbor returns the morning of the *Time* photo shoot, in full makeup, eager to talk to reporters.

"Sorry," the woman says, "but this is about me," and shuts the door on her friend.

II.

People were still milling with sweating glasses in their hands when we got to Stanley and Gloria Kastle's. Milling and speaking in soft voices over the melancholic and refined tones of Erik Satie's *Gnossiennes,* which were a soundtrack to the lives of the types of people who came to dinner at the Kastles'. If not the life they actually lived, the one they imagined for themselves and wanted to draw from for inspiration. Gloria, in a head wrap, her black handcuff eyeglasses, and a caftan, came toward me with a hug. Many women were afraid of Gloria, as I had been, but I was becoming less afraid. I sensed she was coming to understand that I was part of Sandro's life and that there was no choice but to accept me.

Votive candles flickered behind her, giving the loft the feel of a strange and magical chamber. On every surface were delicate little flowers—weeds, I saw upon closer inspection, clover and dandelions, with sprigs of ailanthus—in little transparent vases, which contrasted with the old, wide-plank floors, the high ceiling stripped to the framing. The loft had once belonged to the painter Mark Rothko, and knowing this gave it a despairing and enlightened aura. It was almost better than going to the Met and looking at the Rothkos. It was the afterimage of that: sad tones of the *Gnossiennes,* Gloria in a head wrap, looking feline and fierce, Stanley's mysterious martyrdom, for whom or what I never understood.

On long metal tables that Stanley had welded sat various collections of semi-industrial objects: early-twentieth-century lightbulbs, antique Bakelite telephones, an Olivetti typewriter given to Stanley by Sandro, who knew the family, and a cap-and-ball pistol, also a gift from Sandro, but as a kind of joke. It was a replica of an early-nineteenth-century Colt revolver that had been remade by the Valera Company for spaghetti Western productions. Stanley was terrified of it and had put it out, with its complicated boxes of ammunition and parts, hoping Sandro would take the cap-and-ball pistol home with him when we left tonight.

"This is Burdmoore Model," Gloria said, steering me toward a slump-shouldered man in a blazer that looked like he'd balled up and used as a pillow the night before. "You'll be seated together at dinner." An auburn beard tumbled down his chin like hillside erosion. He was short and pot-bellied but had a kind of blunt virility. He nodded at me with bright, sad eyes, tucking a lock of stringy red hair behind one ear.

"Mod*elle*," he said. "The stress is on the second syllable."

But after meeting him that night I never heard anyone pronounce it that way; they all said "Model." Gloria introduced me as "a motorcycle racer," which made me blush with embarrassment, not only because I wasn't one but because I felt it made me seem young and unserious compared to the Satie and Rothko mood of the room.

"Well, all right," Burdmoore said, nodding. "That's cool."

He took a sip of wine and accidentally set his glass down too forcefully. Red flew upward and doused his hand and sleeve.

Ronnie came over to say hello to Burdmoore—they seemed to know each other—and I went to help Gloria. Despite her feminist claims and enlightened look, the caftan and the chunky African jewelry, I always sensed from Gloria that female guests were expected to help in the kitchen. But Gloria had ordered out, from one of the Indian restaurants on Sixth Street, so there wasn't much to do. As she and I moved chicken tandoori and various sauces and side dishes from white paper containers to ceramic serving bowls, she told me Burdmoore was a motherfucker.

"He seems nice," I said.

"I mean *the* Motherfuckers," she said. "They were a political street gang. Late sixties. They went around pretending to assassinate people with toy guns. I think they 'killed' Didier de Louridier, who's coming tonight. That should be interesting. Eventually they put away the toy guns and stabbed a landlord. It was all so lurid and we wouldn't even know about it except the father, Jack Model, was a friend of Stanley's, a janitor who worked around the art department at Cooper Union when Stanley was teaching there. The two of them became close. Stanley hated academics and said Model was the only person he could relate to at Cooper, this blue-collar guy from Staten Island who lived on vodka and cigarettes. The darkest phase of Burdmoore's wasn't this 'Motherfucker' business but when he gave up being an anarchist tough and started making papier-mâché sculptures. Burdmoore got it in his head, in the wake of his landlord-stabbing phase, that art would put him in contact with some . . . *thing*, some kind of emanation. He had no permanent residence—he was on the lam, for all we knew. Stanley let him keep his art supplies and a bedroll here, gave him a small work space, and we tried to suffer through the phase, this art-as-transcendence crap. He'd work furiously on these ugly figurative constructions, and make us listen to his confused rants about the female body and Mother Earth. Shaping crude forms and talking about art moving up the thigh of Mother Earth. Art 'parting her labia' and so forth. It was a real regression for someone whose father had pushed a mop, worked like an animal in hopes his son might get a high school degree, maybe join the police force. Instead, he was a dropout, and with such tacky ideas about art."

Gloria had a way of insisting that I track her comments, agree with them, as she spoke. I nodded in assent as she went on about how bad art could not save itself and could not *be* saved, as she spooned sauces, all of them the same ocher-orange color, into bowls. Helen Hellenberger, just arriving, peeked her head into the kitchen and blew an air kiss to Gloria. Helen looked around the kitchen, passing over me as if I were Gloria's assistant, hired to help out for the night, and then left the room, to chat with the men.

As Gloria went on about Burdmoore and bad art, I nodded and

privately hoped I was on the side of good art. I was not making papier-
mâché, obviously. Or declarations about parting labia. And I was safe
in another essential way: I had not put myself out there yet. I could
delay it until I knew for certain that what I was doing was good. Until
I knew I was doing the right thing. The next thing would be this Valera
project. It was half art and half life, and from there, I felt, something
would emerge.

Gloria was still talking, something about how shooting people was
in a sense *safer* than making art, in terms of avoiding serious lapses
in taste. She said the Motherfuckers' actions were interesting, in the
context of the dreadful hippies of that era. The Motherfuckers were
about anger and drugs and sex, and what a relief that was, Gloria said,
compared to the love-everyone tyranny of the hippies.

As we all took our places at the table, Sandro came over to kiss me,
say hi, because he was at the other end, next to Didier de Louridier,
victim of the Motherfuckers. I didn't mind being seated so far from
him, although sometimes Sandro would speak later to whomever I'd
been next to. "So-and-so said you were very quiet." As if I had some
duty—to Sandro—that required me to be more assertive, to entertain
his friends. So-and-so talked nonstop, I'd say, and he'd laugh. They all
talked nonstop. That is, if you didn't intervene. They were accustomed
to being interrupted. Whoever was hungriest to speak, spoke. I wasn't
hungry in that same way. I was hungry to listen. Sandro said I was his
little green-eyed cat at these parties. A cat studying mice, he said, and
I said it was more like a cat among dogs, half-terrified. "You shouldn't
be," he said. "You always have something interesting to say, but you
withhold it. The only one besides me who knows you," he said, "is Ronnie." Which sent a curious wave through me. I wanted to believe it was
true that Ronnie knew me.

We were at a massive, outdoor-use picnic table with ancient-looking
messages knifed into its top. "Kilroy was here" and "eat me" and "fuck"
and "fuk." Its gouged surface was lacquered over in glossy black. The
Kastles had purchased it from P.S. 130 in Chinatown, which, Gloria
announced somewhat triumphantly, was selling everything but the
smoke alarms to keep from closing down.

Burdmoore turned to me. "That's who you're here with?" He gestured in Sandro's direction.

I said yes.

"What are you, eighteen years old?"

"No," I said, laughing. "Twenty-three."

He was looking at Sandro and about to say something more when Gloria started in about the purchase of the table, how they'd found someone to strip it and lacquer it, and how it had to be lifted up the elevator shaft, end-on, with ropes and pulleys. Burdmoore concentrated on the chicken tandoori, the problem of its sauce in his beard.

"Enough about the fucking table," Stanley said.

He and Gloria squared off in lowered voices. As they argued, Gloria got up and went to a sideboard and I had the terrible thought that she was going to pick up Sandro's cap-and-ball pistol and point it at Stanley. But she retrieved a tea towel and a bowl of water and set these in front of Burdmoore so he could clean his beard.

Sandro raised his glass and said he wanted to make a toast. He gazed warmly at me across the table, his smile punctuated by dimples, and I thought perhaps he was going to toast me, my ride across the salt flats.

"To Helen," he said, "and to the future, our future. Let's hope it's a long one."

As I drank to Helen, I understood that her elegant Greek air, like Gloria's stern air, was not an attack on me. The important thing was to be patient. To not make enemies. I would even try to befriend Helen, I thought.

The common table conversation had lulled and people were breaking off into smaller groups. Burdmoore and I glanced at each other awkwardly. Each time I thought we'd speak, he smiled in a stunned or stoned way, nodded enthusiastically, and said nothing. I heard Ronnie tell someone that if you weren't sure where the camera was focused in an image you were looking at, as a general rule you could assume it was the crotch. A man named John Dogg was talking to Helen about his art, too excited to tone down his sales pitch. Only a certain kind of pushiness works in the art world. Not the straight-ahead, pile-driving kind, which was the method John Dogg was using.

"Malevich made the white paintings," he said in a loud voice. "And then we had Robert Ryman. Ryman making them, too, more academic and provisional than Malevich, the religion subtracted from the facture. Little test canvases of white, like bandages over nothing. White on white. Now what I do is I make white *films*. Just light. Pure light, and what's fascinating is—"

He didn't seem to notice that Helen's face had gone blank, as if she'd been summoned elsewhere but had left an impassive mask behind, for his self-promotion to bounce off. John Dogg pressed on, hoping to recapture her attention. It wasn't going to work. But I admired how convinced he was that his work was good, good enough to show to her, and he simply needed to get it seen. As if that were the main stumbling block, and not the problem of making art, the problem of believing in it.

"They made the white paintings. I make the white films. I've been rather protective of the conditions of display but I'm coming around to the idea of making my work more accessible. In fact, I'm open to showing them to you. I'm enormously busy but I could make time. I could bring the reels by the gallery. No projector? Well, I could bring a projector. Oh, I see. Or perhaps to your residence, then. I'm not opposed to the idea of making a visit to your home. Why don't we say tomorrow?"

"I used to paint," Stanley said to no one in particular. "I had to give it up. I lost contact with the paintings."

"Although it's true that there is a powerful enough idea behind the works," John Dogg said, looking for a signal in Helen's blank face, "that you could just get the idea, and not necessarily see them. The main thing to understand is that I deal in light. I mean I deal *with* light. It's a way of portraying light—light that is a lit picture of some other, original light. Like happiness is both an experience and an afterimage of something else. An original happiness—"

"I tried to keep it going," Stanley said. "Some relation to painting, to the hand, by drawing. I tried to draw pictures and could only draw boobs. I used up all my good drawing paper and a full box of Lumigraphs and every day it was the same thing. Boobs. Just boobs."

Didier was talking to Sandro. As he spoke, he ate and smoked simultaneously, puffing on his cigarette and then transferring it from his hand to his lips as he buttered his bread, a blue box of Gauloises next to him, ashes fluttering and mixing with his rice and curry and meat.

"It's best you gave it up," Gloria said to Stanley.

"But sometimes I want to cry."

"My films are not about bringing people together," John Dogg told Helen. "They're about dividing people into for and against."

I turned to Burdmoore. I said Gloria had mentioned he'd been involved in a movement that sounded interesting.

He looked at Gloria and said it might be something Gloria snickered about but it was real. He had been a Motherfucker. Lowercase, too, he said, according to his ex-wife.

I tried to reassure him that Gloria had not said anything insulting, but he waved my words away, as if to say don't bother, no hard feelings.

"We took over the Lower East Side," he said. "Place is dead now. If you could only have known it then. But you're too young."

"The Lower East Side is full of people," I said. "There's all kinds of stuff going on there."

He smiled at me like I was endearingly naive.

"I'm talking," he said, "about insurrection. There isn't shit going on in that regard. It was armed struggle, and the cops"—he said "cops" with a tough, flattened New York accent, as if he were beheading the word with the chop of his voice—"had come in with tanks, and dirtier methods, informants, heroin."

"No kidding?" I asked.

"Yeah," he said, and some people even suspected that narcs had deliberately introduced sexually transmitted diseases. "Every one of us had the clap. It gave us a bad rep. Although we wanted a bad rep."

They fought the cops, he said. Drove out the dealers. Fed the people of their neighborhood. And lived a life that felt free, "given the police state we live in," he said in his flat accent, which was growing on me. He seemed so much tougher, more streetwise, than the usual dinner company at the Kastles'.

"In a way it's worth explaining this," he said. "I mean to anyone who wasn't there for it. Did she tell you we loaded our guns under the soda counter at Gem Spa?" He nodded his chin at Gloria. "We carried these black flags. We had switchblades and guns hidden here and there. No shoulder holsters—that was a kind of unwritten rule. Shoulder holster not cool. No hip holsters, either. It's way too NRA fanatic, that style. We all had the same kind of hand-cobbled Peruvian cowboy boots. There was a guy who sold them for cheap on Saint Mark's, and you put the gun in the shaft of your boot. Fucking beautiful boots. I wish I had a pair now."

"Why were you called Motherfuckers?"

"Because we hated women," he said. "You think I'm joking. Women had no place in the movement unless they wanted to cook us a meal or clean the floor or strip down. There are people who've tried to reno- vate our ideas, claim we weren't chauvinists. Don't believe it. We had some heavy shit to work out. But we were idealists, too. We saw a future of people singing and dancing, making love and masturbating in the streets. No shame. Nothing to hide. Everyone sleeping in one big bed, men, women, daughters, dogs."

"Who wants to do *that*?" Sandro said later that night when I told him that the detail of men masturbating had seemed particularly sad. But he said he respected Burdmoore. That the Motherfuckers were something formidable. He told me the first time he met Burdmoore, he didn't know anything about that history. He remembered the jani- tor Stanley would go on alcoholic binges with, a tough old guy from Staten Island whose eccentric redheaded son was an equally unlikely pet project for Stanley to have chosen, a dropout freeloader. Burd- moore had answered the Kastles' door in his socks, wearing the kind of cheap team jacket you send away for after purchasing so many cartons of cigarettes. Sandro said the Kastles let Burdmoore drink their good whiskey and run roughshod over the loft. But that he brought some kind of life into their house and the Kastles would probably have killed each other without the distraction of a fugitive from the law.

A wave of laughter overtook the table. Ronnie was recounting the episode of his trip to Port Arthur. Stanley said Ronnie had killed Saul

Oppler's rabbits unjustly but that the rooster, it sounded like it had wanted to die, and so Ronnie hadn't done all bad.

"The most you can hope for," Stanley said, "is that someone will have the guts and know-how to kill you with a two-by-four."

"What kind of know-how do you need for that?" Didier asked.

Which made Stanley laugh. He was laughing so hard he had to wipe tears from his eyes, and suddenly he was really crying, his head in his hands, the table quiet, Stanley's body shaking as he sobbed.

"Come on, Stanley," Gloria said. "You devalue the tear when you do this. You really do."

She looked around the table, perhaps seeking consolation. *See the maudlin bullshit I have to put up with?* Then again, she might have been saying, *You better not think this is funny.* This was the way with them. It was all very grave and dramatic, and you didn't know if it was a joke or if it was real. Sandro said their gloom was almost mathematical, an endgame that Stanley had created. All Stanley had to do, at this point, to keep his art career going, was order neon tubes in various colors from a manufacturer, and his assistants arranged the tubes according to an algorithm he'd invented long ago, as if to subtract himself from the production of his own art. He was rich and well respected but he had forced his own obsolescence. The art made itself. Sandro said that Stanley's work had outmoded him the way the postindustrial age was now robbing the worker of his place and that this truth made the art more powerful.

The Kastles had spent the summer in East Hampton, although apparently Stanley never stepped foot on the beach. He slept all day and spent his nights drinking and making monologues on a reel-to-reel tape recorder.

Ronnie asked if he could hear a bit of one of Stanley's recorded reels. We ate silently, listening to Stanley's voice.

"Without clothing nudity loses context," it declared as the tape wound forward, one large wheel tracking the other.

"And yet to give the body partial context . . . a belt around the waist of a naked woman, a bow tie on a naked man . . . you see what I mean.

Accessories take away nudity's dignity. Cheapen it. I know a man, a husband, whose wife enjoyed *Playgirl* calendars. Each year she bought one and tacked it up in her area of the loft that she and the man shared. Each month offered a different theme. A doctor, nude, with stethoscope and lab coat. A logger in Red Wing boots and a hard hat, an enormous dingaling hanging down between his thighs. The wife was always careful to turn the calendar to the new month, as if the previous one had not been enough of an imposition on this poor husband she lived with, who suffered enough as it was, from unknown causes. One day the husband decided he'd reached his limit. He took the calendar down and removed all the genitals with scissors. He put the calendar back up on the wall, careful to return the page to the proper month, the model's genitals, previously outsized and healthy, now a jagged absence, a peek of wall from underneath, as if the nude model himself had forgotten to include his own dick and balls, or had lost them someplace, or had them taken from him in some unwholesome arrangement where he'd bet them or traded them away, and had to suffer the consequences, posing without a crotch area. The wife said nothing about it and yet in the way she proceeded, as if nothing were amiss, the husband knew he had deprived her. This made him happy for a while. But it wasn't enough, this husband discovered. Calendars were only a touchstone for the endless fantasies that were doubtless running through his wife's mind and he could not get in there with scissors to remove them and so he cut the cord on his wife's personal massager—that was what she called it, but we can say vibrator. Vibrator. But I've digressed from the original subject of partial nudity, which is what I aim to discuss. I'm not the first to point out its tasteless nature. Diderot said something about the consequences of putting stockings on the Venus de Milo. Which brings me to another, related matter, her limblessness, so obviously part of the allure. It would be unthinkable kitsch to fit the Venus de Milo with arms. Her missing limbs are a *positive* attribute, not an absence. Really quite strange, as a concept. I once knew a man who played a hanky-panky with his wife that involved pretending she was an amputee. She would strap her lower leg up behind her thigh, with his assistance, and go around in a knee-length skirt and crutches, hopping on the one serviceable leg, and people assumed she had lost the other one in a terrible accident, or an illness of some kind. The two of them would have these 'erotic weekends' in towns where no one knew them. They would pick a place on the map and arrive in their respective play-act roles, a stoic amputee crutching her way into a motel office with the help of her doting caretaker. They would check into their room and then go to a restaurant, where they received looks of shy condolence from the hostess and waiters and the other clientele. They would order as if they were on some kind of significant date, an anniversary, say, in these hickville special-occasion establishments where the waiter comes to the table with a pepper grinder that's five feet tall. You know what I mean. Heavy and oversized furniture, ugly American Colonial lighting, either too bright or too dark, places where the wine is some kind of grapy burgundy served in a carafe by small-town goobers trained by the management to congratulate you on your order. Excellent choice, sir. As they ate their chops and drank their burgundy and took in the shabby ambience, the husband covertly fondled his wife's stump under the table, her not-real stump, her play stump. The two or even three carafes of burgundy staining in, blurring inhibitions, they would return to the motel. The man, drunk now, and good and ready to get into the real business, would remain ever patient and solicitous with his handicapped wife, help her to the room, carry her over the threshold like a child bride being airlifted into a territory of freshness and anticipation, the lightness of his wife's body in the man's arms somehow exactly the weight of her light compliance. He would set her softly on the bed. Proceed to undress her slowly, with meaningful pauses and great care. Eye contact, deep and even breathing. Extra attention to her knee stump, the surface of it, rounded but with shallow areas, like a very smooth rock, the knee. And then touching the cold bed below the knee, the emptiness of it. A complicated thrill, which I myself can only imagine. 'Not for the layperson' was what this man said of their game, an advanced level of fantasy and humping. The idea of her missing leg was a shared space between them; it was practically a religion and they didn't want to give it up. At the end of these dirty little weekends, when for the return home she released her hidden leg, unstrapped it so that her 'stump' was yet again just a normal healthy knee, the sight of it there in front of her was beyond painful for both of them. The real leg contradicted everything. It ground the memories of their romantic jaunts to nothing. The wife, her two healthy legs stretched out, would sob inconsolably all the way home. This distressed her husband, as you can imagine. And he had his own interest in hoping to find a solution to their problem. So they began to inquire. They saw various doctors at various clinics. Nobody was interested in helping them. One or two medical professionals even threatened to call the police, suggesting that the man could be arrested. Which is another topic for another discourse. But briefly, why is the common good dependent upon preventing these two semi-free individuals from removing something that belongs to them, and that they both agree must be disposed of? What interest do we have in her leg that she herself does not have? Because I must confess I am among those who would want it to stay attached to the rest of her, even as this seems an abuse of governance, and an imposition on the victimless sexual satisfaction of two people, as I said, semi-free. Last time I talked to this man, we have lost touch, the reason for which you'll learn in a moment, anyhow the last time I heard from him he and his wife had finally found some kind of doctor down in the Yucatán who was willing to perform the operation, and apparently there was a community there for rehabilitation and general lifestyle support. They were planning to relocate. The man wrote to me and said, 'Our dream will soon be coming true.' And here I arrive at my point. The point is that everyone has a different dream. The point is that it is a grave mistake to assume your dream is in any way shared, that it's a common dream. Not only is it not shared, not common, there is no reason to assume that other people don't find you and your dream utterly revolting."

After a pause, Stanley's recorded voice began to sing to us from the machine:

Oh, dreams coming true in Quin-ta-na Roo
Where we will cut off what's making you blue.
We'll take it away, and you will feel whole.
Oh, dreams coming true
in Quin-ta-na Roo.

Stanley got up and fast-forwarded the reel. His voice became a high-pitched ribbon until he lifted his finger and it quavered back down to the speed of regular talking.

"The great thing is, it's a buyer's market right now," his voice said from the machine. "Then again, if you want to sell, it's a great time to do so, because it's a seller's market right now, too.

"*Home.* We say 'home,' not 'house.' You never hear a good agent say 'house.' A house is where people have died on the mattresses. Where pipes freeze and burst. Where termites fall from the sink spigot. Where somebody starts a flu fire by burning a telephone book in the furnace. Where banks repossess. Where mental illness takes hold. A home is something else. Do not underestimate the power in the word *home*. Say it. 'Home.' It's like the difference between 'rebel' and 'thug.' A rebel is a gleaming individual in tight Levi's, a sneering and pretty face. The kind Sal Mineo wet-dreams. A thug is hairy and dark, an object that would sink to the bottom when dropped in a lake. A home is maintained. Cared for. Loved. The word *home* is savory like gravy, and like gravy, kept warm. A good realtor says 'home.' Never 'house.' Always 'cellar' and never 'basement.' Basements are where cats crap on old Santa costumes. Where men drink themselves to death. Where children learn firsthand about sexual molestation. But cellar. A cellar is where you keep root vegetables and wine. Cellar means a proximity to the earth that's not about blackness and rot but the four ritual seasons. We say 'autumn,' not 'fall.' We say 'The leaves in this area are simply magnificent in autumn.' We say 'simply magnificent,' and by the way, 'lawn,' not 'yard.' It's 'underarm' to 'armpit.' Would you say 'armpit' to a potential buyer? Say 'yard' and your buyer pictures rusted push mowers, plantar warts. Someone shearing off his thumb and a couple of fingers with a table saw. A tool shed where water-damaged pornography and used motor oil funneled into fabric softener bottles cohabitate with hints of trauma that are as thick and dark as the oil. I'm not talking about *Playboy* or *Oui*. Harder stuff. Amateur. Pictorials featuring *married* people with their flab and bruises and smallpox vaccines, doing things to each other in rec rooms and sheds like the one housing these selfsame magazines. Middle-aged couples who get trashed on tequila and document with a supply of flash cubes. You have to be careful about words. You're thinking about your commission, your hands are starting to shake at the idea of the money, and meanwhile your client hears 'yard' and sees himself nudging icky amateur porno with his foot, potato bugs scattering from their damp hideout underneath. Again, it's 'lawn.' 'Lawn' means crew-cut grass. It means censorship, nice and wholesome. It means America. And you know what I mean by America, and by the way, 'cul-de-sac.' Not 'dead end.' If I have to explain that, you'll never pass the exam to get your license. We say 'dinner.' Never 'supper.' 'Dinner' is the middle class, semi-religious . . . Christian . . . Christian*esque*. 'Dinner' is a touch-tone doorbell with a little orange light glowing from within the rectangular button. The bell is there for expected guests. People carrying warm dishes covered with gingham checked cloth—the cloth, needless to say, has been laundered with stain remover. The type of people with stained old dishrags are not going to press this doorbell. No one with a beard. No one with a grievance. Only people who share the values of the hosts. 'Thank you for having us to dinner in your lovely home.' Say 'dinner.' Say 'home.' Say 'lawn.' Don't be afraid. Like prayer, through repetition and habit, these words will begin to—"

Stanley shut off the reel-to-reel machine.

"Indeed, indeed," Didier said, nodding at Stanley and stubbing a cigarette butt into his food. He retrieved another and lit it, blowing smoke across the table but waving it from in front of his own face as if it were something unwelcome that someone else had just put there. He continued to nod at Stanley, smoke going up in a tight spiral from the end of his held cigarette. Everyone else was quiet, waiting for Didier to make his comment.

Stanley peered at him as if from a great distance. "Why do you look so amused, Didier?"

"Because I enjoyed your little ramble there, Stanley. And I know what you're getting at."

"What am I getting at, Didier? Because I'm actually not sure myself."

"The power and emptiness of words. And yet they rule us nonetheless. Are the sole horizon. Language as the house of being. The *home* of being, excuse me."

"That wasn't my point. I, uh, don't know what my point was, except that men over fifty can't stop talking. It's an illness, I mean a real epidemic, and I'm trying to cure myself with this recording project, sicken myself of talking by talking it all out, like the Schick Center method for quitting smoking. But since you bring it up, Didier, you know what I think of language? That it's a fake horizon and there's something else, a real truthful thing, but language is keeping us from it. And I think we should torture language to stop fucking around and tell it to us. We should torture language to tell the truth."

Gloria let out a long, dramatic not-this-again sigh.

I felt Sandro looking at me. I always could. I turned and met his gaze. His mouth slightly curled in amusement. "*We should torture it to tell us the truth,*" he whispered to me much later that night, or rather, it was close to dawn by the time he whispered that in his feather-light accent, as I lay next to him, feeling his warm breath on my bare shoulder, his arms wrapped around me. *Let's torture it.*

People began to chat in subsets. Gloria served dessert. Didier rested his cigarette on the edge of his plate of almond cookies, dispersing ashes and cookie crumbs and insisting that Freud was correct that language was the only route to the unconscious. Stanley countered that language was given to man to *hide* his thoughts, and that all you could do with words was turn them on their sides like furniture during a bombardment.

Sandro got up to greet his cousin Talia, a woman I'd never met whose late arrival he had been expecting. Gloria led her in, and she and Sandro embraced.

That first moment, as I watched them, her dark eyes shining at Sandro, I knew that Talia Valera was going to take something away from me. Burdmoore was watching them, too, and I had the disturbing sense that he was sharing my thought, knew by his long experience with trouble that it had arrived, but specifically for me.

Sandro brought his cousin Talia around the table. Her hair was short and carelessly chopped, as if she'd cut it herself, but she was pretty enough that it didn't diminish her. She had a husky voice and dirt under her fingernails. She wore a black tank top and karate pants. The effect was meant to seem boyish and nonchalant but something else came through, a refinement maybe, a kind of calculation.

I should have gotten up to speak with her, but I stayed where I was and focused on Burdmoore, who was talking again about the Lower East Side. He said that while I might think it was the same, rubble piles and squats and graffiti, dope dealers and artists, that it could not be more different. They'd had it all *mobilized*. Even the bums, he said, were their own cadre—WFF, Winos for Freedom—with a cache of weaponry scared up by Fah-Q, a comrade in the group who Burdmoore kept mentioning. He and Fah-Q were the lost children, as Burdmoore put it. They were *awake,* he said, while most of America slept. And those awake are the nightmare of the sleepers. "We were their nightmare," he said.

"Now everybody says, *but be reasonable*. We never pandered to that reasonableness bullshit. 'Those who make peaceful revolution impossible make violent revolution inevitable'—that's John F. fuckin' Kennedy. A clown who didn't do shit but he was right about that one thing. Plus," Burdmoore said, "he had a pretty cool wife. I still think urban insurrection is the only way, but not in New York City. Not at the moment."

There were still some major issues to be worked out, he said, and I nodded, wanting to hear what they were, but unsure what it was we were talking about, worked out for what purpose.

"A lot of people think the city is decadent emptiness," Burdmoore said, "empty of potential. It's dead now, I mean currently. But the day will come when the people of the Bronx wake up, the sisters and brothers out in Brooklyn, and I can hardly wait."

Sandro's cousin had seated herself next to Ronnie and was asking him what he did.

"Have you seen those signs around town, green and yellow with red lettering, and they say Blimpie?" he asked her.

"No," she said with a laugh. "I guess I missed those."

"Well, then it won't mean as much to you. But that's my family—we make the tastiest sandwiches in New York City. You might be the Valeras, but we—see, we're the Blimpies. My name is actually Ronnie Blimpie but I changed it. Because we own a sandwich empire and I didn't want to forever be the sandwich guy. I can tell you because you don't have us yet wherever you live."

"London," she said.

"Yeah, we're not in London yet. At the moment we're not expanding. We're focusing on subsidiaries. Like how Valera isn't just tires, we have another business, which is actually enormous. You know those plaid plastic laundry bags that are ubiquitous in Third World countries, crappy plaid bags that you see in every town from one end of the African continent to the other, and in Asia, and all over Latin America, too? Rectangular bags with zippers? Which Gypsies drag around and live out of, in First World countries? And people cart from project housing to Laundromats? Well, we make those, all of them. There are huge profits in semi-disposal goods like that."

"You're joking," she said.

"It's true. I mean it's true that I'm joking. We don't own the Blimpie chain. And we don't manufacture those bags, but whoever does is making a killing. We're Fontaine. We don't own anything. But I was not raised Fontaine. I was really at sea."

"Everyone's like that when they're young," she said.

"No, I mean I was actually at sea. On a boat."

Didier de Louridier and Sandro had stood, as Didier inspected Stanley's collections of bric-a-brac on the small tables that lined the room. Didier paused before the cap-and-ball pistol.

"Pick it up," Sandro said. "Nothing to be afraid of. You'd have to shoot someone in the eye to actually hurt them."

Didier picked it up and looked down into the barrel.

"What about the others in your gang?" I asked Burdmoore. "Are they still around?"

"There are remnants," he said. "Remnants and debris. Fah-Q lives with his retired father in Miami, got so paranoid he can't do anything but throw pots. He's really into that, making pottery. One guy became an anti-fluoride crusader. Another is a Guardian Angel. Those guys are complete psychos. They've adopted state power as *volunteers*." As Burdmoore spoke, he was watching Sandro explain to Didier how the cap-and-ball pistol worked.

"Your boyfriend likes guns," Burdmoore said.

"It belonged to his father," I said. "His family used to manufacture that gun. There's a logic."

"Right. A logic."

"He doesn't *use* it. It's not stuffed in the cuff of his boot."

"And yet I'd wager he is the type of man who would enjoy the feeling of that," Burdmoore said.

He leaned his chair back on its hind legs and looked at me. The chair was creaking and I worried he might hurt it and that it would gouge marks into the soft wood of Gloria and Stanley's pine-plank floor.

"And I think you might be . . . oh, never mind," he said.

"I might be what?"

"I think you might be the sort of sister who likes that type," he said.

His chair kept creaking. I was convinced it would break from the strain of bearing his weight on its hind legs.

"You like a guy who puts a gun in his boot," he whispered, "*don't you?*"

In fact I had once *watched* Sandro put a gun in his boot. I did not admit this to Burdmoore. We had been in Washington, DC, for Sandro's show at the Corcoran Gallery. DC had some kind of weapons ban that Sandro was secretly protesting by showing up to his own opening armed.

His interest in guns had never bothered me. I was around them all the time growing up. My uncles, my cousins, all shot guns. Reno's main thoroughfares were lined with pawnshops, and I understood the pawn-shop to be a kind of forge that liquidated objects into money. The things that could be most quickly converted were guns. When someone in our family died, the big inheritance question was who would get the guns. Relatives would stake a claim based on sentiment. "Your dad's nickel-plated Browning meant a lot to me," Andy had said after my father died. "First gun I ever shot." He knew my father better than I did, because Andy was older than I, and my father had left Reno when I was three, had gone to Ecuador to build log cabins on someone's get-rich-quick scheme, and when that didn't work out, had gone on to other get-rich-quick schemes. I didn't know him and I didn't want his guns. I gave them to Andy. A few days later they were in a pawnshop window downtown.

Click-click. We watched as Sandro showed Didier how to pull the cylinder and unscrew the nipples on the cap-and-ball pistol, how to load the chamber.

"Black gunpowder goes first," Sandro said. "Then you press the lead ball down into the chamber."

Didier asked what the attraction was to such an antiquated thing.

There was a loophole, Sandro said. Anyone could own one. Carry it concealed.

"It's not considered a gun," he said. "But it is one. And it fires very, very straight."

Burdmoore didn't say anything more, but I felt a need to explain away Sandro's interest in guns.

"His work is all objects that are what they are, and something else, at the same time," I said. "A gun can be an idea, a threat, or a thing. As Sandro would put it, imaginary, symbolic, or real, all at once."

"Oh, sure," said Burdmoore. "I mean, it sounds good. Except you can't brandish a gun *and* shoot it."

Didier was directly behind us now, practicing quickdraws with San-dro's cap-and-ball pistol like a Western gunslinger, gazing into the mir-ror that hung on the wall behind Burdmoore.

"A gun is either symbolically enlisted or it's enlisted enlisted," Burd-moore said, watching Didier, who froze with the gun drawn, admiring his own reflection. "Threats are for people who aren't willing to risk anything."

Didier laughed. "Oh, right," he said, turning to Burdmoore. "But wasn't it someone from your little gang who shot at me with blanks? Is that not a kind of hysterical threat?"

"That was . . . it just happened. You were not on our list of targets."

"But what was the purpose, if not for intimidation? Obviously you didn't intend to kill me. Or you would have used real bullets."

"Look, man. You fainted, is what I heard. Which, for an esoteric guy like you, is a kind of death."

"A kind of death—what crap," Didier said. "You guys were a bunch of image-obsessed poseurs. Sorry. If I recall correctly, Antonioni wanted to put you in his youth cult film, the one with the Pink Floyd soundtrack. Or am I mistaking you for some other group of cinema-ready toughs?"

Everyone was listening now.

Burdmoore smiled. "That's true. It was us. But we turned him down."

"*Zabriskie Point?*" John Dogg said from the end of the table. "You can give him my name if he's casting for something."

"And didn't you guys have a kind of sit-in in front of the UN, with your faces wrapped in bandages, pretending you were survivors from a platoon that had been accidentally napalmed in a Vietnamese jungle by an American bomber?"

"We were bringing the war home. Would it have been better not to stage our dissent?"

"But that's exactly it! You 'staged' your dissent—just as you say. I'm remembering more now. I heard about it from someone who was there. You all removed the bandages from your faces as this coordinated act of protest, strip by strip, ever so slowly." Didier gestured with his hands, as if lifting bandages from his own face.

"Reporters all around you. There to see the terrible damage as you unveiled yourselves, the few survivors who managed to plunge themselves in a river, jellied gasoline clinging to their cheeks and arms and ribs, the smell of charred flesh—"

"Sounds practically like you were there, Didier," Ronnie said.

"No, Ronnie. I just think it's important to draw distinctions between real violence and theater. So there you all were, screaming, 'Look at us! *Look* at our faces!' The bandages fell away. And surprise: no one was burned. *You* didn't go to Vietnam. None of you did. It was a hoax."

"It wasn't a hoax," Burdmoore said quickly. "It was theater. Real theater. Like Brecht."

"What does Brecht have to do with it? I think you should leave Brecht out of this—"

"The people who watched? They wanted to see our burned faces. And if we'd shown them burned faces they would have turned their heads away and flinched, but left satisfied that we were burned, end of story. We thwarted their expectations, left them *disappointed*. The observers are promised disfigurement, are led to the crime of having *wanted* to see it. And then a question lingers: *where is the violence going to show itself?* By removing the thing the mask is meant to cover, we were making a point. The thing the mask is meant to cover can't be covered or seen: it's everywhere."

"Blah-blah-blah," Didier said. "My advice would have been to give up the street theater and drop below the radar. Go underground. Isn't that what they're doing in Italy, Sandro?"

"I don't keep up on it, Didier," Sandro said. "And I'm not sure what you mean. There's a youth movement. It's out in the open."

"Don't play dumb, Sandro," Didier said. "I'm not talking about *students*. I mean the factory militants."

"The Red Brigades," Burdmoore said. "We never could have been like that. Our trip was not about rigor and self-sacrifice. Anyhow, those people are Leninists. We were more like libertines."

"Followers of the great windbag Moishe Bubalev," Didier said.

"Say what you want, Didier," Burdmoore said. "He was the main thinker advocating a shift from theory to action in the late 1960s. A lot of people were reading his stuff."

"I've got a good story about that guy Bubalev," Ronnie said. "There was a certain group looking for guidance. A famous group. They had a hostage and needed insight on how to proceed. This is in Bubalev's diaries. This group showed up at his place, pestering him. They brought liquor and a good-looking female, stayed for the afternoon. Drank as the girl waggled her ass around. When it was time for them to go, Bubalev was sad they were taking the pretty girl away, but at least they left their liquor behind. That's all he says about them: they took the girl but left the booze. It was the Symbionese Liberation Army, with Patty Hearst."

"Since when do you read Moishe Bubalev?" Didier asked Ronnie.

"Since never, Didier. Someone told me that story, actually. I have no idea if it's true."

"Could be true," Burdmoore said. "But look, Bubalev wasn't a priest. He was a professor and probably didn't get a lot of brainwashed chicks visiting him in faculty housing. It's best not to look at personal conduct. Take Allen Ginsberg, decent poet, had an important moment. But when you actually know him, a complete charlatan. He hung around our scene. One night, this rich kid shows up at Gem Spa with ten thousand bucks in cash. He wants to burn it in Tompkins Square Park, to take that share of capital out of the system. He was trying to convince me and Fah-Q to come watch him burn this money. We all troop over to the park, thinking there's no way he'll really do it, but it was our job to encourage extreme acts. So we're saying, *burn it, go ahead*. Allen Ginsberg was in the park that night. Someone told him the kid planned to set this large sum of money on fire and Ginsberg, in his loose, cotton guru clothes, goes rushing over, trying to convince the kid in a rabbinical and pushy tone to give *him* the money. In the end, the kid decided not to burn it. He gave it to me and Fah-Q."

"So what happened?" Didier asked him. "You guys had ten thousand bucks. Followers. Energy."

"Ten thousand bucks was nothing to us. We had steady sources of funding."

"From where?"

"Can't say. But it was very steady and very generous. We had accounts all over town that we withdrew from, ten, twenty, thirty thousand bucks a pop. We gave a lot of it away. The reason we pulled the plug had nothing to do with money. Things got hot and some of us split. Went to the Sonoran Desert and lived on horseback."

"Like real Marlborough men," Didier said.

Burdmoore laughed. "Hardly. We weren't peddling addiction as rugged independence. It wasn't nearly so romantic. A couple of us almost died from hypothermia. Another barely survived a bobcat mauling. We were attacked by wolves. Fire ants. Chiggers. We suffered scabies. Impetigo. Rope burn. Hong Kong flu. Paranoia. Near-starvation. It ruined my marriage, the end of me and Nadine."

"Nadine?" I asked.

I had never seen her again, after the night with her and Thurman and Ronnie.

"My former wife," Burdmoore said. "Ronnie knows her. Didier knows her."

Didier cleared his throat. "I knew her once. Just in passing."

"Dogg knows her."

We looked over at John Dogg, who was saying his good-byes. He approached Didier and handed him a business card, determined to make his connection before the night was over and it was too late. "I am not at all opposed to working with art writers," he said to Didier, "if you'd like to do a project with me. I mean write about my work."

"I think they're involved," Burdmoore said after John Dogg had left. "Which is fine. It's been a long time. Too much happened."

Nadine had told me practically her entire life story over the course of that evening, and now her voice came back. High and soft. Her voice and her legs and her long hair, strawberry blond, like ale. The ex she had complained about. It was Burdmoore. Burdmoore who had told her that after the revolution everyone would work two or three hours a week. That's all that would be needed, with all the robots and automation. "I don't know if it's revolutionary not to work," she had told me, "but it's better. When you sell your body you are what you do. You're yourself and you get paid for it," or so she had thought at the time, still semi-brainwashed by the ideas of her husband's group. He and his friends said hookers and children were the only people in the world who logically should be idle. Children because they were busy being children, and hookers because the labor happened on the surface of their body. The labor *was* their body. A man who does what he is is useless, her husband said. Despicable. Though he'd hoped to become despicable, and to survive doing nothing. Nadine had told me it wasn't a bad time in her life. She loved walking on Hollywood Boulevard, where a banner said, "Wake up in the Hollywood Hills." An ad for condominiums. And she'd looked up at it and thought, yeah, that's right—that's what I do! But waking up in the Hollywood Hills sounded better than it was, she said. She had almost died. "I was slapped," she said. "Punched. Shaken. Hung from a balcony over the 101 freeway, and yet look." She'd leaned toward me, revealing nothing more, just plain beauty, magnified. "I am still . . . so . . . *pretty*. Let's not pretend. I don't have to fake modesty. I have other problems. I am still pretty, never mind that I was burned with cigars. Raped. I snorted Drano by accident. But the really messed-up thing is that I am *still. So. Pretty.* After all that? How is it possible?"

She was beautiful, it was true. With large hazel eyes, speckled like brook trout, and the hair, reddish-gold around her white face. But I had seen, the night I met her, that her beauty was going to leave her like it does all women. For the face, time relays some essential message, and time *is* the message. It takes things away. But its passage, its damages, are all we have. Without it, there's nothing.

III.

We shared a common drunkenness departing the Kastles' loft together, as if the group of us—Ronnie, Didier, Burdmoore, Sandro, his cousin, and I—carried a heavy blanket or rug over our heads, each supporting a little of the weight, which rested on all of us, and resulted in our slack words, our swaying and knocking against one another in the freight elevator. Time had stretched like taffy, the night a place we would tumble into and through together, a kind of gymnasium, a space of generous borders. Or else why would we have gone, at one in the morning, to Times Square? I didn't know why, or whose idea it was, only that the night felt roomy and needed to be filled.

We broke into two groups, climbing into taxis, and reconvened on Forty-Second Street, where red light leaked like a juice from the theater entrances. A giant thermometer rising along one side of the Allied Chemical building shifted eerily from red to violet, red to violet. Below it was a frozen planet Earth cradled by a polar bear.

My group—Ronnie, Burdmoore, and I—stood under a marquee on a broad wedge of pink carpet that flopped out to the sidewalk like a tongue, creating a semi-indoors, almost domestic ambience. There were posters lining the entrance, a woman's face and bare shoulders against a black background, *Behind the Green Door*. It was all over town, the advertisement for that film. She looked like a nude astronaut floating in space, too sensual for anything like a breathing tube. A stark, look-at-me expression, solemn possibility. *I used to be a nice girl.* That was required, the just recently having been one. The actress had been a laundry flakes model for a brand of soap that was extra-gentle for baby's tender bottom.

You had to look the part for such a spectacular fall. I had never looked the part. The gap between my two front teeth, as Ronnie said, spoiled my cake-box appeal. Or as Sandro put it, gave a certain impression of mischief. I never thought I looked mischievous, but I'd always been told this. I could see this kind of thing in women with slightly crossed eyes, some breach in symmetry suggesting another kind of breach, in judgment or morals. Like the actress Karen Black, one eye slightly amiss in its focus. The women in *Hustler* cartoons were drawn with crossed eyes like Karen Black's. The mind is off duty but the body is open. There was that movie where poor Karen Black utters the fatal question at dinner with her lover's higher-class family: *Is there any ketchup?* At the end, she waits as the man goes into a service station bathroom while their gas is being pumped. A logging truck pulls up between the gas pumps and the restroom. When the man emerges from the restroom, the logging truck is there, blocking her view of him. He approaches the truck's driver. We hear only the freeway and the idle of the truck as he and the driver speak. He gets into the cab of the truck. It pulls out, climbs the highway on-ramp in low gear. The woman waits in the man's car. Gets out, looks around, waits some more. The credits roll.

"Triple X," a man said to us, pointing toward another entrance, large photographs of women stretching upward and backward like pythons. Why did snakes rear up like that? Every moment, poised for killing.

"We got only the hardest-core rating," the man called out. "Trip*pel* X."

"Triple X isn't a rating," Ronnie said. "They rate themselves that. To make the movies sound better."

Burdmoore had wandered off, and came around the corner toward us, light flashing over his noble profile and matted beard. He looked like Zeus lost in a casino.

A taxi pulled up, and Sandro, his cousin, and Didier got out. I glanced at Burdmoore, whose face registered the cousin's beauty. He watched her with interest, but also caution. It was the expression of a man who had handled beautiful women and could still admire them but never wanted to handle them again.

She bounded toward us, not at all aloof, as I expected her to be. I hadn't said two words to her at the Kastles'.

"Come on! Who's coming in?" she asked. "I want to see a show." She turned to Ronnie.

"Not my kind of thing," Ronnie said.

"What *is* your kind of thing?" she asked.

"That's a tough one," Ronnie said.

"Why?" She sparkled her dark eyes at him. He seemed not to notice.

"Because there's no market for what I want to see."

"Then it can't be that bad," she said. "For the worst things, there's a market."

"You're probably right about that." He looked at her as if he were making a new assessment, now that she'd said something possibly smart.

I thought of the girl in the photo in Ronnie's studio, the one on lay-away. She was probably waiting for him this very moment, somewhere downtown. Checking the clock, applying lipstick, concentrating her-self into an arrow pointed at Ronnie. Doing the various things women did when they had to wait for something they wanted.

Sandro was counting bulbs on the marquees. He was never wait-ing for someone else, he was simply in the world, doing, acting on his interests. He said that Times Square was all soft rhomboids, that this was part of the experience, the shapes of modern stamping technology reproduced here, in the shapes of signs and marquees, all rectangles with softened corners, streamlining as an attitude.

"It's funny they call it *Times* Square," Sandro said. "There's a nude magazine in Italy called *Le Ore*. The hours."

"Makes sense, actually," Ronnie said. "Pornography as a way to mark time. You dictate when and how. There's no chance in it. It's clockwork. Daily habits. Control. It's the opposite of sex. Which is pure freedom, in all its horror. You never know when you're actually going to sleep with someone, and when it does happen, the character is of surprise: this is actually *happening*. There is no surprise in simply getting off. It's sched-uled activity. Three p.m. Midnight. The morning shower. You know those marital aids, so-called? The thing about those products is they promise enhanced sensitivity, increased pleasure, and it's just numbing cream, to make you go longer. They add *time*. That's all they do."

Sandro and Ronnie speculated on whether you could love pornog-raphy simply as a cinephile, and on the unit of the quarter, because everything here was twenty-five cents. A quarter to peek through a quarter-size hole. Ronnie said the peep show was based on the Advent calendar. That it was a Christian tradition, this kind of looking, open-ing a window onto Jerusalem, a peek at the manger for each day of December. Sandro laughed, as if Ronnie were full of it, but also as if nothing pleased him more.

"You see it all through a hole," Ronnie said.

"Then I'm an Adventist," Didier replied. "I believe in that kind of isolated viewing, the focus on parts. Metonymy. Does anybody have quarters?"

A change man heard him and moved toward Didier in his coin-dispensing belt.

"Adventist," Ronnie said with faked wonder. "Does that mean you believe the end of the world is . . . imminent?"

Sandro had told me that Ronnie had a long-standing grudge against Didier, something to do with a negative review Didier had once written of Ronnie's work.

"Everything and nothing are imminent," Didier said. He handed the change man a five-dollar bill, cupping his hands for that amount in quarters. "This moment now? Imminent. Wait. Oh, gosh. Now, past. It all depends on how you experience time. Time is a function of pleasure, as you just crudely pointed out. The experience of it, I mean."

His blazer pockets weighted with quarters, Didier turned to Talia Valera. "Are you coming?" He said it somewhat insistently, as if she were obligated to go with him because he alone, among the men, was willing.

"No," she said, glancing at Ronnie.

Didier shrugged and went up the pink tongue of carpet and into the theater.

Somehow the decision was made to leave Didier there and go down to Rudy's. We got in another cab. Talia was about to sit on Ronnie's lap when he leaned forward and flipped up the jump seat for her. It wasn't that I would have minded if she'd sat on Ronnie's lap. But I would have noticed it, while Ronnie himself would have been oblivious to the echo, me on his lap. So many women on so many nights, flirting with him and ending up in his lap. Ronnie, who always had lovers and never girlfriends and did not kiss and tell. It could have been for this reason alone that I still felt something for him. And who could say that one reason was more valid than another? Unavailability was a quality, too.

As we rode downtown he was murmuring to Talia quietly in fake Italian, taking an Italian suffix, adding it to every word, and then repeating them. "Andiamo in un taxi-dino a Rudy-miendo's, con innu-endo in un taxi-dino—"

Sandro was telling Burdmoore, who was up front, about my motor-cycle crash on the salt flats, and how I'd ended up driving the land speed vehicle that his family sponsored, and I sensed he was framing the story as far-fetched, outlandish, but I could have been projecting, since there was a divide between us on the subject. Burdmoore turned around and looked at me with a certain amusement, not unsexual, but not lustful, either. The facts of the story made him a little curious, that was all. A funny thing about women and machines: the combination made men curious. They seemed to think it had something to do with them. This should have been amusing to me, the expression on Burdmoore's face as Sandro recounted the story. But I was focused on Ronnie and Talia, on the way he was making her laugh. *Taxi-dino, innuendo.* Pointing out a green-and-yellow Blimpie's sign, "There! One of ours!" Her laughter penetrating his fake sincerity like carbonation.

Rudy's was packed. People were arriving in buoyant swells, pushing in and talking loudly, bringing the energy from wherever they'd just been, different groups merging together like weather systems. Talia ran into two friends—girls I had seen around, at art openings, sitting at the Café Borgia or Graffito or Looters, an after-hours club where you had to pound and yell and hammer on the door to be let in. Neither of her friends was as pretty as Talia, which made sense. She got to be the pretty one. And the least compromised, the least dutifully feminine, with her husky voice, her karate pants, her low and complicitous "one of the guys" laugh.

Giddle came toward us and I realized she had been at the bar all those hours since we'd left in the early evening. She shone like something wet, a piece of candy that had been in someone's mouth. Up close, I realized it was glitter, here and there on her face and arms. It must have rubbed off from someone else. She hugged me in a cloud of cucumber oil. As a rule, the later it got, the more drinks she'd had, the more cucumber oil Giddle applied. It was so cloying and dominant a scent that I'd started to smell it when she wasn't even around. I smelled it on my own clothes. Even on Sandro's clothes. It got stuck in my head the way a song might.

After hugging me, Giddle took the drink in her hand and poured its remnants over Sandro's head. I was shocked, but strangely, Sandro was not. He simply blotted his face with cocktail napkins from the bar. I felt it was my fault for having such an eccentric friend, but Sandro didn't make a big deal out of it. "She's drunk," I said, watching her hug everyone we'd come in with. Ronnie was next. Then Giddle moved on to Burdmoore, seeming not to notice that Burdmoore was someone we didn't already know. She threw her arms around his neck. He didn't object. Their lips touched and kept touching. They gripped each other like two people having a reunion in the international terminal at JFK.

We all danced. Sandro, with his hand on my waist and the other on my shoulder, guiding me. "He Hit Me (and It Felt Like a Kiss)," a mainstay on the Rudy's jukebox, filled the room.

> If he didn't care for me
> I could have never made him mad
> But he hit me,
> and I was glad.

I responded to dips and twirls too late and felt like I was trying to sing along with a song I didn't know, mouthing each word just after hearing it sung. I didn't care. Sandro was a good dancer; it was part of his role as the older man, the teacher.

Henri-Jean wove his way around the edge of the dance crowd, carrying his striped pole, raising it high so he wouldn't hit anyone. Whenever there was any mass of people in SoHo, at Rudy's or a loft or an art opening, Henri-Jean made his scheduled appearance. "The sentient automaton," Ronnie called him, like Chaplin. Sandro said he was nothing like Chaplin.

Smoke collected above our heads, red-lit and infused with a bright, jangly, early sixties girl-group sound, rising toward the ceiling like an evaporating valentine. Rudy didn't always turn on the red light, softly emitting colored neon tubes arranged in an acrostic that hung from the wall, made by Stanley. Until a year ago, the red light glowed continuously during open hours, but then the bulbs for it were no longer manufactured and had to be handblown by a glassmaking studio in Washington State. Now Rudy only plugged it in on occasion, but it wasn't clear what the occasions were. "A mood on the street," Rudy said. "I just know."

Burdmoore was dancing with Giddle.

"I don't like the beard!" she shouted over the music.

"Why?" he shouted back.

"Because it's not *you*," she said. "You never had that beard—"

Burdmoore grinned. "I've never *not* had this beard, sister."

"You should shave it," she said, "go back to your old look, *you*." She grabbed the lapels of his rumpled blazer and shoved him in an affectionate manner.

"I will shave it," he said, his face brimming with a kind of amused joy as he held her by the waist to stop her from shoving him again. "I'm going to. Tomorrow."

More oldies came on. The Marvelettes. The Feminine Complex. Those girl groups would always remind me of Sandro, his light, careful steps, his way of politely overlooking my inability to take cues. He learned to dance at boarding school in Switzerland, where they'd had proper ballroom lessons, each boy taking his turn with the teacher, a Chilean woman whom Sandro had dreamed about for years afterward. He had tried to contact her through the school but she'd disappeared. "Maybe she simply went on to do something else," I'd said when he'd told me about her, "which isn't really disappearing. It's living." Sandro remembered all the steps. People said Mondrian had been a good dancer. And Yves Klein, too. There was something to it, artists who could dance. To be either a good dancer or a good artist the decisions needed grace and improvisation, an ease of bodies, of matter, in space. Like the old painter who had been a mentor of Sandro's. An artist he had pilgrimaged to see in New Mexico. She was living in an Airstream trailer and made paintings in an uninsulated outbuilding with no electricity. Got up before first light, worked until dusk, ate food from cans, slept alone. She told Sandro she had gotten the idea for her most important cycle of works when she was walking with her sister on an empty Texas plain one summer evening, a single star in the sky above them. They were teenagers. This was before cars, before World War One. "My sister had a gun and kept throwing bottles up in the air and shooting them," she had told Sandro. "We walked under the big empty twilight and that star." There had to be an element of chance. But also precision. An occasional dead-on hit. My sister had a gun.

The jukebox was turned off and a band called the Soviets started to test their equipment, saxophone erupting in blurts and squiggles, cymbals crashing down over the room. Giddle and Burdmoore retreated to a dark booth where they seemed to be working out some ancient connection, never mind that Giddle had possibly mistaken Burdmoore for someone else.

We were at the bar having one last drink. Sandro and I had meant to leave but he and Ronnie got involved in a semi-argument. Ronnie brought up Italy. He said I should go to Monza and that Sandro shouldn't be a stick-in-the-mud about it. "You're against it," he said to Sandro. "I get it. It's your family. But the thing is, she's the fastest chick in the world, Sandro. And you're slowing her down." He said it lightly, teasingly, drunkenly, and Sandro went sullen.

"Thanks, Ronnie," Sandro said. "I spend my whole life trying to get away from Valera, and I end up with their spokespersons, my best friend and my woman, both against me. Why don't the two of you sell me a set of tires while you're at it?"

I felt bad. But I wanted to go to Italy and hadn't possessed the courage to push for it. Ronnie was doing it for me.

But why? I wondered. For what motivation? And then I realized he was convincing Sandro that Sandro and I should leave New York, and I thought, won't you miss me, Ronnie?

At the confusion of that, I assented to the next round of drinks, while Sandro and I argued about Valera and Italy. "Why can't you just do something here? Focus on the photographs you have," he said. "Of Bonneville."

I wanted to carry the project through, I said. Going t[o]
part of Bonneville; it was one project.

Ronnie ended up in a nearby booth with Talia and
pretty accomplices. My discussion with Sandro was put
watched them. The girls had gotten the idea to slap and h
with Ronnie's encouragement. They were laughing, goi[ng]
table, each girl slapping herself. The first round of sla[p]
light pat on the cheek, the heel of a hand on the forehe[ad]
girls slapped herself, and with each slap they all erupt[ed]
When it was Talia Valera's turn, she punched herself in
closed fist. She had especially large fists, like a puppy wi[th]

Sandro went over to the booth and tried to reason [with]

"Calm down, Sandro," she said. "It's just a game."

"You'll end up with a black eye," Sandro said.

She didn't care. Ronnie had his camera and took pic
at the lens in a frank manner.

I thought again of the girl on Ronnie's layaway pla[n]
a bath and given up, gone to sleep? Or put on more l
looking for Ronnie, but to the wrong places?

Flash. Talia posed again for the camera. Her eye
and had the taut appearance of polished fruit. There[']
her eyebrow, probably from the silver rings she wore,
that shone prettily against her tanned skin. I detecte[d]
as if she felt that the gash and swollen eye were r
essence, deep and profound, for Ronnie and his cam

"This is great," Ronnie said. Click-click. Flash. "J

"He refuses to grow up," Sandro said to me as we w

But was that what he refused to do, or was it s[o]

Either way, while Ronnie acted like an asshole a
Sandro and I were on the street getting mugged.

11. THE WAY WE WERE

*I*n *the rain. In a squat. In an orgy. We meet again.*

By late 1966, the year the movement formed, the way they were was armed. Armed and ready to battle the Man and his Pigs. They were a Lower East Side street gang with a theory, a call, to liberate people and zones of strategic importance, to colonize an entire quarter of New York City as a network of crash pads, soup kitchens, and arsenals.

They were prepared to requisition all goods that met their needs. The way they were was ready to advance the struggle by any means necessary. The way they were was dangerous. Ecstatic. Angry. Occasionally stoned, but ready to put down the joint and take up the gun at any moment. *Taking the City, from Riot to Revolution* Bubalev's treatise was called. From riot to revolution was the point of their arrow. They were looking for people who liked to draw. Who were ready to draw. Pull back the hammer and fire. If you didn't believe in lead you were already dead. The way they were was unafraid to shoot a Pig in the face. The police were *structurally* bad, in Bubalev's formulation. They ratcheted that analysis: the Pigs are assholes, they are the enemy of us and our brother.

The way they were was done with a shitty police state where action was no sister to dreams. The way they were was unafraid. Ready to defend a new and total freedom from Amerikan capitalism and its wars, its deadening effects, its slaveries.

What happens between bodies during an insurrection, Bubalev said, *is more interesting than the insurrection itself.*

In the rain. In a squat. In an orgy. We meet again.

Fah-Q Motherfucker declared in a 1967 flyer printed in their squat on Tenth Street that in Amerika life is the one demand that cannot be fulfilled. We are here to live, said Fah-Q. To demand our life. Not to request that the needs of life be met. We are here to meet them ourselves, to meet the demand for *life.*

Among the Motherfuckers' many actions in that potent five-year run, 1966 to '71, some storied, others unknown except to their participants, the following represent a few choice cuts:

Requisitioned uniforms from an army surplus place on Canal Street, to meet their needs for revolutionary dress: black Levi's, black T-shirts. Took an entire pallet of each as they were delivered by a wholesale supplier.

Occupied the squat on Tenth Street, what would become their famed headquarters, in the last days of 1966 and then held a New Year's feast for their neighbors, burying an entire pig, which they stole from the Meatpacking District, in the sand of the children's playground in Tompkins Square Park, an effigy of the most hated neighborhood denizen, the uniformed Pig. "Pig roast! Pig roast!" neighborhood children yelled, running up and down Avenue B, bordering the park. The Motherfuckers core group took a lesson from that day, their first big community gathering: the children of the Lower East Side, under-fed, runny-nosed, of black and brown complexions, robbed of a lice-free, misery-free existence, robbed of most aspects of childhood, were

already soldiers partaking in the struggle. Fah-Q understood, as a sur-
vivor himself of the ghettos of Miami, Florida, who and what they were.
But he did not recruit them. They joined on their own, a breeze of play,
of life, who defended the perimeter of the Motherfuckers' compound.
The Pigs were afraid of those children, who had nothing to lose. In
May of '68 they were breaking up pieces of sidewalk (just as Fah-Q,
who gave them pickaxes, had seen it done in the newsreel footage from
Paris). That summer the kids heaved concrete and cobblestones at Pigs
on their big Harley-Davidson Pigcycles as they rode up Avenue A, one
of whom crashed, a big, beefy fellow in short sleeves and knee-high,
shiny jackboots. Later that year the children stole an idling ambulance
as two paramedics were picking up Chinese food on Houston Street.
The kids brought the stolen ambulance straight to the Motherfuckers,
who converted it with matte black spray paint and new plates and a
removal of most identifying marks. It became their official van, useful
for requisitioning goods from appliance stores along the Bowery, items
stocked right there on the sidewalk, which they claimed for their own
store on Tenth Street, called Free, where they gave everything away.

Robbed a Chemical Bank on Delancey Street. The bacon bank, they
called it. Smoky vaporized bacon grease from the deli next door per-
meated the carpets, air, walls, everything. The bacon bank never did
not smell like bacon. It had been easy: two P38 pistols, pantyhose over
their two heads (which gave their faces a blurred intensity, encouraging the tellers to meet their needs, and quickly), one note, with clear
instructions. Their stickup appeared nowhere in the news, which was
a lesson to the Motherfuckers, useful: banks were robbed daily. It was
not a difficult task to rob a bank. It was easy and that was why it happened every day. Every business hour you could be sure a bank somewhere in New York City was being quietly held up and that you were
never going to hear about it, know about it, unless it was you who had
robbed it. The banks did not broadcast these robberies. If everyone
knew, they would rob banks instead of work.

*   *   *

Beat up a rock band from Detroit called the Stooges. Beat the shit out of them for not being tough enough, and having a reputation for intensity though it was unearned. The Stooges had played at a rock club on Second Avenue, and just after their set ended word spread that the band was piling into their limousine and heading off to Max's Kansas City for dinner with rich people and celebrities. The crowd became enraged, dragged the singer and his bandmates from their limousine and forced them back inside the club. The Motherfuckers concentrated on pummeling the singer and then pissed on his satin pants. Which he was still wearing as he lay on his side, groaning. Not quite in the same way he had groaned and yowled onstage, trying to peddle his fake intensity to the young girls, among them Love Sprout and Nadine, Fah-Q's and Burdmoore's respective womenfolk. Fah-Q and Burdmoore crossed streams of urine over the body of the singer, and Burdmoore knew that brotherly pacts ended badly. But he was in it to the end. He was ready for badly.

Firebombed a retailer of Thom McAn Shoes the week before it was scheduled to open on Saint Mark's Place, accidentally burning down the community center next door, where Alcoholics Anonymous met. No apology was issued. They hated Alcoholics Anonymous anyway. Talk to the flames, Fah-Q said. The Motherfuckers started things. Sometimes the things they started finished themselves.

Ransomed Maury the Slumlord's miniature whippet ("minwhip"), sending a note with a demand for five thousand dollars to be dropped with the bartender at McSorley's. *Listen Maury you scumbag,* the note went, *if you want to see this stupid arachnid creature again pay up.* Maury owned vast holdings on the blocks surrounding Tompkins Square Park, including their own large tenement building on Tenth Street, which had been empty and boarded before the Motherfuckers decided it would meet their needs. Rumor had spread that Maury was in the process of having it condemned to get them out. Instead of paying the ransom for his minwhip Maury called the cops, who referred him to animal control, and it turned out he didn't have a pet license for the dog. The Motherfuckers, meanwhile, had developed an attachment to the minwhip, formerly called Basket and now rechristened Bonanno, after Alfredo Bonanno, an Italian anarchist who was currently doing time in some Italian prison somewhere and Burdmoore had never read his stuff but understood that his name carried a kind of weight because Bonanno had tried to burn down the Vatican. Bonanno the minwhip could leap incredibly far, he was a long jumper, and also a biter. The Motherfuckers trained him to hurdle flaming barricades and attack the Pigs.

A few actions remained merely dream actions, but very few. Like the day they went to dangle their erections in the faces of tourists. They went to the Statue of Liberty to carry this out. It was Valentine's Day and freezing, but no matter, hundreds of families were lined up to enter the big lady. The Motherfuckers unzipped and found themselves shriveled to nothing. There was little point in wielding their weaponry that cold morning. Instead, they semispontaneously pissed an important movement message into a snowbank on Liberty Island. Burdmoore did the *N* and started the *E* but ran out of fuel. Luckily one of them had brought beer along, which they passed around, taking long guzzles to complete the message. NEVER WORK.

Smashed up a Cadillac Brougham that was parked on Tenth Street. Burdmoore had identified the car as belonging to Thurman Johnson, a fuckhead Southern gentleman who was sleeping with Nadine, and even if the movement was down on couplism, this bothered Burdmoore, because Thurman seemed not to appreciate Nadine but to employ her in a sadistic power trip. The trees on Tenth Street reflected on the windshield of the parked Cadillac like a leafy silkscreen before Burdmoore shattered its glass with a sledgehammer. It felt great to smash that wind-shield, even if the car turned out not to have been Thurman Johnson's.

They killed only one person. Maury the Slumlord, who had come at them with an aluminum baseball bat, did not count. That was war and you don't call it murder when the other side takes casualties. The only person they deliberately killed was Twilight, a neighborhood heroin dealer. After a sixteen-year-old girl OD'd they went to Twilight's place on Clinton Street. Fah-Q, having lost his two older brothers and a girl-friend to horse, had the lowest tolerance among the Motherfuckers for dealers and their negative impact on revolutionary potential. "When you are offered only abjection and misery as so-called life," Fah-Q said, "you sink into yourself. Feels good, but it's a lot like death." There was a line halfway down Clinton Street when Burdmoore and Fah-Q arrived. Sniffling junkies waiting like for bread during the Depression, wiping runny noses on the cuffs of their dirty suede jackets. There's a movie title for you, Burdmoore thought, *Snot on Suede*. He and Fah-Q cut the line and went up. Those waiting didn't object, perhaps due to their degeneracy, but also, Fah-Q was six two and weighed two hun-dred pounds, and people had a tendency to move out of his way. They shot Twilight with a P38, the semiofficial weapon of the Motherfuck-ers, came back down, that was it. No blowback, because it turned out no one cared if Twilight lived or died.

Robbed a Chemical Bank on Seventh Avenue, Burdmoore's para-military garb for that action involving nothing but a ski mask and a black satin bikini. *Incognito* was how he later remembered the rationale behind the decision for the bikini, which had been requisitioned dur-ing the accidental robbery of a Courrèges store on Madison Avenue. The bikini fit, and the feel of its stretchy material had grown on Burd-moore, so much so that he was seldom not wearing it. Seldom to never. The silky bikini had become for him a sacred undergarment, the way it snugly held his junk, made him feel . . . *gathered*. Perfect for a stickup, he'd thought, stripping down in the van.

Took in escapees from Bellevue, sisters in hospital gowns who weren't going to recover in mental wards. And escapees from the foster home on Fourth Avenue near the post office. Gave these girls and women clothes, beds, meals, and showed them the way to noninstitutional bliss. A good time was had by all. *What happens between bodies during an insurrection is more interesting than the insurrection itself.*

Took in escapees from the Order of the Golden Daughters, like Juan, who had no arms, his T-shirt sleeves empty and flapping. The Order of the Golden Daughters brainwashed children by sharing the white smoke of the drug dimethyltryptamine, or DMT, as a highway to God.

Raided the Order of the Golden Daughters after the leader gave herpes to Love Sprout, who was only fourteen. The church was in an apartment. Burdmoore's own street-level quarters in the squat on Tenth had a dirt floor and six unfixed Manx cats who infused his lair with the eternal smell of cat spunk. The church apartment was squalid in a different way. One hairy fatso, the leader, freebasing in white robes that had fallen open, a face almost entirely masked by an unkempt beard, the leader's wet red mouth connected to a glass pipe. Burdmoore took one look at him and almost puked. Two teenage boys lay on the floor moaning about the light filling them up, as a pigeon on a sill above them with pushpins in its wings tried to unflap them from the pins. Fah-Q and Burdmoore picked up the leader by the scruff of his robes. Knocked over his freebasing gear. Doused the place with kerosene and lit a match. Carried the moaning, moony-eyed boys back to HQ and treated their DMT highs with orange juice. Fah-Q and Burdmoore did what they could to balance out the bad morale in the community. The pushers, charlatans, proselytizers, and Pigs. They did what they could to offer care. Care with strength, call it armed love. Fah-Q did.

Brought garbage to Lincoln Center. Garbage for Garbage, the action was called, which took place on the ninth day of a garbage strike in the summer of '69. As they moved north up Broadway with bags of garbage in the back of the van, Burdmoore had it in his mind that they were riding up Jackie Kennedy's tanned leg to the Lincoln Center fountain, her panties.

They upturned their garbage bags into the fountain, filling Jackie's underpants with coffee grounds, beer bottles, sour, crushed milk cartons, all variety of stinking muck. Burdmoore wondered if he should be sorry, but then he knew Jackie must be digging it. Every chick wants her panties filled. Name a chick that—

Burdmoore didn't share with any of the Motherfuckers what he secretly felt they were doing with this action, cramming garbage right up against Jackie's high-class snatch, trash held in place by snug fabric, the way he himself felt held in place by the black Courrèges bikini. He'd had to lock himself in a bathroom afterward and jerk himself vigorously. Jackie turned him on so much he wondered if he were actually *gay*, but he shoved the thought away and focused on yanking down her fancy underwear and thumping his cock against her plush, tanned pussy. Oh, God. Was her pussy *suntanned*? Did it make him gay that Jackie was an icon for the fags? A question that came at exactly the wrong moment and he found himself coming while picturing big, pink, chintz-covered buttons. The Motherfuckers' next big action came quick because he needed to engage in something indisputably macho and so they

Knifed a concert promoter on Second Avenue. The promoter was refusing to let them use his club for community events. "This is for Jerry fucking Garcia," Burdmoore said, as Fah-Q jammed the spike of his knife under the promoter's ribs.

*   *   *

Robbed a Chemical Bank on Broadway and Seventy-Ninth Street, wearing wigs. Burdmoore's was brunette with bangs (this is for you, Jackie), and then splurged on groceries at Fairway. Returned to the Lower East Side and fed the people. Fed the people for a week. Chasing after junkies and alcoholics and teenage girls with hollow eyes, Dominican and black children who otherwise lived on chocolate Yoo-hoo and Cracker Jacks, the Motherfuckers passing out paper plates with grits, pinto beans, rotisserie chicken, salad. Families of every racial type included in the New York census came to their address on Tenth Street and ate the food the Motherfuckers cooked and served, drank the juices they made and ladled into Dixie cups and for which they asked nothing in return. They even fed the hippies, who were unpolitical hedonists hated more or less by the Motherfuckers. But the Motherfuckers did not turn anyone hungry away. Your hunger is your dignity is your payment, they said as they handed out the plates of food and the cups of fresh juice, beet, carrot, pineapple, wheatgrass. Food. Grace. Love. Dignity. Enjoy. Enjoy. Enjoy.

Stormed Veselka, the overpriced rip-off Ukrainian diner on Second Avenue and Ninth. No territorial borders anymore between kitchen and restaurant, customer and bum, waiter and thief. The women who were with the Motherfuckers (it may as well be stated: no women were Motherfuckers. Women were the sisters of action, dreaming. Bedmate, janitor, cook, nag), carrying out plates of hot food and everybody noshing. Later they upgraded this concept and stormed the Four Seasons, ate and drank whatever they wanted, and then walked out after creaming a maître d' for the hell of it with the contents of a fire extinguisher. *Comiendo,* as Fah-Q, who was Cuban, liked to say, *comiendo a la fuerza.* Eating by force.

Called in security geese, or rather some geese randomly ended up in their squat, which Juan trained and oversaw, along with looking after

Bonanno the minwhip (Juan loved animals, and had he not been arm-less, homeless, neglected, afflicted, abused, molested, and left for dead on Avenue D, Burdmoore felt he might have become a veterinarian). The geese honked their heads off and bit anyone unapproved who came to the compound as well as offering a lively, dynamic presence to their scene. The downside was that they shit all over the place in dark, oily squirts, and everyone had to be careful where they stepped.

Called in the Hells Angels when news came of an imminent raid, to be led by Captain Fink of the Ninth Precinct, with reinforcements from other precincts. The Angels met their needs, for the most part. They barricaded the corner of Tenth and B, and from inside, launched Molotovs, and later, when the police arrived with the usual—riot gear and billy clubs, baton rounds of various sorts, mostly rubber and bean bag bullets, stench darts, smoke bombs, water cannons, flashbang and sponge grenades, tear gas—the Angels put together a huge tower of burning tires to neutralize the tear gas. The Motherfuckers held their ground and the Pigs had to regroup and find a new tactic to try to flush them out. The hitches were few but unfortunate: drunk and caged in too close of quarters, one of the Angels committed a forcible act on Burdmoore's wife, Nadine. The cause of whose tears, Burdmoore understood, could not be found in the traces on her cheeks. My hands are tied, Burdmoore said, frowning, as he and Nadine both looked at his hands. What could he do? Not much. Little. In fact, nothing. Even as he knew the source of her tears was endless. Bottomless and endless and not to be found in their traces.

In the rain. In a squat. In an orgy. We meet again.

Made end-time plans, with sixty-eight charges brought between the two of them, Burdmoore Model and Fah-Q Motherfucker (whose real name on official police documents was Hector Valadez, which no one knew until the warrants were served. Fah-Q said you should hear in your name nothing of yourself, nothing but the voice that calls it).

It was time for the diaspora, the wandering, Fah-Q said, Burdmoore agreeing, but on what the wandering was, how it related to struggle, to revolution, they did not agree. For Fah-Q, struggle was a historical process with specific phases, stages, ruptures, plateaus, and victories, all leading to an eventual classless society. Burdmoore was more of a mystic, an intuitive sort of dude. For Burdmoore, there was *only* waiting—that was how you prepared for the future, by waiting for cataclysm and you would know it when it came. It might blow up in your face, but hopefully your enemy's face.

Fah-Q said the city could no longer be the site of an insurrectionary seizure of the means of life. It was 1971 and not only was the heat on him and Burdmoore, the factories were closing. The worker was leaving the city, and the city, according to Fah-Q, was *only* the worker, the factory, the reproduction of the class relation. It was time to drop into the void, the desolate mountains of northern Mexico.

Burdmoore went with him, taking Nadine, but only to evade the police. Burdmoore believed still in the city, which he felt sure was the only place for love and violence. Whoever goes into exile *exiles,* he told himself on the day of their hasty departure. Does not the stranger who leaves take with him the inhabitable city? *I take it with me,* he thought, *and I will return it and myself in due time.* At the right moment. History, Bubalev said, happens in cities. Not elsewhere.

In the meantime, with sixty-eight charges between them, it was time to go.

Six months into their hardship, Nadine having ditched him for a ride to Los Angeles, Burdmoore lucked out and found legal aid. Returned to New York and worked out a deal with the DA. Regrouped and waited for the rupture he knew was coming.

With or without him, it would come.

12. THE SEARS MANNEQUIN STANDARD

It was simply our night. People were mugged every night of the week in SoHo, where the streets were dark and empty—no streetlights, no open stores, just deserted loading docks.

We'd walked with a kind of pall over us, Sandro annoyed at Talia for letting Ronnie goad her into punching herself in the face, annoyed at me for announcing to him that I was going to Monza, which was what I said on the street, outside Rudy's, drunk and pushing the limits.

"I'm going," I said. "I was invited and it's not about you. It's about me."

"Great," he said. "That's great. Maybe for your next act you can show them your tits."

"That's nice," I said.

"It's as nice as the Valera Company gets," he said. "Actually, it's nicer, because it's a region of human qualities. Of females. But never mind."

We walked along in the dark, our silence thick with two minds that were not going to reconcile easily. He wanted me to forgo the trip, and I thought it was unfair to pretend that my driving the *Spirit of Italy* was nothing. It was not nothing, it was actually incredible. And yet I was being forced to choose, now, between a genuine opportunity and Sandro. The more I thought about it the angrier I got, and then our mugger emerged from a doorway.

He was holding a knife out in front of him like it was something hot, flashing it at us in jabs. He demanded our wallets.

Sandro reached for his, in his back pocket, and instead withdrew the cap-and-ball pistol.

"Drop the knife."

The mugger didn't.

"You aren't going to *shoot* me," he said to Sandro. "What the fuck is that man—"

He reached toward Sandro. Sandro pulled the hammer back and fired.

A ball of smoke went up. The knife clattered to the sidewalk.

The mugger shrieked, holding his hand, his body folded around it. He looked up at Sandro from his crouched position, clutching his hand.

"You fucking shot me! I can't believe you fucking shot me!"

I felt the mugger's horror as mine, too.

I said I was going to call 911 and get the guy an ambulance. We were only a block from our loft. "You better wait with him," I said.

"Sure," Sandro said, and shrugged like I was making a minor and fussy request, asking him to retrieve a candy wrapper he'd just dropped on the ground.

I was on hold, 911 flooded with calls on a Saturday night, New York so full of emergencies that the wait was ten minutes.

"Did you see the gunman?" the operator asked me.

"The gunman?"

"The person who shot the victim," she said.

The victim?

"Hello? You're going to have to make a report—"

I hung up the receiver. Cooked old spaghetti, and as the water boiled I heard the ambulance.

I kept expecting Sandro. He didn't return. I wasn't sure what to do. I ate the spaghetti and drank a glass of warm white wine because these were what we had and it was late and there had been a lot of drinking and I was hungry for a second dinner. The ambulance had come and gone and now I heard nothing. I decided I'd better go back out. There was no one on the street. It was dark and quiet, as if we'd never been there getting mugged. I walked down to Houston Street, where an occasional taxi sped past. Returned home and waited.

I sat on a daybed in the living room, a plywood platform that Sandro had built, listening through the open windows to the airy tone of the sleeping city. Not a single car disturbed the loose cobblestones on our street. I turned on the television. The three a.m. movie was just starting. A baby crying in the arms of a woman whose face was puffy from sleep, her hair matted and pillow-dented. The scene was familiar but I could not place it. The camera moved to a prettier woman on a couch. She sat up, thin and blond with a weedlike vitality, looked out the window at a front-loader pushing coal waste around. I realized I'd seen this movie in a theater with Sandro. The prettier woman had ditched her husband and kids and was about to set off on a series of sketchy adventures with a jumpy, anxious man. The point of the film was not the stark life in a coal-mining town, although that was how Sandro had read it, the human element of industry. It was about being a woman, about caring and not caring what happens to you. It was about not really caring.

Coal came in different sizes, Sandro had explained after we saw the film. Names like lump, stoker, egg, and chestnut. Sandro liked knowing those kinds of things. He and Ronnie both did, although, as Ronnie joked, Sandro *owned* factories and Ronnie had worked in them. Or at least that was what Ronnie said, that he'd worked in a textile mill. But sometimes he said he'd only ever worked on boats. And yet the stories Ronnie told about working in the textile mill seemed real. I decided that if he hadn't worked in one, well, *someone* had. Someone had lived the experience Ronnie narrated to us. "We pissed behind the dye house," he said. "Because there were old lushes hiding in the bathrooms, hovering and waiting for you to pull out your young cock."

Ronnie's job was stirring a dye vat. He worked with another kid, tall and skinny with a goiter on his neck the size of a tennis ball. One week, Ronnie said, this kid with the big goiter on his neck didn't show up and Ronnie stirred the dye vat alone. The next week the kid was back, a large bandage where the goiter had been. Ronnie said they had a secret medical clinic in the subbasement of the mill so that no one would file workers' comp. "When my hand got caught in a roller," he said, "these guys wheeled me down there and left me for dead with a big male nurse who fed me MREs and morphine."

"Is he telling the truth?" I asked Sandro. "He's complicated," Sandro said. "You have to listen closely. He'll say something perfectly true and it's meaningless. Then he makes something up, but it has value. He's telling you *something*."

The woman in the movie goes to court and tells the judge she's no good, her kids are better off without her. Her calm and snowy face: a person quietly letting her life unravel. Because of her beauty, there would be no unnecessary detours through vanity.

I have other problems, Nadine had said.

The woman in the film was already beautiful and had to confront her life directly. She was driven to destroy herself, and because of her beauty, free to do so.

She tries to collect the rest of her pay at a sweatshop.

What can I do for you, lover? The shift boss in thick glasses, his eyes big jelly orbs rolling over her.

Behind him, centering the frame, the employee punch clock. Ronnie and Sandro's friend Sammy punched a time clock on the hour every hour twenty-four hours a day for a year. Sandro said it was one of the great artworks of the century, that and Ronnie's declared project to photograph every living person. Sammy who had lived outside for a year, which was far more grueling, more extreme, than driving a land speed vehicle. But both meant shaping your life around an activity and calling it a performance. And so why should I not go to Monza?

I heard the garbage trucks outside. Ronnie was probably making his appearance at the young girl's, the one he was keeping on a layaway plan. Not as he had doubtlessly promised, hours earlier, but now, in the final moments of night, to take what she offered.

The woman in the film drinks in a bar. She's in hair curlers, a chiffon headscarf tied over them like a tarp over a log pile. The hollows of the curlers, spaces for hope: something good might happen.

There was no sign of Sandro. I watched the film to keep myself awake while I waited.

A man bought the woman a beer. She took dainty sips in her hair curlers, in preparation for no specific occasion. Curler time seemed almost religious, a waiting that was more important than what the waiting was for. Curler time was about living the now with a belief that a future, an occasion for set hair, existed.

But then she was putting on her ratty underwear and the rest of her clothes and chasing a traveling salesman out of a motel room, abandoning the curlers for good.

Hey! Hey, wait up!

I came to rehearse parts of this film, my memory of the scenes returning in more detail as I watched. I began to anticipate. Not the lines, though I remembered a few of them, but looks on the woman's face.

Gazing at department store mannequins as if they possessed something essential and human that she lacked. Mannequins were carefully positioned to look natural, looking off in this direction or that but never at us. This was part of the Sears Mannequin Standard. My mother had worked for a short time as an assistant window dresser at the Sears in downtown Reno. She was given a booklet with a list of instructions, the most important being the no-eye-contact rule. If the mannequins made eye contact with shoppers they would disrupt the dream, the shopper's projection. A mannequin's job was to sell us to ourselves in a more perfect version for $19.99.

The woman peered at the mannequins for guidance. Examining their enameled makeup, a purse dangling from a stiff arm, a pole supporting each life-size figure from behind, disappearing into a hole cut into the rear seam of her slacks. They each have a pole up their ass, says the sudden wryness in the woman's face. How about that.

Her face when Mr. Dennis, the jumpy man, tosses her new lemon pants out the car window: childlike disappointment.

When you're with me, no slacks. No slacks!

Tosses her lipstick.

Makes you look cheap.

When you're with me, no curlers. Why don't you get a hat?

You don't want anything, you won't have anything, he tells her. You don't have anything, you're nothing. You might as well be dead.

Everything goes wrong when they try to rob a bank. It was like poor Tim Fontaine, Ronnie's younger brother. Tim Fontaine, who had robbed a bank and then waited at a crowded bus stop when the ink bomb in the money bag went off. Why didn't he take a cab? I'd wondered. "Because that's my brother," Ronnie said. "If he was smart enough to take a cab he might have figured out some other way to finance his drug habit." Ronnie said that before his brother robbed banks he sold heroin in Bushwick and that it was a stupidly hard job, sixteen-hour days, and his only pay was a morning and evening fix. "That's the thing about junkies," Ronnie said, "they work like dogs, it's all day out on the streets and they think they're cheating the system. I told my brother, you make twelve cents an hour." "How much do you make, Ronnie?" Sandro had joked. And Ronnie said, "I don't make a *wage*, I'm an artist. I'm not part of the system." "Neither is your brother," Sandro said. "So you have to tack on something to his twelve cents an hour, some added value."

I once met Tim Fontaine. I'd had ideas about what he'd be like, as a brother of Ronnie's, and as a person who'd spent several years robbing banks and armored cars before he was caught. I pictured sideburns like Ronnie's, swaggering and handsome like Ronnie, the never-washed and greasy Levi's, the motorcycle boots. The sarcasm. Sunglasses propped on his head and the slightest, barest touch of a grace that was almost feminine, because Ronnie had a pretty mouth. In other words, I pictured Ronnie. Tim Fontaine was nothing like Ronnie. He mumbled and shuffled and stared at the floor. He wore the stiff, ill-fitting, and too-new-looking work clothes I later learned is the universal wardrobe of ex-cons. The severe, barbershop hair. A mustache that covers some kind of pitting or scarring. The awkward bulk of prison yard muscles. There was a sense with Tim Fontaine that it was all uphill from here. Twelve steep steps, then repeat. He barely looked at me when I met him, just stared at his hands, the pads of his fingers crusted and shiny. "The dumbfuck removed his fingerprints with acid when he turned eighteen," Ronnie said. "As if that won't instantly ID you as a criminal."

Nearing the end of the film, morning in a deserted quarry. The woman wakes up in a car, a soldier unzipping his pants and forcing himself on her. She escapes, runs screaming into the woods in her white sandals, slingbacks Mr. Dennis had borrowed from the trunk of a car in the Woolworth's lot. By luck they had fit her perfectly. She tears through the bramble, scratched, frantic, half-dressed, half-raped, and falls, facedown, crying.

Night at a roadside tavern. Someone fits an unlit cigarette behind her ear. She's given a hot dog. Chews it, meek and grateful. Her beer glass is filled and refilled.

Honky-tonk music plays, fiddles eking out cheer as people shout and smoke and drink, their voices pelting the woman.

You don't want anything, you won't have anything. You don't have anything, you're nothing.

The cigarette in her long-fingered hand. Her snow-faced beauty, the light of it dim.

I am still . . . so . . . *pretty*. Nadine, leaning toward me to prove it.

The camera frames the woman, her eyes toward the table.

That's it. End of film.

As if on cue, I heard our freight elevator climbing toward the top floor on its chains.

*   *   *

The elevator rumbled and squeaked slowly back down to its resting position on the first floor. I turned off the television and got up.

Sandro was sitting in the dark, on a chair in the middle of the large entrance room. I went for the light switch.

"No," he said, "leave it and come here."

He buried his head against me. I was flooded with sympathy for him. The only fair thing, I thought, was to try to share the psychic fallout for his mistake. And yet as I stroked his hair, his warm weight against me, I felt separate from what he'd done, defending eight dollars plus a phone number scribbled on a hardware store receipt—the contents of his wallet, I later saw. The number was the Trust E. Ordering takeout, probably. He'd shot a person in the hand to defend eight dollars and a phone number I knew by heart.

He picked me up and carried me to the bed. There was a bed in that room that we didn't normally sleep in. It and the single chair were the only furniture. Sandro liked to have a bed in every room, freestanding, never pushed against a wall. Even on the floors below, which were only for displaying his finished works and the works of his friends, Stanley Kastle, Saul Oppler, John Chamberlain, a few pieces of Ronnie's, there was a bed in each open room, islands of domestic comfort in spaces otherwise so spare that an old steam radiator in the corner, its silver paint flaking, seemed homey and domestic. The only person who used these beds was Sandro. He liked a surface for lying down and thinking, for feeling the space of a room, for looking up at the high, repeating pattern of stamped tin, listening as the cobblestones made their hollow *clomp*-clomp when trucks passed on the street below. Its austerity gave Sandro's loft the feel of a very clean machine shop. Everything in it was coated in a fine residue that had a greasy sustenance to it, like graphite shavings, dust that left a blackish smear if you tried to wipe it from a windowsill, or if you sat on a chair in light-colored pants. Sandro's loft would never be clean like a regular home. Machine lubricants and the solvents and by-products of fabric treatment were stained into the floorboards in ghost-dark shadows. In the building's former life it had been a dress factory. When Sandro first bought it, Gloria Kastle was working for him as an assistant, one aspect of their "long history," which Gloria took pleasure in alluding to and Sandro rolled his eyes at. Dress pins had been packed into the spaces between every floorboard, and Gloria's job had been to pull them out, crouching on her knees with a handheld magnet. It took her a week and her back hurt for months afterward, but she said she grew attached to the task, consolidating stray pins. "When I closed my eyes at night," she said, "I saw pins being coaxed from cracks and crevices with a very strong magnet, the pins sticking to one another like a chain of paper dolls." Sandro had done the brute work, unbolted and javelined the scores of industrial ironing boards into an open dumpster in front of the building, whose sea level of discarded machinery rose each day and was magically lowered each night as nocturnal scavengers climbed into the dumpster and carried things away.

We lay on the bed in the entrance room. It was five in the morning and the streets were silent, nothing but the sound of one basketball bouncing in the courts across the street, occasionally bonking the backboard. It was my habit to picture a lone person playing with the single ball, dribbling, bringing it to the netless hoop, retrieving it. Someone unable to sleep who had gone out with his ball to pensively shoot baskets. There could have been two or three or even a whole team of people shuffling around in the dark, dribbling, passing, shooting, and yet whenever I heard a ball echoing on the little court I thought it was the sound of a single player.

Sandro stared at me as if to confirm we were in the same register. I stared back, unsure what the register was. It seemed important to convey that I understood. Isn't that what intimacy so often is? Supposing you understand, conveying that you do, because you feel in theory that you *could* understand, and you want to, and yet secretly you don't? Then he was pulling my underwear off and I didn't need to understand. In that large open room, my thoughts wandered as Sandro descended, his breath against my thighs, a sensation that always embarrassed me a little, as if I were a frigid teenager. I had the vague feeling that consenting meant approving of his act of violence and I did not approve, but then again this was simply sex, not approval or forgiveness, and I'd already decided I wasn't going to reciprocate. Too tired, too late, I didn't feel like it. Sandro never cared about reciprocity. Sex is not about exchange values, he said. It's a gift economy. I relaxed and let my mind wander. I was thinking about the woman in the movie, her snowy face. Daintily sipping her beer in its short glass. I was half-removed from what was happening, from Sandro's mouth, an asymmetry that was meant to be read as connection, a man's face, tongue, and focus, between a woman's legs, and her focus on fruition. Not gratitude, not intimacy, just fruition.

The woman in curler time, sipping her beer, was readying to lose herself. She would do it. She was not afraid.

The sky lightened through the loft windows, the trucks on Grand Street beginning their daylong stream of bangs and rumbles as they hit the large steel plates that lay over the street.

Sandro had waited with the mugger, he told me, a fourteen-year-old kid with a shattered hand. I was quiet. He took my silence as an accusation. A guy with a knife was *threatening* us, he said. How could we have known he wouldn't harm us? There was no way to know. The only sure thing was the revolver, which, because of Sandro's demonstration for Didier, was loaded.

When the ambulance wailed toward them, Sandro left the scene. He went walking down Houston to Allen. Down the Allen Mall, as we called the pedestrian walkway between north and south traffic, to Delancey. Past Ratner's, which was filled with late-night diners. He climbed the steps of the Williamsburg Bridge and began to cross. He could see the yellow neon of the sugar refinery across the East River, the halogen safety lights of the Navy Yard, the electrical substation to the south of the Navy Yard, its dark smokestacks blinking red. He'd forgotten how magnificent that view could be. But passing along the graffiti-pasted walkway he felt the gun in his pocket and began to wonder if he was going to be mugged again. Surely it couldn't happen twice in one night. The odds were totally against it. It should have been impossible, given that it had already happened. He saw a clump of dark figures lurking on the walkway at the next concrete anchorage and decided that being mugged had nothing to do with odds. Nothing to do with what had already taken place. He had no desire to use that gun again. He turned around, descended the steps of the bridge, and wandered into Chinatown, over the hose-sprayed sidewalks in front of closed fish and produce markets. He found a bakery on Hester Street that had its interior lights on, the windows slicked with a veil of white steam, so much steam it was collecting in rivulets that ran down the interior of the glass. Inside, workers were filling display cases from large bakery pans. He rapped on the window and talked them into selling him a lotus paste bun. It was just out of the oven and its warmth and aroma, he said, transported him to me. Nothing mattered except coming home to see me.

"And there you were," he said. "In your cotton-underweared splendor. Your leggy splendor."

Helen Hellenberger called in the morning with the name of a lawyer for Sandro.

How does she already know what happened? I asked.

Sandro rubbed his head like he was overwhelmed by technicalities and the trauma of the incident and said, "I telephoned her when I got home. But what does it matter? The whole thing is a kind of blur. A fuckup and calamity. I'm really mad at myself."

He put his head in his hands, and then I was busy comforting him and told myself not to be paranoid about Helen.

The lawyer informed Sandro he would have to choose, either go to the police and tell them exactly what happened, or decide not to go, to do nothing.

"But what happens to me if I turn myself in?" Sandro asked him.

The lawyer explained that Sandro had it all wrong. There was no reason to worry. They would want to make him a hero. Hero vigilante chases down mugger, takes back night.

Sandro relayed all this to me at the Ukrainian diner we liked to go to on Second Avenue and Ninth Street. Then we drifted east down Ninth toward Tompkins Square Park. It was a beautiful fall day, a quiet morning, oak trees with their leaves going burgundy, the smell of woodsmoke from someone's fireplace.

We were near the strange little storefront congregation that gave out free doses of DMT, communion for anyone hoping to get closer to God. Ronnie had pointed it out to me—a door with an ugly brown mandala painted on it, a place you had to already know about in order to find. He'd once gone in for the experience, not God, just DMT. He said the preacher was "fair," meaning he gave everyone and himself the same amount. Ronnie had taken his hit, which was instant and hard. He floated up to the ceiling. He wanted to come down but it was too late and the preacher and his congregation were haranguing him from below, yelling something at him about Jesus and the true inner light. It was terrifying, he said, really unpleasant, and there was nothing he could do but wait it out up there on the ceiling. "If that's God," Ronnie said, "he's deranged."

Sandro and I passed the ugly mandala of the little DMT church. Beyond it, a group of hippies sat against the chain-link fence of an abandoned lot, drinking beer out of clear forty-ounce bottles.

The impulse to shoot someone in the hand. To hide a gun in your boot. What was it? I felt free of that. Like I could float up to the ceiling, unweighted by the burden of a male ego. I would float on up and not be afraid.

"So that's what we'll do, okay?" Sandro was talking, and I had not been listening.

"Call them as soon as we get back. Because they're Italians and you have to plan things months in advance and deal with tons of bureau-cracy."

I should go ahead and schedule the publicity tour with the Valera team, and he would come along.

I was happy. I had never really considered not going, but Sandro supporting it made everything so much easier, even if his sudden sup-port was about him, the mugging, and had little to do with me.

"You can protect me," he joked, "from Italy. I'll hide behind you. Cling to you in a way that will drive you nuts."

Sandro had a show at Helen's in February and wanted to leave right after. The tour with the Valera team was supposed to begin in March. We could use his mother's country place as a base. I would go to Monza and then other racetracks in northern Italy, and possibly France and Germany. I would make a film about the tour, about my own encounter with speed.

"You can flirt with Didi Bombonato," Sandro said teasingly, and did a play flip of his hair.

I tried broaching the subject with Marvin at work the next day. My hope was that he'd say I could take a leave and come back and be assured of a job. But Marvin heard "Italy" and started off on a story.

"In the summer of 1967," he said, "a friend of mine was working for the company that was going to distribute *Contempt*. He spoke Italian and French, so he was assigned to prepare the subtitles. When the print was ready, this friend invited me to its first showing. There were some funny errors in the subtitles. The *Odyssey* kept coming up 'odious.' Later this same friend did other Godard films, and there were more typos in his subtitles. My favorite was from *La Chinoise*. Hegel came out 'Helga.'"

"Marvin, I want to go to Italy," I said. "For three or four months, probably, enough time to travel with the Valera team. I'm hoping to make a film."

"It's not unusual for subtitles to run off onto the leaders," Marvin continued.

Had he heard me? Was he responding in some coded way?

"Just a few frames from the girl cut into the negative as a calibration tool. You, or some other, there with a bit of accidental subtitle. Helga."

When Eric came back from lunch, I told him I was hoping to go to Italy in the spring. He said it was fine, that I could keep my job as long as I returned by midsummer.

To be in Italy with Sandro and with the Valera team—it would be the grand tour compared to my time as a student in Florence, when I had no money to travel and lived in the walk-in closet of a fruit seller. Marvin gave me sixteen-millimeter film stock at such a discount it was practically free. There would be a demonstration of the *Spirit of Italy* at Monza and they were going to have me drive the car. I had an idea for the film, of filming up close, in dilated view, the poster of Flip Farmer. Going close to his face, scanning his body, the flameproof suit, his arm over the helmet. A meditation on that stilled image, the monstrously white, pure smile. And then intermixing myself. The Valera team. My own driving gloves. My helmet.

"He likes me to beat his ass," Giddle said when I asked how things were going between her and Burdmoore.

We were at Rudy's for the usual experience, as well as a final good-bye before Sandro and I left. It was winter, and dirty snow scuffed the curbs.

"It's hard to imagine," I said. "You're so petite."

"Not beat him up. Literally beat it. With a Ping-Pong paddle."

"Oh."

"He calls me Mama," she said.

"I'm sure."

There was new graffiti in the women's bathroom at Rudy's:

"Whoever talks about love destroys love."

Someone had crossed out "love" and written "Ronnie Fontaine."

"Whoever talks about Ronnie Fontaine destroys Ronnie Fontaine."

The women's bathroom often became unisex late on a drunken night. I wondered if it was Ronnie who was writing this stuff. Messages to himself.

Ronnie showed up and slid into the booth as we were talking about Burdmoore. "Oh, yeah," he said, "that's still on?"

Giddle said she was flattered Ronnie was interested, and yes, it was still "on."

"I'm not that interested," Ronnie said. "I just want to know if you tug on his beard. Apparently Brancusi, when he slept with Peggy Guggenheim, which is more than once, as I understand it, he told her not to touch his beard. It was forbidden. Anything else she could touch. Any body part or tuft. Not the beard."

But Burdmoore had lost the beard, I saw as he made his way toward us through the crowd at Rudy's. He'd lost the stringy locks of red hair, too. He'd cut his hair short and was clean-shaven. I found it hard to understand what he looked like now, because in his smooth face, his cropped hair, I saw only an agreement with Giddle, hair removal in exchange for something, unlimited sex maybe, and not a man who had decided to look a particular way.

Giddle made a toast, and gushed about how fabulous it would be to think of me in a racer's suit, on a track, how thrilling. Also, she said, how necessary it was to spend time in Italy, that it was part of a gamine's coming-of-age, a sort of finishing school, and she became her older-sister self with me as young protégée, which was a role she often played, and she was, in fact, probably ten years older. I had spent almost an entire year in Italy as a student, but I didn't point this out to Giddle. She knew it, or at least I'd told her. She said I should consider coloring my sandy-blond hair red, that Italian women hennaed their hair. Nothing else was fashionable there but dyed red hair. Dyed hair and palazzo pants, she said. We have to get you some palazzo pants.

At some point she mentioned she'd never actually been to Italy. "But I can imagine it," she said. "A place where old women scrub stone steps with a stiff brush and a bucket of soapy water. Where someone is always scrubbing stone steps, a widow in mourning clothes. No one does that in America. Scrubs steps. Wears mourning clothes."

It was late and dark and smoky at Rudy's. The booth had broken into several conversations, Ronnie next to Saul Oppler, who had fully forgiven him for killing his rabbits. Ronnie was looking at Saul's hands. "Saul," he said, "you have no fingerprints." Saul looked at his own hands, old and giant and strong, hands that looked like they could pulverize rocks. He examined his smooth fingerpads and shrugged. He said he *used* his hands. To make paintings. Just worked the prints right off, he said.

Ronnie said he never knew it could be that easy.

"What do you mean, *easy*?" Saul said. "I've been in the studio for forty-eight years. You call that easy?"

"I meant getting rid of your—"

"I didn't get my first solo show until I was thirty-seven years old! Easy. To hell with it," Saul said.

Sandro was at the bar, ordering more drinks. Burdmoore was next to Giddle, mutely watching her with a kind of wonder as she and I spoke. He seemed to feel no need to win her, to make her smitten with him. He just watched her with a steady gaze, like he was already thinking about later, what he and she would do later. I looked up as Sandro appeared with more drinks. Behind him, in the middle of the room, a girl stood alone facing our booth. Young and pale and thin and straw-blond, with a large face, a large head like a child. She stared at Ronnie, who was talking to Saul Oppler and didn't look up, didn't notice her. It was the girl on layaway.

"I'm so excited for your trip," Giddle continued. She gazed into the glass of slivovitz that Sandro passed to her, turning it in her hands.

"I see octogenarian transvestites who are devoutly Catholic and may invite you over for tea," she said. "You'll go, wearing your palazzo pants. We have to get you some at Goodwill." She took a sip of her slivovitz, and then peered back into the glass. "The old trannies will have curious furniture stuffed with horsehair, lace doilies draped over everything to cover the black mold."

She'd known an Italian transvestite, she said, a player of chess and turn-of-the-century German opera recordings who had once told Giddle that every night she dreamed about popes. Popes in pure dazzling white, floating on clouds. And Giddle had asked which pope, *the* pope? Was it Paul VI? And the transvestite became disgusted and said no, certainly not! Not the one in the Vatican. Just *popes*. All in white, she'd said to Giddle, restoring her dreamy reverie. Beautiful popes, floating on clouds. Giddle thought that was really great. "Her vision was not molested by actual power," she said. "It was just men floating on clouds."

The girl on layaway was standing in the middle of the room, facing us.

I wondered if I should say something to Ronnie. I decided not to. If she were ready to alert him to her presence, she would do it herself. Instead, she stared at him with narrowed eyes, training her sadness on him.

Ronnie didn't notice and kept entertaining Saul.

She turned to go. I watched her move toward the exit, taking her sadness with her.

13. THE TREMBLING OF THE LEAVES

said as much about what would happen, according to the Brazilian overseer Valera hired. The overseer said you could not predict. You would not know, by guessing, which of the tappers would come in at quota, which of them would come in under quota, and which of them would die.

Yellow fever, the *patrão* said, they die of yellow fever.

A rubber worker with a .22-caliber hole in his head:

Yellow fever, it's written in the booklet.

Another with a hole in his back:

Yellow fever.

A third with an ice pick pushed through his neck, because the patrão's flimsy muzzle-loader, with its cheap wire-wound barrel, unraveled:

Y.f.

The Valera Company guns the patrão was given were good for fifty shots and then they fell apart. He wrote to the company's contact in São Paulo about the faulty equipment but was told there was nothing to be done about it.

It was important to keep these Indians on edge, so the patrão had to find ways. The Indians needed threats. They needed to be afraid. They might run away. Or sell the rubber to rubber pirates who roamed the edges of the encampment, and then the patrão would lose his profit share. You could hear these bandits, their cracks and rustlings in the jungle. The patrão's job was to keep the Indians in line. His tools were the cheap muzzle-loaders, mock drownings with water poured over a facecloth, and various further entrenchments of the Indians' peon status. They owed a fee for having been brought to the Amazon. They owed for their purchase on credit of goods at the company store. They were forbidden subsistence activities. No collecting Brazil nuts. No growing of crops (anyone caught farming: *y.f.*).

This life, the tapper's, rushing, sweating, exhaustion, waiting. Rushing, sweating, exhaustion. You wait while the patrão inspects your taps to be sure they're clean, inspects your trunk incisions to be sure they're correct (not too shallow and not too deep, in order not to damage the tree's soft part, the cambium, and not circular—rather, you make a half spiral in the trunk, from lower right to upper left, tracing with your gouge the latex tunnels inside the tree). If the patrão is busy, you set down the milk-loaded pails while you wait. If you run with pails full of latex and spill some, you are said to *skedaddle* it. If you carry the latex pails uphill and because of the *titubation of your gait,* you slop some from the pails, you are said to skedaddle it. Slop it from your pail and the day's work, so unmatched to the scale of the body and its limits, is wasted. It isn't just a loss down to zero but below it. You didn't know how low a person could get below zero, down under the roots of it, until you found this life, or it found you.

It is one hour's walk with the heavy slop-promising pails, *sloppossible,* back to the man with the scale. Twice a day you go to the scale, at noon and then again at sunset. At noon, a whole day, a day's life, a reality, has already been lived. Waking at dark, deep down under daylight, hurriedly preparing lunch to eat in the jungle, running to the taps, opening them as quickly as you can. The closer to daybreak the more likely you'll make quota because the trees flow better at dawn.

You have to know which trees to return to (you can't tap the same tree two days in a row), running from tree to tree to get the taps open and by the time every one of them is flowing you race back to the first tap of the morning, the one you opened in total darkness, by feel alone, and you return to get your yield, pour it from the cup at the bottom of the tree into your pail, clean the tap, and get to the next tree. That's how it goes, this zigzagging from tree to tree, coated in sweat and jungle damp, zigzagging until noon, when you are ready to collapse, feeling like your head is in a cloud of ammonia, dizzy, confused, pain shooting up your spine, your muscles twisted into torn rags.

The man who puts your pails on the scale is against you like he was born to hate you in a natural way that won't be corrected with fuller pails, less slopped on their way to the scales. He was lured by good money, easy money. He'd been told proper housing, electricity, hot meals. You carry his water—sloppossible but not measured like the latex is, just eyeballed, and so less calamitous if slopped. He isn't so bad off, not at all, in fact, compared to your life, heat and pain and exhaustion, little sleep on dirt floors under canvas tarps, eating cold food when it rains, because the cooking is all outdoor. He is there to mind you. That is his job, and it is your fault. He frowns with hate, weighs the pails of latex, and puts down a number in the booklet. You don't get paid for the pails. You get a number in his booklet. If the number is under quota you get no credit. If your pail is at quota they say you're breaking even, and you get another number, for the credit, the amount owed against the amount collected, resulting in a handful of stale manioc flour, for which you must have your own bag, or the flour goes straight in your pockets, or, if you have no bag and no pockets, you run toward camp with your fingers sealed together in a bowl, like a hungry, desperate fool, leaving a trail of powdered manioc behind you. If your pail is over quota, you get the flour, and they say you'll get something when the job is finished. Rumor has spread that the booklet is a lie. The job is not going to finish in the sense of an accounting and a payment. Someone says, *Let's burn it.* But then you really won't get paid.

You and the others had made a four-month journey to a living hell and the patrãos knew it. All the way from Belém, where you enlisted. They kept their guns pointed so you would not escape. But you tried. The patrão who stood with the man working the scale was distracted, drinking from his canteen and trying not to look at the long line of men holding their pails, waiting. He sat on a cut log. His muzzle-loader hung from a strap on his shoulder. He closed his eyes and rubbed them. The man who weighed the pails was writing in the booklet. Because the jungle made the pages damp, he had to draw out each pencil line slowly. The pencil didn't like damp. Or the page didn't like it. You, almost at the end of the line, set down your pails and dove into the brush, off the path that led to the scales. Not sticking to your line, off the page like a pencil that would not write.

And then you were running and looking up through the green fringe of tree ferns. Panting and huffing and feeling your throat go cold with shortness of breath, the green fringe pounding above you as you ran.

How was it, the thought entered your mind as you ran, that God could love you and the patrão and the man who weighed the pails, at one time? How was that possible? Your bare feet had gone numb with running. It was important to try to run lightly to keep quiet, but you could not feel your feet, like you were bobbing on two rubber bounce balls instead of feet, deep in a jungle four months' journey from your village. Running on feet you could not feel. Bounce balls. And working with the numbness, pulling your legs up to step lightly, because small cracks and rustlings echo in the jungle. Sound travels cleanly, is made louder as it relays through the spaces among the trees, like through those bullhorns they put on the trucks on Sundays to get everyone herded into church, back in your village, which seems not so bad a life now, drought and God and stomachaches from unripe fruit. There was nothing to do but at least there was time. Now you are short on time and running. Weaving among the trees. The trees, thick and strong and sturdy, blocking out the sunlight, but themselves reaching up to it. If you step on a branch by accident the trees give away your secrets. Crack-*crack*, the sound of you sent back through the jungle to the patrão. The trees, reaching up to the light they blocked, were not part of God's matrix. They went from their roots to the sky without any part in heavens and hells. The trees just were, and they relayed your secrets if you stepped on a dry branch while trying to escape. Not because they wanted you caught, but because of sound, and the way it traveled. They were no part in God's matrix. They were the wood His Son was nailed to. That was all. They would not suffer like you did, wondering if God loved you and the patrão at one time. You and the man who weighed the pails. Wondering if God could hate. If He could love. If He could not hate, like the priest said, well, then. He couldn't love, either. And what help could He offer now? He was as good as the trees (no help at all).

Runaway logic: if you run in the night and sleep by day, you might make it to the river and build yourself a raft. Or you run with no plan but the slim moment, the patrão's back turned.

Most runaways were caught. The ones who weren't died alone, among animals, watched by those huge trees that weren't in God's matrix. If the Earth is something whole, its wholeness is of no comfort. Some suffer. Others don't. What is God's harmony? That you have a gun pointed at you, and the patrão is aiming it. By the laws of harmony, you cannot both have guns.

The green tree ferns pound into and out of view, branches scrape you, your feet are numb. You trip, you fall, you get up, you keep running.

14. The Rules of Violence

We were in low chairs around an outdoor fireplace as dusk settled over the villa, the light tinted pink and made hazy with woodsmoke. Lake Como, far down below us, was a spill of silver. The men were elegantly dressed, in crisply tailored suits and buttery-looking Italian loafers, probably just the kind that Ronnie had coveted when he was driving Saul Oppler's E-type Jaguar down to Texas with a load of dead rabbits.

There was the gravelly throated Count of Bolzano, a little man whose round belly pressed against his mint-green shirt, which was monogrammed on the lower left, over his spleen. He was an old friend of Sandro's mother's. On my other side was a man named Luigi, an industrial designer who peered at me through large, square eyeglasses, looking like a character from a Fellini film. And lastly Sandro's brother, Roberto, who was as unfriendly as Sandro had warned he would be. Roberto lived down the road from the family villa in a recently built glass-and-steel house. Sandro and I had visited him there two days earlier, on the afternoon we'd arrived in Bellagio. We'd walked down the little road, cicadas surging from the green underbrush that banked the narrow lane. Sandro held my hand, and I'd felt light and strange, partly from jet lag, but the feeling opened me to this soft, lush place, where everything was so carefully tended.

Roberto had greeted us in his weekend clothes, new designer jeans and a double-breasted blazer, his manner as stiff and guarded as his clothes. I tried to thank him in the awkward moments of our introduction for the Moto Valera I'd gotten from the Reno dealership. At first he seemed to have no idea what I was referring to. Then he remembered and said, "But you crashed it," and turned to address Sandro about something else before I could respond. Sandro had tried to apologize for him afterward, explaining that Roberto was in a tough position. There was massive upheaval at the Valera plants and though Roberto had worked out deals with the trade union, the workers were now rejecting their own union and striking anyway. Good for them, I thought, and anyway it didn't excuse his brother from being rude.

Tiny orange lights were beginning to twinkle on the lake's darkening shore, the lights mirrored in the water, the hills above them spreading out in reverse. The villa was at the top of a steep incline, just a fifteen-minute drive from the lakeside promenade of Bellagio proper, with its double-parked Lamborghinis and its women in furs. Its regal-looking car ferries, which arrived from Varenna, across the sparkling water. And along the waterfront, its white tablecloths, cold prosecco, rich and subdued families gazing off. But in that fifteen minutes traveling uphill from the lakefront to the Villa Valera, one left that world behind, passed horses and cows grazing lazily, handwritten signs advertising farm-made honey and yogurt, and roads choked with blackberry and young chestnut trees.

This was a different Italy from what I had experienced during my two semesters in Florence, hanging out with Italian bikers in a bar near the train station. The Valera villa was of such a grand scale it suggested a life that was more like I'd seen depicted in paintings at the Uffizi than on the narrow and chaotic streets of Florence. The villa was nestled in the high wilds above Bellagio, but its grounds, on a broad, flat promontory overlooking the lake, were landscaped and formal, all geometric lines and classical motifs. The iron entrance gates were abutted on either side by tall cypress trees, their tips ending in perfect points like obelisks. The long private drive up to the villa was lined with more cypress, and classical statues, nymphs and satyrs, pieces of roman ruins or what looked like them, and huge urns engraved with cryptic Latin phrases. On the flat expanse at the top was a vast carpet of green grass bordered by color-shifting beds of rhododendrons. Various patios and arbors were covered by trellises of grape and climbing roses, and underneath, marble furniture and patio swings with striped seat cushions. Sandro said his mother had done all this landscaping, brought in the classical statues and ruins and urns after his father died, that old Valera had loathed this sort of thing.

A warm wind rustled through the pines that bordered our view of the lake, their tender green pinecones bouncing up and down as the limbs moved. Above the hearth around which these men and I gathered was a statue of Pan playing his flute. Something about his posture, the way he lifted the pipes to his mouth, made him look as if he were wetting the glue on a Zig-Zag in order to seal a joint.

"Of course you should recognize Luigi's name," Roberto said as he introduced me to the others, "he's the most famous industrial designer in Italy."

"Yes, I should—"

"If you *haven't* heard of him, you might wonder what they taught you in art school," Roberto said.

"So you're from the West," Luigi said to me, the firelight bouncing from his eyeglasses. His tone was kinder than Roberto's, although I didn't sense in it that he was offering himself as an ally. "I have a few friends out in Hollywood," he said. "I try to make it there once a year or so. A strange place, but magical in its way. I take a mud bath at the Bel-Air Hotel."

All I knew of Hollywood was Marvin mutilating Paramount films with meat cleavers, Nadine inhaling Freon from old refrigerators. Having been to a fake McDonald's in the City of Industry didn't seem like it would count. I said I was from Reno, Nevada.

"The real West, in other words," Luigi said. "Ranchers. Drifters. Divorcées. A poetic dignity there."

"You've been to Reno?"

"No, no," he said, as if I had misunderstood. "I saw *The Misfits*. And I have a wonderful book of photographs by Bob Avery. Do you know it?"

The Count of Bolzano turned to Luigi and told him that I was into car racing. That I was going to be doing something with Didi Bombonato. Hearing the Count of Bolzano speak of the publicity tour to Luigi, it sounded like a silly novelty, something kitsch.

"Ah, there you are." It was Sandro's mother, coming toward us in the dim light.

Her voice was friendlier, softer than I expected, from the interactions I'd had with her so far. I realized she was looking at the Count of Bolzano. The "you" was he, the softness for him. She had been at a beauty salon in Bellagio in the afternoon, and I could see that her hair was sprung a bit too tightly. She wore a long, brocaded tunic like something purchased from a Turkish bazaar, with espadrilles whose constricting ties crisscrossed up her ankles, as if the ribbons were meant to compensate for the swollen and blotchy appearance of her old legs. She seated herself, touching the curls that clung to her scalp like Mongolian lamb's wool. It was obvious she had been beautiful when she was young, with eyes that were the splendid gold-green of muscat grapes. She was in her seventies now, her complexion like wet flour, clammy and pale, with the exception of her nose, which had a curiously dark cast to it, a shadow of black under the thin tarp of skin, as if her nose had trapped the toxins from a lifetime of rich food and heavy wines. Her French bulldog, Gorgonzola, scampered after her and plopped itself at her feet, licking its tummy, its body in the shape of an egg cup, and whimpering the way little dogs did, with needs that could not be met simply, with food and company, which was all that larger dogs seemed to need. Actually this was Gorgonzola II, the Count of Bolzano said as I addressed the dog. Gorgonzola I, the Count of Bolzano told me, was buried near the swimming pavilion, in the family plot.

Sandro had shown me his father's headstone. T. P. VALERA, ARDITO,

FUTURISTA, PADRE, MARITO. He'd died in 1958, just after work was begun on his dream project, the Autostrada del Sole. He'd been through two wars, had been a member of the Fascist Party, and had risen from the ashes of that disastrous era to become a huge postwar success. Ardent or not, he was buried next to Gorgonzola the First, who, I saw the next morning when we were down at the swimming pool, had a pink marble headstone that was as grand and ornate as T. P. Valera's.

There was a toast all around the fireplace with what the Count of Bolzano commented was a very good Trentino wine, which solicited from signora Valera a lament about how it had been difficult recently to locate Trentino wine, and about all that was wrong with the situations in which one found oneself, where people didn't know about it or about the best Nebbiolos, such as Barbaresco and Barolo. I understood most of what she said, but she spoke quickly and her words were punctuated by the echoed pock-pocking from the battle that was taking place under the huge sycamore tree down the lawn, where Sandro and the old American novelist were slamming a Ping-Pong ball back and forth. The old novelist had arrived that morning. "Chesil Jones," he'd said, and extended his hand to me, "but you can call me Chevalier." Sandro's mother had held a pretend bugle to her lips and then they both laughed. Was I really to call him Chevalier? I was getting used to proceeding without answers, unsure if I was the butt of jokes.

I could hear the old chevalier grunting and heaving as he leaped to whack the little ball. Sandro was going to defeat him at Ping-Pong, and Chesil Jones had decided to make Sandro's win as difficult as he could. I'm better at Ping-Pong than Sandro. At least I've beaten him at it. And yet I was left to discuss Trentino wine, which I knew nothing about, while Sandro played my game.

"She looks lovely," signora Valera said, and looked me up and down.

"Yes, she does," Luigi said, glancing at me. Not in a salacious way, more as if he was taking inventory of what I had on, in the same way she had. These people cared about clothing and appearance. I understood this was a cliché of the Milanesi, but it also was true. In Milan, it had bordered to me on comedy, women riding bicycles through a downpour in platform heels and tight skirts, holding huge black umbrellas. Florence had been similar, except that the women in Milan seemed more like women in New York—hard and professional, exuding capability. Also, in Florence they dressed well but all women dressed alike, in minor variations on the same theme, and I'd had the feeling they owned only one or two outfits and wore them every day. While we were in Milan, strolling the Corso Buenos Aires, Sandro had stopped in front of a shopwindow and pointed to a dress of pinkish-beige velvet. He said it would look good with my hair, and began carefully brushing my hair away from my neck and looking at me and at the dress. "Why don't you try it," he said. It was a very expensive-looking boutique, Luisa Spagnoli. I had wondered if he was momentarily confused about women, about what they want or think they want. I said it was beautiful but seemed formal for a stay in the country, a place he had told me so much about, the meadows and muddy streams and hiking. He said his mother liked everyone to "dress" for dinner. It was an old-fashioned rule, he admitted, but perhaps I could just try it on. In New York Sandro would never submit to a social rule of how anyone should dress. But we were not in New York anymore. We went in. A salesgirl fetched the correct size. The fine silk velvet fell in a lovely way, as only very expensive cloth, cut correctly, does. And it did look good, the rose-beige making my dirty-blond hair more honey in shade, closer to that of the dress. Now I was in it, sleeves to the elbow and little velvet-covered buttons that fastened there.

"You look lovely as well," I said to Sandro's mother, unsure if I were meant to respond to the compliment, since she had referred to me in the third person.

"Me?" she asked in a surprised tone. "I am hardly dressed up. This is what I normally wear. You've made an occasion of it, I can see that."

"The dress was a gift from Sandro."

She turned to the Count of Bolzano. "But of course it was a gift from Sandro," she said to him. "A last-minute refurbishment before he brought her here." She had forgotten, once again, that I understood

Italian, although she only seemed to forget, and to say something cruel, when Sandro was not around.

My eyes had begun to tear from the cruelty of her remark. The man who maintained the grounds was putting more wood on our fire. I focused on him, on his hands, the wood, the flames, and the strange phrase chiseled into the flagstone above the hearth: FAC UT ARDEAT. "Made to burn," the old novelist later told me. The wood popped as it caught fire. I gazed into the flames and told myself not to say anything, not to be angry. The groundskeeper silently arranged the logs with an iron poker and then he turned and looked at me. I looked away but could feel his stare. In the two days we had been at the villa I'd caught him staring at Sandro and me several times, not in a friendly way. There was something about his gaze, an intensity, that made me nervous. The entire staff of the villa seemed to harbor a kind of collective hostility toward us. At first I thought it was due to their resentment of Sandro's mother. But the reason was actually the opposite. We were not deserving of the same treatment as the lady of the villa, to whom they were deeply loyal. We were in some sense freeloaders, especially me, an unpedigreed American they were meant to serve as if I were a Valera, when they knew that I was nothing of the kind.

The cook set out a cutting board loaded with various cheeses, tall, soft wedges that listed this way and that. Did you use the cheese knife to spread what you cut onto your cracker, or were you meant to deposit a dollop onto one of the little plates, and use some other knife to spread? I hadn't eaten all day, because Sandro and I had gone on a long hike and we had forgotten to bring the picnic lunch the cook had prepared for us, but I was afraid the cook would reprimand me if I went about serving myself the wrong way. With the encouragement of the Count of Bolzano, I helped myself to the cheese. I used the common knife to spread it on the crackers. I thought of something Ronnie had said, that rich people didn't follow the letter of the law. Only strivers did that, Ronnie said. Doggedly following rules emphasized that one did not belong, according to Ronnie. It sounded right. Although there was *some* way of following them, while not submitting to them, but it required a mysterious touch, and you had to be from that class to possess the special touch. Like me in that Luisa Spagnoli dress. Even it was beautiful, and such a flattering cut: by wearing it I was submitting. "You've made an occasion of it." While Roberto and Luigi and the Count of Bolzano were not dogged in their finery, but natural. And what did the dress have to do with me? Nothing, while the clothes of these men had everything to do with them.

Signora Valera asked if our room was suitable for me.

"Yes, certainly," I said. She had already asked me this question two or three times.

"You're in the company of Ettore Valera," she said, "Sandro's grandfather."

I said yes, and that Sandro had explained this to me.

"It was commissioned," she went on as if I had not spoken, "by King Fuad of Egypt, in appreciation of Ettore's work on the Suez Canal. *King Fuad whispered*," she said, suddenly whispering hoarsely herself, "because he had a hole in his neck. From a bullet. My husband remembered that very clearly, from when he was a boy. The way the king whispered."

They had once gone back to Egypt together, she and Sandro's father, T. P. Valera, but all signora Valera could recollect of it now, she said, was the overwhelming stench of urine in the tombs and temples at Luxor. They were there to visit her husband's mother, Ettore's wife, who was living back in Alexandria, having fled Italy in protest when the king was dethroned at the end of the war. "She was a monarchist," signora Valera said, "and now I can't say that her view seems unreasonable, though yelling, 'Save the king,' from the window of a Rolls-Royce probably wouldn't go over well now, either. What a mess things were. Actually my husband made a lot of money, but you couldn't *buy* much. We were eating cold polenta while my mother-in-law lay stretched out in her African compound, Negroes around her holding torches. That's another thing my husband loved to tell about Egypt, the way electric lamps were for those who could not afford a full staff. If you could afford it, you had Negroes with torches, not lamps, not electricity."

After Egypt, there was talk of other relatives, an uncle of T. P.

Valera's who had kept a bear as a pet, which one afternoon mauled him viciously, leading to this uncle's morphine addiction and eventual death. Another relative of some kind who slipped on wet tile and fell into a sulfur bath in Lourdes, the bath having been accidentally heated to boiling. Someone else who was killed in Capri, when picnickers dropped a canned ham from a high cliff to the beach below, rather than carrying the thing down a switchback trail. A cousin who went to sub-Saharan Africa and was bitten by a tsetse fly and got elephantiasis in his buttocks. He'd had to purchase special-order trousers with a gigantic seat, Sandro's mother said, and he slept with a platform extension at the side of the bed, to support his ass.

She narrated all of this with no hint of irony, but she must have known it was funny. I smiled at her.

She looked at me coldly. "You're amused only because you're American," she said, "where people die of old age, or in car accidents." She turned to the Count of Bolzano. "They don't *have* histories there. They barely know what history is!"

Again I stared at the fire, as if to hypnotize myself and melt her words to nothing. *Fac ut ardeat.* I could hear the little Ping-Pong ball being knocked and slapped back and forth in the near dark down the lawn. The edges of the lake below us glittered. The moon, white and full, was rising over the olive grove beyond the patio, twisted little trees spaced apart in such a way that they looked like dancers on a dark stage, each holding its pose, waiting for the music to commence.

When Sandro had suggested a hike that morning, I'd jumped at the idea of leaving the villa for the day. I was feeling stifled inside its walls, ancient and clammy and six feet thick. For keeping out intruders when it was built, in the seventeenth century. Some kind of lord had lived there and the pleasures of it—those shaggy, towering pines, their branches sweeping the dense carpet of grass, their huge pistachio-colored pinecones, and the acacia, which were covered with blooms, little white bells bobbling against the windows where Sandro and I slept, green leaves pressing the glass like decoupage—all this beauty led me back to a sense of cruelty, to the people kept out, and those kept in, in the kitchen, the washing shed, the servants' little stone cottages. As a guest, you weren't allowed to do anything for yourself. Our first morning, we waited for the maid to bring us coffee on a silver tray, with a basket of chewy, coarse bread I assumed was baked somewhere on the property, probably in an elaborate outdoor oven and by a method peasants had developed over hundreds of years. The breakfast room was sunny and beautiful, but I could not relax the way Sandro did, casually flipping through his *Corriere della Sera* as though it were normal to wait in your own house for a servant in uniform not just to bring your coffee but also to pour it. Sandro seemed unable, or unwilling, to acknowledge how different this place was. Servants pour the coffee and you act like that's normal, I thought at him, but all he did was rustle his pages, his posture asking or instructing that I not acknowledge the change, or his comfort and familiarity with this alien place, where it was typical to hear no people but to understand that they were everywhere, watching you eat, waiting for the moment you might put down your cup, in order to appear suddenly and refill it. There was always someone nearby, the strange groundskeeper, or a maid or cook or some other household employee quietly moving about. There was one servant, a woman who wore a huge wig of grayish-lavender curls that seemed like a practical joke, whose only purpose that I could detect was to cut flowers from the garden, make little arrangements and place them here and there, and then to scurry around managing these arrangements, clearing away dispensed petals and replacing drooping flowers. She and the others moved through rooms with no hesitation, whether they were occupied or not. They didn't knock, or announce themselves, but instead, in their noiseless corduroy servants' slippers, they acted invisible, meant to dust or replace dead blooms as if they themselves were of no consequence to the privacy of others. I asked Sandro about this, after the woman in the lavender wig came into the bathroom while I was bathing. She had begun stocking a cabinet with soaps and toilet tissue and never once looked at me. "They're used to people," he said.

"They're domestics. It's not a big deal." Later I realized they weren't a big deal to Sandro because he didn't register their presence as judgment. Only I did, which, as his mother might have pointed out, was a problem of class, of being from the wrong one, too low for a servant to feel I was an appropriate object of their attentions, for their flower arrangements and ironed sheets, and that was my problem, not hers or her servants', and she was probably right. It was my problem. The groundskeeper was the one who unnerved me most. He said nothing as he went about his business, up on a ladder, pruning the wisteria that wrapped up and around the cypress trees, or fumigating a wasps' nest. He watched us and glowered, while the others didn't look at us at all. He would stare at me, a certain wryness in his face that I couldn't decipher. I might have stared back had he not been handsome. He was, if in a plain and obvious way, and it was that—his looks—that unnerved me, made me look away whenever we crossed paths.

This morning, our second one in the villa, Sandro had slept late and I'd gone to breakfast alone. Signora Valera was there at the table, but it was too late to turn back. We drank our espresso in silence, or what I hoped would remain so, until she asked if I was going to marry her son. Because, she said, she had not been informed of a wedding.

"We're not getting married, no."

"So what are your plans?" she asked. "I mean, for when you are no longer together. If he has not asked you to marry him, it's temporary. A temporary arrangement."

"I don't have any plans," I said.

There is a certain type of older woman who pretends to be doddering and meek when in fact old age has made her strong and vicious, but signora Valera was not that type. She did not pretend to be meek.

On our hike, Sandro and I lay in a sun-dappled patch of wild chamomile, resting and gazing up at the sky framed in branches. We ended up entwined, his jeans unbuttoned, mine down around my knees. A kind of urgency was what he liked, and making love in a field, in various sorts of public places, was something Sandro was into. It made the act that much more thrilling and directed. But it had been my idea this time, my cue. The villa was so oppressive, and his mother made me feel so minimized that I had not really wanted to make love to Sandro inside its walls. When I had returned from her breakfast assault, Sandro had grabbed me and I'd said no and pushed him away, his mother's voice in my head, as if submitting to him were submitting to her idea of my disposable status. Here, I felt a bit more free and probably I thought screwing her son in a clearing in the woods was a way to defend myself, my autonomy, from her judgments. I looked from the sky, the breath of blue that opened above the crosshatch of chestnut trees, to Sandro, in whose face I detected an apology.

He picked crushed little chamomile flowers out of my hair as we continued our hike, and pointed out a matted place among the underbrush where a wolf had slept. We stopped and looked together at the indentation that was the wolf's bed. There was something tender in seeing where a wild animal slept, the choices it made to seek softness, and I felt a twinge of envy for that wolf, its self-preservation, its solitude. We came out of the woods on a rise above the *limonaia* that had been planted when Sandro was born. He laughed and said it was an absurdity for the region and that each tree had to be individually wrapped in burlap for the winter season. He put his arms around me as we gazed from our rise over the tops of the lemon trees below us, which had taken root when Sandro had, experienced the same amount of lived time. *This is also me,* I felt him say, *you have to understand that it's also me.* I leaned back, into him. *I love this also-you.* Even if his mother intimidated me and meant to, and even if their house, if you could call such a place, thirty rooms, a house, was not the least bit inviting. There in the woods, his cashmere scarf wrapped around my neck for extra warmth, I felt like everything was going to be okay. I was with Sandro. It didn't matter if his mother, when we were introduced, had smiled in a strained way as if I were a disappointment. Or that she had laughed when Sandro told her I spoke Italian, and insisted on speaking to me in English or what she thought was English but was a strange hybrid language that sounded more like German. No matter. In a week his mother would return to Milan and we'd have the villa to ourselves.

Soon after, I'd go to Monza. Sandro had said he wanted to come, and for once, he would be tagging along with me, and not the reverse. In the meantime he would be the bridge between me and this odd place, and maybe at some point we could laugh about it together.

Laugh about his mother? How foolish I must have been.

By the time we were returning along the road, in view of the high, stone wall of the villa, flowerless vines spilling over it like concertina wire, I felt relaxed and happy in a way I had not since we'd arrived. San-dro had suggested we use the garden gates and not the main entrance, and we had passed the groundskeeper's little stone cottage and strolled among the olive trees holding hands, Sandro as my protector from this world of rooms and servants and customs, fortifying me against it as he guided me into it.

It was very cold in the dining room, almost colder than it had been outside. Later I came to recognize the particular cheapness of the very rich. Sandro's mother was not concerned with saving money. Rather, she seemed to enjoy creating conditions that were slightly less than hospitable, even a little hostile, with rooms that were fifty-five degrees Fahrenheit. And despite all the talk of the diminishing elite of people who knew (or *knew* to *know*) about the right Nebbiolos, wine in a box was mostly what we drank. We would see the same bread at dinner that we'd passed over at breakfast, stale and hard then, in the morn-ing, and by dinnertime tooth-breaking. I thought of Ronnie's discourse on bread. Ronnie was amused that you could find only whole-grain breads now in New York's gourmet markets. Not that Ronnie shopped in gourmet markets, but one had opened in SoHo and he perused the aisles to fuel his running commentaries. He said it was an irony that people had decided collectively that whole grains were more desirable than white bread, which, for centuries, had been the bread of the gentry. "Everything's like this," he said. Refinement followed a certain course and reverse course. In this case, the literal refining of flour, until super-refined white bread, light and fluffy like only kings and queens had once been able to obtain, was widely available, and so rich people had to go back to eating the crude whole-grain breads they used to leave only for peasants. Now no educated person would be caught dead eating white bread. Not even a middle-class person. Sandro was always amused by these rants of Ronnie's, but here at the villa every custom was normal to him. He ate the stale brown bread and said nothing about it.

Eventually a servant came and started a fire in the dining room hearth and the room warmed up, but a haze of suffocating smoke hung over the table, a mesh of white tangles that thickened as dinner dragged on, making it difficult to breathe. On the ceiling above us was a fresco of Lake Como. In the lake, a circle of popes or maybe bishops in white gossamer robes. The fabric of their robes hung down below them like tendrils as these religious clerics treaded water. They were jellyfish popes, not unlike the lonely transvestite's popes floating on clouds, pure and pristine goodness. Or perhaps these men were the mirror image of that: they didn't seem like they could help anyone, occupied as they were with trying not to drown. As a servant came around to refill our glasses, the old novelist Chesil Jones, who was seated at my left, leaned toward me and said he used to be a drinker but had given up booze. His breath reeked of alcohol. He and I were behind an enormous branched candlestick that blocked my view of Sandro. I asked the old novelist about his books. He narrowed his eyes at me as if I had insulted him. "You'd like to discuss the most recent, wouldn't you? *The Sole of a Whore* was what I originally called it—not her spirit but the bottom of her shoe. And what do they come up with? *Mrs. Dollface,* for godsakes. If you want to revisit the idiotic responses *Mrs. Dollface* has gotten, we can do that."

I said I was simply curious about what sorts of things he wrote.

"Oh. Why of course, yes," he said, suddenly solicitous, realizing that I was not a hostile critic. "There is a small library. I can have them brought to your room. The ones you should start with, in any case."

Beyond the huge candelabra, the subject of tragic or tragicomic death continued, not that of a relative in Egypt but of an Italian industrialist or the heir of one, who instead of amassing more riches had spent his family's money publishing pro-Soviet literature and support-ing underground groups that wanted to overthrow the government. The man's name was Feltrinelli—like the chain of well-known bookstores. I remembered them from my time in Florence, but had no idea that Fel-trinelli had been electrocuted, as the Count of Bolzano explained it, trying to sabotage Milan's power supply. He was found dead under a pylon. It had happened five years earlier. I got the feeling these people had discussed it plenty but because of its mysterious circumstances weren't ready to give up the subject. It wasn't clear if his death had been an accident, a suicide, or if he'd been murdered. Roberto said it didn't matter *how* it happened, that Feltrinelli's death had been a resounding defeat for the Communists and a victory for anyone who felt it was a mistake for party boys to hemorrhage money to radical causes.

"He was a semiretard, even if he published Pasternak," Chesil Jones said. "Semiretarded. He got his negative and positive leads mixed up."

Sandro said that was nonsense and that Feltrinelli wasn't stupid. What happened had been a terrible tragedy.

"Have it how you want," Roberto said. "I find him to have been a clown. You find him to have been tragic. Either way he's dead, and that in itself is neither tragic nor clownish, it simply is. He asked for trouble and found it. What was he doing, for godsakes, on a pylon?"

"He didn't know negative from positive," the old novelist said, and put his hands together as if holding two leads, then shook like he was being electrocuted.

"So it's of no consequence," Sandro said to Roberto, "whether he died by accident or was murdered."

Roberto shrugged. "He was a problem. To business. To Italy. To the entire Ministry of the Interior. Not to mention the CIA. A lot of people wanted him dead. And then he managed to die on his own. Anyhow, who grieved over the death of Giangiacomo Feltrinelli?"

"Roberto, eight thousand people were at his funeral," Sandro said. "It was in the *New York Post*. And his death helped nothing. If he was killed, whoever killed him can count themselves responsible, at least in part, for the violence since."

"What do you know about the violence since, Sandro?" Roberto said. "You've been in New York making metal boxes, going to cock-tail parties, or whatever it is you do, while Mama and I get phone calls about the latest round of sabotage, the latest work stoppage, the most recent supervisor to be killed. Are you aware of the problems?"

"I'm saying martyrs give cause. They create sympathy. But you're right, I don't get those phone calls. I take my inheritance and give noth-ing back. I have never denied that. I think I'll stick to what I know."

"What subject is that, Sandro?" his mother asked.

"Metal boxes, Mama."

"I thought you were going to say American girls," she said, not look-ing at me. "How many have we met, at this point?"

Chesil Jones put his two hands together again and shook erratically.

I felt like hurting this old woman, and I believe she knew it, and that she felt, in reaction, both afraid of my anger and also morally defended against it, against such crude low-class aggression. I never asked about Sandro's previous girlfriends. He teased me about that, wanted to know why I didn't ask, which made me sure it was wise not to. Or at least sure that it bothered him that I didn't, because he wanted to make me jeal-ous, and so I gave him no opening.

Sandro told her to stop acting rude and then they were arguing, speaking very quickly, and I could no longer follow. It was either about me or about some general failing on Sandro's part.

Chesil Jones leaned toward me. "Just ignore it. She's . . . what can I say? I'm fond of her. Quite fond of her, actually. But late tonight, after the staff retires? She'll be bent over the open refrigerator, count-ing slices of ham to be sure the servants haven't taken more than their allotment. She's tortured, bless her. Anyway, I can appreciate you. I can tell you're good folk," he said, nudging me and laughing. "I've been to Reno, by the way. I wasn't looking at a fucking Bob Avery book like Luigi won't shut up about. I skied Mount Rose."

"My ski team trained there," I said, assuming Sandro must have told him I'd been a ski racer. "It's a place I know so well."

"Did a bit of racing myself," he said. "Nothing major. A sort of subpro league. Nastar, it's called. Actually rather competitive. I have a bronze medal someplace, knocking around in a box of ribbons and whatnot, from various hobbies of mine. I did retain something of a feel for the slalom course. The motion of it. It's in the knees, like this, see. A bit in the hips as well." He swiveled back and forth in his chair, holding out his hands as if gripping ski poles.

"Women have a tough time learning to ski," he said. "They don't have the mind for the physics of it. But they can learn by feel. I've been a pretty good instructor, I've got good form, a perfect stem Christie. Though my last wife got up to the top of the mountain, we were in Chamonix. 'Sham-o-nicks,' the nitwit kept calling it. 'Sham-o-nicks.' We took the cable car up and at the top, we're ready to go, boots laced, skis strapped on, and she just freezes, stiff as a corpse."

Sandro and his mother had finished arguing. Chesil Jones had everyone's attention. Noticing this, he cleared his throat, and his delivery changed, became magisterial, as if he were duty-bound to part with some of his profound and cloistered knowledge, for our benefit.

"The thing about skiing is that it's suited to men. Partly because it's a great metaphor for other endeavors. Endeavors of the mind. Martin Heidegger was a skier, did you know? The little hut in Todtnauberg where he wrote was right next to the chairlift. Legend has it that he gave his seminar at Freiburg directly from the slopes, going on about the being for whom being is a question while wearing a parka and boot gators. As a young man, I had a wonderful writing teacher who was a terrific skier. I'll never forget my first class with him. This was in Hanover, New Hampshire, dead of winter. 'Your assignment,' he says, 'each one of you boys, is to drink a case of beer and ski yourself off a cliff.' He wanted us to *feel* the terror. Not of the cold, of the speed, but of our talent. Just . . . do with it what you must. What you will. With my own students, I—"

"Why didn't you say anything to that bastard?" Sandro asked me later that night as he dove playfully under the covers and grabbed me with his cold hands. There'd been a giant moth in our room, which he'd successfully shooed out a window. He didn't care about moths. He did it for me. I was the only American girl here, I reminded myself as he chased it around our room in his underwear. The only one.

"You were a racer, for Christ's sake," he said, shivering under the duvet, his arms around me. "And he's instructing you on the basics. 'Ribbons and medals from my hobbies.' What a moron."

Sandro didn't understand why I let this old man go on at length as if I'd never been on skis, but my experience had nothing to do with Chesil Jones. It wouldn't have interested him one bit. He didn't bring up skiing to have a conversation, but to lecture and instruct. I'd seen right away he was the type of person who grows deadly bored if disrupted from his plan to talk about himself, and I had no desire to waste my time and energy forcing on him what he would only will away in yawns and distracted looks. And anyhow Chesil Jones probably hadn't skied in the twenty years since the stem Christie had been a popular technique. What was I to say, we make parallel turns now? The boots have buckles instead of laces? The bindings are quick-release?

After dinner, we retired to the living room. While his mother sneaked off to bed, Sandro put records on the old German phonograph, and more wine was poured. We listened to Stravinsky, harsh but stirring strings, sounds that were like stiff brushes dipped in paint and used to make a geometry of lines in stark black. Signora Valera must have then switched on the television in her room upstairs, because over the strings we heard distortedly loud voices interspersed with a laugh track. Wealthy Italian or Reno pensioner, it didn't matter, she was like any old person with her TV too loud.

Roberto had gone home. Sandro told me Roberto's wake time was four thirty a.m. It was one of the reasons his wife stayed in Milan when Roberto came to Bellagio. She couldn't take his schedule, Sandro said. It was difficult to imagine that Roberto even had a wife, that he would be interested in women, he was so austere and clean and rigid.

There were catalogues of Sandro's work on the coffee table, and the industrial designer Luigi began flipping through them, looking at Sandro's spare, aluminum sculptures. Sandro had whispered to me, in a moment alone in the hall, that Luigi also was a soft-core pornographer with a foot and leg fetish, and sold that work in editions of very limited print runs that cost thousands of dollars.

"I am stumped," Luigi said when he'd looked at every image in the two thick catalogues. "I just don't get it."

Sandro was used to this. Minimalism is a language, and even having gone to art school, I barely spoke it myself. I knew the basic idea, that the objects were not meant to refer to anything but what they were, there in the room. Except that this was not really true, because they referred to a discourse that artists such as Sandro wrote long essays about, and if you didn't know the discourse, you couldn't take them for what they were, or were meant to be. You were simply confused.

"I'm going to just come out and ask you, Sandro," Luigi said, "since I cannot infer from the work alone: Are you an ass man or a leg man? Which is it?"

I could tell from Sandro's slow, quaking smile that this would be immediately assimilated as a favorite story. There needn't be an answer. There need only be the story itself, archived in the asking. Although later that night, after the matter of shooing out the moth and diving under the covers, Sandro declared that he was both an ass and a leg man, a breast man, also. Interested in knees, the lower back, the neck, the little place where the collarbones meet. The mouth. "Your mouth," he said, pressing his fingertips to my lips. Sandro said it was limited to think in terms of such *metonymy*. Didier's word, plucked like a ghost from our life in New York.

The next day was quiet and serene and unseasonably warm. The groundskeeper had cleaned out the swimming pool at signora Valera's request, because Sandro loved to swim. He'd heated it to eighty degrees, and with the air about seventy, steam rose from the water's surface in periodic light drifts, ghostly apparitions veiled in gauze. Chesil Jones was already down at the pool when Sandro and I arrived. He was lying on the stones next to the edge, nude except for a hand towel that was folded into a small square and balanced over his privates, his eyes closed as though he were encased in a tomb of sunlight. Sandro flashed me a look of amusement and tugged me toward the open pavilion next to the pool, a raised platform with couches. He picked me up and tossed me into a pile of throw pillows on the couch. When I giggled a bit too loudly, the old novelist sat up and glanced at us, squinting against the sun and holding his inadequate hand towel over his crotch like a tiny curtain. He began gathering his things. Leaving the young to their privacy, I felt him think. Although Sandro wasn't all that young, which made his departure a generosity. The young drive out the old. He was leaving by choice. But before doing so, he stood in front of the pavilion, preparing, I sensed, to deliver one of his minor speeches.

"A splendid aspect," he said to me, "the swimming pool. Wonderful that you're getting the opportunity to use it. Notice the patio stones. That was Alba's idea. *La signora,* I mean, ha-ha. The stones are actually for grinding polenta. They're the tools of a peasant's existence, a peasant's meager fare, bland mush you cook in a copper pot. A few years ago she and I were rambling around the hills above Argegno and she saw a stack of them next to a quarry and asked this fellow if she could buy an entire lot, to make a patio. It's very original, and quite funny in a way, a patio of stones that give the swimming pool its elegance, place it so beautifully in its wild setting, and yet their rough-hewn softness is from thousands of hours of peasants toiling away. In any case, enjoy."

"Thank God," Sandro said, watching him make his way up the path toward the house.

I assumed he and Sandro's mother were lovers, but sensed this would be a taboo subject with Sandro, who rolled his eyes at Chesil Jones and didn't say anything more than that he was a blowhard.

When he had disappeared up the path, Sandro pulled me toward him. He wanted to fool around there, in the pool house, but I was nervous about it.

"What about the groundskeeper?" I said. He had been skimming the last few leaves from the pool's surface when we arrived. Perhaps he was still lurking around.

"Oh, he's really going to object," Sandro said. "Maybe he's watching us right now. Let's give him a show."

"No."

"Well, then we'll have to be discreet," he said softly, staring at me, his fingers grazing the back of my knee.

"I'll just help you out," he whispered, and pulled me down onto his lap, working the zipper of my jeans, fitting his hand into my underwear. *"And no one will know. I promise. Not even your groundskeeper."*

Sandro was generous that way, seemed not to tally what he offered against what he got in return. I had chalked this up to his age, as if maturity meant that pleasing others gave back to him in certain ways. But there was power in this, for him, to watch my face with such scrutiny, to observe the effects of his own touch, as I sat over him on that couch, the two of us silent, me trying to hasten things, because I could not shake the feeling that the groundskeeper was somewhere nearby, watching as Sandro had joked he was.

We spent the whole first part of the day there, reading on the couches in the swimming pool pavilion, Sandro's arm resting lightly around me, stroking my hair absentmindedly. I closed my eyes and heard nothing but wind brushing through the trees and Sandro turning his page.

I could get used to this place, I told myself. If I could just suffer a bit more time with these rude, rich people. Soon they'd all be gone. "We can't just show up and not see my mother," Sandro had said when we planned the trip. "I've got to give her a week." After the family meeting at the Valera factory in just a few days, his mother would return to Milan, and Chesil Jones would go with her. Sandro and I would have the villa all to ourselves, and then I'd go to Monza.

Probably they would just roll out the *Spirit of Italy* and have me pose in front of it, the team manager said when I spoke to him on the phone. Giddle had reminded me to ask how much I'd be paid. That way, she said, whatever you do or don't do with it, you're still making something: money.

I was in the pool, floating on my back, letting my legs sink into the water, when I heard bare feet on the patio stones. The polenta stones. I opened my eyes to the wavering trees, thinking that whoever it was, I would just go on floating and sinking, sinking and floating. A gust of wind sprinkled a few leaves into the water. I smelled cigarette smoke.

"Sanndroo!" a huskily familiar voice said.

It seemed a voice out of a dream, but it was real. Talia Valera, walking toward the pavilion.

"You people swim in March? How ridiculous."

Sandro had not mentioned she was coming. I made my way to the edge of the pool and got out.

"How is it?" she asked me.

"Warm," I said.

"Hey, maybe I'll swim, too. Sandro?"

A moment later she had stripped off her clothes and was naked and walking toward the water. As she took heavy steps toward the edge of the pool, extra flesh on her bottom and the backs of her legs went into a kind of systemwide jiggle.

She dove in, moved across the bottom of the pool silently.

Sandro laughed and stubbed out her cigarette, which she'd left perched on the edge of a table.

She lay on her back, taking large lungfuls of breath in the same way I liked to do, to rise, float, and then slowly sink, then rise and float.

A servant brought lunch down to the pool pavilion, and we ate listening to Talia talk about the various men, and women as well, who had recently become obsessed with her, so much so that she'd had to leave New York. "I was getting bored there anyway," she said. And then she had gone back to London but her old boyfriend had made a habit of standing below the windows of her flat and crying, and the scene there was boring to her, too, so she'd decided to do her mother a favor and attend the Valera Company meeting on her mother's behalf. Her mother had gone to India and according to Talia was not coming back.

"Have you ever been to India?" she asked me, aiming her chin up in a slightly arch manner. I realized she was looking at herself in the mirror that hung down across from us in the pavilion.

I shook my head.

"Then you can't understand," she said, meeting her own gaze, drawing a lock of her hair down along the side of her face, inspecting her reflection with pleasure and satisfaction. "There's a lot about the world, about humanity, you just can't *see*. No, you absolutely *must* go to India. Immerse yourself in its colors and smells, in the cycle of life and death . . . you don't *know* anything about life, Talia. How can you, if you've never been to India?" She changed her tone. "My mother thinks wearing silk saris and burning incense will keep her from killing herself."

I thought of Gloria, when she'd returned from India the winter before, with an air that wasn't too far from Talia's parody of her mother. Gloria had gone to Calcutta and came back announcing to everyone that artists needed to start using more bamboo. She was trying to convince Stanley to work in bamboo. "*You* work in bamboo," he'd said, when Sandro and I went there for dinner, to hear about her trip. "But I dance," Gloria said. "My body is my material." "Then shut up about bamboo," Stanley said.

It came as no surprise that Talia and Sandro's mother got along famously. Not in a mother-daughter way. More like two warriors taking a bit of time off together from rampaging the enemy. Talia had the right confidence and ease for Sandro's mother; I could see that. She walked around the villa picking up little treasures and commenting on them, asking the right questions about various tapestries and busts, to the pleasure of her aunt. They were of the same pedigree, which removed the need for snobbery. They sat together, disarmed, and drank large amounts of wine and vodka and made each other laugh. They even made fun of Roberto, Talia walking stiffly across the lawn in her flip-flops as if with a stick up her ass, talking in a German accent, which was a little unfair, given that Roberto was totally and completely Italian, and yet the German accent had a comic logic that I wished I could openly appreciate, but they spoke in low tones and did not address me, and it would have been inappropriate to laugh along with them.

There were more interminable dinners for which we had to "dress," or rather I did, as we moved slowly through the four long days until their departure. Sandro, as always, wore his one nice jacket, but over his standard uniform of faded black T-shirt, Carhartt pants, and scuffed steel-toed boots. Talia wore various elaborate kimonos and gowns of Sandro's mother's, and came to dinner barefoot, and was much complimented by her aunt for looking ravishing in this or that ancient and brightly colored garment, which she would inevitably take off halfway through dinner, revealing that underneath she wore a leotard and jeans, which was what I wished I had on myself, but I wore the things that Sandro had bought for me in Milan, unable to let go of the idea that I could please his mother by following her rules. I understood, as I followed her rules, that this was only causing her to despise me, but she intimidated me, so I smiled nervously and cleaved to politeness as if it were a lifesaver. It wasn't.

The first night after Talia arrived, I dreamed that Sandro's mother was friendly and open, a woman who spoke to me in the same soft tone she'd used when she said "there you are" to the Count of Bolzano. In my dream I was the you and she said it to me. *There you are.* Her nose was not black. She was not drunk or confused, as she sometimes seemed at the villa. I don't know what language she spoke in my dream, but whatever it was, it was crystal clear, a language that she and I both understood perfectly. We smiled in complicity over something, some ciphered knowledge. "You know he really loves you," she said, and then she conveyed a question to me silently, *What are you going to do about it?* It left a strong residue, that dream, and when I saw her the next morning, her stern gaze was a shock. *Don't think for a second I'm the woman in your dream,* it said. *There's no softness for you.*

"We are so seldom all together," signora Valera said one evening. "We should take a photograph," and she went off to fetch a camera. I offered to take it, to avoid the awkwardness of moving out of the frame. When the photos came back from the developing lab in Bellagio, signora Valera was unhappy. She said she looked old and tired.

"No," I said. "You look beautiful."

"I know what beauty is," she snapped. "I used to be quite good-looking. You wouldn't understand what it is to have that and then lose it. Every trip to the mirror is a nightmare."

Talia burst out laughing. It wasn't clear to me if she was laughing at me or at her aunt.

This inability to interpret was not only unpleasant, it also seemed to perpetuate itself. The less I understood, the less capable I was of understanding the next time someone made a comment that seemed possibly like an insult and someone else laughed. And the signora persisted in forgetting I understood Italian and would turn and say something to Talia, quick, vague, and idiomatic, that I didn't catch. Talia would look at me. "Zia, she understands." Sandro's mother would reply in Italian how inconvenient it was, that usually guests could be discussed openly. I was constantly on alert when Sandro's mother spoke to anyone but me, and when she spoke to me, even more so. You could say I was growing paranoid, but there were reasons for it.

There were place cards every night, even if there were just the five of us—Talia, Sandro, his mother, the old novelist, and myself. "It's important to rotate and intermix the guests," signora Valera said. "If I could, I would have dinners where only some of you were invited, but since you're all staying here, it's a bit awkward. But honestly, that's how I would prefer to do it." I was never placed next to Sandro. "You are a couple! I mean, how dull, how inane, to sit together!" she said when Sandro protested. "What is there to discuss?" I was always to sit with so-and-so, if not the old novelist, some crumbling viscount or count who would apparently like me. "He'll be charmed by you." As if to say, he goes in for that kind of thing (that most of us don't go in for). She always seemed to seat Sandro next to Talia, free and easy Talia, who reached across the table, joked openly about the stale bread, the bad wine in a box, asked the cook to make her an egg when she didn't like what was being served, a regional dish called *pizzoccheri*, heavy and rich with cheese and butter. And she did look good in signora Valera's gowns, of red or purple silk, with her dark hair, which was now a bit longer, wisps of it almost reaching her chin. I imagined that her decision to cut it short, as it had been when I'd met her, was made under circumstances not unlike the decision to punch herself for Ronnie's entertainment. A lark, a dare. A why the fuck not. If she had been nicer to me I would have wanted to know Talia Valera. It was always that way with women I found threatening, that there was some unfulfilled longing to be friends. I didn't know quite why she threatened me. She was full of life and verve and a refreshing bluntness, and yet I wanted her contained instead of celebrated for these qualities I secretly admired.

Her third night at the villa, she appeared at the dinner table wearing what looked like the brown fedora I had given to Ronnie on that secret night long ago. Sandro's mother smiled at the sight of the hat, and the pleasure in her expression was like the softness of her tone for the Count of Bolzano, *it's you,* the way she reserved warmth for certain people in certain moments. The way I had dreamed of her.

"That hat," she said to Talia, "looks absolutely fabulous on you."

Talia took it off to show her aunt that it was a Borsalino. My Borsalino. So Ronnie and Talia were sleeping together. The girl on the layaway plan flashed into my thoughts. Her hopeful, young face.

How stupid I'd been to give it to Ronnie, even if I had stolen it to begin with. It was a naive generosity, to establish some connection. He had given it to Talia. *See how little you meant?* It was possible she'd simply found it in his apartment and claimed it, the way she claimed her aunt's ornate gowns. Or that Ronnie had forgotten who had given him the hat to begin with. None of those scenarios consoled me much.

"Are we wearing hats tonight?" Chesil Jones asked. "Because there's one I've frankly had my eye on."

He got up from the table and reappeared in a curious black fur fez with gold and black tassels that flopped down over one eye.

Signora Valera looked at him sternly.

"Take it off," she said.

The old novelist smiled and began swinging his arms as if to a brass band, humming some kind of official song that the hat seemed to suggest or summon, the tassels that hung over his face bobbing up and down as he jerked his arms.

"Please remove it."

A servant came with pork chops on a huge silver platter. At the sight of the chops, the old novelist shot up his right arm in salute, exhaling a gin-scented wind.

"You'll have to leave this table. I mean it."

"Oh, lighten up, Alba. Why can't a man have a little fun? I'm not trying to fill his boots. I can promise you that. In any case, they are, *ahem,* too small for me, way too small. And from the look of his closet, he wasn't much a wearer of boots. What I have seen are mostly pigskin moccasins by Ferragamo and Hermès, and dainty kerchiefs with the good old 'T. P.' embroidered in the Venetian style—"

"Stop," she said. "Stop it right now. Let the dead rest."

He looked at her in an almost tender way but did not remove the hat. He took a deep breath. I could feel it, the gearing up for a lecture. Stanley was so right about old men. Sandro and I joked about it. "What are you going to do," Sandro asked me, "when I get to that stage when I won't shut up?" "I'll buy you a reel-to-reel tape recorder like Stanley's," I replied.

"All of these silly *categories,*" the old novelist said, tsking and moving his head slowly back and forth as if in disapproval, the tassels drooped over one side of his big, ruddy face. "The way people whine, oh, I can't like *him,* he's a *Fascist.* Or, he's a *Communist.* A Trotskyist. A pederast. A this. A that. I couldn't care less if you're a *that.* If you wear the official hat of the *that.*"

He walked over to the sideboard and lifted the small, trapezoidal shade from the lamp there. He traded it for his fez and said, "Look, now I'm a Maoist." When none of us laughed he took it off and put the fez back on.

"*I* care if a person is attentive," he said, reclaiming his seat. "If they seem to have a brain. If there is a genuine quality to their manner—it's the only way to judge someone."

"And if my husband were here," signora Valera said, "he would judge you an idiot. But I will tolerate your nonsense because you're American and you had a crooked spine, could not fight in the war, and have no idea what you're talking about."

"The spine is not the only part of mine that's crooked," Chesil whispered to me, grinning in a salacious way. "But she never complains about *that*."

He asked the signora if she'd prefer that he'd had a straight spine and might have, who knows, even appeared over Lake Como with the American troops. Could she imagine? Him over Como, under a billowing parachute. "Like an angel," he said. "I could have been your angel, Alba. But since I wasn't fit for combat, I was merely a journalist in Naples when the Americans arrived in 1943, and that's how they came. Softly, on great, white wings. The Italians, what can I say? They were starving, eating boiled cotton, sleeping under rubble. Stepping over their own purple relatives. We didn't have it much better, just meager rations of fried Spam—"

"What's that?" Talia asked.

"The innocence of a question. Spam, my child, is . . . ah . . . it's pig marmalade. It and creamed corn and corpses—these were wartime delicacies. But I should say that we in the press corps did drink wine made from grapes of the Sordo vineyards, and not this bargain-basement rotgut your aunt stocks. But where was I . . . oh, yes, with my crooked spine, stuck merely observing your liberators, these magnificent American soldiers, beautiful blacks who urinated on the king's throne in the Palazzo Reale. While the Italian mothers called out, 'Hey, Joe, hey, Joe,' and attempted to bargain their children on special Allied Forces discount. Conqueror's credit. Also called rape, but what do I know?"

Sandro groaned and pushed back his chair. He wandered into the living room.

If you were one of them, you didn't have to follow the rules. But I was not one of them and was sure it would have been held against me if I'd left in the middle of dinner. Sandro could not accept that Chesil was, as Sandro put it, his mother's confidant. He was clearly more than a confidant, but Sandro could not acknowledge it, even as we sometimes saw the old novelist emerging from his mother's quarters in the morning wearing a robe with the initials of Sandro's father's emblazoned on the breast pocket. Sandro said he couldn't understand how his mother tolerated this ridiculous man in any capacity. I understood that she did tolerate him, and even why. She was lonely, and his ridiculousness was a form of vitality. It brought something to her life. In any case, many men were that way, but I couldn't tell Sandro that men were ridiculous, and since his mother was not a lesbian they were her only option.

"I could have been *your* conqueror, Alba," Chesil said, "I mean your liberator, right here in Bellagio, but as it is, I can only tell you about the Neapolitan mothers eager to sell their children on the *piazzetta* of the Cappella Vecchia. The girls bartered on the cheap to the American soldiers and the boys to the Moroccan soldiers, who fought with the women over the price of these ruined little creatures, snot and melted caramel running down their faces, the single caramel each sucked given to them to preserve an effect of innocence. To be fair, I suppose it is simply the destiny of the young the world over to be hawked in the streets. For hunger and desperation, they should be so lucky. Back home in America, what can I say? They're sold in the streets, too, of course, but not for reasons of hunger or fear. It's worse. Much worse."

"Are you drunk?" Talia asked him. "What's with you?"

He took off the hat and turned it in his hands, folded it closed like a flattened envelope and stroked the fur. "What's with me," he said, "is, as your aunt points out, a bit of scoliosis. But, oh, had my spine been unkinked! To remind you what cowardly shits you people were. Who was in this place, again?" he asked, rapping his knuckles on the table. "I forgot. Who was living here? You did have to clear out for a German overseer, but which? You are never in the mood to discuss it, dear Alba. Was it Dollmann? Kesselring? Or maybe Reder. Like the most rabid Germans, in fact an Austrian. Was it Reder who used this place as headquarters? That's the Walter Reder, I mean, who blazed across central Italy, Pisa, Lucca, Caprara, Casaglia, killing almost two thousand people, according to the 'winners' who wrote the history books, as you might call them, my ardent Alba. Reder burned men, women, and children alive under gasoline and straw. Strange fellow, Reder. Missing a hand, wore a fake one covered in a black leather glove. Anyhow, the suffering of others must surely serve *some* purpose, right? But *what is that purpose*? No one is ever sure of the answer. All I can tell you is that history is a goddamned dangerous place."

"You must stop this," the signora said, "stop it right now."

But he didn't, or couldn't.

"At Casolari, one woman attempted to flee Reder with her newborn babe but was caught. After he finished her off, Reder threw the baby in the air and shot it like a clay pigeon. But of course a baby is not a clay pigeon. There is a thud, a lot of bleeding, a bundle of possibility left to rot in a field, covered with horseflies. I'll end with the little boy of six whose entire family—"

The signora threw a sugar bowl at Chesil. Its top exploded on impact, and he was coated in white sugar.

A servant emerged from the kitchen, having heard the noise, but stayed back when she saw the expression on signora Valera's face. I sat, not sure where to look, resenting Sandro for having been able to get up and leave.

"I guess the genie," Chesil said, wiping sugar from his front, "is out of the bottle. Some things have been said. Decanted."

Signora Valera's face was almost translucent with anger.

"You are the genie," she said, her voice quavering. "You're out of your own bottle. You've only humiliated yourself. That's all."

He lowered his ruddy face toward the table and nodded slowly with dawning regret. He stood up and brushed himself off. Sugar released itself from the folds of his shirt and slacks and formed a residue around his chair.

"I am sorry. My apologies. Mosquitoes bit me today and I think I'm having a bad reaction. I'm feeling dizzy, actually," and he excused himself from dinner.

*   *   *

The next day, the rantings and insults that characterized our meals at the villa all but stopped. Bad news had arrived by telephone.

Workers had gone on strike at the main Valera tire plant outside Milan, blocking the entrances. The scabs the company brought in were dragged from the assembly line and beaten. Even the white-collar scabs, there for accounting and secretarial work, were taken out and beaten. Equipment was sabotaged at other Valera plants, which also experienced strikes.

Over the next couple of mornings, while Sandro and I drank coffee and chewed stale bread, the newspaper reported that a high-level manager at Fiat had been kidnapped and ransomed, another kneecapped on his way to take his midmorning coffee, and a judge who was trying the case of two Red Brigades members was killed.

Roberto and the signora spoke a great deal about the possibility of some kind of calamity, which they didn't name. Sandro felt they were acting hysterical and was, like me, counting the days until they all went back to Milan and we would be alone in the villa. But they weren't hysterical. They were marked people. I see that now.

Then, I would not have called them marked, or known how it was that marked people behaved. But the significance of the armed guard newly stationed at the gates adjacent to the groundskeeper's cottage was not lost on me. The guard, a former paratrooper in stiff, tight jeans, stood around smoking brown cigarettes and alternately touching his mustache and adjusting his balls in the tight jeans. Talia made fun of him, pretending to touch her own mustache, adjust her own balls. "He bleaches the crotch area of those jeans," she said, "to give it a bulkier look."

Neither was the meaning of the armed guard who traveled up and down the short *stradina* with Roberto in his Alfa Romeo lost on me. Nor the hushed discussions that took place between Roberto and the Count of Bolzano, when the count came to dinner on the evening after the judge presiding over the Red Brigades case was killed.

By that point I no longer held any hope of liking Sandro's family, of finding a way to be liked by them. When I had consented to spending a week at the villa with Sandro's mother, I'd had no real sense of what I was getting into, and somehow a week had been stretched to ten days and was beginning to feel like an eternity. I knew that nothing I said would please his mother, that I would be insulted by Roberto, outshone by Talia, and talked at incessantly by Chesil Jones, who'd had a servant place a stack of his books next to our bed, and I'd even been curious about them and had been reading from his first novel, *Summertime,* until I attempted to pay him a compliment and he corrected me for mispronouncing the name of his central character and began quizzing me in an unpleasant manner about the salient themes of his own book, as if it were assigned reading.

I had no sympathy for these people and thought I'd be secretly amused when the calamity Roberto and Sandro's mother were expecting finally arrived. The company, the family, were under attack. I didn't much care, and I never would have guessed that any of the bad news would have an impact on me.

After dinner, just as the Count of Bolzano was leaving, the phone rang. A servant answered and relayed a message to the signora in a whisper.

"Kidnapped?" the signora asked.

A foreman at the plant? A company lawyer?

No. It was Didi Bombonato, who was shopping in the Brera district in Milan, trying on sheepskin coats when he was shoved into a car and driven to an unknown location.

"But is he . . . *ours?*" the signora asked Roberto, the first person she called.

"Then why should we pay to have him released?" she said after a silence. "Perhaps someone else can pay. His family, or the government. What on earth do they want? The answer is no."

The next day it was the headline of *Corriere della Sera.* A high-profile kidnapping by the Red Brigades. That was why they'd done it. When a company president was kidnapped it was buried in the business section, barely news. Didi was front-page material, a national icon. There was a photo of him taken after his capture, a look on his face of pure, childlike fear.

I thought of his separate status that week on the salt, the way he'd simmered with hatred of the mechanics upon whom he relied, and they also seemed to waste no love or loyalty on him. I wondered if any of those mechanics could be involved.

I was supposed to be with them at Monza in a week. I called the team manager but was unable to get through.

Sandro laughed sadly. "I warned you. And not just about my family, but Italy. The place is in shambles."

Sandro said that Roberto had instituted some of the most severe shop-floor policies of any company, and that Roberto was reviled by union leaders and workers, that nothing was going to end well. The workers, he said, came from the south, lived in miserable conditions. Their wives and children put together Moto Valera ignition sets at the kitchen table, working all night because they were paid by the piece, whole families contracted under piecework, which was practically slave labor. Now, poor people all over Italy—in Milan, Bologna, Rome, Naples—were setting their own prices for rent, electricity, bread. The whole structure was unstable, Sandro said, and I understood more clearly, seeing him here, why he kept as far away as he could. Here he was forced to face himself, to be among them. He would go to their board meeting and try to talk sense into his brother and mother, because his would be the only moderate voice in the room.

Two days into Didi's captivity, the Valeras were still not paying. Meanwhile, more bad news arrived by telephone: a security guard at one of the Valera Company warehouses was shot in the legs. And that same day, at another plant, a section boss was beaten brutally while workers looked on, none of them stepping in to prevent it.

With the shadowy presence of our paratrooper security guard and the many recent violent events, Chesil Jones began speaking in alarmed tones about the personal danger he faced. When Sandro's mother implored him to take another slice of veal at lunch, he accused her of fattening him like a hen for someone to nab.

"But you arrived here already fat," she said.

At which point he accepted the second veal slice and said fatness was a mark of moral health.

His fantasy of being taken from the villa became a running joke.

"If it were to happen," signora Valera said, "he'd run his mouth and they'd do all they could to get rid of him. They'd push him from their getaway car, anything not to have to listen to him anymore!"

"Is he famous?" Talia asked.

I hadn't heard of him or the titles of any of the books he'd sent to our room, but I assumed this was my own shortcoming.

"He's famously a pain," Sandro's mother said. "But known in England, I think. His books are more popular there than in America."

Known in England. It sounded like something he might have told her himself. She made fun of him, but it was clear that she took him seriously in a way the rest of us did not.

Chesil announced his plan to flee Italy altogether, down at the pool on the third morning of Didi's kidnapping. It was just the two of us and before he began to speak, I felt a sudden tenderness for him and the burden he bore, of being trapped in his own long-winded narcissism, a burning need for others to *listen*. But this moment of unexpected tolerance may have bloomed in me because they were all finally scheduled to depart the next day, and it is easier to like difficult people when they are leaving, or already gone.

While it's true, he said, that the common people don't run away from death, he himself, not of the common lot, was concerned for his life and would be leaving the country, catching a ride to the airport when the family went to their company meeting in Milan.

I was distracted, thinking about the Didi situation. The team manager, when I'd finally gotten in touch with him, was curt. I'd had to remind him of who I was, which almost left me in tears. I'd come all the way to Italy, taken a leave of absence from my job, worn a frilly dress every night for ten days to please Sandro's mother (and had never pleased her once), and now the Valera team manager didn't remember me or why I was here. And when he did recall, I realized what I was to him, or rather what I was not, and I felt ashamed for asking him to focus momentarily on the least significant of details in the midst of a crisis. Didi had been kidnapped. My own private purpose for being in Italy had been cleaved away.

"Any public person can be abducted at this point. Even up here, in this little paradise, I smell danger," Chesil said, lowering his voice because the groundskeeper was near us now, trimming the branches of a magnolia tree that swung too far out over the pool.

The groundskeeper was on a ladder. He looked at me with what I thought was an upturned lip, the lightest suggestion that he was smiling.

Did he know how silly this man was, whose company I was forced to keep? Yes, I sensed, he did realize. He kept looking at me. I looked back at him. There was something compelling about the groundskeeper, but I couldn't be sure I wasn't imagining it. Silent people can be misleading, suggesting profundity and thoughtfulness where there may be none. He climbed down the ladder and stuffed the trimmed tree branches into a cart and wheeled the cart up the hill toward the gardening shed, abandoning me with Chesil, who was talking about the place he was going to from here, a spa of some kind on a river that fed into the Danube, where Hercules apparently had bathed. I pictured the old novelist seated in a shallow stream, clear waters swirling around his big belly.

"The Roman emperor Trajan conquered that place," he said, "called Dacia, and at that time—"

Lately I had developed a curious habit when Chesil went into these monologues. I closed my eyes and pretended I was skiing. A deep-snow day, the snow coming down, the light dim, and that kind of socked-in, windless quiet when you can hear mostly the fabric of your parka hood as you move your head left or right. I would start to make turns in the dry, light powder. Bouncy, sailing curves in the deep snow, swinging left, then right, floating, shaping my rhythm around the snow-laden trees, deep in the back-and-forth float of fresh snow, and not at all listening to this old man. It was surprising how well it worked. He was still talking.

"—so the King of Dacia slit his own throat, and his head was carried west, to Rome. But east dribbled a trail of Latin, like blood, into Romania, and it's there that I'll go to soak my—"

Roberto postponed their big factory meeting to go to Rome to speak with government ministers about the labor situation. Which meant four extra days with Sandro's mother. The ten days would now be two full weeks. Workers were planning to strike in every sector. A general strike, all across Italy. Roberto didn't want to go, he said. Rome was a mess. The university had been taken over by students, turned into a city within a city. We had been reading about it in the paper. It wasn't just students, Roberto complained. It was people from the slum districts, along with hippies and queers, all occupying the place, eating in the mess halls, doing their laundry in the faculty bathrooms, burning files of documents in big metal trash barrels for warmth.

The evening Roberto was expected back from Rome was a Sunday, which was the staff's day off. Signora Valera complained bitterly that the staff hid from her on Sundays.

"It isn't how things used to be. When you have a staff and they live on the grounds, you don't pretend you don't see them on Sundays! If they are there and something needs to get done, it used to be they would simply do it. They certainly wouldn't claim arbitrarily that because it was *Sunday,* they could not. Or worse, pretend not to see me, or think they don't have to answer when I ring them. Everyone is counting their hours and overtime now. They want to buy a stupidity box," she said, meaning a television, like the one she watched many hours of each night. That was when I had sympathy for Sandro's mother, imagining that it was a relief to be upstairs and alone. Where she could safely feel herself to be what she was, a counter of ham slices. There would be no pretending in her private quarters. She could be done with the constricting ribbons of her stacked espadrilles, which caused her swollen ankles to bulge in a crisscross waffle pattern, off duty from the vigilance of meting out her venom in controlled little gasps. Her bedroom television at an obscene volume, in that cell of noise she could be the kind of person who enjoyed her stupidity box. Every night I heard the familiar harmonica wail, loud and distorted, of *Sanford and Son* leak through the closed door that led up the stairs, the voice of an Italian-dubbed Lamont, *Babbo, ma dai! Smettila, Babbo!*

With the staff off duty, Talia wanted to go down into Bellagio to pick up some things for dinner—cheeses, cold cuts, and rolls. Signora Valera insisted that Sandro go with her. The new safety precautions made all Valeras precious and vulnerable. Although Talia, I'd learned, wasn't a Valera. Talia's mother was a Valera, while Talia's own last name was Shrapnel. She had changed it to Valera because she didn't want the stigma of her great-great-great-grandfather's invention, the shrapnel shell, a thing that was far more famous than the man it was named for. The shrapnel shell came before the name Shrapnel, and not the reverse, and Talia didn't want a name that suggested mutilation and killing.

After they left, Sandro's mother invited me to come and sit with her on the terrace and have a drink. Like the sudden curious tenderness I had experienced for the old novelist, I felt I'd been at the villa long enough to speak comfortably to her, to try to convey something respectful, and be respected in turn. I said it must be nice for her to have Sandro around, that I guessed she missed him when he was so far away, in New York.

She gave me a hard look. "I have a feeling I'm meant to say something here, give an indication that my prodigal son is actually the favorite, and even to suggest I harbor some disdain for the dedicated one and so forth. Nonsense. I greatly prefer Roberto. You'd have to be a fool not to feel partial toward the one who actually takes care of you."

Sandro was probably having a carefree time down in the village. Why did he leave me here? Someone had to stay with his mother, he explained, but the paratrooper should have been enough.

*   *   *

The signora was in her quarters bathing before dinner when I heard a car pull up the drive. I assumed it was Sandro and Talia, and I went out to greet them. It was Roberto. He began talking about Rome. "You've probably never been there," he said.

"I was there once."

"But you can't possibly know Rome by seeing it once," he said, "as a tourist." He was right. I could never know the Rome that Roberto knew. Just as the villa itself, even if unpleasant, was an experience of Italy to which I would have had no access as a student in Florence. It seemed to me that if you were poor and went to a foreign place, you met poor people who weren't all that foreign to you, like the bikers and their girlfriends I'd hung around with at the squalid bar near the train station in Florence. And the opposite was probably true, too. For the rich, the world would be a series of elegantly appointed rooms, similar rooms and legible social customs, familiar categories of privilege the world over.

"Anyway, it's too late," he said. "Rome is ruined. Dirty and chaotic, and there is the feeling of enemies, a population of people who are against you and for no reason. Hateful people who attack us because we are sane, and for order and work and all the good things that Italians once wanted. All the young people are on drugs," he said. "With long, ratty hair and stupefied expressions, like they've figured out how to empty their minds of thought. They have nothing to communicate but the cretinous message anyone can see: *I have long hair.*"

I wanted to ask Roberto about Didi, but then Sandro and Talia pulled up. They emerged from Sandro's mother's Mercedes with a burst of energy vibrating between them, Talia's hoarse voice, a conspirator's laugh. She was tearing off small pieces of a long baguette wrapped in brown paper and throwing each piece underhand to Sandro, who caught them in his mouth. When they reached the kitchen, Sandro grabbed the baguette from her and began throwing pieces for Talia to catch in her mouth, but she couldn't, because he was pelting her with them harder and harder, and it was funny, except that it brought me no relief.

*   *   *

The next morning was the company meeting. I kissed Sandro good-bye in the driveway as signora Valera's Mercedes idled on the gravel, the mustachioed paratrooper behind the wheel, his arm on the sill, bent for access to his mustache, which he stroked in a dreamy way as he waited for their imminent departure, and with his other arm tugged at the rise of his tight jeans, adjusting himself on the leather-upholstered seat.

Didi was still in captivity, but I had put off making plans for what to do until the rest of them were gone. Now the moment had arrived. When Sandro returned, we'd be rid of them. Talia was going back to London. The old novelist, to bathe like Hercules in the Danube. Sandro's mother and Roberto, both back to Milan.

Sandro had wanted me to come with them to the meeting. He explained in whispers that the gates of the factory were being picketed, that it might be a tense situation and I could film it if I wanted to.

Document the problems at his family's company? I had never considered it, given that it was not a subject Sandro was normally willing even to discuss. But now he was encouraging it. Wasn't one of the earliest films, he said, of workers leaving factory gates? This would be angry workers blocking factory gates. "It's actually a much better subject," he said, "than Didi and the Valera team." But I wasn't ready to give up on that idea, and I couldn't bear the thought of spending the entire day with his mother, Talia, and Roberto, of trying to make something in their midst, so I stayed behind.

They departed, the Mercedes moving slowly down the gravel drive. As its sluggish diesel idle faded to insect chatter, I knew I'd made a mistake, that I should have gone with them. I should have filmed. The point was to have interesting footage. I could have decided later what to do with it.

I wandered through the house, experiencing it for the first time in this empty state. While the servants were all downstairs, I peeked into Sandro's mother's bedroom and looked at the perfumes and lotions and powders on her bureau, the silver vase of enormous pale pink roses the maid in the lavender wig must have put there. I felt a curious bristle at the sight of these things. Was his mother not allowed to have feminine accoutrements simply because she was in her seventies? It wasn't her age. It was that she was cruel, and I didn't associate her cruelty with femininity and its rituals. I went into Talia's room, next door, which she'd cleared out of, banging her huge leather suitcase dramatically down the stairs that morning, before Sandro intervened and came to her aid. The bed was unmade, wet towels on the floor. On a chair was my Borsalino. Had she forgotten it? No. She didn't care about it. She was free and easy Talia, and the hat meant nothing. If Ronnie Fontaine had given me something the one night I'd brought him home, if our secret interlude had resulted in a possession, I would have held on to that thing, whatever it was, forever. But Talia wore the hat once, got her compliments, lathered the old novelist into a drunken tirade. That was enough. It probably just took up too much room in her suitcase. I put on the hat, went to the room I shared with Sandro, and lay on the bed next to the stack of Chesil Jones's novels, *Summertime, Men in Trouble, Guilty Pleasures, The Runaways*. I looked up at the portrait of the grandfather. He was trapped in a never-ending vigil up on the wall. I felt like we had that in common, somehow. The predicament of being trapped.

"They went to the factory," I said, looking at him.

He stared out from his dark green void, holding my gaze, or his own gaze, and then the maid in the lavender wig came in, flitted a feather duster around, and began collecting dropped flower petals and stuffing them into her apron pockets. I would never feel comfortable with servants around. I felt convicted by their very presence, not among them and not worth their servitude. I took off the hat, put on a sweater, and went out for a walk.

At the gate I saw the groundskeeper, who was leaning into the open engine of an idling car, a little Fiat 500. I looked at the empty place in the garage where the Mercedes was kept and felt a small wave of anxiety. I couldn't have named its source, a pocket of worry that just happened to pass by, like a flurry of gnats. I walked around the idling Fiat, thinking I'd go down the road and maybe into Bellagio.

The groundskeeper glanced at me. It was not only because he was handsome and possibly contemptuous of us that he made me nervous, but because he was my age. I was self-conscious, in his presence, of being the lover of someone both older and very bourgeois. Every time he was lurking around, I felt a desire for him to understand that I was not with my own people, here at the villa. That I was not one of them. He leaned into the engine compartment. I heard the gentle, rhythmic winding of a socket wrench.

"Why didn't you go?" he asked without looking up. Tools clinked on the gravel. He wiped his hands with a red shop rag, shut the hood, and latched it.

"It's a company meeting," I said. "A family thing. I'm not part of the family. I'm just here."

"You're just here," he said. "Yes. This seems clear."

I turned to walk down the road, feeling like I was performing the role of a girl walking down the road, because I knew he was watching me. The road curved out of his sight, and I was alone, stepping over the broken crockery that formed its surface in lieu of gravel. Crockery instead of gravel. There was nothing wrong with beauty. I thought of Sandro, of making love to him in a field on our hike. Me, smothered by his heavy frame, but floating into the cross-hatching of tree branches. By the time Sandro returned tonight, we would be here alone and everything would be better.

I heard the little Fiat approaching from behind. I moved to the side of the road. The groundskeeper slowed. He said they had forgotten a file of important papers and that he was bringing it to the factory. He'd left the gate open, for me to get back in.

I thanked him.

The reason to stay home, to avoid riding in a car with his mother, had already fallen away. If I went with him, I could film at the factory, the one reason to have gone. I asked if he could take me along.

He nodded and shrugged, as if to say, Sure. What difference does it make?

"You can return with him," he said.

Him. He meant Sandro.

"You're not coming back?" I asked.

"No."

I got in and he took me back up the road so I could get my knapsack, camera, and my passport, because he said I'd have to have proper identification to get inside the factory.

As I grabbed my things, I was thinking how much I'd fallen into a kind of ditch, how eager I was for contact with anyone outside Sandro's mother's loyal little circle.

When I got back in the car, the groundskeeper looked at me as if he knew what I was thinking, but he could not have.

Gray concrete and puffing smoke from huge vertical towers. Concrete-block buildings under clouds that pressed low and dark, promising rain. Those shades of gray: sky, concrete, and smoke were the first impressions as the groundskeeper motored his little Fiat along the perimeter.

At the factory gates was a large group of men with signs. They swarmed around a car that was attempting to pass through the gates. I expected some kind of conflict, but they only handed flyers to the men in the car. The groundskeeper unrolled his window and called to one of the picketing men by name. He and the groundskeeper spoke briefly.

"You know them," I said.

"I worked here."

I looked at the flyer he'd handed the groundskeeper. The strike was tomorrow.

"Sandro said it was today."

"Sandro? That's his name?"

That he didn't know the names of the family members came as a surprise. Sandro was Michele Alessandro, properly speaking, and the groundskeeper probably only knew his full name and not what he went by. I realized the Valeras were nothing to him. Of no consequence. He was as free of them as that wolf that slept in matted briars.

"He told you the strike is today? Workers decide when the strike is," he said.

Factory guards checked the car, the trunk, the groundskeeper's papers, my passport, the camera and knapsack, and let us through.

"They won't let you film, you know," the groundskeeper said.

If I were with Sandro, different rules would apply. I nodded and kept the camera in my knapsack.

Beyond the guard station was a city of tires. Stacks and stacks of them, gleaming like black doughnuts. Shuddering, deafening noises, heavy, bitter air, and repeating rows of textured black O's. The workers had on white coveralls like Didi Bombonato's race techs at the salt flats had worn, "Valera" in red script over the breast pocket, as they operated forklifts that moved these giant doughnuts around. We kept driving. A train yard, cars filled with carbon black, and men, their faces and their white coveralls grimed in it, unloading the carbon black with shovels, silos towering behind them.

We parked and made our way toward a set of interior offices, the groundskeeper carrying the leather valise that Sandro's mother had forgotten. I had my knapsack but didn't want to disrespect the groundskeeper's word by pulling out the camera. I'd wait until we found Sandro.

"Is that how you know signora Valera," I asked him, "from working here?"

"You don't meet the family dynasty when you work on the assembly line," he said.

We walked for a bit in silence.

"I was passing through the area," he said. "A neighbor said she could use me at the villa. That's all. No connection to the factory."

"Do you like working for her?"

"She's a fine person."

As he said it, I realized I'd hoped he would say something negative.

"Everyone respects her," he added.

She wasn't to be messed with. You didn't try to talk about her to her own staff, who, whether they hated her or not, were not going to expose hidden resentments to her son's American girlfriend.

We walked along the exterior of a building. Crossed through an area of parked forklifts and beyond them a series of giant spools, "Valera" printed on them, the letters gone slightly blurry on the rough plywood of the spools. We got to another building, where the groundskeeper had been told they were, but the entrance was locked. He said to wait here, that he'd go around to the other side.

I sat on the steps of the building and waited. I could hear the echo of loud things being dropped from forklifts, the whine of engines in reverse gear. There was no one around, and I decided to film the smokestacks, which erupted with bursts of steam every few minutes. There was another smokestack that sent out a volley of yellow flames intermittently. The length of a single roll of film was three minutes. Short enough that it was worth trying to capture something while he was gone. I panned from one smokestack to another. I was experimenting. If I wanted to make a film of a factory, I would first need to see how a factory looked on film. I wandered along, filming the building's exterior. When I got to the corner, I filmed a desolate alleyway between warehouses. Although not entirely desolate. There were two people down at the far end, leaning against a wall. Two people, face-to-face, as I saw through the viewfinder. A man and woman, and I thought it was odd to see a woman here, because I had only seen men in their white work coveralls. I kept the camera on the two people, watching them through the viewfinder. The man pulled the woman toward him, and then I wondered if I should be filming them. That was my thought. *Should I be filming this?* My first thought was not that the man was Sandro and the woman was Talia, although there was no mistaking. If there would have been a way of mistaking, I would have done so. They were face-to-face, leaned against the wall. He was kissing her, his body pressed to hers. I put the camera down and hit stop.

As I walked hurriedly down the alleyway toward them I heard a voice.

"Don't interrupt them!" An old man in company coveralls, laughing.

I grabbed Sandro by the back of his shirt. The worst part of it, of everything, was the look on his face in that moment he turned around and saw me. Talia stood there, impassive. I went to hit her. Sandro grabbed my hands and held them firmly. He was holding my hands down so I wouldn't hurt her. He was protecting her. Against me.

I pulled away from him and ran. Sandro did not come after me. He did not come after me.

The checkpoints seemed unconcerned with a crying American woman. No one stopped me as I reversed my route and tried to find my way back to the entrance.

I was not thinking, as I moved toward the parking lot, through the blur of the factory grounds, about what I might lose, was losing. There was just flight. Hurt and flight propelling me to the groundskeeper's car.

I sat in the passenger seat watching smoke rise from a chimney and darken the undersides of rain clouds. A simple existence, moving up and out, joining the clouds, dirtying them. Another smokestack emitted a forceful burst of steam, which cauliflowered outward and upward. I remembered that Sandro said the company made petrochemicals for the tires now, that it was much cheaper than natural rubber and more durable.

Rain began to fall. At first lightly, and then it surged, running down the windshield, encasing the car in its noise, and I had the quick thought that the whole world was against me. But the rain, I knew, was not against me. It was indifferent, not the same as the hurtful indifference of Sandro, the look on his face when he realized I was there. His expression showed the fatigue of someone who was only wary of a mess. Not pained. And then holding my arms down—not to touch me but to contain me. Having seen Talia naked, and that she had an awkward body and heavy legs, added in a surprising way to the pain I felt, sitting in a stranger's car in the parking lot of a tire factory thousands of miles from home. Sandro cared about bodies. He liked tall, lean women. He always said so. All of his attention to me, physically, was focused on my body and his praise of it, his gratitude for its proportions. Given that Talia's body was awkward, there must have been real desire there. What he liked was not for me to see or know. In the first few months we were together, I could feel him running his hands over me all night long, even in his sleep. Slender bodies, but not too slender, with a waist, was what he loved. Talia was chunky and short, and yet he had pulled her toward him outside the plant office as if he wanted something. Pressed her against him, and I knew where this led. To quick passion in a public place, which was his taste. His taste whether with me or with someone else.

The day of her sudden appearance by the pool came back to me, the smell of her lit cigarette, the husky voice, her feet slapping over the pool patio, the stones that a thousand invisible hands had apparently pounded. The truth was the thing I had sensed but pushed aside, because it was too obvious to accept.

Maybe an hour passed before the groundskeeper returned. It was almost dark. He showed no surprise to see me.

"I'm going to Rome," he said, blotting rainwater from his face with the sleeve of his coat. I noticed then that it was the same kind of mechanic's jacket, cheap gabardine, quilted red on the inside, that my cousins Andy and Scott wore.

I nodded.

He started the car and pulled out of the lot, and then we were on the autostrada, headlights streaming toward us, blurred by rain.

15. The March on Rome

All the little snub-trunked Fiats on the autostrada, matchbox cars in white, beige, or yellow, a few of them cherry-red and gleaming in the rain like children's plastic slickers. I gazed out the windshield, water running down the glass in uneven sheets. I didn't turn to look at the groundskeeper. He glanced over once or twice, but not in a way that seemed meaningful or sympathetic. Still, his lack of surprise at having found me in his car felt like sympathy. He said nothing.

I wouldn't have guessed that his silence would be so effective. It grafted me in. To a way of proceeding. Of not knowing where we were going except someplace in Rome, not knowing where I would stay or what I would do. I had my passport, the camera, and the equivalent in lire of ten U.S. dollars.

In retrospect, it would have been far easier had I not fled straight to his car, outside the tire factory on the industrial outskirts of Milan.

Not gotten inside, once I found it, unlocked, in the parking lot.

Not sat quietly when he got in, started the engine, and pulled out of the lot.

Each of those moments, if taken, would have required less of me than to separate from what he led me to, once I was there. Once I was there, in Rome, it was simply too late.

It was a long drive, and I let the sound and vibrations of the car motor stun my thought patterns into something uniform and calmed. I wondered if I could still be myself with all context, all my reason for being here left behind, discarded.

We were on the autostrada, nothing but green signs with white letters in a rounded but affectless font. The sulfur lamps that angled high over a divided road not meant for the scale of the human. I thought of Sandro and his youthful idea of making industrial paintings to roll out on the autostrada. On the stairs leading to his mother's stupidity box chamber was the same photo Sandro had, of T. P. Valera with Italian prime minister Aldo Moro, cutting a ribbon for the groundbreaking ceremony of the autostrada. Behind them a motorcade of Valera cycles. "Gas, tires, and oil," Sandro said to me. "*You* would think it's a reference to a Pontiac muscle car. But no. It's an incredible trifecta. My father and his cronies conspired to change the face of Italy. They wrecked the place and made piles of money. Brought in the so-called miracle, the postwar miracle, everyone in his own little auto, put-putting around, well enough paid from their jobs at Valera to buy a Valera, and tires for it, and gas." Here I was on the Autostrada del Sole with a stranger who probably just thought of it as a highway, took it as a given that Italy had a central artery, a car culture, a tire company so large it was practically a public utility.

The groundskeeper and I did not speak until he stopped for fuel, and then only a few words. He showed me where the women's bathrooms were and asked if I wanted a coffee. I patted cold water on my face, hoping it would shrink the puffiness from crying, and when I realized what I was doing, I laughed sadly at my mirrored self for still caring what I looked like, even now. Taking inventory of my face. Wetting my bangs to get them to lie straight. The groundskeeper and I each drank an espresso at the little bar without speaking. His name was

Gianni, but the blank fog of his presence at the villa clung to him and I was hesitant to claim even enough familiarity to call him by his name.

It was night when we entered Rome through narrow streets, everything soaked and shining from rain. Water bubbled along the roadway, carrying leaves and debris. There were metal barricades blocking every side street we passed. Carabinieri in their white bandoliers blowing whistles and directing traffic. I asked what was happening.

Some of the streets were closed, Gianni said, because of the parade tomorrow.

"A parade?"

"A demonstration," he said.

"Gianni Ghee-tarrr!" a girl called out as we entered the apartment.

Everyone looked up. At him, and then at me, and I could see that there was a silent but collective decision not to say anything. Not to ask who I was. Gianni nodded at them in affirmation, but affirmation of what I didn't know.

After many hours of driving through darkness, silence, rain, it was jarring to be in a cramped and brightly lit apartment full of people, mostly men, who lay around on couches, some sprawled on the floor, one strumming an out-of-tune guitar. They weren't a type I could place. They wore dirty clothes, black leather jackets, black turtlenecks. Their long hair was greasy, carefully parted. Most of them had mustaches. They reminded me of the plainclothes cops in Tompkins Square Park, who were always too severe and ominous despite their efforts to pass for hippies.

The girl who had announced Gianni's arrival was sitting on the floor against the wall, curly hair spilling over her shoulders, big white teeth, and a large but delicate nose that made her seem friendly and approachable. I found I could only make eye contact with her and none of the others. "È arrivato," she called out to someone unseen, in another room. A female voice answered back that Gianni was probably working for the CIA now. That was what it sounded like, but it was not spoken in the clearly enunciated Italian I heard at the villa. Everyone laughed but Gianni, who ignored them and asked if I wanted a glass of water.

There was a tiny kitchen filled with cigarette smoke and the sound of frying and of pots being banged around. Gianni went in for the water and then excused himself for a moment, retreated to the room from where the unseen girl had made the CIA comment. One of the men got up from the couch and insisted I sit. I thanked him and asked his name. "Durutti," he said. "Have you heard of me?" Everyone laughed.

Gianni and the woman in the other room were talking. Were they arguing? Only because I was his charge did I take note that he probably had a girlfriend here. That he was talking to her now. In a moment she would emerge and meet the stray he had dragged into this apartment, and I would try to communicate to her that I wasn't any threat.

A radio was turned on and everyone quieted. I figured we were just listening to it. I didn't know it was being broadcast from another room in the apartment. The announcer was talking about the demonstration tomorrow. The parade, as Gianni had called it.

"We've received a tip from a comrade in one of the security police battalions, about their preparations for tomorrow's march." There was a long list of armored cars and weaponry at various barracks that were being readied. All leave was canceled. Gunners with submachine guns would be stationed on roofs. "I think it is safe to say the carabinieri will be marching alongside us. Thank you to the brave comrade who has provided us with this information. See you tomorrow, seventeen hundred hours, Piazza Esedra."

Lou Reed's "Perfect Day" came over the radio, familiar bittersweet piano notes. Sandro loved that song, and it had always reminded me of our first date. Now I thought with sadness of Sandro's departure for the meeting at the factory, the last moment of normalcy. Sandro kissing me. Chesil Jones, stiff and impatient in signora Valera's Mercedes, ready to get the hell out of Dodge.

I felt lost to all that now. Lost to Sandro and to the humiliations of his fabulous moneyed stupid world. To the project at Monza. Didi had been kidnapped and the team manager had better things to concern himself with than me. And anyway I was here, which was . . . where? Someplace in Rome. In a crowded apartment with graffiti on its walls, young people talking loudly over Lou Reed's sad, ardent voice, a boy and girl on the floor kissing. I turned away, not wanting to look. The sound of frying from the kitchen, the voices, the texture of energies, it was an enveloping reality. It filled the emptiness of having exiled myself from elsewhere.

A woman emerged from the kitchen and handed out plates of food. "Spaghetti Bolognese," she said to me and then added in English, "with *the meat* on them." Her name was Claudia, and from that moment she always spoke to me in lousy English, while everyone else addressed me in Italian. At first I was offended, until I realized she simply wanted to practice. Roberto had consistently spoken only English to me during my time at the villa, but his English was perfect and crisp, accustomed, as he was, to talking to finance people in London and New York. I wasn't hungry but I accepted the spaghetti with the meat on them. I chatted with the girl with big white teeth, whose name was Lidia. She asked if I'd come to Rome for the demonstration. I said yes without much thinking about it. Gianni brought me. If that was what he was here for, then yes. Yes. I thought of the way he'd carefully avoided looking at me as I'd wiped my tears away, sitting and waiting in his parked car. How decent it had seemed that he'd said nothing, and included me in his plan, whatever that plan was. Gianni in a quilted mechanic's jacket like my cousins wore. The clink of his tools, such a familiar sound, as he'd tinkered with the little Fiat's engine that morning at the villa. The only recognizable thing to me here among these young Italians was Gianni—who was essentially a complete stranger, and yet I clung to him, alert to his every movement in that apartment in Rome.

People were coming for the march from all over Italy, Lidia with the big white teeth said. Naples, Sardinia, Milan, Turin. "Maybe they would have come anyway," she said, "but now that there's been a murder in Bologna, cold-blooded, they shot him in the back! Now, forget it. Everyone is coming, no? This is a war, no?" She phrased her assertions as questions but they weren't like Nadine's. They weren't shaky ways of having a presence. The questioning tone was as if to say, *You better agree with me, no? Of course, right?*

Gianni appeared with the woman from the other room. They did not look at each other or touch. She went into the kitchen and returned with a plate of spaghetti for herself. She looked at him. "You're not hungry?" He shook his head. Maybe she wasn't his girlfriend. She was petite and blond, but with a dark sexiness, slanted, almost reptilian eyes, and with freckles covering her face, her arms, and her cleavage, visible under a low-necked smock, a kind of faux-medieval hippie dress, but like with the others, there was a toughness I didn't connect to hippies. Her name was Bene. I'm just along for the ride, I thought at her as she introduced herself. I sensed, in the way she peered at me, that she was reckoning what she saw with what Gianni had said to her about me or my situation, whatever he interpreted it to be.

A week ago I had been in the swimming pool of a Bellagio mansion, watching Talia tread across the patio, her extra flesh jiggling with each step. Now the weather was cold and damp, the sky promising only more rain. I wore my same clothes as yesterday. I had slept on a dirty couch in an apartment filled with the type of people Roberto hated, involved in what he deplored: the Movement, as they called it.

The people in that apartment had been kind to me the previous night. There was something about them I could only describe as human. Humane. They didn't ask who I was, why I was there, where I came from, what I did. One didn't present credentials with these people, like in New York. "She's with Sandro Valera." "He shows with Helen Hellenberger." They asked if I was hungry. They asked if I wanted a beer. They made me a bed to sleep on. They didn't know anything about me. I was brought by Gianni, and that was all the information they needed. Gianni himself did not stay. He and the kid who had called himself Durutti went out into the black night, into the pouring rain. No one asked them where they were going. I was bothered that he was gone, and wanted to know where, but I tried to push it from my mind.

The Movement. I knew little to nothing about it, but it showed itself that night as their kindness to me, a stranger. Whether Gianni was in the Movement was unclear. He did not look like the rest of them, working-class handsome in his mechanic's jacket. He was clean-cut, quiet and reserved, almost emotionless, or so he seemed. Before he and Durutti left, he sat reading the dusty-pink pages of *Il Sole 24 Ore,* and I had smiled privately because it was the same newspaper that Roberto read religiously, Italy's version of the *Wall Street Journal.* I think the Valera family even owned part of it, or was part of the conglomerate of industries that owned it. The rest of them moved around Gianni, reading the business news in their free-form bedlam, as if this were precisely his role.

In the morning, there was no sign of him. Bene and Lidia, the girl with the big teeth, took me with them around the neighborhood. The apartment was on the Via dei Volsci in San Lorenzo, an area near the university that was so ugly it almost made me laugh, to think I might have assumed all of Rome looked like the Spanish Steps, the Trevi Fountain. San Lorenzo had been bombed in World War Two and now it was a mass of drab, modern apartment buildings with television antennas jutting from every balcony and roof like hastily stabbed push-pins. Sacks of garbage hung from the windows like colostomy bags. There was graffiti on every building. I was used to graffiti from living in New York, but the graffiti in San Lorenzo was all urgent and angry messages, or ones with a kind of dull malaise, as if the exterior of the buildings were the walls of a prison.

"They throw us in jail and call it freedom."

"They can't catch me. I'm moving to Saturn where no one can find me."

"When shit becomes a commodity the poor will be born without asses."

Underneath, a crude picture of an ass, and *"What do we want?"*

"Everything."

New York graffiti was not desperate communication. It was an exuberance of style, logo, name, the feat of installing jazzy pseudonyms, a burst of swirled color where the commuter had not thought possible. These were plain, stark messages written in black spray paint, at arm and eye level from the street. There were few pictures, with the exception of the occasional five-pointed star of the Red Brigades, which had appeared above Didi's frightened face, in the photo of him in *Corriere della Sera*.

Why was a badly drawn pentagram so much more menacing than a perfectly drawn one? I wondered as we passed one, no message, just the five-pointed star.

It was the hand's imperfection that made it menacing, I decided. But why that was, I didn't know.

Bene didn't mention Gianni. I asked at one point where he was.

"Doing the same thing he does at the Valera place. *Fixing things,*" she said in English, with a look I could not read.

She took me with her to drop off flyers about the demonstration on the Piazza Navona. As we encountered people she knew, she introduced me as an American who told Roberto Valera to fuck off. I didn't want to let her down by saying I'd done no such thing. That rather, his brother had broken my heart, and I'd run away like an injured animal.

The Piazza Navona was lined with outdoor café tables, young people seated around them. Bene said it had been more crowded before the sweep. A lot of the people around here were hauled off to prison, she said. When I asked what for, she shrugged and said, knowing someone who was involved in illegal activities. Or having your name on a lease of an apartment where someone later stayed who was in the vicinity of a bombing. Disrespectful to the state. They can get you for anything, she said, now that they've changed the laws back to Mussolini's.

"If you drive near the prison at night," she said, "you can see torches made of bedsheets hanging through the cell bars. It's really sad. These lights shining into the blackness, at no one. Half the people from around here are there, at Rebibbia, where no one can see them. All they are now is something burning from a window."

I watched a woman who sat with two men who had a movie camera. She was young, a teenager, and beautiful in both a tragic and an unmarked way. It was her smile, dimpled, sweet, and naive, and her patient tolerance of the older men who directed her, that seemed tragic. One of the men filmed while the other spoke to her, asking what her name was, where she was from.

"Anna," she said, and smiled at them. "From Cagliari."

"Wait," the man filming said. "One more time, but slower."

The first man stepped back and approached her again, just as he had the first time, asking her what her name was and where she was from.

"Cagliari," she said again, this time enunciating with more care.

"Cagliari," the man sitting with her repeated.

"*Sì,*" she said, and then she explained that her parents were Sardinian but had moved to Paris. And from Paris she had run away, back here, to the Piazza Navona, because, she said, holding out her wrists and showing them the scars there, they put her in a hospital in Paris. Put her somewhere, in any case, as I didn't know the word they were using—*manicomio,* which I later looked up. Madhouse.

It was clear she knew them already, that they had instructed her to pretend they were strangers for the purpose of the film, but with her dirty clothes, her unbrushed hair, she looked like a runaway living on the Piazza Navona. I had the feeling she was not an actress. That they were directing her to play herself.

"You've been sleeping here?" the man asked.

"Yes," she said, looking up at him with her sweet, open face.

I stared at the young runaway, *la biondina,* they kept calling her. She stood up and put her hands on her belly, which protruded high and round under her poncho. She smiled at me, but in a way that let me know yes, she was pregnant, and that she didn't much appreciate being stared at.

"She's been here for a week," Bene said. "Sleeping on the street, hanging out with drug addicts. Those two bums—I don't know what they're up to, but I can't imagine they'll help her."

They lived downstairs from Bene and the others, in the same building on the Via dei Volsci.

We watched as the one filming followed the other, who walked alongside the biondina, holding her arm. She turned to him. He put his hand on her forehead.

"I need a bed," she said.

"What?" he asked.

The one filming said cut, and asked her to repeat it.

"I need a bed. A place to lie down," she said.

"You have a fever?"

"Yes," she said.

"You're pregnant and you sleep on the streets?" he asked.

"Yes," she said, and smiled in a perfectly guileless way.

My one trip to Rome, when I was a student in Florence, was only for two days and it had been a lonely tour of sights: the Pantheon, the Spanish Steps, where pickup artists worked on young girls, the Colosseum, a great decaying skull whose grassed-over arena was all but lost in a strange haze of thereness, unreal because it existed, now, without its former use. Tourists watched each other and roamed the crumbling edges, unable to feel the scale as a populated place, a mesh of attentions and shoutings, a looking of thousands upon a ring of human violence. It had been empty when I got there. A gray kitten rolled on its back, inviting me to pet its white, furry loins. I'd bent down. There was no sound but the traffic that banded the exterior of the Colosseum, and the kitten, which had begun to purr.

You can't feel a crowd in an emptiness. That had been my thought in the Colosseum.

But here, in the Piazza Esedra, there were so many bodies massed together that they formed a vast shifting texture, a sea of heads filling the square. Above them, fabric banners rippling. Sound swells rolling across the immense piazza like great sluggish ocean waves, voices shifting directions.

All these people and their bright banners, which weren't cheerful exactly, in stoic white, blood red, ink black. A rain-swollen sky pressed down, darkened to slate by the late-afternoon light. The air had an electric feel, as it does when a storm has moved in but has not yet unleashed itself. The electric air and the premature darkness gave those moments, the gathering before this march was to begin, a granular sort of intensity, every color and surface vivid and distinct.

The shops were closed, their corrugated metal shutters rolled down. The one exception was the Feltrinelli bookstore, which remained open. The clerks were handing out free copies of Mao's Little Red Book, cheap plastic-coated copies like Gideon Bibles. I thought of Roberto's insistence that Feltrinelli's death was necessary and good, and Chesil Jones claiming it was an act of stupidity, a mix-up of positive and negative leads. Fools love to declare that they don't suffer fools. It was a lusty pleasure for the old novelist to say the word. *Fool*. Weakness made him say it, even as the word made him feel strong. I didn't know if Feltrinelli got his positive and negative leads mixed up but I felt he must have been a serious person, as Sandro said. In any case, death was death: it had its own gravity. Watching the shiny red books passed through the crowd I had the thought that Sandro, who sympathized with anyone willing to think some other mode of existence besides rich-man-takes-all, would have appreciated this scene. But he wasn't here.

When the Piazza Esedra was completely full, people leaked into the side streets to which the police would allow entry. There were sections. The women's sections, the high schools, the various representatives from factories—Valera, Fiat, SIT-Siemens, Magneti Marelli, who made wiring harnesses for Moto Valera. There were the students from the university, bespectacled and grave, their faces masked with scarves. The Bologna contingent, here to avenge the death of the young radical who had been gunned down by police yesterday. Another group filed in, their cheeks and eyes painted like mimes with black and white theater makeup, hollering like Indians. "We want nothing!" they chanted. One carried a sign that said, "More work, less pay!" Another: "Down with the people, up with the bosses!" "More shacks, less housing!" They were young, and dressed in the most ragged clothes imaginable, old shoes without laces, pants with huge, sagging knee-rips, elbows jutting through their moth-bitten sweaters. I watched as one of the boys eyed a woman putting out her cigarette, and then he walked over, picked it up, asked her for a light, and sauntered away, puffing on her cigarette butt. They spoke in a dialect I could barely understand, words that were quick and slurred and open like their laceless shoes.

The types Roberto was probably referring to. Who he claimed had nothing to say but *I have long hair*. I thought of what Sandro had told me about people setting their own rent, their own bus fare. Kids with no part in bourgeois life. With their perverse messages and ratty clothes, they made Talia's air of toughness seem like princess toughness, nothing but an upper-class performance.

They were from remote slums on the outskirts of Rome, Bene explained. There's nothing to do out there, she said. They're young and it's like they're left for dead. Ronnie would have appreciated them. I had that thought, anyway. But when I tried to sustain the idea amid the waves of sound rolling across the square, the banners rippling, the crowd becoming more and more dense, I decided that this context was too massive for Ronnie. I could not have guessed what he would say about these kids and the feeling they gave off, of life lived in the present moment, an air of nothing to lose. I thought of Ronnie's personal ad, his joke, printed in Sharpie on the bathroom wall at Rudy's. "Looking for an enemy." Really he meant friend. And the scrawled question under it, "But how do we find each other?" Which was probably also Ronnie, something he wrote himself. He loved to talk about the ways in which people were processed and accounted for in the modern world. Numbered street addresses, he said, were relatively new. In the Old World, there was a natural vetting process, according to Ronnie. A stranger enters a village and declares who it is he is looking for. He is either turned away or assisted, depending.

How do we find each other?

It repeated in my head as more and more people packed into the enormous square. The "we" of it: people lost in the vast thickets of the world. People lost among people, since there wasn't anything else. *The world was people,* which made the prospect of two finding each other more desolate. It was like finding a lover, pure chance and missed connections. It *was* finding a lover.

The pregnant girl, Anna, the biondina, wove through the crowd in her poncho, her same guileless smile, which said, "I have nothing to protest. I'm here to be here."

The two men making a movie about her followed with camera and microphone.

"I'm hungry," she said to them. "Let's go eat."

"Say it again," the one with the camera said.

"I'm hungry," she said, and smiled shyly at them.

The one with the microphone leaned in toward the biondina and placed his hand on her breast.

She looked at him with a child's mischievous delight.

"There's milk," she said, holding her breasts up for him.

"Milk," he said, leaning to see down into her poncho. He was in his midforties, I guessed. Balding and scraggly.

She pushed with her hands, squirting a fine light stream up at him.

He took off his glasses, wiped his face, and laughed.

The kids with the painted faces had formed a circle and were doing an improvised rain dance.

"Rain! Rain! Rain!" they yelled. "We want it to rain! Kill the sun! Kill the sun! Harpoon it out of the sky!"

A long row of carabinieri pushed into the square, forming a perimeter. The diagonal white slashes of their bandoliers converged into a vast mesh, as if they were part of a performance. Each held out his right arm, right hand covered in a huge black gauntlet glove, pushing people out of the way as they sealed off the exits to the square.

"Arrest us!" the kids with painted faces yelled at the carabinieri.

"We want to go to jail! Come on—take us to prison! *Rebibbia! Rebibbia! Rebibbia! Rebibbia!*"

They chanted it louder and louder, some of them banging on upturned pots and buckets. Rain started to fall. The carabinieri moved in with their black gauntlet gloves and grabbed the loudest of the kids and dragged him, screaming, to a paddy wagon, wrenched his hands behind his back, kicked him in the ribs, and shoved him inside. The rest of them opened their mouths and hollered in an eerie cacophony. Eerie because it wasn't a cheer and it wasn't a lament. It was ambiguous, or it was both mixed together, an ecstatic warning.

The carabinieri blocked off the large boulevard where the march was meant to take place, using barricades and a row of armored vehicles. Behind the barricades and in front of the vehicles riot police stood shoulder to shoulder, black helmets, visors up. The carabinieri didn't have helmets like the riot police. They wore hats with shiny visors like beat cops in New York City, and like beat cops out in the rain, they had fitted elasticized plastic covers over their hats. The carabinieri blew their whistles, while the riot police—*celerini,* Bene said they were called— tried to move people away from the barricades, pushing them in the direction of Termini, the train station. The celerini were complete bastards, Bene said. I began to film the crowd, scanning across the groups. "But *those* guys," she said, pointing, "can fight back. Untie the fabric, and wham." It was the Valera contingent, raising their banner, a huge white cloth with red letters. The banner, I saw, was supported on each end by tire irons.

Thinking Sandro would have appreciated the free copies of Mao's Little Red Book was naive, I knew. If he were here, he would have wished to be gone and, like his Argentine friend M, to not have to discuss the matter, which both did and did not concern him. But he was elsewhere. I was alone and rootless. I had fallen through a hole and landed in a massive crowd of strangers, this stream of faces, a pointillism of them. Face after face after face. If someone wanted to turn Ronnie's fake mandate to photograph every living person into a sincere proposition, I thought, panning the camera across the piazza, this would be a place to start.

*   *   *

We were moving out of the piazza, down a narrow lane closed to auto traffic, the whistles of the carabinieri echoing in the wet and empty street ahead of us, people chanting and shouting. The women's groups were marching first.

Italy was backward in its treatment of women. Divorce had become legal in 1974. Abortion was illegal. A lot of the women's banners were about rape. That I knew about these issues through Sandro, who would go on at length, made my chest tighten. Sandro, interested in feminism. A sympathizer. A man who apparently loved women so much he had cheated on me the moment it was convenient to do so. And possibly he had been doing it all along. Helen. Gloria. Talia. And for what logical reason did Giddle dump a drink over his head? Did he think I was stupid? Yes, he did. And I was that stupid. Or rather, I willed myself to that state. Lovers offered only what they offered and nothing more, and what they offered came with provisos: believe what you want and don't look carefully at what isn't acceptable to you. Gloria had come to the loft to collect a box of personal effects in the wake of my move to Sandro's. She looked directly at me, the box in her hands, offered no explanation, and I knew, and she knew that I knew, but what would have been the point of making a scene about it with Sandro? She was leaving with her stuff. I was replacing her, and whatever secret complexity Sandro maintained with the wives of his friends was something I preferred not to think about. I took him as he was, not as something perfect that he wasn't. But that tacit acceptance, too, had a kind of good faith in it that he'd trampled. Now, Gloria's direct stare, the box in her hands, it was all one insult. Sandro's insult. Watching these women with their bullhorns, shouting, "You'll pay for everything!" I took their rage and negotiated myself into its fabric. I fused my sadness over something private to the chorus of their public lament.

In the stream of bodies, I lost Lidia and Bene almost immediately. The rain was coming hard. I was soaked through, letting the crowd jostle me this way and that, the police moving alongside the women as if they were a threat.

The people marching up ahead started moving backward. Those

behind us were trying to move forward. There was no place to go, and then the riot police Bene had warned me about, the celerini, closed in, their faces and bodies clad and hidden behind shields, pushing and clubbing the women who were trapped in their path. I felt my stomach drop. It was that moment on the Ferris wheel when the car sweeps backward and up.

People were screaming, trying to flee from the piazza up ahead, where there was a fire. Smoke filled the street. A bus had been turned on its side and was burning like a giant torch. A building in the piazza also was burning. The celerini herded us into a kind of centerless spiral and began arresting as many women as they could seize, pulling them by limbs or hair or handbag, dragging them.

I worked my way to an open side street by following a small group of young women who seemed to know where to go, how to avoid the row of police vans into which others were being shoved.

The march continued up the Via del Corso but differently now, the orderly procession of groups broken apart and scattered after the fire and arrests. There was a palpable anger. The students with their grim expressions and delicate eyeglasses were pulling paving stones up from the streets, walking with the stones in their hands.

Via del Corso was like the Corso Buenos Aires in Milan, an avenue of chic and expensive boutiques. The shop fronts didn't have corrugated metal gates. They were like glass dioramas, chalk-white mannequins gazing imperiously.

"Underneath the paving stones, more paving stones!" someone yelled.

I heard the crash of breaking glass.

"Expropriate! Expropriate!"

Three kids with painted faces came running past clutching fur coats, the war paint on their cheeks dripping down, sweat and rain-smeared, stacks of furs over their arms like midtown Manhattan coat-check clerks.

"Furs for the people!" Plastic hangers dropping behind them as they ran.

Windows were methodically smashed as the procession moved down the Via del Corso. Police zigzagged through the crowd in pursuit of the vandals—jeans for the people, handbags for the people, wine for the people, shoes—but there were too many. A shop was on fire, black smoke pouring out from the rectangle of darkness where the door's glazing had been. There were Molotovs and Moka bombs, as they called them, made the usual way—cotton plus gasoline, add match—but instead of a bottle they used a little stovetop espresso maker. "Better to run with," it was later explained to me by an eight-year-old, the son of someone in the apartment on the Via dei Volsci. "It even has a handle! With glass, it slips from your fingers and that's it," he said. *"Buum!"*

The shop engulfed in flames was Luisa Spagnoli, the same as the place in Milan where Sandro had bought me the velvet dress. "They use slave labor from the women's prisons!" a young woman was shouting. It was women throwing the firebombs now. Dress shops. A department store. A lingerie boutique. Up the Corso they moved.

As I heard another window shatter I saw white balloons, a flock of them, rising.

I took out the camera and filmed.

Why this? I couldn't say. But I watched through the viewfinder as the balloons went up, riding smoothly skyward on invisible elevators. Up, up, passing each floor of a tall building. Balloons pure and drifting, their stretched skin the sheer white of nurses' stockings.

A feeling of calm settled over the Via del Corso. There was a break in the rain. People were quieting one another. Fingers raised to lips. A young girl was going to sing. An area was cleared around her. I kept my camera going.

She wore theater makeup, red and white bordered in black fanning out in triangles under each eye, curious geometric teardrops, wedges of color pulling her expression downward, her pretty face a pictograph of sadness, but a lovely, strange, and playful sadness. Her face was some kind of counterreality, in which play and tragedy had equal parts, or had traded places.

She looked skyward. She, too, was tracking the balloons. They were

from a department store—La Rinascente, it was called, as I saw when
one of them floated low, the name printed over the thin, nurse-stocking
skin of the balloon.

A sound issued from the girl's throat, smooth and unmodulated.

"Sixteen years old with a voice like Callas," someone said.

As she finished her song and we began to clap, a burst of shots
erupted, a metallic pop-pop. People screamed, pushed, ran. I saw
Gianni. Our eyes met and he came toward me. Where had he been?
He never did explain, later, when there was time to do so. There were
more shots. The celerini were there, shields up, batons out, men barely
human under so much gear. Gianni and I ran. People darted through
the crowd in their own "gear," motorcycle helmets with face shields
pulled down. It was the next level of anonymity, from a bandanna over
your face. And it protected the head, just as the celerini, too, protected
theirs. A man ran next to us in a ski mask, those cartoonish eyeholes
like the symbol for infinity. Gianni gripped my arm, yanking me as we
fled. When I tripped and should have fallen I skittered along like his
teddy bear, until he righted me and I could run again.

That face, with the ski mask, the infinity eyeholes. It was another
counterreality, but not like that of the girl who sang. The person in the
ski mask: tall, gangly, in a dirty blazer open and flapping. Running with
a gun in his gloved hand.

He turned back. Aimed his gun at the police and fired.

Gianni and I ran down a side street. Something whistled through
the air. A hissing bloom of smoke filled the street, the air white. My eyes
burning, spilling tears, Gianni pulling me. The camera slipped from my
hands. I stumbled over it, couldn't see. I heard people retching. Gianni
pulled the neck of my shirt up over my mouth and nose. It was automatic, the way he went to cover my face. He turned away, spit up, pulled
his own scarf up to his eyes. Coughs echoed everywhere. The air was
white; it was like being in a cloud that had moved down over a mountain, the vertigo of not knowing which direction is falling and which is
up. I coughed and coughed, unable to make it through the coughing
to its other side, to a place of not coughing. The camera didn't matter

because I could not breathe. Gianni held on to my arm, but his grip was tense and impersonal.

As the smoke thinned, the people around us reappeared, in gas masks of various styles and types, or with scarves tied in complicated ways over their faces, like Gianni. They'd been waiting for this. I had not.

The demonstration had begun at dusk, under stormy skies. One hundred thousand people, a tenth of them apparently with guns hidden in a pocket. By the time Gianni and I reached the end, at the Piazza del Popolo, it was completely dark. People crowded in and told stories of police beatings, of the thousands who had been arrested. Someone gave out lemon-soaked rags, which we held over our mouths. Bottles of Coca-Cola were passed around. You were meant to dribble some over your eyes, as Gianni showed me, to stop the stinging. Guns were handed out among the people in the Piazza del Popolo, looted from a rifle shop. I was passed one and it was far heavier than I would have expected.

Popolo means crowd or multitude. *Popolaccio*: rabble or mob.

I left with Gianni just as the police began arresting anyone on the street who was wet. Anyone in possession of lemons. Anyone who smelled of gasoline. That smell was pervasive. The students smelled of it. Some of the women. All of the men. It was something I associated with Reno kids, my cousins and their friends, always smelling of gasoline. Scott and Andy returning from the filling station in the back of Uncle Bobby's pickup truck with pink gasoline in plastic jugs, or siphoning it from unsuspecting neighbors with a segment of old garden hose, their studious expressions, pulling gasoline, angling the siphoned liquid into a container, sometimes getting a mouthful by mistake. Gasoline was a summertime smell. Long solstice days. The rangy Doppler of a lawn mower. Scott and Andy done with their chores, their dirt bikes up on milk crates, the winding sound of socket wrenches in the suffocating heat of an afternoon garage. Boys who loved the smells of gas and oil and carburetor cleaner, soaking into their hands, soaked into the red shop rags they used to clean engine parts, cleaning these parts in a manner so fastidious it was as if they were cleaning tarnish from expensive jewelry, working the rags over the tiny set-screws of their carburetors. The hands that cleaned carburetor and engine parts, permanently black.

That I could draw no connection between that world and this one, the people who stank of gasoline in the Piazza del Popolo, and Scott and Andy who loved its smell, made me sad for Scott and Andy in a way I could not explain.

That night, the second one sleeping in my same clothes, I lay on the couch and thought of those white balloons I'd filmed, retrieving what I could from memory, since the camera was lost. The sight of them, floating, took me to a park in Reno when I was small. Children were gathered, a group of us seated in an open grassy area. Someone had given us each a balloon. We counted down, and then let go of our balloons. I remembered how the sky had looked after we had opened our hands to let them rise. It was late afternoon, and as the balloons went higher they were set alight by the sun's stronger angle, gold light that only the balloons were high enough to reach. I remembered watching them fade, smaller and smaller, lone voyagers on floating journeys, the sky their ocean, with the ocean's depth and immensity.

I was lying on the couch in that apartment, riding the vast unknown sea with those untethered balloons, when I heard a soft cry, a woman's voice from the other room. Then another cry. The knocking of a bed frame against a wall. I tried to relocate the scene of the balloons and to pretend I was not tracking these sounds, a rhythmic thump, a woman's cries. Durutti was on the couch across from me. I could tell by his breathing that he was deep asleep, and I envied his innocence.

I was awake, waiting for those cries, listening to the thud of the bed frame against the wall. The cries were Bene's. Bene being made to voice those sounds by, I was sure, Gianni, while I was alone on a couch with my childish memory, a person neither in a movement nor of one.

And, in fact, they weren't actually cries. Or rather, the first was a cry, but thereafter they were voiced sighs, so faint I'd had to hold my breath to hear them. The truth is, I was listening very carefully.

The next day, and in the days that followed it, three, four, five—I lost count, surrounded by people who didn't work or go to school or have any compelling reason to care what day of the week it was—I did not think of myself as someone who needed to make decisions. Decisions about Sandro, about New York. I was, instead, one of the people in that Volsci apartment where so many congregated, who had been in the march, who had not been injured or arrested. And by escaping those two outcomes, injury, arrest, I was part of the rage and celebration. One person at the demonstration had died, hit in the neck by a tear gas canister. Many others were beaten by the celerini or by the Fascist gangs that had surged into the rear segment of the march, swinging lead pipes. The kids with gun in pocket, the Valera workers with their tire irons disguised as banner dowels, were, it turned out, merely protecting themselves.

Demonstrations were temporarily banned by the government. There was to be no loitering, no collecting in groups. People all over the city responded to this. Someone figured out how to trip the traffic lights, and they all turned red and stayed red for an afternoon, causing gridlock. Other acts were coordinated by the radio station that was broadcast from inside the apartment, a soundproofed room next to Bene's. Durutti went on the air and invited Romans who were hungry to go out, order food, eat it, and refuse to pay. The radio station was a central coordinating voice. Not a government, but a way to speak to each person, a voice addressing each autonomous person. These are the new figures for rent, the voice said. Pay this amount to the electric company. The things Roberto complained about: this was how they were done. The radio pulsed through a network. A network of people who acted in concert against the government, against the factories, against everything that was against them. We'll take what we can and pay what we want. We'll pay nothing for what is already ours. Bene and Lidia hosted an hourlong morning show addressed to women. One day it was dedicated to the housewives of Rome; the next, to the working prostitutes of Termini. To the women in the armed struggle. The women inside Rebibbia. To the men who have reduced the world to a pile of trash. To our lesbian comrades. The show was called *Everyday Violence*.

"Sisters," Bene said, "men can put you in touch with the world. We see that. Men connect you to the world, but not to your own self."

"To fight with a gun," Bene said, "is to take it upon yourself to think for others. So think clearly and well."

The radio station was jammed repeatedly, the broadcast overtaken by a sudden whistling sound, but Lidia, with Durutti's help, managed to locate another position on the bandwidth and continued broadcasting.

When the police came to San Lorenzo they were fired upon by children and grandmothers with rocks, buckets of water, rotten eggs. There was more of the proletarian shopping, as it was called, that I'd seen on the Via del Corso. Jeans for the people. Cheese and bread and wine for the people. Umbrellas for the people, because rain fell and fell that week.

Downstairs from the apartment was the one in which the two men lived who were making a film about Anna, the pregnant biondina. They had expanded their project and enlisted a crew that included lighting people, electricians, production assistants. Their door was always open, equipment and cords spilling out into the hallway. Passing by, I heard them yelling at the biondina to get into the shower. The two filmmakers were shouting a word I did not know: *"Pidocchi! Pidocchi!"* Because the apartment was open and they were always beckoning, I went in.

The girl was naked, being pushed in the shower by the one on whom she'd squirted her milk.

"You stink," he said. "Come on, it's time to wash."

She smiled in her guileless way. "But I'm shy," she said, trying to hold her hand over her large breasts, the other over her crotch, her full round belly protruding between the two zones of modesty that she was attempting to cover.

She had to be convinced, and finally assented, leaning into the water, soap running over her slippery pregnant form. I remembered suddenly that I was watching, right along with this crew, all male, fixated on her, their subject. I left to go upstairs, ashamed.

Pidocchi were lice, Bene explained. "I hope they get them, too."

Two days later, the filmmakers and their crew were all scratching like crazy as I passed by their downstairs apartment with Lidia, Bene, Durutti.

We were on our way to the movies. At the box office window there was some discussion of what we should pay, the appropriate price for a movie, and then Durutti said screw it, movies should be free. He bypassed the ticket window and yanked open the doors and we crashed on through. The theater was filled with smoke from cigarettes and hash. The movie was already playing, *A Star Is Born*, with Barbra Streisand and Kris Kristofferson. People filed into the dark, yelling the names of friends, hoping to find them. Voices from all over the theater shouted back, "Over here! Over here!" as a prank. Every time Barbra Streisand or Kris Kristofferson opened their mouths to speak, the audience erupted in roars, and the actors' dubbed voices could not be heard. Barbra Streisand was singing, *"Love . . . soft as an easy chair,"* as liquor bottles were dropped, rolling noisily down the sloped theater floor toward the front. *"Love fresh as the morning air . . ."*

I saw a familiar face as we filed out, the soap-flakes model staring down from a poster. The midnight movie: *Dietro la porta verde*. It and she really traveled, a kind of beckoning. Come find out what.

Didi was still in captivity, his face on the front page of the newspaper Gianni was reading when we returned from the movies. I had never told them about Didi, about why I was in Italy in the first place. It seemed like a dream. And maybe an indictment. I was fraternizing now with people who made it impossible for me to think of going to Monza, too deep inside an enemy camp to admit my former allegiance, to think of leaving to pursue the original goal. The day I was meant to go to Monza had come and gone. And who from that realm had cared or noticed? If Sandro cared or noticed, he had not tried to find me. More than a week had passed since I'd left for Rome with Gianni. Maybe I was impossible to find. I heard Sandro's mother's voice, not what she said but a tone: good riddance. And Talia: good riddance. The Count of Bolzano: a shrug, a shake of the head at my crude American behavior, fleeing as I had.

I was estranged now from that world but I felt, as well, an estrangement from this group of people, who nonetheless included me in everything, or at least many things. There were secrets in that apartment. Gianni was often absent and always aloof, quietly reading his *Il Sole 24 Ore* on the couch. He and Durutti would retreat into a room, looks exchanged among the others as the door was shut. At one point, Bene seemed to suggest that Gianni had been in prison but had escaped. I could not tell if she was joking. My Italian was good, but nuance and humor were sometimes lost on me.

There were a lot of gray areas with these people. Roberto and Sandro, despite their political differences, both had presented the issues as stark and tidy, as if there were exactly two groups that opposed the state, as distinct from each other as black and white: the Red Brigades—armed, underground militants. And the leftist youths—open, public, more or less nonviolent. But nothing was simple or stark, I was beginning to see. Guns were issued in the apartment on the Via dei Volsci in virtually the same way the jeans were distributed. It was a world apart from Sandro and his guns. One artist at a shooting range in the Catskills, interested, as Sandro was, in manufacture, protocol, history, the weapon as almost a work of art, an industrial thing of beauty. This was something else, a ragtag mob with guns jammed here and there in their pockets, no concern for make or model beyond pragmatics. The gun was a tool like a screwdriver was a tool, and they all carried them.

A television was liberated by Durutti and two others from a neighborhood electronics store, and we watched the news. The Red Brigades had struck again, killing a Fascist. The Fascists had retaliated by killing an anarchist who was not associated with the Red Brigades. The pope made an appeal for an end to the violence, in his Sunday-morning televised address from the Vatican. He stood on a balcony wearing a huge ornamental headdress that looked like a brushed-metal bullet, a large pointed dome with a row of twinkling stones low around its girth, underneath a spiky gold base.

It was true that we had smoked a little hash. Nonetheless also true that the pope made his plea for peace with a giant bullet propped on his head.

The next day Didi Bombonato was set free, after thirteen days in captivity. That marked time for me in a way I could not have marked it on my own. Thirteen days. A lifetime. For me, anyway, because I had thrown my old life away. At this point I might have gone from the Monza track outside Milan to the German track. That is, had Didi not been kidnapped, had Sandro not betrayed me, had I not run away. And after Monza and then Germany, I would have a lot of footage, possibly enough for my film. I'd return with it to New York, and Marvin and Eric would not be mad about my sabbatical from work, because they'd see what I'd made and as arbiters of the medium would be understanding and supportive.

Instead, no longer the owner of a camera, having smashed and lost my Bolex Pro at the demonstration, I was on a couch in Rome, stoned, watching TV, looking at the face of free and waving Didi Bombonato, whom I had known, but now, would not know.

Didi had been let go after he had agreed to write a defense of the Red Brigades, a letter with a distinctly Leninist tone. The Valera Company was suspicious that Didi had possibly contracted Stockholm syndrome, and whether he had or not, he was no longer quite the image they were looking for to represent and promote Valera Tires, and they pulled their sponsorship of him, according to the news report. No one else in the apartment was watching but me.

Later that day I walked downstairs and saw that the filmmakers' apartment was empty. There was no equipment crowding into the hall. No crew. Just the balding, scraggly one sitting in a chair, smoking.

"Where is the girl?" I asked.

"In a manicomio," he said.

A manicomio. It took me a moment to remember. Insane asylum.

"What about the baby?" I asked.

"The baby," he said, scratching his head almost as if trying to remember. "She had it yesterday."

"So where is it?" I asked.

"Vincenzo has it," he said.

"Vincenzo?"

"The electrician. He fell in love with her. I stepped aside for that. No one can accuse me. I let Vincenzo have her, even as I could have kept having her myself. Because . . . hey, American girl, did you ever have a baby? No? Well, I can tell you what you might not know. Some pregnant girls are very sexual."

He smiled. He had a gap in his teeth like mine. An ugly gap.

"We're editing the film, hopefully in time for Venice," he said, filling the empty room with exhaled smoke as he stubbed out his sloppy and limp handrolled cigarette. "Alberto has a festival connection who can get us in, and—"

A manicomio.

Vincenzo has the baby.

They didn't care about her. The girl who was the center, the cause, the reason for their film.

Venice. They were hoping for Venice.

Vincenzo has the baby.

Durutti and the boys liked me and fought for my attention. It was a good distraction from the problem of Sandro, of what I could no longer go back to. That was something the biondina and I had in common. I didn't have lice. I wasn't going to the manicomio. But like her, I was passing through. A girl who would be around every day for a spell, and then one day be gone.

Gianni did not fight for my attention. He was far too cool, too distant from this whole thing he had brought me to. Bene was his lover, but he showed her no affection in front of others. He was calm, stone-faced, just as he'd been at the villa. Everyone else quieted when he entered the apartment. They lowered the television volume and tracked his movements as he went from room to room, as if they were waiting for him to say something or to make some judgment.

Twice he asked me to take rides with him. On those rides I felt a measure of intimacy between us. He drove, stopped in front of an apartment, parked, asked me to wait. Returned to the car, cool as ever. Once we were stopped at a security checkpoint in Trastevere and Gianni told the traffic officer I was the wife of Sandro Valera, that he worked for the Valera family and was taking me to do my shopping. Hearing this, the officer was eager to wave us on, and I sensed it was my function, for Gianni, to play that role and relieve suspicion. The police were the enemy of the young in Rome, that I understood firsthand, so I didn't think much of it. It was illegal to even plan a demonstration. Discretion, having the wife of a Valera along, made sense.

The third time I went for a ride with him, we had a beer together before returning to the apartment on the Via dei Volsci. He showed me a skeleton key Durutti had made, to insert in pay phones for free calls.

"Want to call your boyfriend?" he asked.

"No," I said.

"Right," he said. "He cheated on you. And right there at the factory, in public . . ."

I felt ashamed to be reminded of it.

"I think Sandro Valera is an asshole for doing that," he said. "You shouldn't feel any shame about it. *He* should be ashamed."

"What were you doing there?" I asked. "Why were you working for her?"

He looked at me. For some reason, we both started to laugh. A strange laughter, airy and heady and off-centering. My face felt red. His wasn't. He stopped laughing and answered me.

"I was looking after them."

"Looking after them," I repeated.

"Keeping tabs."

Of course he was. And why had I not realized? Even when he brought me into that apartment on the Volsci, the heart of the Movement, as I came to see. Why had I not realized that Gianni would have some actual purpose in working for the Valeras? In hovering near their dinner table chatter. Their poolside conversations. The intimacy of the house.

"That family is going to pay," he said. "You'll see. They'll get their justice."

Which was the thing Sandro had promised when he had invited me to his loft for the first time. He'd promised justice, and what I found instead was Ronnie Fontaine. Did Sandro know I'd slept with Ronnie? Did he place him there on the couch as a joke of some kind? I doubted it. But I also knew their friendship wasn't simple. And that when Ronnie chided Sandro about not blocking my way to Monza, it wasn't really about me. Even as it seemed to be. It was between them, a link between them I didn't penetrate. Just as Gianni's threats about the Valera family weren't about me, either. But I was comforted by them. Did I want Sandro to pay? Sure I did.

We returned to the apartment. Gianni and Bene fought. I heard only her, just as when I had listened to them have sex, her voice behind a closed bedroom door, this time loud and upset, righteous.

She came out, entered the kitchen, and ranted to the women gathered there, who were soldering radio parts. She called Gianni various names. The women all laughed.

I stood outside the kitchen, awkward, his accomplice, perhaps the reason she was angry. Bene looked at me. Her face broke into a tight, unfriendly smile.

"Go ahead. Just go with him," she said. "Go on."

I'd spent a few innocent hours with Gianni, and she was shutting me out.

Bene put her hand out, gesturing in the direction of the bedroom where Gianni was. "Go with him," she said.

The other women kept soldering. Not a single one looked up at me. I was being shunned because of Bene. Because of Gianni. Because of something that possibly had nothing to do with me.

It seemed ridiculous, a joke, but it wasn't a joke. They had turned against me in the few hours I was gone.

Bewildered, I walked past the kitchen to the bedroom and opened the door.

Gianni looked up at me.

The rest of it I wish I could erase.

16. HOOKERS AND CHILDREN

John Dogg and Nadine were quite the couple now. John Dogg was showing with Helen Hellenberger. Helen was wild about him. All the important critics were at his debut opening at her gallery. There were slide projections of blank white light. And patterned light from shallow zinc rectangles of water he'd placed strategically on the floor. He'd aimed film lamps at the rectangular pools, which sent reflections up the gallery wall in veined and fractured shimmers.

John Dogg wore a well-cut linen suit and laughed easily and occupied the role of feted artist with perfected naturalism, no sign of the pushy tactics I'd seen at the Kastles'. He moved through the room confident that he was universally adored, and it seemed that he was. I'd met him the previous September and now it was late April, almost May, and he had been reinvented. This happened in New York, and you could never point to the precise turn of events, the moment when the change in human currency took place, when it surged upward or plummeted. There was only the before and the after. In the after, no one was allowed to say, hey, remember when everyone rolled their eyes about John Dogg? Shunned him, thought he was an idiot? I understood all this now. Sandro disapproved of that kind of ambition, said there was no hurry, but it was a lie, a thing successful people said, having conveniently forgotten that they themselves had been in a rush.

I watched as Didier de Louridier pumped John Dogg's hand eagerly and congratulated him on the show.

Nadine stood at John Dogg's side. She, too, was transmitting and receiving on a new frequency. She was sleek and composed, all sheen and stillness. She wore a black, high-collared dress and stiletto heels of black patent leather. Her hair had been cut into one of those waferlike constructions you saw in fashion magazines, a wedge of it, hardened with aerosol lacquer, fanning over one eye. She gleamed like an obelisk, standing next to John Dogg as he shook hands with the people who surrounded them. The concentration of smooth, flattened energy in that wafer of hair, which shaded one eye like an upside-down poker hand. She was nothing like the woman I remembered, sunburned, drunk, crying, something starkly provisional about her enjoyments, Thurman's goodwill, the sense that she would be on hard luck whenever he was bored with her, done escapading, and wanted to go back to Blossom.

I was at the opening with Gloria and Stanley Kastle. Since my return, two weeks earlier, I had been staying with them, in the same spare room where Burdmoore Model had camped out in his fugitive days. I was their current adoptee, and my photographs from the salt flats, at Gloria's insistence, went above the shelf where Burdmoore's sculptures had been displayed. I showed Gloria my short films, which I associated with a naive era, before I'd met Sandro, tracking the row of limousines and drivers on Mulberry Street, a dark walk through neon-lit Chinatown, but Gloria liked them. I was a fresh cause for her and Stanley. They disapproved of how Sandro had treated me. But I understood that they would remain friends with Sandro permanently. I was temporary and Sandro was permanent. They claimed to be angry at him and said if he made an appearance here at John Dogg's opening they would protect me, but there was no risk of running into Sandro. I still knew him, even after discovering that I didn't quite know him. He would feel it was beneath him to come to the opening of John Dogg, so recently scorned and ignored.

Spring had arrived and it was a mild, windless night, the pear trees on West Broadway covered with white flossy blossoms as I had parked the bike and waited for the Kastles outside the gallery.

"She's sleeping with her analyst," Stanley said to me as they approached.

"The couch is there for a *reason*," Gloria replied. "You are flat, horizontal, frontal. They are vertical. The session can either be inert or it can be activated, in which case, Dr. Butz is active."

"She pays him," Stanley said, "a hundred bucks."

"I pay a *negotiated* fee of eighty-five, Stanley."

"Still, she pays him and they do it on the session couch."

"Listen, Stanley, it is the least he could do for me after seventy years of Freud and his patriarchal bullshit. You know what Freud wrote to his fiancée? *Dear darling, while you were scouring the sink, I was solving the riddle of the structure of the brain.* Dr. Butz can scour *my* sink."

"While the riddle—"

"It's your money I'm giving him."

"While the riddle of the brain goes unsolved," Stanley said to me as we walked into the gallery.

Sandro wanted me to come home. He said Talia was just a messed-up and confused girl. I didn't see what her state of mind, her confusion, had to do with anything. Sandro had let me know he was capable of harm, greatly capable of it.

What I'd done, helping Gianni—it was a secret that lived in me, one I didn't know quite what to do with. When I thought of Gianni, his brooding authority, the hurried departure, me driving what turned out to be his getaway car, I felt alone in a way that might be permanent. Secrets isolate a person. In that, I understood one thing about Gianni: the fog of his distance, the burden of secrets, the isolation.

Sandro had picked up the repaired Moto Valera, which had been shipped by the dealer in Reno to one in Manhattan. He relayed through

Gloria that I could collect it if I wanted it. It was in the ground-floor hall of his building, the pink owner's title folded and taped to the gas tank, the key in the ignition. When I went up to get my clothes, Sandro was at his big studio table, drawing. I went into our room, which had never felt in any way mine, and packed my clothes into my duffel bag, the same one I had brought here when I moved from Mulberry Street. I thought maybe Sandro would come in while I packed, try to apologize. He didn't. When I walked past, he looked up. I stopped. Neither of us said anything.

I went down, strapped the duffel to the rear rack of the bike, and rode it over to the Bowery, to the Kastles'. It was my first ride through the streets of New York City, but on a bike I already knew. I had to watch out for potholes, and cabs that came to sudden stops, but crossing Broadway, zooming up Spring Street, passing trucks, hanging a left onto the Bowery, the broadness of the street, the tall buildings in the north distance, the sense of being in, but not of, the city, moving through it with real velocity, wind in my face, were magical. I was separate, gliding, untouchable. A group of winos in front of a Bowery hotel gave me the thumbs-up. At a stoplight, a man in the backseat of a cab, a cigarette hanging from his lips, rolled down his window and complimented the bike. He wasn't coming on to me. He was envious. He wanted what I had like a man might want something another man has.

There was a performance in riding the Moto Valera through the streets of New York that felt pure. It made the city a stage, my stage, while I was simply getting from one place to the next. Ronnie said that certain women were best viewed from the window of a speeding car, the exaggeration of their makeup and their tight clothes. But maybe women were meant to speed past, just a blur. Like China girls. Flash, and then gone. It was only a motorcycle but it felt like a mode of being.

A week after I took the Moto Valera, Sandro came to the Kastles'. His tactic was sternness. He said I needed to stop acting like a martyr. Gloria and Stanley moved in beside me, told Sandro to give me time. He looked at them, nodded in bitter assent. *Yeah, okay. You're protect-*

ing her. I'm the guilty one. He nodded all the way to the freight elevator. Pushed the button, waited for a moment, then took the stairs. It was the last time I'd seen him.

Inside Dogg's crowded opening, Gloria grabbed Helen Hellenberger by the arm and said she should come over to the loft and see my films. Helen was about to make an excuse. Her mouth opened. Gloria said, "Great. We will see you at our place, next week."

When you're young, being with someone else can almost seem like an event. It *is* an event when you're young. But it isn't enough. I was still young, and I wanted something else. I needed a new camera. The Bolex was smashed and I was alone and I wanted my life to happen.

As we moved toward the bar, Stanley said he was terribly thirsty, that he felt like something with rust stains on it.

"That's because you drank nearly a liter of vodka last night," Gloria said. "Your habits are going to be a slow killer of you, Stanley."

"I'm not in a hurry," Stanley said, and turned to watch a girl who pushed past us. She was wearing pants that had clear plastic stretched over her rear, a window for viewing her two butt cheeks, which slid against each other as she walked.

The Kastles had always been engaged in a low-intensity war with each other, but seeing them day in, day out, was to witness the derangement in a new way. One morning Stanley had been drinking coffee when Gloria came into the kitchen area of their loft holding a page ripped from a magazine.

"Stanley," she said, "I want to show you something."

He looked at her fearfully. She held the page in front of him. It was a glossy pictorial of three men and a woman. The men stood over the woman, erect cocks wagged in her face, semen jetting across the image, thick pearls of it on the woman's open lips.

"Should I get my hair cut like this woman?" Gloria asked. "Do you think that style would work for me? Is it becoming?"

Stanley closed his eyes. He shut them tight and shook his head.

"Are you saying no, Stanley, or are you refusing my question?"

When she realized he wasn't going to respond, she left the room. Stanley turned to me.

"A little boy and girl, brother and sister, are looking out the window of a train as it rolls to the platform," Stanley said. "The girl sees a sign on a station door and says, 'Look, we're arriving at *Gentlemen.*' 'You dummy,' the boy says. 'Can't you see we're at *Ladies?*' You see," Stanley said. "The boy will wander around *Ladies,* and the girl will venture into *Gentlemen*. It's the same place. But they will never realize it."

While we were in Italy, Gloria had been given a residency at the Kitchen on Wooster Street. She did a one-day performance called *Alone.* Gloria stood in a small booth with a curtained, pelvis-level opening. A sign invited people to Place Hand in Window. In the window, behind the curtain, was Gloria's naked pelvis.

Stanley had been too prudish to touch his own wife's genitals, as Ronnie announced to me. While Ronnie himself had apparently not just put his hand in the window, but kept it there awhile. "I did my volunteer work for the year," Ronnie said. "I always maintained I wouldn't turn down public service." He put his hand in the window, and barely realizing what he was doing, lost in an interior reverie about the construction "to finger," and how interesting it was that it was gendered, and not reversible, that to finger a man was to pin something on him, a crime, and to finger a woman was to bring her off, and that he was just moving his finger in a kind of unconscious way, back and forth, back and forth, and thinking about those two completely different meanings—not obverses, but maybe not completely unrelated, to finger a man, to pin a crime, to finger a woman . . . suddenly he feels this shudder from Gloria. Oh my God, he thinks, she just had an orgasm! And if that wasn't bad enough, she cheated her own formal precept by peeking to see whose hand it was. As he turned to go he heard this muffled voice from behind the curtain whispering his name. He told the story as if Gloria was somehow presumptuous or overreaching, when he'd put his hand in her vagina. But that was of course the joke, the outrageous pretense of innocence. Of passivity.

"I should get one of those T-shirts that says ORGASM DONOR," he said.

Afterward, Gloria followed him around for a week like a puppy dog. He finally had to tell her she was about twenty years older than his type. "I thought you don't *have* a type," Gloria had said. "You always make a point of that, of not having any type. You don't have one, and I'm not even *that*."

Gloria told me about her residency at the Kitchen, and about *Alone*, but not what happened with Ronnie.

"It was about the fourth wall," she said. "It was also about making an assertion. There. Factual. In a sense *male*. If someone chose to break the fourth wall and place his hand in the box? They brought to the piece any component of sex. They brought it. I offered an object in a box, coldly. If someone placed a hand in the box, it was that person insisting on sensuality, on touching. Not me."

But then she broke down sobbing, and when she had regained enough composure to speak she told Stanley, with me as witness, that she believed she might be in love with Ronnie, and that the terms of her performance of *Alone* had not included that possibility, and perhaps she was losing her mind. She sobbed and sobbed, her body convulsing into the arm of the couch.

The three of us sat, Gloria crying, and then Stanley sighed, cleared his throat, and spoke.

"Dear Gloria," he said, as if he were writing her a letter, "remember how we used to joke about the concept of love? The phrase 'to be in love'? I would say to you, Darling, I believe I may be in love with the woman who announces the time of day over the telephone. Her voice is so calm, and even, and feminine but not artificially sweet, just measured. And she is always available, always there when I call. I can get a drink of water in the middle of the night, while you're sound asleep, furtively dial MEridian 7-1212, and she'll say to me, '*At the tone, eastern standard time will be 2:53 a.m. exactly.*' I could call her whenever I wanted. She was totally available to me, and yet an enchanting mystery, one not to be solved. I could never make anything advance further. And remember that while I held this fascination for the Time Lady, you one day fell head over heels for the man who answered the suicide hotline? Remember, Gloria? You said to me, 'Stanley, he listens to me. He listens.' And I said, 'Gloria, that is his job.' And when you were better, when the temptation to hurt yourself had passed out of your mind completely, you forgot all about him. Remember? You didn't even want to call the man you'd once been in love with, because you no longer were in that frame of mind. Call a suicide hotline? I'm Gloria Kastle, goddamn it—I don't call hotlines. Hotlines call me."

Gloria sniffled, blotted her tear-streaked cheeks with a throw pillow from the couch, and smiled weakly.

"Do you realize how many Larrys are at Dogg's opening?" Ronnie said, coming toward me in a shirt that said MARRIED BUT LOOKING.

"Larry Zox, Larry Poons, Larry Bell, Larry Clark, Larry Rivers, and Larry Fink. And they're all talking to one another! This is some kind of historic moment. Reminds me of a story Saul Oppler once told me. He was sitting with Saul Bass and Peter Saul on a rock in Central Park, and they look down from this rock, and below they see Saul Bellow with Saul Steinberg, *together,* buying hot dogs from a Sabrett cart."

Nadine and John Dogg posed for someone's camera. Nadine turned her head just slightly to one side. The light from the flash lapped at her hair and polished complexion, the black, shiny cloth of her dress. She did not blink. I told Ronnie I almost didn't recognize her. I did recognize her, though. There was no question. I meant to say she seemed changed, altered.

"She looks like a model advertising an expensive timepiece," Ronnie said. "Funny how they try to make it into a separate category. Not 'watch' but 'timepiece.'"

Nadine was close to us now. Ronnie said hello to her.

She said hello to him and then to me, separately, but as if she'd never met me. I didn't press the matter. We watched her walk away.

"Are you still friends with that photographer?" I was breaking the long silence about that night. What the hell, I thought. She's here, and Ronnie's here, and Sandro, Sandro is not here.

"Yeah. Thurman's wife died recently. People say the stupidest things about his work now. Thurman took a lot of pictures of the sky, and now Didier and his ilk claim that this is a kind of mourning. A great sadness, Thurman unable to face the horizontal world, the low material world, because he's pining for his wife and thinking only of death and the heavens. This is a man who slept with everyone but his wife. Took pictures of the sky because he was too drunk to get up. Puked in a church donations box in Louisiana—I was with him. He had a bad hangover and had gone in to photograph something, I don't remember what. He said it was the only time he'd been in a church since he was a child. But now he's gazing at the heavens, in tribute to Blossom. People and their need to interpret."

He waved away the subject of Thurman. The subject of that night.

"Hey, listen. I don't know what you were doing over there in Italy besides having melodramas with Sandro. But the place must suit you or something. You look good."

"Thanks," I said, fairly sure I looked no different. I was in cutoffs and knee-high socks, the men's kind with blue and red stripes around the ribbing at the top. Those socks weren't allowed when I was with Sandro. "Come on, seriously," he'd say. "You'll make me look like your father, like I'm taking you to your basketball game."

I had on a leather jacket; maybe that was the difference Ronnie noticed. And I had the bike, outside, unseen, but it had become a kind of mental armor.

"Yeah, you look like you've grown up a little." He was looking at me from various angles. "See, now you're doing that whole smiling-woman thing. That's good."

I'd had a fantasy, back at Sandro's mother's villa, of saying something to Ronnie, letting him know he was a bastard for giving Talia my hat. But now I couldn't bring myself to do it. Talia wasn't here. She didn't matter. I would make her matter by bringing her up.

*   *   *

Even while he seemed not to focus on me, I felt Ronnie's attention at John Dogg's opening. Even as he spoke to others, performed his Ronnie shtick, I suspected he was secretly performing it for me. Things were shifting. I was no longer his best friend's lover, but a girl he'd once slept with.

Ronnie told John Dogg's parents his name was Sergio Valente. To the girl with the see-through pants, he introduced himself as Albert Speer.

"I hearda you," she said, unimpressed.

Being Albert Speer got Ronnie started on the notion of the uncommon criminal, and then he turned to me and cued himself. What made a criminal common or uncommon? The girl with the see-through pants took the opportunity to wander off. She moved through the room, trapped inside her exhibitionism, unable to pretend she was just another girl at the opening, to get beyond the awkwardness of her nudity.

Ronnie seemed not to notice her exposed butt, even as he stared at it and at her.

"I'm collecting mug shots," he said to me as his eyes tracked her across the room.

"Did I tell you that? I go down to police records on Centre Street. I'm looking for convicted criminals with my name."

How many could there be? I asked.

"A few," he said. Actually, only one so far. But three if you included the Ron Fontana and the Robert Fontaine that Ronnie himself did include. They were doing important work, especially the one with his actual name. The heavy lifting, Ronnie said, the dirty work.

I thought of Ronnie's brother Tim, the single time I'd met him. Too muscular to be trusted. His clothes too new and too boxy, the clothing of a prisoner just freed. He was talking about a partner, the plans they had. He could have meant a partner on a construction job, but "partner" could mean partner in crime, cell mate, or all three: a guy you met in jail and then doubled up with for construction jobs and burglaries.

"I'm starting to believe this guy up at Rikers is doing his time, pacing his cell, for both of us," Ronnie said. "Doing *our* time."

He's talking about his brother, I thought.

Giddle showed up. She and Burdmoore were no longer together. He was too sincere, she said. It had started to drive her nuts. He always wanted to get to the bottom of things. Get to the heart of things. "This supposed heart," Giddle said. The way he talked, assuming it existed, zapped whatever feelings she'd had for him. "This whole 'let's take off the masks and hold each other' thing," Giddle said. "No thanks. I'm just passing through. I said, 'If you want to pass through from some other direction and meet and have a good time, fine, but there is no heart and no fundamental thingie.' He put too much pressure. I started making things up," she said, "to satisfy him. Like I'd tell him I was sexually abused by my brother and that was why I had low self-esteem, which was what led me to cheat on him with Henri-Jean."

"The guy who carries the pole?"

"Yeah," she said. "And the thing is, I don't even *have* a brother and suddenly Burdmoore wants me to start hypnotherapy with this friend of his, a woman who counsels incest survivors. I'm just trying to entertain myself. Keep it light. Have a good time. By which I mean make stuff up and watch how he reacts. He didn't know how to play the game. And then the thing with the pants, oh God."

Giddle had brought a pair of white pants into Rudy's and pinned them up on the wall with an announcement that anyone who fit into them could sleep with her. It turned out the white pants were too small for most of the guys at Rudy's. The artist John Chamberlain got them up to his knees. Henri-Jean managed to get them on but could not zip them. Didier was next to try them when Burdmoore showed up. Burdmoore snatched the pants out of Didier's hands. He held them upside down, gripped each pant leg firmly, and ripped the pants by the crotch seam, tore them clean in half.

"If you could have seen his face," Giddle said. "The guy has a serious anger problem." She left with Henri-Jean, who shrugged as they passed Burdmoore. A mime's shrug. Life is sweet, I'm a helpless neuter. Whimsy is the answer to tears. I'm going to fuck your girlfriend here shortly. Shrug.

"Did he use it on you?" Ronnie asked.

"What?"

"That big pole he carries."

"Ha-ha. He didn't need to, Ronnie."

John Dogg led Nadine past us, holding her hand like she was his little girl. She looked down shyly as he spoke to someone about borrowed light. They seemed like one happiness, a partnership. She'd been reinvented in the glow of his sudden success. And her rehabilitation made her into useful and effective arm candy for him. Just as you weren't supposed to point out that John Dogg had recently been considered a clamoring outsider, one was not meant to approach this gleaming version of Nadine and ask if she remembered pissing in a bathtub, or letting Thurman Johnson rub the barrel of his starter pistol between her legs. It was more unseemly of me to think of these things than it was unseemly for her to have done them.

She and John Dogg had made it into the castle just before the gates shut. And the point was not how they got in, or that they almost didn't, or to wonder if they deserved to be there. It was, here they are. Welcome. The point was that they were in. They were in.

"I bet you wore a long coat tonight, and took it off when you got here. Is that right?" It was Gloria, accosting the woman with the butt window.

The woman looked quickly at Gloria and then turned away, but before she did, I saw the distress in her face.

"I just wanted to know," Gloria said to me because I happened to be passing by, as if she would have spoken to anyone passing by and barely registered who that person was, "how committed she is. I wanted a sense of her commitment.

"When the revolution comes it won't make any difference," Gloria said. "They'll have a special guillotine for girls like that. With an even rustier blade for the artists who ogle her. These people here don't matter. It's MTA workers who need to see her rosy butt cheeks. But no, she wears a trench coat on the subway and reserves her hot little ass for us people who have already seen any number of hot little asses. Barbara Hodes was making see-through dresses in 1971. Eric Emerson wore chaps and a jockstrap upstairs at Max's, and Cherry Vanilla *only* goes topless. It is so done. Done done done."

But it's new *to her,* I should have said but didn't. She's on *her* timeline, Gloria, not yours or anyone else's.

After the opening there was a party on the roof of a building around the corner from the gallery, and John Dogg's band played. That was what he'd wanted, a performance of his own band. It was a way to get a gig, using his newfound popularity in the art world to shoehorn in his music project behind him. Once you wedge the door open, push as much of yourself through as possible. They were called Hookers and Children. Bass, drums, saxophone, and John Dogg playing guitar and singing. They wore suits, and the drummer had a silver-sparkle drum kit like an entertainer from the mezzanine of a midtown hotel. They covered a Donovan song, "Young Girl Blues." Dogg wasn't bad. In fact, he was good. He sang like he really meant it, wavering his voice just like Donovan.

> *It's Saturday night. It feels like a Sunday in some ways*
> *If you had any sense, you'd maybe go away for a few days*

The tender but slightly paternalistic love of whoever was addressing the young girl.

Stanley and Gloria had gone home. I stayed. Partly because Ronnie stayed. But I didn't hover around him. We were two coordinates on that crowded roof. I was aware of him and I felt his awareness of me even as he mingled with others. It was a clear night, three stars glinting through a suspension of smog and city glow. I recognized a lot of the people on the roof, but because I'd been away, I felt I was watching them from some remove and didn't have to engage, didn't have to say hello the way you needed to when you had seen everyone the week before, that hello of having mutually decided you would permanently remain mere acquaintances. I stood back, hands in the pockets of my leather jacket, leaning against the railing. I felt like a balloon, like I could just float off the rooftop. I weighted myself with beer from the keg. Watched Giddle dance with Henri-Jean. Leaned over the railing periodically to be sure the Moto Valera was still there.

I didn't want to think about Sandro. I didn't want to think about Gianni.

"The three passions," Stanley had said to me that morning, "are love, hate, and ignorance. Ignorance is the strongest."

I had a hard time getting Bene's face out of my thoughts, her barely concealed smugness, as if to say, *he's all yours.*

I had not wondered, why is she passing him over? Why is she letting him go so easily? I had not wondered.

Bene had put her hand out, steering me toward the room where Gianni was. To the right of her, the other women soldering, hoping to repair a transmitter the carabinieri had smashed. When I passed them, Lidia and the others had not looked up from what they were doing and I understood that I had been shut out. I had not done anything wrong, but that was it. Bene had shut me out. What other choice did I have? I had no money. No friends. Gianni had brought me there, and it was to him I turned.

He and I, listening to Bene's steps on the landing as she departed.

Gianni's face, unreadable. His distance, which I had interpreted as chivalry, a form of respect. When in fact it was just what it seemed: distance.

"I need to take a trip," he'd said. "I want you to come. We'll go together. You want to see the Alps?"

His question confirmed or explained or simply filled the space of tension I'd felt all along with Gianni, from the first moments at the villa.

He took out a cigarette and lit it, in no hurry for my answer. Probably in no hurry because he knew, somehow, that my answer would be yes.

It was a North Pole, the same brand of cigarettes that Giddle smoked. It struck me as funny that Gianni smoked Giddle's brand, but there was no witness who would understand why this was funny. Giddle and Gianni, from opposite sides of the globe featured on the cigarette packet.

I had no other world to turn to now but this one, the roof, Dogg's band, Giddle's antics.

Hookers and Children filled the night. There was a lot to say on these two subjects.

They were playing their own stuff now. Dogg's earnest voice, but with more dissonance in the chords.

Henri-Jean wrapped himself tightly against Giddle and they swayed from side to side. Their dancing seemed especially obscene for the fact that he was out of character. He wasn't supposed to grind against women. He was supposed to be this lone figure in the cityscape, jester and outcast with his idiosyncratic burden, the pole over his shoulder. But in fact he was a man, bending his knees to lower his pelvis to the level of Giddle's ass.

Nadine was talking to Helen. Smiling in a remote manner that was probably nervousness but would be read by Helen as reserved, attractively reserved. Helen said Nadine looked familiar and asked if she, too, had by chance gone to Dalton.

"No," Nadine said in a dispassionate tone, almost like a corpse, no expression on her face. I sensed that she had been coached by John Dogg to remain aloof or to pretend to. She held herself perfectly still. By revealing any animation to her face or body she would spoil the effect of the hair and the dress and the patent leather heels, which shone on the roof's gravel like wet ink. Watching her hold tight to sudden elegance, hold it like it was a religion that could save her, I understood that Nadine had told the truth and Giddle had lied. Giddle had never been a prostitute. I didn't know where she went in the velvet jumper she kept in her work locker, but it wasn't to a midtown hotel.

While Thurman Johnson and an unidentified Ronnie had gone out to buy scotch that night at the Chelsea Hotel, Nadine had told me about the first time she turned a trick. It was with a very old man. He wanted a blow job. "Five dollars a minute, I told him. I knew he had a lot of fives in his wallet." This was an important part of the deal, she had explained. You made an educated guess of roughly how much money they had on them, and how much more they might be able to acquire if they ran out of what was in their wallet. You priced accordingly, tried to divide time into segments that corresponded with a complete emptying of their wallet. "You have to think in totalities, as my ex-husband used to put it. The larger view. So I said five a minute, figuring he had about a hundred dollars. The first minute goes by. I take his little pud out of my mouth and he says, *Oh please, oh please.* 'Five more dollars,' I say. I made about eighty bucks. My mouth was numb. It's actually not so simple when they stay soft. It's like slurping on the corner of a plastic bag that has a little bit of air in. He never came. It was just minutes and fives. Another thing I have done to make money is cry. Some men will do anything to get you to stop crying. They don't like to see women cry, nuh-uh. Nice guys will do whatever they can to get you to stop. The problem is most guys aren't nice."

Giddle's lie didn't matter. Giddle lied about everything. I didn't even know if her name was Giddle. Her lie was not a claim to a life like Nadine had lived. It was something else, whatever Giddle naively imagined to be the glamour of the call girl, the secret power, a cliché, champagne and silk teddies. The way Giddle said "businessmen," daubing cucumber oil on her neck. The way she said "midtown," and flipped her hair out so it lay evenly and full like she was Rita Hayworth. It was play-acting. It wasn't that different from my childhood fantasy of the Mustang Ranch as an actual ranch, grand and Western-fancy, and not various ugly trailers. It was like saying "timepiece" when you meant watch; there was no such thing. Only minutes and fives.

"This one's called Bud's Doughnuts," Dogg said into the microphone. "Our Second Avenue home away from home." It sounded like surf rock. A psychedelic projection behind them. Hookers and Children were like a slightly ironic prom act.

"I *know* Bud," Ronnie said to someone. "It's a real dude. I know him from high school. We both moved to Manhattan and he opened Bud's Doughnuts on Second Avenue. His brother Tom opened a car wash."

"Tom's Car Wash, out on Myrtle Avenue?"

"No, man, that's not the same one."

There was a guy on the roof with a Polaroid camera, getting girls to show him their breasts. When he approached Nadine, she gave him a terror-stricken look and shook her head. She was again with Helen Hellenberger, who politely said, "No thank you."

Burdmoore had talked about the lost children. The times to come. The times that had been to come but that had not come.

There was the matter of who was awake and who was asleep. The question of it. The ambiguity inherent in this way of dividing people one to the next, awake or dreaming. *We were their nightmare.* If one group was dreaming the other, there couldn't be certainty as to which group was which.

After Burdmoore and Fah-Q had withdrawn themselves from battle, retreated to the mountains of northern Mexico, Fah-Q had a vision, Burdmoore had told us that night at Gloria and Stanley's. After the vision came to him, Fah-Q broke from their grim, secret encampment and traveled all the way back to New York City. He needed to speak with Allen Ginsberg. Fah-Q was certain that Ginsberg had an important message for them, Burdmoore had recounted to us. A message about their clandestinity, about the revolution. "So what was it?" Didier had asked, a lightness in his voice, the joke being that whatever the message was, perhaps it might still be of use. Fah-Q found Ginsberg, Burdmoore told us, and indeed, Ginsberg had a message for the Motherfuckers. The message was that they should all quit smoking. They should give up cigarettes. Didier, seated across from Burdmoore at the Kastles' dinner table, had narrowed his eyes and sucked wetly on his Gauloise and nodded, understanding that Allen Ginsberg was truly the idiot Burdmoore had claimed he was.

More and more people crowded onto the roof as Hookers and Children finished their set. All the other roofs around SoHo were dark, occupied by squat water towers, rickety and hand-hammered spacecraft set down for the night, dormant and crouching on spindly legs over dark, flat expanses. This roof was noise and movement and shifting silhouettes. Empty plastic cups sent over the edge. The hopeful, gaspy pumping of an empty keg. Ronnie telling someone a story about a Japanese stripper named Shomi.

The air was cool and breezy now. I checked again on the bike as a gust loosed pear blossoms from the trees, invisible hands stripping branches of their little white petals, scattering them on the sidewalk.

"The thing about songwriting," John Dogg was saying to someone, "is that you can address things *obliquely,* but no matter. You can't get away from the content that is the essence of the form. All songs are about unrequited love."

"Except 'Green Onions,'" Ronnie said. "Which isn't about love at all."

It must have been Tim Fontaine, and not Ronnie, who'd had to live with that song in his head. Tim had spent a decade in prison. Got out, violated his parole, and was now back inside, as far as I knew. It was Tim's experience in prison that Ronnie had spoken of. Tim, who was doing Ronnie's time. Why couldn't Ronnie just say so? Why did he have to present these elaborate stories, and some of it was true and some wasn't and you were never going to know which was which. Either he'd worked in factories, or on boats, or both, or neither, and whatever he had or had not done, there were a lot of stories. Sandro had always protected Ronnie's evasions. "You don't know," he'd tell people. But Sandro didn't know, either.

"I'm talking about songs with lyrics," Dogg said. "Not instrumentals. 'Green Onions' is an instrumental."

"'Take This Job and Shove It,'" Ronnie said. "Tell me that's about unrequited love."

"Oh, but it is. It is," Dogg said. "It is. *Take this job and shove it, I ain't working here no more,*" he sang. "He's quitting because his woman left him. And she was the only reason he withstood the lousy treatment in the first place. He's done being abused by the factory foreman now that his heart is broken."

John Dogg was not a complete idiot. He had merely seemed like one. It was wanting something a great deal that made people embarrassing—which was why I'd hidden my wants around Sandro and his friends, and Giddle, too, pretended I didn't want an art career when I did. Pretended I wasn't jealous of Gloria, of Helen Hellenberger, of Talia, when I was.

I wove through the crowd, heading for the fire stairs. Giddle was flirting with John Chamberlain, who made precarious sculptures of crushed-up car parts. She was drunk and kept asking him if he had a driver's license. That was a particular mood of Giddle's, heckling as flirtation. When that didn't work, she said she knew his secret, his dirty secret.

"What is it?" he said, suddenly interested, looking her up and down in stark assessment.

"You used to be a shampoo girl," she said.

He laughed, grinning at her broadly. "So come on back to my place and I'll shampoo you."

I passed Ronnie. He was talking to a girl I didn't know. "Have you had any contact recently with people from other planets?" he asked her. His voice got louder as I passed. He turned in my direction.

The stairs were behind the water tower, where the drinks table was. Nadine was there alone. She poured wine into a keg cup all the way to the top. It was dark and she didn't see me. I watched as she drank the entire thing in one quick and continuous series of gulps, then wiped her mouth with the back of her hand, looked around nervously like a hungry animal eating some other animal's food, and refilled the cup.

Don't you remember me, Nadine?

Don't you?

But why would she. She was on her way down, or up, or down, and not looking for friends. She wasn't shopping for experience. She was trying to survive. I was the one shopping for experience. I who remembered her and everything she had said to me, and that was enough. It was enough that I remembered her.

The bike would not start. I couldn't get it to turn over. I pushed it off the centerstand and figured I would try to bump start it, coast and get some speed and hopefully it would catch. It had been fouling spark plugs. Maybe that was it.

"Engine trouble?"

I realized, hearing his voice, that I had hoped Ronnie would follow me out. He bent down. "Could be this."

One spark plug lead was dangling. A simple thing that anyone could see. He plugged it back into the cylinder head.

"Thanks, Ronnie."

"Well, maybe you could give me a ride. I mean, if you can start it."

"I can start it."

I'd given rides back in Reno, when I'd had the other, older Moto Valera. A lot of passengers didn't understand that you leaned with and not against the driver. That you put your hands on her waist, never on her shoulders. But Ronnie had ridden plenty. He owned that Harley when I met him, and he knew how to be a passenger, to lean with me when I cornered. He held me snugly, his arms tight around my waist, his chest pressed to my back. I couldn't tell if this was deliberate or not. Scott and Andy had told me that boys became connoisseurs of breast size, shape, feel, having girls pressed against their backs as they cornered and braked. Andy said if you weren't sure, you stopped short, so that your passenger mashed into you, which gave you a good idea of what was underneath her sweater.

I drove Ronnie to his place on Broome Street. "You can come up," he said, hopping off. His tone wasn't exactly enthusiastic. It was as he said, you can if you want to.

It had been two full years since the night I'd spent with him, a night that had opened out, self-expanding, into a world of infatuation and innuendo and games, and finally, the two of us in my old apartment on Mulberry Street, innuendo had turned to assertion. We had lain down. Faced each other and let our lips touch, and I had felt like we were two shirtless kids, sibling and casual, done with our paper routes and relaxing on the grass. Later, our bodies entwined, we weren't casual, or like siblings. I had been sure it meant something. Even if he had shown no vulnerability, nothing even close to it. I had mistaken physical passion for passion.

Ronnie's loft had the same high ceilings and industrial grime as Sandro's, but it was more cluttered. The cakey smell from the fortune cookie factory on the ground floor filled the room, a rising sweetness in the middle of the night. The floor Ronnie occupied had been an Asian import foods warehouse before Ronnie took it over, and he had kept a lot of what had been left behind. Huge barrels that said MSG on them, where he stored the clothes he bought and wore and then threw away instead of laundering. Against one wall were crates of canned lychee packed in heavy syrup, whose labels he said he found beautiful, and meant to do something with at some point. There was a 1954 calendar on the wall, an Asian woman whose prettiness was meant to promote some product, her face faded to grayish-green, smiling under all that lapsed time.

I opened Ronnie's refrigerator. He had gold boxes of Kodak film and three cans of Schlitz. We each opened a can and joked about how no one had food in the refrigerator. I would have thought married people like Stanley and Gloria might have food in their refrigerator, but no. Film canisters, margarine, and Kraft Fluff. Generic brands had just begun appearing on the grocery store shelves. What would they call Fluff? Ronnie wondered. Schlitz could be "Beer," and Fritos "Corn Chips." But Fluff was its name and what it was. "Whipped Marshmallow Puree?" I said. Maybe, he replied, but it lost the effect of simplicity. It sounded like an industrial product.

He was telling me about the state the loft was in when he signed his lease. "These guys did not believe in banks." He bent down and opened a door hidden in the wall. "A safe is an adjective as a noun. Probably a very old concept."

He could have been talking to anyone. Where I had felt his attentions at the opening, now I felt the old distracted and performing Ronnie.

"What do you keep in there?"

"Secrets," he said, shutting it. "And deeds. This guy whose boat I worked on as a kid gave me some land and money. I never claimed any of it. I keep the deeds in this safe."

"Why didn't you claim it?"

"It's a long story."

"Like all your stories."

"This is the longest. But listen, I think I need to hit the hay."

I said I should go anyhow, it was late. But I hesitated, hoping for some way to make it through the distance, to reach him.

"The guy in Rikers with your name," I said. "It's about Tim, isn't it."

I detected a faint crease of irritation in his face.

"That's right. It's about Tim," he said. "Guy I shared a childhood with."

"Why can't you just say, 'I feel bad about my brother'?"

"I feel bad about my brother," Ronnie repeated in a robotic tone. "I feel bad about my brother."

I stayed quiet.

"You think you're the first person to think of that? That I feel bad about my brother? Let me introduce you to a concept. Two concepts, actually. Important tools for surviving the human condition. One is called irony. Say it with me. *Eye-ron-eee.* Now, the next is harder to pronounce, but let's try. *Diss-sim-you-lay-shon.* Giving the false appearance that you are not some thing. Like a hustler pretends that he is not a skilled player of pool. One may, in a quite different circumstance, give the false appearance that he does not suffer from guilt about his own brother's incarceration, but instead, simulates an interest in the incarceration of not his kin but phantom subjects with which he has only one tenuous but coherent link: a name."

He lay down on the couch.

"My brother got out of prison a month ago," he said, looking up at the ceiling. "He was keeping his appointments with his PO. He was trying to get into the welder's union. I loaned him a thousand bucks to buy a Trans Am. I said, 'Why do you need such a stupid car?' And he does this, *Come on, Ronnie, come on, big bro, I've been in the joint ten years. What broad is gonna be interested in an ex-con? I need the car to put me back in play. I need it to keep me good. I won't be just some asshole looking to screw up his program and get back inside.* Who could argue with that? I gave him the money for the car. He totaled it on the New Jersey Turnpike. Chest right through the steering column. He crashed the stupid car I bought him and died. So I feel especially bad about my brother. But that is my business. And I'll mention him or I won't as I choose."

He stared at the ceiling.

"Ronnie, I'm sorry."

When he finally spoke, his voice was gentler. "I used to tease Sandro about you," he said. "Sandro playing coach. Or dad. You just seemed too young. And you were. But honestly, I don't even know if you'd be different older. I like you. But there's something you never seem to get."

And that's why I can't love you.

Ronnie didn't say that. And yet all the way back to the Kastles', and lying in the dark loft, the sound of someone kicking a metal garbage can down the Bowery, I felt the sting of that phantom phrase.

I was the girl on layaway. And it wasn't Ronnie who'd put me on layaway. It was something I had done to myself.

The news hit about Roberto Valera the next week. I didn't see it in the newspaper. Helen mentioned it when she came over, on Gloria's insistence, to see my films. I'd borrowed a projector from Marvin and Eric. In the way Marvin had gravely made me memorize the proper procedure for loading my reel, I understood that he and Eric were invested in me. They liked my films and were saving "damaged" but in fact perfectly good roles of Kodachrome for me to take home. I had just loaded the first film, *Waiting*, I had called it, the footage of the patient Mob chauffeurs on Mulberry, when Helen asked if we had heard what happened to Sandro's brother.

"He was kidnapped!" she said.

My film flickered on the screen that Gloria had put up for me, a white bedsheet. The first driver. Sweat rolling down his face.

From my terrified position I was able to see that to Helen it wasn't a big deal.

"Kidnapped," she said, "and Sandro has been in my office talking to people in Italy nonstop. No one can get through to the gallery now, never mind that it's costing me a fortune."

Helen watched the films and said they had something. "Maybe for a group show I'm thinking of," she said, "for next summer."

I nodded but it went in one ear and out the other. All I could think of was Roberto.

I went to the international newsstand on Astor Place and bought all the Italian newspapers they had. It was not major news, not on the front page. Deep in the business section of *La Repubblica*, one incident of many. Roberto Valera, taken on May 1 from his countryside home above Bellagio. Armed combatants had entered in the early-morning hours and then driven him to an unknown location. There was a photograph of Roberto holding up the previous day's newspaper, May 2, proof he was alive, that he existed inside time. He gazed at the camera, looking like the Roberto I knew. Irritated, a man whose patience was being tested.

A call had been made to the police in Rome, the article reported, the caller declaring the kidnapping the work of the Red Brigades, not by accident on International Workers' Day. It had been confirmed that the anonymous call had been placed from inside Rome's Termini train station, from a pay phone right next to the police kiosk. A comical, taunting gesture. The playfulness of it reminded me of Durutti and the others in the Movement. But Durutti wasn't kidnapping anyone. The people on the Volsci carried guns, but as defense, they said, against Fascists, who also carried guns. They shared an attitude about life, a lightness. They weren't clandestines. Only Gianni was possibly that. Gianni, who had been watching Roberto. That was why he had been there, at the villa. To form an impression of schedules and habits.

The anonymous caller from the pay phone near the police kiosk said Roberto Valera was an enemy from the enemy class. He was being detained by the people's army. Held in a people's prison, at a secret location. He would be tried by a people's court. If he was found guilty, the punishment would be severe.

There were other kidnappings and attacks that had also occurred on May 1, according to *La Repubblica*. A SIT-Siemens manager was shot forty times in the legs outside his home in Milan. I remembered what Roberto had said about the kneecappings, that it was a bumpkin method borrowed from the Mafia, who would do it to cattle to destroy a farmer's herd. Roberto had shaken his head at the savage stupidity of borrowing a technique meant for cows. Another manager, from Fiat, had been kidnapped that same morning, with a three-billion-lire ransom.

Why Roberto would be tried and the other ransomed I didn't know. When I looked at his image in the newspaper, the impatient gaze, holding the newspaper up, a wave of nausea passed through me. Not sympathy, just nausea. It was possible he might die.

I thought of Gianni telling the carabinieri I was married to a Valera, his employer, and that he was taking me shopping.

I thought of that long and bewildering day, waiting for Gianni on the other side of the Alps. How cold it was as the light drained away, and Gianni did not appear, and I could not seem to answer my own question of how long it was a person was meant to wait.

The day after I learned Roberto had been kidnapped, Burdmoore Model came to visit. The Kastles were out. I invited him in. "Oh, uh, okay," he said, slightly unsure of why he should stay since Stanley and Gloria were not home. He asked about Sandro. I said we were no longer together. There was an uncomfortable silence. I said his brother had been kidnapped by the Red Brigades. Did he know? Had he heard about it? I imagined in him some silent sympathy for my involvement with Gianni. I wanted his sympathy.

"They are trying him," I said.

Burdmoore nodded. "This brother of Sandro's, he runs the company? What business are they in again?"

I said, "Rubber, mostly. And motorcycles."

"I'd imagine he'll be guilty," Burdmoore said.

"And then what?"

"After the death sentence?" He scratched his chin, thinking.

"Like in Brecht's *Der Jasager*," he said. "After a fate has been decided, it's customary to ask the victim, the sacrifice, if he agrees to his fate. But it's also customary for the victim to say yes. So maybe he'll be given that option. I mean the mandatory option of accepting his fate. Then again, maybe they'll just let him go. One thing I'll say about these kinds of militants, which I do understand, from my own history. These are people who consider the means they use to be the same, morally, as those of their enemy. In other words, no less justified. One's own means are always justified. To them, the capitalist, like in this case your boyfriend's brother—"

"Ex-boyfriend."

"Either way, the capitalist isn't a marionette serving some other, larger system of evil. He is power himself. Evil itself. And they've nabbed him."

I went back to check *La Repubblica* on the newsstand at Astor Place a few times and didn't find anything. I realized that if I wanted to follow that kind of news, I had to read *Il Sole 24 Ore*, the financial and business paper Gianni was always holding in front of his face. I went to the library on Forty-Second Street after work and read it on those wooden dowels in the periodicals room, rustling pages as old men smelling of liquor slept in club chairs, a woman shuffled around trying to look purposeful, but the wrong kind of purpose for a library. She circled the room, moving with that particular way that homeless women had of seeming like little girls, taking steps with their toes turned slightly inward, chewing on a frayed sleeve, little girls shuffling down the hall to their parents' bedroom in the middle of the night. I read through *Il Sole 24 Ore*. After three days of no news except that the Fiat manager had been released after his family produced the ransom, Roberto appeared again in the paper. There had been a statement by the Red Brigades that he could forestall his trial, and the possibility of a guilty sentence, if the government was willing to trade him for eight militants currently imprisoned. Roberto had written a statement encouraging this. Insisting on it. It was, he said, the only way to save his life.

"He's not himself," an article headline in *Il Sole 24 Ore* announced the next day. The quote was from his own mother. Signora Valera said her son deplored any negotiations with terrorists and never, *never ever,* would have advocated such a thing. "He's not himself." The photo of him holding the newspaper the day after his capture appeared next to the article.

Not himself. It seemed a kind of death sentence. If Roberto was killed, it wasn't the old Roberto. It was some other, who was now begging for negotiations that he hadn't approved of until it was his own life in question. There was silence the next day, and then an article on the question of where he was. The police in Rome had apparently hired a psychic who held a séance that the investigating team attended. The planchette had produced only the word *Cinzano*. A dead end. On the seventh day of Roberto's capture, the chief constable in Rome stated that priority should be given to investigating the organized wing of the autonomist youths in Rome's San Lorenzo, from which he believed the Red Brigades found support and cover.

I told myself that the question of Roberto's life had nothing to do with me.

I had been back in New York a month. I was not in contact with Gianni. Not in contact with Sandro, had not seen him since the week after my return, when he walked out of the Kastles' loft nodding angrily.

My guilt concerning the question of Roberto's life was a fantasy, I told myself. It was not reality.

If Gianni was involved in Roberto's kidnapping, that was not related to anything that was related to me. If Gianni had said the family would pay, that was something Gianni had said. I was just a girl who went to a factory to meet her boyfriend and met him by accident with another woman.

If Gianni was keeping tabs, well, that was Gianni. And if the family paid in some form, that could be Gianni. It certainly was not me.

This is what I told myself. And then repeated. And then said again. I ignored the part where I drove Gianni's getaway car—or maybe it was his hearse.

"So in the fall of 1967 I went to Los Angeles," Marvin said. I was on the white divan for a new round of prints, something to do with emulsions, different emulsions.

Roberto had now been in captivity for a week. I kept expecting to run into Sandro, waiting to. Marvin was speaking in the flat, nasal, unmodulated tone of his, almost a drone, indicating that he was going to recount in great detail some aspect of what he considered his critical personal history. I had just said that Sandro's brother had been kidnapped by the Red Brigades. It was impulsive, but I figured maybe we could talk about it. It was Marvin who had introduced me to Sandro in the first place.

Marvin said it was terrible news. He shrugged and added something about it being a high-profile family and then there was an anecdote and we were suddenly, it seemed, going to talk about Marvin instead, about his own history.

"The first job I had was as a stock footage researcher. I was employed by a director doing preliminary work for a feature. The script called for documentary scenes of people dying violent deaths. That's to say, actual people dying. The stock footage vaults where I did my research had the negatives of the Pathé newsreels from beginning to end. I went through, looking for violent deaths. What I found overwhelmingly were executions, almost all of them by firing squad. I gave the director all the scenes I'd had printed. Nothing ever came of the project, and that director disappeared off the face of the Earth, as people tend to do, change their names, become Hare Krishnas, drink themselves to death, whatever. I never heard from him, wouldn't have thought of him again, but one of the scenes I'd given him was, according to the newsreel caption, the execution of an Italian Fascist by a partisan militia, and when I met Sandro in 1968 or '69, I had a déjà vu about his name. Was the condemned man in the stock footage also Valera? Because that would be an incredible coincidence. In the summer of 1974 I was back at that same vault and tried to find out. But in the intervening time, things had changed. They used to make a viewing print for just a lab charge. Now they charged a fee for each phase of their service. I didn't want to find out badly enough to spend a lot of money. Really it had nothing to do with Sandro Valera. It was about something specific becoming stock footage. I always had this feeling there were two worlds. The one we live in, you know, just streaming along, future into present into past, recorded distortedly in people's minds, and this *other* world: stock footage. Small integers of life, I mean life in quotes, which represent whatever did take place, whether or not what's on the stock footage actually occurred. Cropping can make outcomes so ambiguous, but it doesn't matter, see. It's stock footage. A reference file to reality. Like you're a reference file for Caucasian skin tones; it doesn't matter that you exist. For the technician or projectionist, you're an index for the existence of woman, flesh, flesh tones. Which brings up the question of race, unaddressed. You, as *you*, have nothing to do with it."

Marvin took pictures of me holding the color chart. I began to feel like I was made of lead, heavy enough to sink right through the divan. If he had touched on the subject of Roberto, even in the most glancing way acknowledged the possibility that Roberto could be harmed, he would have helped me out. But he used the subject as a pretext to talk only about himself.

"I tried to explain this idea about two worlds to the people who worked in the vaults. One of them said, 'If you love stock footage so much, won't any piece of it do?' And the thing is, I had to agree with him. Even if they were just trying to get rid of me. He reached into a fireproof safety container and retrieved a role of negative that had started to deteriorate. He gave it to me for free, since they were discarding it anyway. And here is the kicker. It was of . . . uh, hmm. Actually, I can't recall. That's funny. It's gone, just . . . *poof.* I guess it wasn't that important to the story. The story was about how it doesn't matter what they ended up giving me. Also that violent deaths are part of stock footage, even if someone had to be killed, I mean originally, to generate the reference. You look different, by the way. Did you dye your hair or something?"

On my way home from work, I ran into Giddle on the Bowery. It was too late to avoid her.

"Want to come drink old overheated coffee and entertain me while I get paid and you sit and listen to me?" she said.

"No," I said.

We could meet later, she said. She was going to park herself at Rudy's and drink after her shift was finished.

"That kind of drinking where you make a wilderness," she said, "and tear a path in. You meet someone else there, deep in the woods. Go home together. Claw your way toward each other through the booze, confusion, misery, horniness."

"Sounds like fun," I said, "but no thanks."

"I bet you're going to Ronnie's opening," she said.

I said yes. It was tonight.

"You know what it is, right? His show? Pictures of beat-up women."

Stanley and Gloria would be hosting a dinner for Ronnie after the opening. When I got back to the loft, Gloria had assistants running here and there, moving tables, putting out flowers, preparing food.

"What a mess," she said. "It's not the time to entertain but I cannot let Ronnie down. I won't. But it could not be a worse time."

I asked why.

"They killed his brother," she said.

Sandro had called earlier that afternoon to tell them the news. "He says they weren't close. But he's in terrible pain. He's leaving tomorrow for Milan. But he'll only be gone a few days—just for the funeral. And when he comes back, we need to be there to support him. Stanley wants him around. You can stay until you find a place, but perhaps find a place soon."

I called Sandro's number and got the machine. I hung up, unable to bring myself to leave a message, and went to lie down in the little guest room, the Burdmoore room, as I thought of it, my own photographs, the white on white of the salt flats, on the walls above me. I closed my eyes, but with the noise from the party preparations, the news about Roberto, the jangle of thoughts in my head, I felt like I was trying to rest on a freeway overpass. I tried Sandro again and got the machine. I went out for a walk. I'd seen a FOR RENT sign on a fire escape on Kenmare, near my old apartment.

As I left the Kastles', I decided to walk over to Sandro's. Who else knew Roberto? Only me. Sandro never spoke of his brother. He downplayed his family, the company, in every way he could. I rang the bell. No one answered. Gloria had said he was coming to Ronnie's opening. I would see him in an hour. We'd speak then.

I had not guessed Ronnie would use the photos he'd taken that night at Rudy's, of Talia Valera and her friends. I should have. He did. The show was called *Match Your Mood*. Talia and the other women mugging for the camera with their faces roughed up. They'd gotten drunk, and instead of meeting a stranger in the dark wilderness that lay before them they met themselves, in slaps and punches.

Talia was larger than life, with her bruised, swollen eye. She stared out from the glossy black-and-white image with a look of calm satisfaction, as if Ronnie had revealed her profound nature by asking of her this task, to punch herself, and she had, and look, she was not afraid, she was undamaged, still beautiful. But she *was* damaged; they all were.

I thought of the pregnant biondina. The biondina told to strip nude, deloused for the camera, and what was the difference? *Vincenzo has the baby.*

There was no sign yet of Sandro. We would be speaking in front of a huge image of Talia's battered face. She was just a confused girl, like Sandro said. Roberto was dead and maybe it was time for me to come home.

Helen Hellenberger had not wanted to show the work. Ronnie had left the gallery and was now represented by Erwin Frame, on Mercer Street, which was Sandro's old gallery. I walked around the show with Gloria, who told me Helen had felt the work was too misogynistic.

Gloria started glancing behind me as we talked. I turned around. Sandro had arrived.

He was with a very young woman, practically a child. She might have been eighteen years old. A friend's daughter, I thought. Someone's daughter, petite and delicate, a blonde in a black sliplike dress, tiny shoulder blades like a bird's wings, a child someone had dressed up for this event. But they were holding hands, she and Sandro. Walking together, her hand in his, and then he pulled her to him and kissed her on the side of the head. It was the girl on layaway. I hadn't recognized her dressed up, the blonde in the photograph in Ronnie's studio, who had stood in a cave of noise and smoke and gazed sadly at Ronnie that night at the bar, and no one had noticed her but me.

From that moment I began to drift, to really drift. I felt light and queer and untouchable, by people or things. The huge black-and-white photos of beat-up faces receded and blurred. They were too large, like tribal masks or billboards. Gloria's hand was on my arm but I could not really feel it, just a vague pressure. "Let's get you some wine."

I better leave, I thought. Go to Rudy's and get drunk with Giddle, as much a stranger as any of these people but she never really professed to be anything more. Go and enter the dark and tangled wilderness, a different one than Giddle's, each of us tumbling in, in, in.

I was outside, pondering Rudy's, when Ronnie appeared.

I felt keenly aware that it was the second time in a month he'd done this. Followed me out when I'd left someplace alone. But I knew his game, showing just enough interest to keep me hooked in.

"You're ditching my opening."

"Fuck you," I said. I was unsure where it came from but it seemed appropriate.

He laughed. "You really are growing up. Just come to dinner. Sandro won't be there."

"That's not why I'm leaving," I lied.

"We both have dead brothers now," he said. "But no one knows about Tim. You're the only one I told. You can be my date tonight. What do you say?" He grinned stupidly, showing that broken tooth. He never had explained how it had happened. "Walk with me. It's my dinner and I want you to come. To be my guest."

Ronnie held my hand as we walked, and I wondered if he was doing it to console me because Sandro was holding the hand of a child bride, Ronnie's layaway plan transferred to Sandro. Did a pink owner's title go with her? The strange competition and sharing of friendship. *We both have dead brothers now.*

He squeezed my hand. Then he squeezed it again.

"I never understood you," I said.

As Ronnie had promised, Sandro and the girl did not come to dinner. I assumed they did not come because he was grieving, but the thought crossed my mind that it was also because he wanted to be affectionate with his date without the censoring element of my presence. The day I had caught him with Talia and left for Rome was only two months earlier, and he was already with someone else. What I had considered an open issue, the question of me and Sandro, was closed. I hadn't been ready for that. I had forgotten that he was free to move on, that he would seek comfort. A new girlfriend to help bear his sadness about Roberto. Roberto, whose death I felt connected to in a way I would never be able to disclose.

Most of the Larrys whom Ronnie had found so funny bunched

together at John Dogg's opening had been invited to this dinner for Ronnie. And Saul Oppler, who seldom attended these things. And Didier, puffing his Gauloise and taking bites of the fish Gloria served, his plate a mixture of fish and ashes and cigarette butts.

Erwin made a toast to Ronnie. Gallerists needed so badly to believe. They were not allowed the skepticism the rest of us harbored. The photographs were tasteless and mean. They were as questionable as a documentary about a pregnant girl with a fever and no place to lie down. The movie director sleeping with her as a way of offering her a bed. And because Ronnie's photographs were so obviously tasteless, Erwin talked about their tastefulness and surprising tact, their great *humanity,* Erwin said, their honesty, an unexpected tenderness—

As he spoke, he searched the table for us to agree with what Ronnie himself would have called bullshit hagiography.

We clinked and sipped.

Ronnie cleared his throat.

We waited quietly for him to speak.

"When I was a kid," he said, "I was messing around at a construction site and got whacked on the head by a railroad tie." He looked around. "Have I told any of you this story?"

We shook our heads. Wind came in through the open windows of the Kastles' loft, and the little candles on their long schoolhouse table dimmed and flickered, as if in anticipation.

"I got whacked so hard I forgot who I was. Twelve years of life, gone. I wandered with a headache, stunned and aimless, for a couple of days, sleeping in public parks, competing with pigeons for old french fries, relieving myself in bushes, drinking from plaza fountains—"

"Ronnie," Gloria said, "they *recycle* that water. You're not supposed to drink from fountains."

"For crying out loud," Stanley said, "Ronnie just told us he hit his head and *forgot who he was.* What does it matter about the water?"

"I came to a small marina," Ronnie said. "Probably I'd been there before, but everything looked new to me. The ocean flashed and glistened. A salty breeze riffled my hair. The gentle slap of waves against the boats docked in the marina was a voice beckoning me. The sound of the rigging. Of sun-bleached, heavy canvas snapping in the wind. The creak of rope knots—"

"Where did you grow up again?" Didier asked skeptically. I felt skeptical, too. Was he making this up?

"Connecticut. Anyway, it was a place of real logic. A logic of the senses. Stunning, really, and I can still recall the scene in precise detail, the shimmer of blue tarps, the heady fumes of deck paint and turpentine vaporizing in the warm air. The green algae that flocked the dock moorings like furry hip waders from the waterline down. I was overcome by a sense of openness, an open destiny. Easy to say, of course, since I did not remember a single element of my old life, not one fucking thing. But actually," he said, "I did remember *one* thing: after the log came down on me, the only image I held on to, strangely, was of a woman drying her hair with a bath towel. Rubbing vigorously, just out of the shower, with a dingy pink towel, like a white towel that had been washed with red T-shirts. I could only see her from the back, head bent forward, water-clumped strands that were the color of wet sand. Her neck. Her wet hair revealing the shape of her head and something more, a general strippedness, though I can only see her from the shoulders up as she towels her wet hair."

"How oedipal," Gloria said. "Let me ask: what color is Mrs. Fontaine's hair? And I mean your mother. Not that teenager from New Mexico you were married to for a couple of weeks."

"You married a teenager from New Mexico?" Stanley asked with barely concealed envy.

Ronnie shrugged. "She was a hitchhiker. I couldn't help myself. She was just so adorable. With these bangs that hung down into her eyes. But she started to get on my nerves. It was like being a legal guardian, I had to tell her to eat her vegetables, to put on a sweater—"

"Ronnie," Gloria said, "are we to assume your mother had sandy-blond hair?"

"No," Ronnie said. He was staring at me across the table. "No, she doesn't."

It was a searching, scanning gaze. Like he was trying to discern something.

I had taken a shower that night that Ronnie stayed over. I'd put my hair in a faded pink towel, my Pickwick towel. I had lain next to him, thinking, so naively, that this would be the first of many moments with his fingers in my wet hair.

"I walked along the dock and considered each boat. Their names, one after another, appeared to me as the names of different lives I could choose. *Me and Mrs. Jones. Loan Shark. Come to Papa.*"

There was laughter. Ronnie waited for quiet and continued.

"There was one especially beautiful boat. It singled itself out. It was the rich color of eggnog, a fifty-foot cruiser called the *Reno.*"

So. He was speaking to me from across that knife-scratched table. A story for twenty with a message for one. But what was the message? Could it be that Ronnie loved me? Or was his use of our secret history one more hoax? Yet another layer of the joke?

"The *Reno,*" Erwin said. "That's an odd name for a boat." He said it with the confusion of someone who concerned himself with the naming of boats.

"This older couple sat on the deck. I shaded my eyes and looked up at them. 'Well, hello,' the man calls down. I said hello back. 'The wind is just perfect,' he says. 'We're getting ready to go.' I asked where. He said to see the world. Was I interested? I guess I thought he meant generally, and I said sure. I mean of course. He asked if I liked the open sea. 'Well, sure I do,' I said, but what did I know? I liked the words *open* and *sea*. I still like those words. He said to call him Commodore. He told me they were setting sail that afternoon. I said, 'Just you two?' looking from him to his wife—he had introduced her by name but I forgot it immediately, and soon we were all chummy-chummy and it was too late not to know it. No one ever called her by it. He called her 'dear,' or 'my wife,' and everyone else simply said the commodore's wife. 'Just us,' the commodore said, 'and our first mate, Xerxes, who also cooks. And maybe you.' And then he tamped his pipe, one of those meerschaum pipes, and something shifted or brightened in my mind. I didn't know then, I mean I could not have recalled, that my own father smoked a pipe."

"Huh," Didier said, nodding. "Classic displacement."

"Maybe. So he lights the bowl and puffs his pipe," Ronnie said, "and tells me, 'You look like you'll work out just fine for us. Just fine. When Mr. Sneeks said he had a cabin boy for me, well, I imagined someone just like you. I thought of *you*, and here you are.' 'And here I am,' I said, and as I said it, the world went clean and orderly in a way it almost never does."

Ronnie paused, took a drink. Everyone was quiet, unclear where we were headed. They'd been expecting a funny escapade, like the one about Oppler's E-type Jaguar.

"We set sail later that afternoon. I felt what I can only call a mystical vibration when we lost sight of land. The commodore said I brought luck on board, as the winds were such that we sailed wing and wing, with both jibs open at an angle and filled with air, so that the yacht looked like a huge white cabbage butterfly. The commodore explained that this manner of sailing was not only fast but also the most balanced and pleasing kind, because of the steady way the boat moved through the water. In the evening, Xerxes prepared our dinner on a gimbal stove, and we ate on the aft deck, in the bright, gassy glow of a Coleman lantern. The commodore and his wife talked about their lives, and having no memories or interests of my own, I was fascinated by their stories of tax shelters and cocktail parties, tennis elbow, summer compounds, and disowned children. Now, of course, this kind of thing couldn't interest me less, though it's often the artist's duty to listen to exactly these sorts of details and to pretend they matter."

Erwin Frame laughed uncomfortably, glancing at the two collectors he'd brought to dinner, a husband and wife much too polished and fancy for downtown Manhattan, the man's platinum watch, his timepiece, glinting in the candlelight. The collectors' faces were pleased and vacant, like they had already decided that this artist whose work they were buying was going to entertain them and he was. Whatever Ronnie actually said didn't matter. They were surfing the experience of a loft on the Bowery, an environment foreign to both the man and his wife, but with the charade that for the man, it was not foreign. He would guide his wife. He was the expert. On downtown and painting and the art market and when to laugh and so forth. Just follow my lead, honey, his body language instructed his wife. Both looked at Ronnie with broad smiles.

"That first evening, the commodore gave me a private lesson on night sailing. He showed me how to flip on the red port light and the green starboard light. He said it was the law of the sea that these shine until daybreak, to warn ships of our presence. 'The law of the sea' was a phrase the commodore would invoke frequently, and each time he said it I felt his awe before the notion of a larger agency, a cosmic governance. But later, I mean much later, I came to wonder if the law of which he spoke was sometimes in truth not that of the sea but of the commodore, his own law, or even more arbitrary than law, and more fickle, the commodore's private fancy. But this abuse, shall we call it, of his position, was never explicit. Even now, his ethics on our journey are a mystery to me. On that first night, he was a great teacher. He got out his sextant and explained how to take a star fix, although I didn't get the precise method, overwhelmed as I was by the sensations of the night sea. There were stars overhead in a brilliant scatter, and we sailed on stars, too, which shimmered up from water so smooth and inklike that the heavens were reflecting back at themselves, as if the sky were underneath us. I heard the commodore's voice and felt that we were in an open-air capsule or sleigh, traveling through the vast universe, a great, pin-speckled sphere, a black egg rolled in glitter."

"Beautiful, Ronnie," Gloria said. Her tone presumed he was making this up. We waited, and Ronnie continued.

"We docked in the Keys, and the commodore golfed while his wife directed the purchase of a new wardrobe for me. She had particular tastes, the commodore's wife, and a methodical sense of how shopping is done. I needed a certain number of boys' cotton shirts, and sweaters of various blends of wool and cotton. I needed three bathing suits. Duck pants. A tie and jacket, just in case, she said, ports of call led to formal situations. Canvas Top-Siders and a pair of beautiful hand-tooled wingtips whose leather was the dark stain of boysenberry syrup. I can tell you now it wasn't a typical cabin boy's wardrobe, but I had nothing to compare it to. The wingtips had been crafted by the finest English shoemaker, according to the commodore's wife. They came in their own chamois sack, with a tin of saddle soap and a silver-plated shoehorn. They probably wound up decorating the feet of an otherwise naked Polynesian, or resting on the bottom of the sea. I actually never wore them. I grew so accustomed to going barefoot on the boat that wearing any kind of shoes felt too constricting.

"Before we left the Keys, the commodore and his wife picked up one more crew member, Artemio, who, it was fairly clear, would be fulfilling the actual duties of cabin boy. I pretended not to notice, and in part of my mind I didn't. But in some deep space, I knew he was the cabin boy and what I was. I knew what I was, and yet I didn't. I was a blank and innocent boy who'd wandered onto the *Reno*. We made our way—"

"So what the hell *were* you?" Stanley asked, breaking the spontaneous code that had formed, that we would let Ronnie tell the whole story before we attempted to figure out what it meant.

"Come on, Stanley," Didier said, "just let him talk."

"We journeyed south, all the way to the Panama Canal. The commodore was thrilled for me to witness our transfer through the locks and channels. Although he'd gone surly with the Canal Zone Police when they'd boarded our boat. He instructed me to stay in my berth, because I had no papers or passport. I did as he said, and listened through the closed cabin door as he tried to intimidate and scoot the police off the boat. The police were not so easy to scoot. They said they'd heard he had a boy with him. 'We don't like funny business,' they said, and the commodore assured them that neither did he. And then he did something strange. He asked if they would like to see his wife. 'Where is she?' they wanted to know. 'Sleeping,' the commodore said. 'Like a baby.' And then I heard him walk past, down to her berth, and after him, the heavy footsteps of the police, with the extra weight from their guns, holsters, batons, and radios. From what I could gather, the commodore opened his wife's door and let the police into the room where she was sleeping. I heard him say something, and then he closed the door again, and I heard no more sounds. Sometime later, the police slunk past quietly, as if they were on tiptoe.

"The commodore's wife looked unusually radiant at dinner that night, and she told me that life was full of surprises, and also that it was not full of surprises, and that this was one of the surprises, that you could often predict exactly how people were going to behave in a given situation. 'The commodore and I make bets,' she said. 'But the thing is, we never risk losing anything we weren't secretly interested in getting rid of anyhow.' The commodore looked at her and winked a dirty little wink. I didn't like it. I don't know how I knew it was a dirty wink, but I connected it to the police, with their epaulettes and gun holsters. For a moment, I wondered if she and the commodore were a positive influence on me. I was, after all, so impressionable, with no memories or experiences to draw from. The commodore's wife called Artemio to bring out dessert, a quivering flan whose surface was not flat, as one should expect, but angled like a slipway, because it had set as we traveled at a tilt, tacking starboard. The moment of wondering had passed. I spooned the crooked flan and did not think again about what might have happened in the commodore's wife's berth to make the footsteps of the policemen so light."

"They shtupped her," Stanley said.

"Probably," Ronnie said with measured tolerance, as if he were annoyed at having to pause and reward Stanley for declaring the obvious.

"Thanks to the commodore, I knew, by that point, how to take a sun fix, and as we approached zero degrees latitude, which I confirmed with the commodore's sextant and his gentle coaching, I became, through a ritual that remains vague in my memory, an official 'shellback,' which is what you're called once you've sailed south across the equator. Soon we hit the doldrums. The air was sweltering, and we didn't make much headway, but no one seemed to really mind. The commodore and his wife sat under a canvas shade on the aft deck drinking English gin, and

Xerxes occasionally furled the sails and dropped anchor so I could swim in the warm and placid water. When I climbed back onto the boat, Artemio had sandwiches, iced tea, and a fresh towel waiting for me. Giant sea turtles knocked and clacked against the sides of the yacht, friendly and lethargic, as heavy and dense as bowling balls. I was feeding one of them my sandwich crusts when Artemio whacked its head with a mallet. It made a delicious soup.

"Sailing into Polynesia, we encountered our first serious weather, a real squall, and huge waves, combers, the commodore called them, rose up and curled over, foaming and crashing onto the boat, which was thrown violently around. Artemio, Xerxes, and the commodore bailed like crazy. Night came, and the storm continued. 'All hands on deck!' the commodore shouted, and even his wife bailed. Waves socked and pummeled and heaved the *Reno,* which creaked and shuddered as if it were going to burst apart. My fear was primitive and desperate. I asked out loud what we had done to deserve this. I shouted it. The commodore took hold of me and said the sea was not for us or against us. 'It doesn't know we're here,' he said. 'It doesn't know.'

"The storm passed and we sailed toward the Friendly Islands under calm skies. We dropped anchor in the leeward harbor of Puka-Puka and spent several days relaxing, having a good time. The commodore taught me all about shell meat, which was tastiest and which highest in protein, which was deadly poisonous. I dove for murex, purple conch, cowries spotted with chocolate freckles. We cooked on the beach and shared our meals with the local people, who brought a drink called *quee-qum,* which we passed around in a single coconut shell. It was my job, as the youngest male, to drain the coconut shell and then holler *'Maca!'* which means finished, or empty, or more, please. I can't remember exactly. But I remember how I bellowed 'Maca!' and the natives all laughed and smiled, and one of them scampered off to refill the coconut shell. Also I remember that the commodore wore a kind of special woven basket around his waist, like a weight lifter's belt, not unlike the special woven belt that the local tribal chief wore. I wasn't sure what it

signified, if anything, but the commodore seemed to know these people, and they treated him almost as if he were a kind of visiting king
from a nearby island.

"We continued south and west. As we dipped into Melanesia, we
were all deep in the rhythm of the journey. We would make the world
round by circling it. Then one morning we woke to discover we were
taking in water. The *Reno* had sprung a slow leak. Fortunately we had
a transmitter and were able to send out a distress signal. A devious
cruising tug from the tiny island of Kokovoko managed to find us. By
the time we spotted its smokestack, chugging merrily in our direction,
we were loading supplies into a rubber dinghy, just in case we had to
abandon ship. The tug captain advised us to ride with him, to be on
the safe side, as he towed the *Reno*. He was jovial and friendly to us,
at least to me, the commodore, Artemio, and Xerxes. He didn't much
like the commodore's wife and even suggested she remain on the *Reno,*
despite having already said it was dangerous to do so, since our boat
was technically sinking. Much later, when I worked on a tug in New
York Harbor, the captain wouldn't let his own daughter on the boat.
Said it was bad luck. He used to tie her to the dock with sandwiches
and some cans of beer. Pretty girl, but sort of spent looking, even at the
age of twelve. Once I saw that girl at Magoo's, all grown up and dead
drunk. She dropped her cocktail, picked it up, and fit her hand into
the broken glass to dig out the maraschino cherry. Put the cherry in
her mouth and ate it. I said, 'Hey. Hey, I know you. You're the tugboat
captain's daughter, aren't you.' You know what she said to me? 'Fuck
off,' and walked away. Can you believe it? Anyway, the tug captain from
Kokovoko eventually agreed that the commodore's wife could board
the tug if she rode in the very back of the boat. The tug captain had
wanted her to put a burlap sack over her head because he said if she
faced the spray the water gods would be furious and drag us to our
deaths. The commodore eventually got the tug captain to agree that
his wife would ride unhooded, but would remain astern and keep her
eyes on the wake. The commodore's wife was upset about this, and in

truth we were rather annoyed with her, too, for disrupting the flow of our rescue. I sensed the magical spell among us begin to evaporate just the slightest bit.

"That night, in a thatched hut on the island of Kokovoko, I woke with a start. I was disoriented in the dark hut and had to struggle to recall where I was. I listened to the squeak and rustle of palm fronds, the soft, crashing metronome of the sea. Images from my old life started rolling in, one by one, each welling up like sudden kelp in a wave break. I knew who I'd been when I was struck at the construction site: Ronald Franklyn Fontaine of 1331 Castle Peak Drive. Son of Lee Anne Fontaine, homemaker, and Fred Fontaine, Chevrolet salesman, and big brother of Tim Fontaine, who had not yet, but would later, rob several banks and a Brink's vehicle.

"The commodore was always talking about sailing sense, and how many nights he'd woken, suddenly, having realized somewhere in the depths of sleep that the rhythm of water lapping the prow was different than what it should have been. He would get up and discover that his boat had sailed off course. I had a similar feeling lying there in the dark: the rhythm of the commodore and his wife was lulling and seductive but wrong. It was the wrong rhythm. Still, I felt a lot of regret. Because it wasn't a bad life, this new one, even if it might have been more dignified to have remained a properly paid cabin boy, or to have at least resisted complying with the commodore's requests, when complying gave me a bad feeling."

Didier snickered. It didn't seem funny to me, even if Ronnie was making it up.

"It's just that kind of thing," Ronnie said, pointing his chin at Didier, "that I associate with the commodore. A smirk. A muffled glee. He said everything he wanted me to do, or did to me, was for my good, but often it seemed like it was for his good. If it was for my good, why did he muffle his glee? Was I a slave of some kind? I suddenly wondered as I lay there in the dark between the two of them. All existence is slavery of one kind or another, right? Who isn't a slave? And whatever dignity I sacrificed by accepting their gifts, by doing what they asked, still, I was sailing the world with only the smallest of worries: the water is a little cool for swimming this morning, and where do we keep the Band-Aids, because I spiked my toe on a bit of coral.

"I heard Artemio quietly snoring from his station on the floor, there in our hut, in case one of us needed a glass of water in the middle of the night. Did I have to reject this new life simply because something else had come before it? I had no chores and no homework. I swam whenever I wanted, and every so often explored a new port of call, with the paper currency of its government slipped into my pockets by the commodore and also by his wife, each of whom seemed to believe that they alone delighted in spoiling me. Did I want to sail the world, explore remote islands? Or did I want to mow the front lawn, jerk off to the illustration of the lady in the Hoover vacuum replacement bag manual, and get beaten on occasion with Dad's leather belt? Obviously, these were two different realities. I could simply choose between them. And yet I felt the crushing sense that there was only one correct choice. And so I didn't really have a choice, because I had to choose correctly.

"The natives were resealing the *Reno*. Once it was repaired we were onward to the Coral Sea and then the Cocos Islands. Who knew what the Fates had in store. I did not face them. I could not shake the feeling that I had wandered off the track when I chose the *Reno* from among the yachts that reared up in my vision that day. I could no longer suppress the old life. With its drab and dull brutalities, I knew it was the real one, my real life. I'd lost the toehold on my new life, with the commodore and his wife. I didn't understand it anymore. Lying in the dark hut that night—an endless night, a night of great confusion—the commodore snuffled in his sleep and nuzzled close to me. I felt his humid breath on my shoulder, in two little streams from his nostrils. His wife stirred as well, and turned her face in my direction. They breathed on me asynchronously, as if it was their duty to cool me in their sleep. All of a sudden I panicked. Who *are* these people? I wondered. *And why the hell are they naked?*"

We all should have laughed. Because if it wasn't true, it was surely funny. But none of us did laugh. Outside, rain began to fall, but softly.

Cooler air came in through the loft's big open windows, and there was a sound of wet tires on the Bowery.

"I got up and crept out of the hut without waking them. The surf pounded like a heart. I walked barefoot along a dirt path until I found a larger hut with ceremonial shells hanging from the front door. The local tribal chief. I knocked and explained my situation the best I could. We walked over to the municipal government headquarters, where there was a switchboard, and I cabled my parents.

"As I waited for my mother and father to arrive, I pretended everything was normal. I swam open-eyed over the coral reef, which curled and fluttered along the seabed, fleshy and white as skate fish. I ate lobster and crab, cuttlefish and breadfruit. I lay in the hut and listened to the surf, dreaming up errands on which to send Artemio, as my hours of having a servant at my beck and call were dwindling. And here I could begin to invent and you guys might not notice, not even Stanley and his bullshit detector. I could tell you, for instance, that the commodore and his wife both died under mysterious circumstances, and lead you to believe that it was at my own innocent boy's hands that they died, and I could even declare my reasons for murdering them in a way that would leave you satisfied, in fact more than satisfied, that I had done the right thing and that the commodore and his wife had met an appropriate end. Even if you weren't convinced of their guilt, or didn't believe in such a crude moral axis as that of guilt and innocence. Still, your judgment would be informed by a simple fact that we can all agree on: that the notion of the sea and sailors *by itself* suggests the notion of murder. What is sailing, after all, but an extreme form of criminality? I didn't kill them. Like I said, I'm letting you know that I could start inventing. But even if I did kill them, you would feel no sympathy for the commodore in his suspiciously crisp clothes, his wife, calculating and lustful, calling to the drunk and obscene monkeys hanging above her in the trees, flashing their swollen red anuses while she opens her legs for the tribal chief of Kokovoko, who lifts her dress with one hand, and grips, in the other, a phallus of scrimshaw—"

"Ugh," said Gloria. Nothing else. Just "ugh," but Ronnie got the message.

"Okay, okay. As the facts stand, my parents came and took me home, end of it. I resumed my old life, Malt-O-Meal and Fruit of the Loom, model glue, cut grass. Feel of soft flannel and coarse denim, crackly leaf piles and thumbed comics. Our dog Ansich and our cat Fürsich. Everything was normal again, except that I suffered from occasional headaches. And when I twiddled the knob of my shortwave radio, tuning in to late-night transmissions under the blankets, the Tongan news hour or Sumatran music, I closed my eyes and rode the equator, like I was living my own lost life.

"Then, a few years ago, I was installing an artwork at Helen Hellenberger's and this elderly woman walks into the gallery. She puts her old hands on either side of my face. 'Julian, Julian, it's you!' she cries. 'I've found you after all these years!' Apparently, during our time on the boat, they named me after their dead son."

"Heavy," Gloria said.

"Or I think he was just dead to them, disowned or something, maybe for being gay. I can't quite remember. We went to a restaurant together and over lunch she filled me in on the details of our brief life at sea. I had forgotten a great deal of it, in the interest of reconnecting with my family. She actually had a photo of me in her billfold. I looked like myself, but bronzed and barefoot, in ragged shorts. Also, this was the weirdest thing: I was wearing a sturdy-looking four-point leather harness over my chest."

Saul Oppler said, "This is like Robert Louis Stevenson meets Tom of Finland. I never would have guessed, Ronnie."

Ronnie either pretended not to hear or wasn't interested in responding.

"I asked about the harness," he said, "and she claimed it was a safety precaution, in case I fell overboard. A memory, the clammy feel of wet leather on my bare skin, came back to me, but I didn't know if she was telling me the truth. In the photo, she and the commodore weren't wearing harnesses. 'You were a minor,' she said in accounting for this, 'we were responsible for you.' There are a lot of unanswered questions. I close my eyes and see either electric blue water and wind-flapped sails, feel a sense of sunny goodness, or I see something else, nights spent with the commodore and his wife, lessons that continued into some-thing I can't revisit. But I could be making that part up."

"*That* part?" Stanley asked. "And not the whole goddamn thing?"

"They still send me a Christmas greeting every year, those cards that are on color photo stock, with a sprig of holly printed on the white trim of the photo paper. It's strange. They never get any older in the pictures. I think it's actually the same picture they're sending every Christmas, but reprinted with the updated year."

"How bizarre," Gloria said. "That's so odd they would do that. Send the *very same* Christmas photo every year."

"You think *that's* bizarre?" Stanley said. "What about the fact that Ronnie was in bed with two naked people, for Christ's sake, yachting around the world as their semiadopted son?"

"But that sounds *exactly* like something Ronnie would do," Gloria said, and she got up to begin clearing dinner plates.

I needed to talk to him. That was how I felt as we ate dessert and the subject shifted, Didier poking his smoked-down cigarette into the center of an uneaten chocolate truffle and listening intently to Stanley, who was saying something about the old Indian in fringed deerskin who canoes past offshore oil rigs in that public service announcement on television, which ends with the Indian's single shed tear when gar-bage is dumped at his feet from a car window.

"Iron Eyes Cody," Ronnie said. "Actually Sicilian, but it's a good ad, this uncaring world of garbage flingers. And their garbage is not even in a bag. It's actual garbage, crumpled debris that fuck-you's to a stop at the old chief's feet. The message is clear."

"What is the message?" Stanley asked.

"The litterbug is responsible for the genocide of the American Indian."

*   *   *

Ronnie was the last to leave that night. I walked him out, said I needed to make sure I'd locked the Moto Valera.

"I plan to work for a bit, but do you want to come over?" he asked. "Keep me company, as they say?"

On the walls of his studio were cut-out images and articles from a magazine called *Boy's Life*, all about sailing and what to do if you capsize.

Don't abandon your boat! It may float
long enough for someone to rescue you.

An empty bucket can work as a flotation device.

Take off your pants and blow air into them.
Tie off the waist and ankles.

On the far wall was a sheet of butcher paper with a long list of phrases. They were titles, Ronnie said.

"For what?"

"My autobiography," he said.

"Why do you invent?" I asked, scanning the list of titles. "Invent, and tell lies?"

"They aren't lies," Ronnie said. "They're a form of discretion."

He was organizing his worktable, putting things into piles.

"Ronnie," I said, "what were you trying to tell me tonight?"

"I wasn't trying to tell you anything. It was just a story. To entertain those moneyed rubes Erwin brought to dinner."

"The woman toweling her hair. She . . . it could have been me and you know it. Tell me the truth."

"It could have been you, yeah. And then what? You think you want to be with me? Act on some desire you felt long ago, that we both felt?"

I bit my lip.

"Look," he said, and petted my hair. His expression held something like pity. "I have no problem carrying around a small curiosity about lying down with you again. About more than that, okay? Okay? About looking at your cake-box face and your fucked-up teeth, which make you, frankly, extra-cute. About some kind of project of actually getting to know you. Because I honestly don't think you know yourself. Which is why you love egotistical jerks. But I'll tell you something about us, about me and about you, and what happens when two people decide to share some kind of life together. One of them eventually becomes curious about something else, someone else. And where does that leave you?"

My heart was pounding. I felt an ache of sadness spreading through me, down to the ends of my fingers.

"You want another Sandro, and I can just screw whoever I want, to keep myself entertained? Because it wasn't just Talia that he was gifting himself with. It wasn't just Giddle, either, who, well, see Giddle is like a piece of furniture, necessary but ultimately insignificant, something to lie down on occasionally. And it wasn't merely Gloria, who has been Sandro's leftovers for at least a decade, picked up and discarded when he wants. In fact, gee. Name a woman you have met through Sandro, or that he has met through you, and you'll find that—"

"Stop it," I said, tears rolling down my face. "Stop. Why are you doing this?"

"To show you the uselessness of the truth," he said.

17. Match My Mood: The Life of Ronnie Fontaine

Table for Two for One: An Autobiography

The Other Side of Tender: A Life

Married but Looking: My Story

Manhandled: An Autobiography

Who Ate All the Pussy? One Man's Journey

Friendly Fire: My Trials and Triumphs

Potato in a Ski Mask: The True Untold Story

They Took the Liquor but Left the Girl: My Life

Partial View, Obstructed: A Memoir

Third Place (Victory Is a Seven-Letter Word)

Hamburger in Paradise: My Adventures

Bars and Stripes: Doing Time

Green Onions: Getting Out Alive

Can a Brother Get a Table Dance? My Life, Uncensored

Still in Love: A Confession

Patent Pending: My Becoming

Too Rich to Be Bothered (The Life of Sandro Valera,
    as Told to Ronnie Fontaine)

Suicide by Cop: The Path Not Taken

Suds and Duds: Clocking Time with Beer and Laundry

How to Pray and Get Results: The Diaries of Ronnie
    Fontaine

I Lived (He Died)

You're Soaking in It: My Secrets

18. BEHIND THE GREEN DOOR

I was alone again, like when I first arrived in New York, but it was a different alone. Things had happened. I'd walked under the plane trees with Sandro in the gardens of the Villa Valera in Bellagio. I'd tried to chew inedible bread under a fresco of drowning popes. I knew what it felt like to be teargassed. I'd been drawn in by three different men, Ronnie, Sandro, Gianni, and one woman, Giddle, and it would seem that I knew nothing about any of them. I owned a motorcycle. I rode it all over town. It wasn't just transportation, it was an experience. I was a girl on a motorcycle. And I finally discovered what was behind the green door.

One overcast July evening when the heat and humidity became unbearable in my top-floor walk-up on Kenmare, I filled my tank at the Gulf station on Lafayette under a low and heavy sky and went north, not looking in the windows of the Trust E Coffee Shop, a place I now avoided. I didn't hate Giddle for sleeping with Sandro. It was one more performance, a performance of betrayal. You couldn't hate someone who saw the world so differently. And I knew she must suffer. I had never encountered anyone so alone as Giddle. Really alone, no audience to what she was doing, since it was so much like life, and no real friends, since they were merely an audience to her performance.

On Twenty-Third Street, traveling west, big humid gusts blew against the bike. Lightning flashed, the city sky clicking from off to on to off. Pedestrians scattered as the thunder cracked. I went north, up Sixth Avenue, and at each light wondered if I should turn south, go home, and avoid the downpour. I kept going north.

At Forty-Second Street, I headed west toward the orange colors of Times Square, so bright against the blue-gray of storm clouds. There was another flash, a distant rumble. Drops began to fall.

I pulled the Moto Valera up on the curb, thinking I'd find someplace to wait it out. I rolled the bike onto its centerstand, took out the ignition key, and there I was, under the face of the soap-flakes model.

Behind the Green Door

I looked at her and at the old ticket vendor, the showtimes. The next viewing was in twenty minutes. I traded two dollars for a stub.

No one buys popcorn for a porn film. They didn't sell it. I passed through the lobby curtains into what looked like a regular movie theater, red vinyl seats, slightly sloped floor, a stained screen, smaller than I expected. Sparse audience, all male, each with a safety buffer of empty seats around him. A few glared at me, rustled bags, which lone people were for some reason required to do in movie theaters, to rustle paper bags no matter what genre of film, Chinese opera or Mature Audience Only.

I sat on the aisle in the last row, close to the exit.

In the beginning, a truck, a truck stop diner. A woman who could have been Giddle, gray uniform with crisscross-backed apron. But unlike Giddle, who was, in essence, a crypto-bohemian pouring coffee, this woman was just a dour-faced waitress, not ironic. *This* woman, I thought, was what Giddle impersonated. It somehow did not occur to me that the waitress in the film was even more of an actress than Giddle was. She was *acting*. In a *movie*.

The daytime television voices of porn actors.

A man in resort wear, white shoes and yellow socks, saying, Sour cream, borscht, herring, chicken, and bananas. Gimme a break. Sour cream, borscht, chicken—

Cut to the soap-flakes model driving a Porsche 356 cabriolet up winding mountain roads. Not with a dubious clandestine, a Gianni. On her own. In a ski hat, maxing the gears on hairpin turns. Smiling, private, solitary, in her cutely boyish wool hat, red like the car.

These things were behind the green door:

Rules and codes.

Crotchless white stretch-Lycra tuxedos. Somehow not funny, not meant to be.

Fat people in masquerade ball masks. The people in masks seemed to believe they were hidden, like a baby who hides its face. "When baby Kotch covered his own eyes," Nadine had told me, "little thing thought he'd disappeared to everybody else. *Where's Kotch?*" The fat people up on the movie screen acted hidden, leaned back in their chairs with the unselfconscious posture of watchers, their hands unzipping their own zippers and pulling up their own skirts, shifting in their chairs for maximum access to self. Efficient hand flicks.

What the masked masturbators behind the green door watched:

Live sex, the soap-flakes model and a man in tribal makeup. She and the man both seemed deep in the moment but also hyperalert to how they looked deep in the moment. There was something stoic about them, a shared feeling between them that sex was miraculous, that it was a strange and incredible thing people did to each other, that it never lost this strangeness, its thrill. They had that reverence, she and the man in tribal makeup. It remained, even as the sex became pure repetition, gliding and hardness and softness and pushing, their faces up close, his beads swinging, the masked voyeurs who surrounded them, the small and obscene movements of their hands, *local* movements, and we, the Times Square voyeurs, in the theater, and who knew what the men seated sparsely around me were up to, their own local movements, and then the screen went dark.

Paper bags rustling. Someone saying, Hey. *Hey.*

A few minutes later, the film started up again, the sound warbling to life, and then almost immediately it shut off once more. No image, just the projector's insect rattle.

An usher's flashlight bounced down the aisle, his voice next to me, intimate in the dark, echoless against the carpeted wall.

"Movie's over. Save your ticket. We're having a power short. Exit slow and calm."

I felt my way up the sloped aisle, moving through the curtain into what I expected would be light, but it was only more darkness. The men who'd parked themselves far from one another in the theater were all crowded together, finding their way to the exit. Emergencies bring people together. The porn theater was not a place for that. The men dispersed like rats, fleeing through the theater doors into the dark.

No lights shone or jumped in Times Square. There was no skyline of gridded, glowing windows, no blazing billboards, no silken glide of LED.

A half-full moon, egg-shaped, glowed up above, polished and white, the dull white plastic of dark theater marquees visible in its light.

People flooded the sidewalk. It was dense with the heat of them, clustered in large groups but speaking in hushed voices.

Taxis and trucks moved slowly and did not use their horns. Not a single car honked. Traffic edged along in caution and doubt. Horns were about the opposite, righteousness behind the wheel.

The vehicles passing through Times Square were the only light sources, except for the prostitutes who had flashlights, which they swung around, calling from doorways, It's good in the dark.

It's everywhere, someone said. Cigarette cherry zigzagging as he spoke.

Lightning knocked it out.

The murmur of a transistor. Wait, I'm tuning it in.

Shit. I thought the Russians nuked.

I wove through the crowd, crossing the sidewalk to my motorcycle. A woman brushed by. I felt but didn't see her, a body moving past, and when I looked again I saw only white short shorts. A black woman whose body melted into the darkness, her short shorts hip-height and bodyless, the leg openings stretched wide like rigatoni.

I could have stood there watching and deciding for hours. There was no city actively guiding me, the shops and walking masses and traffic lights giving their deep signals of what to do, where to go, who and what to see, what to buy, how to feel, what to think. All flow and force as a city had been suspended. People on the sidewalk talked in quieted tones as if darkness called for a new level of discretion. Some of it talk of the moment, the blackout, but most of it just life.

She's already committed herself.

The thing I learned was I'm my own worst enemy.

Well, I tried writing her a letter.

I started the bike, flipped on the headlight, stupidly amazed for a moment that it worked, as if all units of power were directly connected to the city's grid.

I popped from the curb and joined the shy traffic inching south on Seventh. We were like those vehicles that roll along the floor of the ocean, marking out volume with their headlights against a dark void. Everyone drove haltingly and slow. An eerie echo of sirens, louder the farther south I went.

At Union Square, women were pulling shopping carts out of Mays, multiple carts tied together and crammed with merchandise, their metal wheels making the clattering bright sound of poured money as the women dragged them along the street.

Merry Christmas, motherfuckers! a man shouted. Then he shouted it again.

Merry Christmas, motherfuckers!

Satin sheets, one woman called to another. Always wanted them.

Satin sheets, a fantasy cooked up for the poor. Rich people slept on cotton, dried in the sun, ironed and fresh like at the Valera villa.

I was on Fourteenth, going slowly, when I heard the sound of security grates forced up. Plate glass broken. It was a Thom McAn store. People pulling boxes and boxes of Jox tennis shoes out onto the sidewalk, bouncy brand-new tennies tumbling from the boxes, glowing white in the dark. You couldn't get from A to B in New York without an ad for Jox or its redoubling, someone wearing them.

I heard the short whoop of a police siren, but there was something impotent about it, that single, short whoop.

Traffic was almost at a standstill. I could have gone between lanes, but I had no place I was trying to get to. A group of people wheeled racks out of Says *Who?* Plus-size Styles. Farther down the block, two men backed through the broken window of an Orange Julius, each lifting one side of an industrial juicer. They struggled along the sidewalk with it and then swung one two three through the plate glass of a pawnshop.

WE BUY GOLD ANY CONDITION

People knew what they were doing. Like they'd been waiting for the lights to go out.

You had to believe in the system, I thought, to feel it was wrong to take things without paying for them. You had to believe in a system that said you can want things if you work, if you are employed, or if you were just born lucky, born rich.

The city was in the process of being looted. Chain stores and mom-and-pop stores that owners, families, tried to defend with baseball bats, tire irons, shotguns. People said it was despicable that looters would turn on their own, and target struggling and honest neighborhood businesses. Their own. But they misunderstood. It didn't matter whether looters hit a chain or the local jeweler. To expect them to identify particular stores as enemies and others as friends was a confusion. We buy gold, any condition.

Looting wasn't stealing, or shopping by other means. It was a declaration, one I understood, watching the juicer crash through the window: the system is in "off" mode. And in "off" mode, there was no private property, no difference between Burger King and Alvin's Television Repair. Everything previously hoarded behind steel and glass was up for grabs.

Jox are lightweight. Built for speed.

* * *

I parked the bike in front of my building on Kenmare. The Italians were all outside, domino games and drinking and full-volume news radio.

We're getting reports from all five boroughs, the announcer said. Commanding officers tell us the vandalism and looting are so dispersed they simply cannot prevent individual crimes.

Listeners were calling in to describe trouble in Harlem, the Bronx, Bed-Stuy, Crown Heights.

"Bushwick is being destroyed," one caller said, "by niggers and spics."

"This guy dies in custody and these animals go nuts, destroying everything on Broadway, but he was robbing a liquor store—"

The old Italians playing dominoes weighed in on this.

"They don't know how he died. Probably he was on drugs."

I left the Moto Valera securely locked where my bigoted neighbors could watch over it. No looting would occur in Little Italy, a self-governed fortress, armed, punitive.

I wanted to walk. It was a night to be on the street, where everyone else was, listening to radios, trading stories, marveling at the uncanny dark—natural, but not for a city. I crossed Kenmare and walked down Mulberry, which still reminded me of my arrival to New York, two years earlier, when the sight of a woman smashing a cockroach under her slipper was an exciting urban novelty. Every New York sensation, heat, firecrackers, the humid grit coating people and things, even the smell of chicken blood in the hall, meant possibility then.

At the corner of Spring and Mulberry, by the little park where I used to sit, I saw Henri-Jean. This was his haunt, his quadrangle. But he wasn't in the park. He was standing in the street, directing traffic, using his striped pole like a semaphore, nodding and beckoning with dramatic enthusiasm at the cars. He smiled and directed as if he were a cheerful usher volunteering to put everyone in their rightful seat, the official host and steward of Mulberry and Spring. There was a type who came to life in a blackout, those who would use the suspension of normal life to finally become their full selves.

I went east down Houston Street. There were bright flames over the dark rooftops ahead of me. I heard sirens. The surging horns of emergency vehicles. They passed, heading toward the flames, a building on fire down by the river. As I approached First Avenue there were small fires burning in the street, from dumpsters rolled into the intersection and knocked on their sides.

I passed a little playground where a group of people, mostly children—boys, little ones and older ones—had sledgehammers. They were breaking concrete and scurrying around to pick up pieces of it as it ricocheted, putting heavy chunks of it into knapsacks and plastic shopping bags. One kid had bolt cutters and was using them to sever the seatless chains hanging from the swing set in the little playground. Every time I'd passed that playground on my way to visit Giddle, who lived nearby, I noticed those chains dangling, useless, no swings. The kid was making use of them. He wrapped the freed chain around his hand, with a loose end for swinging. Another took the bolt cutters and began tearing out pieces of the chain-link fence that bordered the playground. Other boys helped him drag out rectangular sections of fencing and toss them into the street.

A man was with them, his face covered with a black bandanna, the only adult, it seemed, caught up in their fury and even directing it a little, and for that, odd and somewhat out of place, because it was a youthful fury. He was dressed all in black, only his eyes showing. He held a long pole in one hand. The pole had something metal and sharp on the upward tip—it looked like a knife, maybe, duct-taped to the end of this pole, which towered over the man. He held it like a staff as he spoke to the kids, gave low-voiced instructions as they hunched and listened, self-consciously, almost vainly, pulling their own scarves and shirts and bandannas up over their young faces. I couldn't hear actual words but his emphatic tone, his flattened and tough New York accent, was familiar.

A grocery store nearby had been looted and people were streaming past with bags and shopping carts filled with goods. Another blaring fire truck headed toward the building burning near the East River. A

Mister Softee truck parked at the curb and the driver opened his window to sell ice cream. People surrounded the truck, saying that it was a blackout and he should not be charging for his cones because they were giving it out other places for free. A teenage girl in cornrows, shopping bags on the handlebars of her white ten-speed, said, "Shit is going to melt anyhow." The Mister Softee driver yelled back that his refrigeration was working just fine. He peeled out as the children with scarves over their faces began hurtling chunks of concrete at his truck.

The man dressed all in black was leading a chant, holding his weird pike or pole aloft, jabbing it upward, the children chanting with him,

"*El pueblo! Armado! Some*thing *some*thing *some*thing."

He was chanting with the kids but his eyes met mine. He was looking directly at me, his face covered. I stared back, sure now of who he was.

I walked closer. The bright, sad eyes.

"What did I tell you, sister?"

Before I could answer, a boy was calling that he and the others needed Burdmoore's help. A park bench had been unbolted from the ground and angled up, and they were trying to drag it to their elaborate pile of smoldering debris and fencing stacked in the street. Burdmoore went over to assist. They moved the bench onto the pile and squirted something flammable over it. The fire blazed up, its light bathing the boys' masked faces. They looked to Burdmoore, who directed. It didn't make sense to wait to speak with him. We were on different planes of existence. He was deep in his blackout self, activated.

"Burn the schools," he called out to his masked brood as they surrounded the fire.

"Burn the schools!"

"Burn the banks."

"Burn the banks!"

"Burn the precincts."

"Burn the precincts!"

"Yeah, fuck the pigs!" added a child's high-pitched voice like a grace note.

They were gone. They had finished their chant and fled down the street in a loose wave of bodies, some slower, some faster, all of them turning a corner and disappearing.

I opened the windows of my studio on Kenmare wide, lay down on my mattress and tried to sleep, floating on a cushion of wailing sirens.

I thought about that long day of waiting and waiting for Gianni. I'd looked up and searched for human color against the white apron of snow: Gianni's red jacket. Any sign, any brightness against the mountain's sameness of face. I had looked and waited, not exactly hopeful. I did not feel hope. I felt expectant. They were different. I waited, not wanting to turn away, to leave without his arrival.

If he never arrives, I had thought, looking up at the blank and impassive white, he's either hurt, or possibly dead, or he has deceived me, and I won't ever know which.

I woke to a red sun pouring into my curtainless windows, the electricity still out. My night came back to me in pieces almost as if I'd been drunk, the people behind the green door and the way the movie's mysteries, unveiled, gave way to a night of suspended time, a city unmasked by darkness.

A Chemical Bank had burned on First Avenue and Fourteenth Street, I heard when I went out in search of coffee (no luck: I bought a warm RC Cola). There had been no available fire truck to come and put out the fire, a suspected arson. The fire had swept through and gutted the building rapidly. Three Chemical Bank employees, either forced under threat of termination to remain on site for security, or voluntary recruits who'd been offered triple overtime, were inside. What was the difference? All three died.

19. THE DAY ROME WAS FOUNDED, APRIL 21,

but April 21, 1937. And so it was movies and Rome and babies and Mussolini and Papa the great industrialist, all together for a photograph.

Sandro wasn't yet born, not for two more years, but he'd been told about it: the grand opening of Cinecittà, his father and the Duce and little Roberto at the ribbon cutting.

What Sandro did remember was when the Allies bombed it, in 1944. Cinecittà, his father explained, was where they made the frivolous films Sandro's mother liked, the ones she took Sandro along to. He was five years old and could not really follow what was happening on-screen. He ate his snack in the dark and then fell asleep holding his mother's hand, his neck against the cold armrest, his wool coat covering his bare legs. White telephone films, they were called. *Telefoni bianchi.* There was always a white phone next to a bed. The tension of the scenes, the thing that gathered them taut, was whether it would ring. When the white phone next to the bed rang, through its earpiece came bad news, or a promise of devotion or a breach of it, this white instrument with flares at either ends of its handle, ear and mouth. The white telephone kept life's pleasures and disappointments arriving to a lavish and dead surrounding, not unlike the lavish and dead surroundings of Sandro's own home—the one that he and his mother returned to after their outing to the movies and then Passerini's for hot chocolate—their villa in the Brera, so clean and ordered there was nothing for the servants to do but look nervously at Sandro's mother and pretend to polish polished things.

Why did the Allies bomb the place where they made movies? Sandro had asked his father as they looked at the photographs in the newspaper of its collapsed roofs, German tanks on the destroyed soundstages, German officers carting the still-usable cinema equipment away. His mother loved the telefoni bianchi, and young Sandro had felt that the Allies bombing Cinecittà, the Germans looting it, were attacks on her, and possibly on them, because the people in the films, the vulgar escapist fantasies that Sandro later understood them to be, depicted more or less his own reality.

After the war ended the movies were different. The directors went out in the streets to film "real" life. Which was convenient, because Cinecittà was destroyed, and in addition to that problem there were people living in its ruins. From 1945 to 1950 displaced people, mostly children, lived in the film studios. If your parents died suddenly, Sandro understood, your home was wherever you were, and now you were from nowhere. Your parents were your provenance. Dead, you had no provenance. You lived at Cinecittà, so be it. Sandro saw pictures in a magazine, orphans crammed into little warrens divided by hay bales and corrugated cardboard. They were using huge props from costume epics about ancient Rome as makeshift furniture.

"They're extras," his father said, "for Rossellini," when Sandro asked why children were living in the bombed rubble of the movie studios. Extras for Rossellini. It was actually funny, Sandro later thought, when he understood the joke. Rossellini was too busy casting regular Italians to *play* wretches, too busy casting them to portray the actual wretches who were living in the former kingdom of elaborate fictions. We must confront our reality directly, or so the idea went. And yet the idea— "reality directly"—was there at Cinecittà: children who had lost their transport during the war. Lost their parents. Who had dysentery. Who did not know their own last names, nor what country they should be returned to. The whole displaced nightmare of World War Two, there among fake Roman columns, and it was too incredible and strange to be dealt with by the neorealists.

While real people suffered in movieland, the great neorealist director turned away from movieland to capture the supposedly real people, and what were they like, the Italians in Rossellini's *Open City*? They were brave. Noble. Moral. Religious, humane, strong resisters to their German occupiers. Hilarious. This is fucking hilarious, Sandro thought, watching it with Ronnie when it played at the Coronet on Third Avenue in 1963. Practically all of Italy had celebrated Mussolini, and then the war had ended and suddenly everyone was an anti-Fascist, except for the bastards in Salò. As if the entire problem could be isolated to a few rich families in the lake district, where Mussolini had set up his exiled government. Families like the Valeras, whose villa was occupied by Germans. After the war, walking to school in Brera, Sandro and Roberto were pelted with rocks. Their father moved them back up to Bellagio, where the boys were pelted with cow chips, and once misled into a swarm of angry bees that stung and restung them more times than Sandro had thought possible. Was he stung because he lacked natural virtues, ones the children who pushed them into the bee swarm possessed? Had those children stood up to Mussolini? No. Did it matter who possessed natural virtues? No. A blend of good and bad characterized all humans, and to pretend to sort that out was an insult to human complexity. But at the same time, Sandro understood that people only tended to allow their own contradictions, and not those of others. It was okay to be murky to yourself, to know you weren't an angel, but other people had to be more cleanly divided into good and bad.

Roberto joined a youth chapter of the neo-Fascists, the MSI, praised Mussolini, and defensively recited the bad-luck contingencies that had led to their own disgrace. Sandro took his licks on the road home from school and did not fight back. He dreamily wished he could perch himself in the spear of a cypress tree that bordered their enormous garden and from the cypress's pointed tip fly north, cross over Lake Como, and continue into the mountains. In the Alps, it would be the time of his father's glory, World War One. Sandro would join the Alpini, the mountaineering troops who had seemed to him, in his youth, so fine and brave, with stiff eagle feathers in their caps.

He had an entire set of World War One assault units, the Arditi. They were paper dolls, with all the accessories and clothing for each unit, and little cardboard tabs so you could remove and replace parts of the uniform. The little paper belt with cartridge pouches and the dagger and scabbard and even a *bersagliere*'s helmet with a paper flume to one side, black cockerel feathers inked onto it. The felt cap of an Ardito, a *scodellino* they called it, a little dish.

Colonel, I don't want bread. I only want lead for my musket, his father would sing to him on the rare occasion when he was in a friendly mood.

The Arditi were called the Black Flames. The Alpini were the Green Flames, his father told him. Bersaglieri were Red Flames, sharpshooters who ran instead of marched.

Sandro moved his paper Alpini around and pretended he was a Green Flame, a thing burning that wasn't meant to be, a thing releasing its poison, like the flames that licked over the plastic bedside clock he'd melted to see what would happen, and his room had filled with a noxious odor he'd waved out the open windows with towels so the servants wouldn't know.

He had the dolls and the full-color catalogues that listed which items belonged with which doll. To make them run he lifted and lightly bobbed them along the dresser edge, dun-dun-dun, instead of a more plodding and rhythmic march march march. They did not come with wristwatches, and having been told by his father that the wristwatch was an invention of war, for aiming a pistol and not having to fumble with a pocket watch, he drew them each a watch with a pen. There were units with different skills and missions, and each looked different and wore different hats and did different things, used different kinds of weapons and caused different kinds of deaths and destructions. The game was keeping them straight. Knowing which hats and badges and daggers went with which unit. That was how Sandro liked to play it and if things got mixed up it was enough to make him cry, because what about war as military order, as the invention of the wristwatch and so forth? Roberto came in and jumbled everything and said Sandro was a sissy and a fool. It's not like that, instructed Roberto, an authority because he was older and could better understand the terribleness of the subject matter. Roberto clanged cymbals against Sandro's ears before the sun had risen. "Wake-up call for Arditi is oh six hundred hours!" Roberto announced, "And by trench mortar round!" At breakfast he ate Sandro's pastry and declared it the way of an Ardito to be a plunderer.

Included with Sandro's dolls was the cycle battalion, like Papa's. Papa had been an Ardito and he rode a cycle called Pope. A gold cycle and the white skull-and-crossbones on the jacket, a Carcano bolt-action rifle on the rear, and on the hips, a file-handled dagger on one side and a Glisenti automatic pistol on the other. Machine gunners behind him with water-cooled Fiat 14s.

His father said the Glisenti was no good, when he saw Sandro using it to kill an entire regiment of enemies hiding under his bedsheet. No good? It was a meant to be like a German gun, his father said, a Luger. But it was a beggar's Luger. A bastard's Luger. A pimp's Luger and it constantly jammed.

"But mine doesn't do that," Sandro said. "It doesn't jam."

"Well, okay," his father said. "But I see you have wounded on stretchers."

"Yes," Sandro said, "this one needs a medic."

"But they are assault troops."

"Yes."

"We were on the couple system. There were no medic units or stretcher-bearers. You had to carry your partner if he was wounded, and it was easier if he died. So that was how you helped him, by finishing him off."

His father's insistence on inglorious details. Sandro pushed them aside and focused on the splendid Arditi patches in gold and silver with oak leaf and laurel, the large pocket each Ardito had on the back of his

tunic for storing hand grenades. And the privileges they enjoyed, such
as hot meals, while the soldiers in the regular battalions ate cold ones.
Hot meals and no camp chores, no guard duty, no trench duty. They
rode nifty vehicles like the gold motorcycle called Pope. They zipped
along with a huge dagger in a leather scabbard and blam-blam weapons,
the Bodeo with the folding trigger and the Glisenti, Thevenot grenades
they could pull from the pocket on their back and free the pin and toss
aside lightly because they themselves were *moving*, with motors under
them. You tossed the grenade, it went off where it landed, and you, you
were far ahead at that point. You didn't toss it and run frantically and
duck, you tossed it and rode proud and straight with your hand on the
throttle of the gold Pope cycle—zoom and boom. Boom.

The flamethrowers with their twin tanks and their gas mask were
Sandro's favorite of the assault company dolls. The asbestos sweater
and balloon pants and gauntlet gloves you could outfit them with so
they would not carbonize when they set a woods on fire. A woods or
bunker or enemy machine gun nest, depending. A supply line of trucks
or a laddered stack of bodies, depending.

The flamethrowers could have been from a different century, both
brutal and ancient and at the same time horribly modern. The flame oil
in the twin tanks they carried was five parts tar oil and one part crude,
and they had a little canister of carbon dioxide and an automatic igniter
and a belt pouch with spare igniters. The flamethrower was never, ever
defensive. He was pure offense, overrunning enemy lines. He surged
forth, a hulking creature with huge tanks on his back, a giant nozzle in
his hand, hooked to the tanks. He was a harbinger of death. He looked
like death, in his asbestos hood with the wide cowl, and he squirted liquid fire from a magnificent range—fifty meters—into the pillboxes and
trenches of the enemy and they had no chance.

But then his father told him the flamethrowers were a hopeless lot.
Their tanks were cumbersome and heavy and they were obvious and
slow-moving targets and if they were ever caught they were shown no
mercy. That's not a thing you want to be, his father said, after which
Sandro continued to love the flamethrowers best, to reserve for them

a special fascination, in their eerie, hooded asbestos suit, the long and evil nozzle they aimed at enemy holdouts. But he didn't know if his interest was reverence or a kind of pity.

Roberto yelling, *"Kaiserschlacht!"* and pouring gasoline over his paper men.

Sandro, eight years old, his face wet with tears, saying, "Why? Why Kaiserschlacht?"

Because, Roberto said, half of them died in the offensive and the others had to be executed for pillaging. Don't you know what happened? This is the retreat from the Isonzo to the Piave, after a poison gas attack by German storm troopers. If you want to play Arditi you have to do it properly, how the battles actually went. The Arditi who survived looted and pillaged as they retreated and had to be killed by their commanders, they had to be killed as a punishment, and if you want to play the game you have to do it right.

An older sibling's function was to bring in swift and unpleasant justice. Roberto had dumped gas from a bottle he snuck from the garage, and then lit a match. The little dolls and their cardboard tabs. The tiny asbestos sweater. The scabbard for the file-handled dagger, which fitted itself in easily because Sandro had been so careful not to bend or crease it. All carbonized to ash.

Ardito! Your name means courage, as their first commandment went. *Run into battle! Victory at any cost!*

Switzerland for schooling.

Holidays at Como. Waiting in short pants. Waiting for a shiny car to come and take him. His father's driver.

The occasional weekend in Brera. Trips to Rome with his father, twice visiting Cinecittà to see producers his father knew. Movie stars. Sports cars like wraparound sunglasses. Umbrella pines above the studio café, Sandro unsure how to speak to his own father. Sipping his *aranciata* as a camera slid past on a dolly—it was a big black heart, with its two film reels, a heart or an upside-down ass, and the cameraman peered through its viewfinder, trailing the slinky steps of a woman in a white dress.

He never liked his father much, an old, strange man who relished in dampening Sandro's fun in the same way Roberto did. They were alike, his father and Roberto, in that one way, and unalike in other ways. Roberto did not care how things were made, as their father did. Roberto liked to dominate, and he liked it when other people showed their weakness. Sandro cared how things were made, and what you did with made things. He liked machines. He liked guns. He never loved motorcycles the way his father had, but Sandro's father was busy running Valera operations and barely rode motorcycles by the time Sandro was born. What Sandro remembered was his father posing for photographs on the new Moto Valera sport models, an old dapper man in his Brioni suit, clutching the handlebar grips.

His father was cruel to his mother, and this might have been cause for an intimate alliance between mother and son, but he never liked his mother much, either, so he allowed no alliance. Because she was mean. A naturally mean person. Only once did he feel something like sympathy for her. The war had ended and they were back in Milan, at the house in Brera. Sandro was ten. His father, just returned from Brazil, was in the hall removing a woolen scarf that sparkled with raindrops. He looked up at his wife's open, eager face as she stood on the landing, the geometry of its balustrade, perfect right angles and folds repeating themselves up and up, bending out of view, and her anticipation, her own oppressive need for order and right angles and patterns all there, exposed, as if the landing were a stage. His father had looked at his mother, at the dress she had on, layers of transparent material that altogether were shiny and opaque, the heels and pearls and her hair curled under on each side of her face like two treble clefs, and Sandro's father had frowned.

"You should take a lover," he'd said. Then he went into his study, to the right of the stairs. Shut the door and latched it.

Sandro's mother gripped the banister. She was crying and didn't bother to wipe the tears. That was the only time he ever really felt any-thing for his mother, who had prepared so intently, with such foolish hope, for her husband's return and was punished for being eager, in front of her children and the servants. She had gone off to the kitchen after that and yelled at the cooks, really let them have it. As she called them idiot and cretin Sandro felt each insult, not as the recipient but the one who delivered, his mother's anger like bullets shooting from his own fingertips.

She never did take a lover as far as he knew. Now she had the Ameri-can writer, the old blowhard, but Sandro could not imagine they were intimate, it seemed somehow impossible, but he knew the impossibil-ity was in him and not between his mother and the writer. It saddened him to think his mother had gone from an imperial force like his father to a silly man who thought his incessant blather was proof of anything, virility or knowledge. The moment the mouth opened the mind shut down, was Sandro's feeling. But his mother had power now, which she never did when Sandro's father was alive, and that was something. To make your own decisions.

He thought a lot about the man who had drowned, or tried to, in the East River. Sandro had saved one man and shot another in the hand and the one he'd saved had not wanted to live. The look on the man's face, trapped with the living. Lost and alive. The layers and layers of the man's drenched winter coats, too heavy for Sandro to lift him out. He had weighted himself to guarantee his passage to death. All those coats pulling him down had reminded Sandro of a tribe his father had told him about, deep in the Amazon of Brazil, who weighted themselves with stones so that their souls would not wander away. Sandro had asked more, but his father brushed him off. It became an obsession for him as a boy, this idea of people trying to keep their souls from escap-ing. He read about other tribes in other parts of the world, Borneo and New Guinea, people for whom the soul was a contingent and skittish thing that could be chased out or lost or worse. It might run away. It had to be kept from leaving you, whether with seduction or stays or hooks or with heavy stones.

That the soul was not a fact, a simple thing you were, and possessed, had seemed to Sandro so reasonable. Still he believed it. That reality, in a sense, was not an objective place where you were thrust. You had to maintain your hold on it by vigilantly keeping watch over whatever slight and intangible thing gave your life its meaning. Call it a soul, or presence. Whatever it was, a prisoner or guest and you had to trick it or petition it into lingering.

People weighted themselves, Sandro knew, if not with stones.

A movie, a lover. Friends. Complicities. A certain amount of success. These were decent crutches, provided they could be changed up often enough. And art, of course. Making art was really about the problem of the soul, of losing it. It was a technique for inhabiting the world. For not dissolving into it.

As a child, his soul felt airy and evanescent, something that was filled only with longings and boredom he knew to be Italian and Catholic. Church with his mother and brother. Women sweeping the sacristy steps with sorghum brooms. Lifeless Madonnas in their blue shawls, always that same shade of blue: piety, sky, forgetting. The hope that comes of mystery and emptiness (hollow plaster). The organ's resounding pipes as the congregation sang the "Stabat Mater," which overflowed its subject, the sorrows of Mary, her suffering an image all men could look to, the tear-streaked face. The music surged in and widened the space of his little soul. It made him light. It filled him with something, sadness and jubilation for experiences that were not his own. Or they were his own, but they had transmutated to sweet and overwhelming song.

Fac ut ardeat cor meum in amando Christum Deum.

Make my heart burn with love for Christ.

But the translation sheet said "soul." "Make my soul glow and melt." For young Sandro mouthing these words in his high voice it was enough to want to burn ardently, not a secular plea, but neither a plea to merge with a mother's suffering, even the wife of God. To make the heart burn. With *something*.

FAC UT ARDEAT. A phrase his father put above the hearth. A clever command, To make burn. And wood was deposited there. But probably it was not merely a joke, and related to his father's own past as an Ardito. An ardent one. Who had burned with the ardor that made him dash into war, toward death, and then toward money and power. The phrase could not be reduced to its imprisonment in the literal, above the hearth. The burning *of*. The soul, glowing and melting—there or gone, lost or escaped—was what mattered.

But if you let your soul go? Let it wander? Would it eventually come home to you? Was it like love in that sense? A thing you had to set free to experience? Even to encounter? Whoever encountered love was so lucky. He meant encountered it not as a might have been but as it was. There was maybe no such thing. His father said history was always late for its date with itself. It was late, it was early, it was before and after its own time. Italy was always missing its rendezvous with itself. The timing of its becoming a nation had not worked, and no one believed in the Risorgimento. The North and the South were never in sync. People had their revelations too early or too late. They were always missing their appointments with themselves. Well. With each other, too. Ronnie was the only appointment Sandro had managed to keep, a friendship he'd recognized the moment they met. He had maintained it all along, it was a connection that happened *in time*. Not in fantasy, not in hindsight. But he hadn't exactly managed anything, it was just luck, like love was luck. It was chance. They knew when they saw each other what they were each looking at. He and Ronnie were almost mirror images, meaning opposites. It was love at some wry distance. Rivalry. It would outlast actual love, he knew that, there was no question of it.

He was at the TWA terminal.

Trans World, Ronnie would have said, hypervigilant to words and branding.

New York to Milan via London.

Sandro both loved and hated that terminal.

He had promised his mother six months. She had only one son now, and he could not turn away from her. He could not. His mother had begged him to come home, and he was doing it and fully—not partially, by bringing a buffer, a girl. He felt like he was both reentering the womb, against all instinct, and also, finally, and way too late, growing up and facing himself.

He wondered about her, what she would do with her life. He never asked his friends about her, even as he knew they were in contact. Discretion was a mode of survival. It was his history, his loss, and none of anyone else's concern.

He looked up at the sailing white arc of the terminal, lines sinuous as Ingres, the swallows flying through, lost inside, and he thought about Brasília. Which was conceived of by a different architect entirely, and yet the TWA terminal always reminded him of Brasília. Same white concrete parabolas and huge glass bays and they were born of the same idea, a proscriptive lie about progress and utopias and born the same year, too—1956. When, as well, the Autostrada del Sole was born. What a year, 1956. Brasília was surely worse than an airline terminal. It was not to human scale and you could see one wretched Indian walking some godawful distance in dire heat with a basket of grain or laundry on her head, casting a shadow on a blank and baking concrete wall two hundred feet high, no shade, no trees, no people. Brasília was not to any human scale, and the inclusion of a Formula One racetrack, in the wake of a generous bid from Sandro's father and Valera Tires, was one more insult to the Indian with a basket on her head.

His father had brought Sandro along because he was in his seventies and in ailing health and needed someone to look after him but could not resist the ribbon cutting. Sandro, eighteen by then, flew from New York to Brasília.

This is what we do, he had thought, holding up his frail father. We cut ribbons. We're ribbon cutters.

He had both liked and hated Brasília's stiff white meringues, which perfectly blotted the ugly history that paid for them. His father's rubber-harvesting operations in the Amazon had made the Brazilian government enough money to build an all-inclusive concrete utopia, a brand-new capital. The money had poured in. The rubber workers were still there—they were still there *now*, in 1977—and there were many more of them because their children were all tappers as well. Neither Sandro's father nor the Brazilian overseers and middlemen ever bothered to tell the rubber workers the war was over. They simply kept them going, doing their labor up there in the remote northwestern jungle. The tappers didn't know. They believed that someday there would be an enormous payment, if not to their children, maybe to their children's children. "What is time to an Indian?" his father had said to Sandro that night in the hotel, the Palace of Something or Other, another interplanetary meringuelike building for industrialists and diplomats. "What *is* time?" his father asked. "What the hell is it? Who is bound to time, and who isn't?" Sandro became angry. What am I doing here with this old bastard? "Go tell them, Sandro," his father had said. "Go on up there. It's only three thousand kilometers, most of it on dirt roads. Go let them know the war is over and they can all go home, okay?"

It was the last time he saw his father.

Everything a cruel lesson. This, what fathers were for. His father taking Sandro, four years old, to the tire factory gates during a strike. The workers carrying a coffin and Sandro saying, "Papa, is it a funeral?" His father laughing and nodding. For me. I'm dead, right? Holding up his hands, slapping his own cheeks, then holding up his hands again. What do you say, Sandro? Do I look dead to you?

The scene at the gates turned ugly, and next Sandro knew, his father's driver was clutching him against his fat stomach and then he was pushed back into the car and the car pounded on by fists and other things, rocks, as his father's driver motored them away from the gates with a bloody face and a lapful of shattered glass.

An argument between his parents when they returned, and he understood that his father had taken him for a purpose, to be caught in what occurred. His father never took Roberto to the gates during a melee. He trained Roberto in the details of profits and losses. Took only little Sandro to see the workers coming at them with clubs. But why? Sandro asked much later, after Roberto had left for his university studies. Because you are going to be an artist, his father said. And it was important to establish that you aren't suited to anything else. That's what artists are, his father said, those who are useless for anything else. That might seem like an insult, he said, but it wasn't, and someday Sandro would understand. Each child was unique, and destined for something different, so why should they be treated the same?

Roberto. For his death Sandro felt something. For his mother, who would be so alone now. You should take a lover. He had always felt he could never go back there to live. But he would go back. He was going. The flight would board soon, and in a way he was relieved to get it over with, to be banished from his own pathetic tendencies. When he had shown up to the funeral with Ronnie's castoff, his mother had said to cut it out. Cut what out? And she said, abusing these young women. You don't love them. You bring them to place between you and your life. That was in May. It was July now and he was officially free of entanglements. Alone.

They would announce boarding at any moment. Going back to Italy would be the death of him, and he was ready for it. Eager, even. His own casket, like the one the factory workers carried for his father. He'd have to occupy a role, be his mother's adored son now that her firstborn was gone.

Probably that girl, Ronnie's castoff, was relieved. He couldn't have been much fun to be around. Moody. Quiet. Domineering. A winning combination. Her curious, catlike autonomy had reminded him in unpleasant ways of his imploded relationship. How badly he'd fucked everything up. The disastrous moment at the tire plant. Even if he had tried to explain himself, explain about Talia, apologize, fix everything, it wouldn't have worked. He'd wrecked things, and maybe it was intentional, by letting his cousin take him back to the place he'd been so many times in his youth. She had been his lover and it was like going home. When were people not attracted to cousins? It had been his right to act on it when he was in his twenties, Talia sixteen, but such an old sixteen. He had tried to distance himself when she showed up in New York. Look, he said, I'm living with someone. And Talia had responded with raucous laughter. You think I want to live with you, Sandro? Don't be an idiot. You're my cousin, for fuck's sake. He had managed to stay away. He told her no like you talk to a dog. No, he'd said firmly, and she had smiled, content in her knowledge that the firmness was for him, not for her, a firmness for his own benefit, a reminder of limits he was trying to impose.

The horror of that day, of having to be in the car with the novelist, that old faggot, not actually gay, so be it, who dared to place his hand on Sandro's mother's thigh and right in front of him. Sandro and Roberto and Talia in the back. Good God. Like children, sibling warfare all over again. Roberto ducking, convinced he was going to be gunned down in his mother's Mercedes. Sandro had said, you're being ridiculous. No one gives a shit about you, he wanted to say but didn't. It would have justified Roberto's fears, that no one cared much if he lived.

Driving in through the gates. Valeras at Valera, and everything he had left Italy to escape was on offer for him. The only thing that wasn't from that Milanese world was Talia. Because she had an English father and had gone to boarding school in the States, and spoke with a slight English accent that reminded him of a recording he'd once heard of the poet Sylvia Plath reading a short, cunning thing that began,

First, are you our sort of person?

The lilt of Sylvia Plath's voice. A question she repeated that became the poem's refrain, Will you marry it? intoned in a way that was gentle and severe and knowing. Will you marry it? He'd fused that stern, sexy voice with Talia's, and this was later, after they'd already been lovers and the combination made her almost a part of him.

How about this suit—
Black and stiff, but not a bad fit.
Will you marry it?
It is waterproof, shatterproof, proof
Against fire and bombs through the roof.
Believe me, they'll bury you in it.

Talia became a thing he could not reject when it arrived periodically on offer. She talked like Sylvia Plath and looked a bit like her.
And her pushy and insistent sexuality—he liked that, too. It became
a habit he relied on. Her pale skin and moon face and the hair, black
like an Ardito's cockerel feathers. She didn't offer the kind of wretched
devotion Italian girls didn't know better than to supply, they wanted to
win your heart by adoring you, cooking you a meal, sleeping with you
as maternal care. It was a nightmare. I don't want maternal care. I can
care for myself, and in New York he met these . . . viragos, who wanted
servicing, like Stanley's wife, and what a relief it was. A vacation from
the self, to attend to their needs. Like Giddle, the so-called best friend,
but a betrayer who barely had a self, who had a sociopathic freedom
from any need for relating. He enjoyed that kind of thing. On occasion.
Or rather, he let himself be enjoyed by these women who dictated. He
needed a break from his devoted girlfriend, who submitted to his generosity and demanded so little. She was like a daughter. Young Reno.
She was both innocent and ambitious and looked to Sandro for direction, and fine, but not all the time. Sometimes he just wanted to forget
himself. Doesn't everyone? Talia was something different, not like an
American girl, either. Proof against fire and bombs through the roof.
They went out together that afternoon at the factory for air, that was
what she said, "for air." And once outside, with no one around, she had
taken the opportunity. Gone right for the zipper. Reached in with such
forthright disregard that it made him sad for his sweet young girlfriend
who did not know you just reach in and grab it and it's not cheap or
crass, it just is, a hand on a cock, that's all it was and some women knew
what to do, his own black-haired cousin among them. If young Reno,

unlike his mean mother and cruel extended family, if she'd known to be rude on occasion, to just take, he might not have strayed. But that was a lie, too, because the truth was that he had liked her as she was, the way she had looked up at him so wide-eyed, searching for some sense of herself, a cue.

He wasn't worth looking up to. Talia understood this, Talia, who didn't look to anyone for anything. She was unafraid. She didn't need to please others. She didn't love herself or anyone else. She knew better than that. She was an evolved human, a Shrapnel. And he understood it. He liked people who didn't give a shit but you can't surround yourself with that, it was only for sometimes. Like a day when he was exactly where he didn't want to be, a Valera at Valera, and Talia had unzipped his trousers and put her hand on his cock and she, it, had promised escape.

He wasn't choosing to wreck his relationship. He couldn't have known his American girlfriend would have found her way to the drab industrial outskirts of Milan, and be there at the factory, right *there*. How could he have? He never could have predicted her appearance. Just as she surely had no idea what it felt like to be him in that moment.

He had hurt the person he did not hate. A person he might have loved. He didn't want to say he loved her, because is that how you treat someone you love? He might have loved her. Leave it at that. Something that might have been but was not, that he could have sustained but didn't.

His father had said to him, "As you get older, you tolerate less and less well women your own age." "You mean *you* do," Sandro had said. "Yes, I," his father said. "That's right. And I used to think it was because I'd escaped time and women didn't. But that's not the reason. It's because I'm stunted. Many men are. If you are that kind of man when you grow up, Sandro, you'll understand. You'll go younger in order to tolerate yourself."

That's what it was about, at the end of the day. His father was right. It's what you can stand of yourself.

He'd grown up to be at times an asshole, he supposed. And it was so much easier to call yourself that after you'd acted like one, rather than to trot out a lot of remorse and do all the work needed to distance yourself from the acts that defined you. In that way, he and Ronnie were perhaps not opposites but twins, or becoming so.

He'd looked at her face, so sad and angry. And he had thought, I'm an asshole. Which was a kind of remorse, but not the kind with any hope in it.

Maybe the way she had insinuated herself—by accident, he understood—with the company, staying with them in Utah, or Nevada, wherever it was, had not been much to his liking. And then the publicity tour, derailed, so be it. She'd disappeared, he didn't know where. One of his mother's employees, the groundskeeper, had gone off to look for her that day at the factory. He said he'd take her back to the villa in Bellagio, but he had not. Probably she'd insisted on going elsewhere. She and the groundskeeper had not been there when he returned. Sandro hung around the villa for a week, alone with the servants and the thump of giant moths against the windows at night. Where was she? She never came back. He telephoned Ronnie in New York, who told him *Time* magazine's cover that week was a plate of spaghetti with a gun in it and the words "Visit Italy."

A boarding announcement for his flight. He stood up from his seat as the blanketing echo of many small conversations ricocheted around the high-ceilinged terminal, Trans World. A great white puff through which sailed both swallows and the underside of modernity. Even if the association was not direct. Because TWA was not Oscar Niemeyer but Saarinen. Still, its melted meringue lines told him Brasília equaled death, a nasty little message, private, from the terminal to Sandro.

"Stupidest people on earth," his father said of the rubber tappers in the Amazon, who made him rich, whose slavery paid for the stunning paean to modernism like the one he was in, the terminal. So dumb and uncivilized that they had weighted their souls with stones. An act whose grave sophistication still impressed Sandro. It suggested they understood what was at stake, how fragile presence, true and felt and lived presence, really was.

Sandro and M, his Argentine friend, once had a long conversation about culture and violence. He should call M, he thought. M would understand the position Sandro was in and what happened to his brother. But why have that kind of conversation? While waiting around the villa that week she never returned, he had seen the images in the newspaper of the demonstrations, the tanks in Bologna, the masses of people in Rome, human foam filling the Piazza Esedra, and he felt nothing. Or rather, he did feel something. A reminder that he was born on the wrong side of things. The anger and radical acts of the young people in Rome were a kind of electricity, an act and a refusal and a beauty, something Italian that was, for once, magnificent. But it was against him as long as he occupied his role as a Valera. It was against him and he had no right to take part.

After that week alone at the villa, he had returned to New York. Resumed his life, but single. Then Roberto was kidnapped, and Ronnie's castoff had somehow been around in all the right moments, one of those women who had a skill for that, good timing. Ronnie had hurt her and made her cry and was grateful not to have her following him around anymore. Then suddenly Roberto was dead. And his mother caught him and called him out. You don't love them.

Now Sandro was going back to Italy alone. The flight was boarding.

He was in his window seat, ready for the strange, intermittent sleep he'd have on a jet whistling through the night. Hurtled along in a dark sky, so many thousands of feet up that the Earth was an abstraction, a nothing. The periodic waking—no place, no place, no place, and then the approach, Heathrow. He took off his blazer, the one jacket he owned, rolled it up and placed his cheek against it. Looked out the window, tried to ignore a passing memory, Ronnie's comment that airplane windows were toilet seats, they were the same shape, which had led, at the time, to a declaration that the Guggenheim looked like a toilet and everyone knew it but was afraid to say. I won't hang my work in a toilet, Ronnie had said, and it was that attitude that would get him a show there eventually, Sandro knew.

They were on the runway, in line for takeoff. He pressed his forehead to the glass, the plastic, whatever it was, and looked out at those melancholic yellow signs, glowing and numbered, that indicated runways.

The sad yellow signs clicked off. They were gone, all at once, lost to darkness. The entire disorganized smattering of runway lights was off. Also, the lights from the terminal. And the ones that had flashed in an arc from the control tower.

Everything was off, everything dark. The lights on the plane were on, but it was a plane in a sea of black.

The airport had lost power. They would wait until it came back on. There was no telling, the cabin attendant said. It could be just a few moments. Please be patient. And everyone was. The plane wasn't hurtling yet, but it was already in the no place they had to pass through to get to where they were going.

20. Her Velocity

L e Alpi," he'd said when the subject of skiing came up.
He'd asked if I liked the mountains and I said sure, that I used
to ski-race, and he nodded in his grave way like he nodded gravely at
everything and I said, "Do you?"

"What?" he said.

"Do you ski?"

"Perhaps."

Le Alpi, he'd said. We'll go together.

I hadn't known he was serious. That he meant sometime soon.

We'll go to the Alps.

Maybe Gianni himself hadn't known what he meant. Hadn't known it
would be later that same day, when I'd been snagged on the wrong side
of some kind of argument, and Bene had all but forced me to stick with
Gianni in an obscure divide between them, between him and Bene.

But he must have known. Because he told me to bring my passport
before we left the apartment. I always carried it anyhow. The carabinieri
loved to stop me for some reason and you were expected as an American to have it on you even if you were just out for a quick walk.

It wasn't at all like Bene seemed to think. She had practically steered me into his arms but nothing had ensued. It was all extremely proper and in that I almost, for a moment, wondered why, simply because anything else was so foreclosed by Gianni. He dictated what our association was and it was proper and stayed that way. Just as when he had taken me from the tire factory parking lot, me in tears, the rain pouring, and hadn't looked at me, said little, I felt from him only privacy and respect.

We were at the trattoria downstairs, where they often ate, that group. The owner is a comrade, they all said.

I was nervous about running into Bene. Maybe it was not a bad idea to go, as he said, to the Alps. Go somewhere.

We saw Durutti just outside the trattoria.

"It's time," Durutti told Gianni.

It was evening, already dusk, a flat violet-colored light descending over the ugly buildings of San Lorenzo, with their hatchwork of TV antennas.

Accompanied by Durutti, we got into Gianni's white Fiat for the second time that day and drove to a bourgeois district that was unfamiliar to me.

We were in a large and beautiful apartment, bookshelves to the ceiling along every wall, glass windows that were double-paned so you didn't hear any traffic, just the creak of the rambling apartment's old wood floors, the papers on a desk stirred to rustle by a ceiling fan. The man who'd led us in seemed like a professor type, wire-rimmed glasses, gray hair and sideburns, a certain way of rubbing his cheeks before he spoke.

Durutti said Gianni needed to disappear. The man took Gianni into another room. The door, as soundproofed as the windows, it seemed, was shut behind them.

Durutti had a nervous energy, like a young boy who has been asked to sit but is not physically capable of maintaining that kind of stillness. He bobbed his knee up and down. Whistled. Picked a book up off the coffee table as if he had never read one before, looked at the cover, looked at the back, whirred the pages under his thumb like it was a flipbook, and then set it back down.

He looked at me. "It's mostly just sitting around," he said.

What is, I asked.

"The life," he said. "Being underground."

We sat quietly.

"And trying to stay invisible. Seen, but not noticed. Gianni is visible now, so it's a good thing he's got you."

"Me," I said.

"I wish I had cover like that. The wife of a Crespi, say. They own the newspapers. Shit. If you want to get things done, you have to find a way to get the police off your back."

He took a lighter from his pocket and began flicking it lit, flicking it lit, flicking it lit. Then he burned his thumb, because the metal flint wheel had gotten too hot.

"Actually, no. You know what this life mostly is? Not Gianni's," he said, "but mine. Gianni is some other thing, no one knows what, really. The rest of us play pinball. A lot of it. Too much. You get very good. It's insane how good we get at pinball. Racking up eight hundred thousand, nine hundred thousand points. And if you're top score at the bar on the Volsci, you get to put your name up on the side of the machine. But we can't put up our names. So all the top scorers, the list there, are made up. None of those people exist."

He was bobbing his knee and looking at me as if I were meant to respond.

"But Gianni doesn't play," I said.

"No, no," he said, shaking his head. "Gianni is more like, ah, more like this: Turn the pinball machine on its side. Produce from nowhere, by magic, a bit of plastic explosive. Also by magic, from nowhere, a roll of duct tape. Wire. A timer. And—"

He looked up and began to whistle his tune again. Gianni and the gray-haired professor were emerging from the other room. Durutti sewed his knee up and down, not nervously, just spastically. Maybe he was eighteen. Maybe he was sixteen. Suddenly I couldn't tell. I'd lost the ability to know who was a child and who was an adult.

Gianni, though. Gianni was an adult.

The man went to a drawer and began to retrieve things.

"Even if you're a novice," he said to Gianni, "you just push along. And watch out for cliffs." He smiled. "I joke, but you must be very careful about crevasses. And there are seracs, which will be starting to shift and melt since it's now late March. Don't stand under one, in other words."

He had maps that he spread on a table. He showed Gianni and Durutti how Gianni should go. The man was calm but serious, tracing a line over the map with a pencil.

"Here," he said, "the top, where the tram lets you out. You descend there over the face, but the main way down isn't steep. Just take big, slow turns. You will come upon a large kidney-shaped rock, and there the trail goes left, down to the Mer de Glace, a glacier like a grooved tongue. The glacier will be soft this time of year. Nothing to worry about. You'll see a little kiosk at the bottom. Take the trail through the trees, which brings you right into Chamonix."

He had telephoned a friend who was bringing over gear. It was in the hall as we left, a pair of skis, poles, men's boots, gloves, a hat, and goggles. The gray-haired professor gave us two warm parkas. We loaded everything into the little white Fiat. The man reminded Gianni to be careful and take it slow because of the crevasses.

Durutti did not come with us. He walked off like he didn't know us, the sky now dark.

Once again I was on the autostrada with Gianni. I was wearing clothes that Bene had either loaned or given me, a pair of faded green corduroys, a black cotton turtleneck. Clothes that made me look almost Italian, and symbolized to me my acceptance among the group, to be dressed like the women in that apartment on the Via dei Volsci.

Because he had worked for the Valeras probably and because he had taken me to Rome and insinuated me with his group, Gianni was a kind of guardian to me, or at least that was my feeling. So if Bene opened a divide between them—angry at him for something that, I guessed, had to do with his situation and what to do about it—and if she put me on the side of Gianni, what was I to do?

I'd walked past, gone to Gianni. My secret guardian, whose silence had pulled me in. I'd been listening to men talk since I arrived in New York City. That's what men liked to do. Talk. Profess like experts. When one finally came along who didn't say much, I listened.

We were on our way to the Val d'Aosta and Mont Blanc. I understood that this was about borders, getting Gianni to France before the police picked him up.

"You're helping me," he said. "I couldn't do this without you. You're a good girl."

Brava ragazza.

His cover. A way to get the police off his back. A mistake—not for him but for me, and I knew it, all at once. But it was too late to back out.

The car up- and downshifted through mountain passes. At the coldest point of the night, just before dawn, there were signs for Courmayeur.

Beyond it was Entrèves and then La Palud, where we arrived at first light. A red-and-white tram went steeply up a mountain cable. The first ride would be at eight a.m.

We drank coffee together in the lodge as old men in wool ski knickers did their stretches, waxed skis, looked out the large windows at the mountain, wind whipping the snow that had settled in its rocky creases, the snow like smoke, drifting and resettling. The sky was an opaque white with a certain brightness to it. A storm was coming in.

Passamontagna, the balaclava was called in Italian, and in this case,

Gianni needed it not to obscure his face like the people at the demonstration in Rome but to protect it from frostbite.

The tram would take him in three stages up to Punta Helbronner. From there he would ski the Vallée Blanche down into Chamonix. No passport checks, no police, no one. A no-man's-land of snow, wind, steeps. The crevasses the gentle man with the nice apartment had warned of. The precarious chunks of ice. Gianni would pass from Italy into France, to some kind of exile.

I had the keys to the Fiat in the pocket of the down parka the man had loaned me, a curious sort of lending, never meant to be returned. The clothes under it also borrowed, their faint lavender smell from her soap a reminder of Bene.

The wind was picking up, blowing snow sideways. Before Gianni got on the tram, I asked if he really knew how to ski.

The question was a joke, but I had wondered it for part of the drive, up and up in elevation. A guy who had worked on the assembly line at a tire plant might possibly not ski.

"Good enough, I hope," he said, and smiled.

I followed the signs toward the tunnel that went under Mont Blanc and through the border.

The signs were in French, the border guards, in their black leather gloves, puffing little gasps of steam from their mouths as they spoke to me. One of them flipped through my passport, stamped it, waved me on.

As I entered the Mont Blanc tunnel, under its perforated stream of white lights, I already sensed what would happen. I felt cut free, under the glare of those runny lights, in a tunnel through the bottom of a high peak. The lanes, one in each direction, were so narrow that each time an oncoming car passed I thought we would collide.

Fifteen minutes later I exited. I was in France. It was snowing.

*   *   *

At Chamonix, I parked where the man in Rome who'd helped us, or helped Gianni, had told me to, near the little Montenvers train station, a sign that said MER DE GLACE, the train's scenic destination.

I got out of the car and tipped my face up into the blank white sky. There had always seemed something miraculous to me in the way snow-flakes formed. As if they simply materialized about twenty feet above the earth, into these falling lacy clusters. The snow came toward my upturned face in a continuous symphony. Big dry flakes. There was no wind. Snow fell and collected in drifts. I was supposed to meet Gianni at the bottom of Les Planards. I asked a man scraping a walkway with the blunt end of a flat shovel. I spoke no French, just "Les Planards?" He pointed. It was a bunny slope, trees on both sides. Mont Blanc, high above it, was shrouded in clouds.

It would be hours, given the tram rides, the skiing. I walked to a little bar next to the train station. Heard only French. Chamonix, with its hotels, mountaineering shops, bakeries, was so different from the tiny station past Entrèves, on the Italian side, where I had waited with Gianni for the tram to open. I felt again what I'd experienced as I entered that tunnel through the mountain, a sense of being cut free, plunged into the unknown.

I ordered a coffee with milk. Sat at a table and waited. All the time spent in ski lodges growing up, the dreamy feeling of a crowded open room when you're little and tired, people clomping up and down metal stairs in ski boots. Our coach buying us hot chocolate that I let burn my tongue, too impatient to wait until it properly cooled. Trapped inside lodges during a whiteout. When our race was rained out. Or when I'd crashed, did not finish and wasn't getting a second run. Disqualified and wasn't getting a second run.

Gianni and I had been awake all night. I let myself sleep, my face in my arms, there at an empty table in the bar next to the little train station.

I woke up to an enveloping din. The lunch crowd. A man and woman came and sat at my table, speaking something Scandinavian. I zipped the parka and went out to wait where I was meant to, at the bottom of Les Planards, where Gianni would ski down. I stared up at the mountain, blearily visible through the wet mist of snow-loaded clouds. I walked back and forth to keep warm. Gianni did not appear.

Wind gusted, stirring the snow-laden branches of the pine trees that clustered along the sides of the slope. The wind moving those trees sent an exhilarating loneliness through me. I looked up, waiting to see the red jacket. Snow stung my face. Visibility was poor. Vapory drifts blew across the open slope. The beginners had now abandoned it. Almost no one was skiing.

For a brief period snow stopped falling and the clouds parted, revealing Mont Blanc, my first real view of it. The sun burst in between low, lumbering clouds, which cast dark shadows over its glaciered face. I tracked them and hoped, as if the shadows were themselves faint images or messages of Gianni. *Arriving soon.*

Mont Blanc, above, was still and serene. A steep white desert peopled only by clouds and snow. Jagged and stark. It refused my question, Where is he?

Late afternoon. The opening in the clouds closed, obscuring the top of Mont Blanc. Snow was coming down. Windows glowed yellow. Two children ran, shrieked, looked up, mouths open to melt falling flakes on their tongues.

How long was I meant to wait?

Dusk, and my feet numb as I paced at the bottom of Les Planards, the run going dimly gray, harder and harder to see.

The yellow lights of Chamonix were blazing now. There was a smell of woodsmoke.

The woman in the movie who had thrown her life away had waited, but for nothing specific. In hair curlers, sitting in a bar. For a man to pick her up, buy her a beer, take her somewhere. The curlers that meant some occasion to come, not yet named.

I wasn't in that kind of time, curler time.

I didn't know if Gianni had ditched me, or had an accident, fallen into a crevasse. I knew only to wait.

Soft clumps of snow dropped from tree branches. I heard a door open and shut. A bus motored by, with external slots filled with skis, black clouds of diesel behind it, illuminated by an orange streetlamp.

It was almost dark now, and much colder. I could see the jagged lines of Mont Blanc's peak, its steeples and snow-filled cracks. A huge mountain, dark and present, but nothing like human presence. It was a monolith of doubt.

You can think and think a question, the purpose of waiting, the question of whether there is any purpose, any *person* meant to appear, but if the person doesn't come, there is no one and nothing to answer you.

It's dark. I hear a small group of men call to one another in German, see them pass by, their pom-pom ski hats bobbing, a squeak of fresh snow under their boots.

They're gone now. The wind whistles through the trees, branches floating up and down with slow, wild elegance.

I'm alone at the base of the run, almost too cold to move.

The answer is not coming.

I have to find an arbitrary point inside the spell of waiting, the open absence, and tear myself away.

Leave, with no answer. Move on to the next question.

ACKNOWLEDGMENTS

I would like to thank Susan Golomb, Nan Graham, Marisa Silver, Nam Le, and most especially Jason Smith, each for invaluable insights. Thank you also to Daniel Burgess, Claudio Guenzani, Hedi El Kholti, Rémy Kushner, Knight Landesman, James Lickwar, Vittorio Morfino, Susan Moldow, Katie Monaghan, Gianluca Pulsoni, and the Santa Maddalena Foundation.

The monologues of the character Marvin are inspired by the voice-over in Morgan Fisher's elegiac and beautiful 1984 film *Standard Gauge*.

The cover image is from issue 10 of *I Volsci* (March 1980), a newspaper of the Autonomia Operaia group I Volsci, named after its headquarters on Via dei Volsci in San Lorenzo, Rome.

This page constitutes a continuation of the copyright page.

Credits